The Commandment

AN AUSTIN GRANT OF SCOTLAND YARD NOVEL

Scott Shepherd

THE MYSTERIOUS PRESS

THE LAST COMMANDMENT

Mysterious Press
An Imprint of Penzler Publishers
58 Warren Street
New York, N.Y. 10007

Copyright © 2021 by Scott Shepherd

First Mysterious Press paperback edition: 2022

Interior design by Maria Fernandez

Library of Congress Control Number: 2021908561

ISBN: 978-1-61316-310-8
eBook ISBN: 978-1-61316-229-3

10 9 8 7 6 5 4 3 2 1

Printed in the United States of America
Distributed by W. W. Norton & Company

For Holly,
because of you there is never
a Lonesome Day

On Your Marks

I

He fell in love at the exact same time every night.

Ten minutes before eleven o'clock.

That was when Billy Street, lead singer of the Blasphemers, launched into "Ain't I Good Enough for You"—their only hit. The audience came out of its alcoholic daze and the chitchat faded as he prepared for his nightly lover's leap.

He had played the song thousands of times and it almost never failed—there was always one lass who'd bump her way to the stage's lip, plant herself beneath Billy's leather-clad spread legs, and stare up at him with lustful adoration as he furiously strummed his Fender Telecaster.

This night's lucky lovely wore snug diamond-patterned leggings and an even tighter AC/DC T-shirt that clung to her ample-sized chest. She knew all the words to every song in the group's catalog, even the obscure and unreleased ones. Either she was a Super Groupie or just a sad girl with time on her hands to memorize the repertoire of a band that most of London (and alas, the record industry) had long cast aside.

Billy couldn't give two shits. In that moment, he was playing only for her—*his* AC/DC girl, *his* devoted fan. He sang his hit, then launched into the covers the Blasphemers always ended their set with, all the while keeping his well-worn rock-and-roll eyes on that evening's object of his brief desire.

II

"That's it?"

AC/DC girl was disappointed.

Billy let out a final grunt; what did she expect? It wasn't like they were going to spend a cozy weekend in Bath or end up in his dingy flat—there was barely enough room for *him* there. Plus, Billy knew if he woke up to googly-eyes and cooing sounds, he'd want to slit his wrists.

"Afraid so, sweetcakes," Billy mumbled as he pushed her off him and squiggled in the driver's seat to zip up his leather pants.

The restored MG convertible wasn't ideal for a shag but the Wooten's dressing room was the size of a dustman's closet and his bandmates weren't leaving anytime soon. So he'd ushered AC/DC girl out into the alley and the MG. He handed her the red-diamonded leggings she'd shed less than three minutes earlier.

"Off with you, now."

Humiliated, AC/DC girl lowered her T-shirt so the band's moniker spread over the pendulous breasts that had occupied Billy's full attention until thirty seconds earlier. "I didn't get to . . . you know . . . finish."

Billy gave her a pat on the rump. "But it'll give you a good story, won't it?"

"That I dropped my knickers for some has-been who lasted twenty seconds?"

"Was it that long?" Billy cracked.

"You really are a fuckin' bastard!" cried AC/DC girl. Mercifully, she crawled out of the car and hiked the leggings back up under the T-shirt.

"I've been called worse."

Billy definitely had.

Not in the early days—back when the Blasphemers had gotten their first and only decent record deal. That debut album had sprouted "Ain't I Good Enough for You," an honest-to-God smash. That meant the next two albums sold well enough, even if the numbers were square roots of that maiden effort. Sub-mediocrity followed; the record company dropped them and there wasn't a single label on the planet that would pick up the pieces.

Now, two decades later, the band was relegated to dives like the Wooten, which bordered a Piccadilly Circus alley where Billy was lucky to grab a groupie fuck.

Case in point—the disheveled and disillusioned AC/DC girl who had choked back a sob, flipped Billy off, then tromped down the alley, her heels clacking rhythmically on cobblestones as she disappeared into the misty London night.

Billy opened the glove compartment and dug around for a half-finished pint of Bushmills, uncapped it, and took a deep pull of amber-colored sustenance.

THUMP.

Something had just hit the back of the MG.

"Holy crap!" Whiskey spilled onto his multicolored silk shirt. His first thought was the girl.

"We're all done here! Go home!"

The car jolted again.

Someone had *opened* the trunk.

Visions of scorned female rage raced through his head—tire irons on body parts, starting with private ones. Even worse—smashing his beloved Fender housed at the bottom of the boot. That got him scrambling out of the MG.

"Done means done, bitch! What don't you get about that?!"

He got no response. Billy realized he hadn't heard her high heels clip-clopping their way back on the cobblestones.

A figure flew out of the fog, swinging a familiar object.

The Fender Telecaster.

Pried from its case and suddenly used on its owner—a washed-up rocker who was soon bleeding out on the cobblestones of an alley in the heart of London.

His attacker hovered above, then straddled him—much like Billy did with his 10:50 women—wielding the Fender as a seductive scepter. For a moment, it seemed like he was going to tear into a searing solo of his own—instead, he ripped off one of the metal guitar strings with a savage jerk.

Within seconds, it was wrapped around Billy's neck.

As he felt the life seeping out of him, Billy heard his killer softly begin to whistle "Ain't I Good Enough for You."

Billy really hated that song.

III

The Heath.

Austin Grant still strolled through it each Sunday after church, though he'd been doing it alone for over a year. Hampstead Heath had been their favorite spot on Earth, a gigantic park plopped atop a hill over London where he'd proposed to Allison over three decades ago.

They'd gotten married on a spectacular spring afternoon when the purple lilacs, pink hydrangeas, and blush roses were in full bloom. He'd been amazed she'd agreed to take him as her husband after a one-month courtship. Grant had been certain her late father wouldn't hand his only daughter to a man with no prospects. Miraculously, Allison saw enough in Grant to accept his proposal and had subsequently cheered him on from a front-row seat through his entire career.

A career that was almost over.

Walking down the manicured path on this blustery December day, Grant kicked himself for not heeding Allison's suggestions to pack it in five years earlier.

When had he finally let her show him the brochure? The month before she took ill? The small house in Todi—an hour's drive northeast of Rome where vineyards flourished and life slowed down to a blessed crawl. "We'll rent it for a summer," Allison had said. "You'll see if you can stand it. Reading a book, taking an afternoon nap; Lord knows—maybe even a drink before dinner."

Grant had been dubious—he took his two weeks a year like clockwork and drove Allison crazy calling work every day while they were supposedly on holiday. More than once they had scrapped a trip altogether because he couldn't tear himself away and would promise to make up for those lost days.

"Makeup" days gone forever when she had taken ill and never recovered.

Highgate Cemetery had been the obvious choice for Allison's final resting place. It had broken his heart when she had told him that it would be a place she knew Grant wouldn't mind visiting her until the time came for him to lie down beside her. Indeed, this was the only place where he could find peace, on the cast-iron bench that, just one year after Grant had donated it to honor Allison's passing, already sported a coat of rust from the pervasive London dampness.

He placed a bouquet of her favorite blush roses on the plot, as he did every Sunday. Hard to find in the winter, Grant was determined his love would always have the same flowers that had surrounded them on their wedding day. He had an arrangement with a florist on the High Street; if the proprietor carried them year-round, Grant could arrange for the steep parking permit in front of the man's shop to be waived. It was one of the few job perks left for Grant.

ALLISON REBECCA GRANT; *Beloved Daughter, Wife, and Mother.*

The simple tombstone inscription always turned Grant's thoughts to Rachel. He wondered what she was up to, how things had gone so terribly wrong. He hadn't seen their daughter since the funeral. Shortly after Allison had been diagnosed with lung cancer, Rachel had flown in from New York and holed up in the bedroom with her mother. She had left the house barely uttering a word to Grant. The one time he had tried to get his daughter to talk, Rachel had laid it out pure and simple.

"Mom is dying. There's nothing more to say."

Why she refused to ever have another conversation about it was a mystery to Grant. She'd stopped responding to his emails a while back and had even changed her cell number. If it weren't for coming across an occasional feature piece she wrote in the *New Yorker* or the *New York*

Times Magazine, he might think that Rachel had dropped off the face of the Earth.

He traced his fingers over the inscription, remembering those final days.

He was forever haunted by that last memory: seeing Allison carted off to hospital, unable to touch her, not realizing in that moment he would never see her again or even get a chance to say goodbye.

Grant sighed and glanced at his watch, the same Tag he'd been wearing for three decades, and spied the tiny window on its face with the date.

The eighth.

Twenty-three more days till year's end. Three weeks and two more days until he didn't have to get up and go anywhere. He certainly wasn't going to rent a house in Todi. Not by himself.

He knew he would end up right here—on this bloody bench. At least he would be rid of his current troubles and wouldn't have to deal with situations like the Fleming mess earlier in the year.

"Sir?"

For a second, Grant thought he'd drifted off and fallen asleep. He couldn't come up with another reasonable explanation for hearing Hawley's voice.

He turned around to see the man himself standing on a path among the graves. Hawley seemed nervous and a little jiggly, still carrying the extra weight Grant had urged him to lose for the job and his health.

"What are you doing here, Hawley?"

"You didn't answer your mobile, sir."

"That's because it's Sunday and I don't have it on."

"Well, I know you come up here every Sunday."

"And how would you know that?"

Hawley hesitated before answering. Grant felt sorry for the man; he knew he still intimidated him, even though he'd been Hawley's superior for over a decade.

"Because you told me this is where you go," Hawley finally explained. "In case I really needed you—if something important came up."

"Then I presume this must be very important."

Hawley swayed back and forth. Waiting, as if for permission to speak—which Grant mercifully gave him. "Out with it, Sergeant."

"There's been another one."

An icy chill ran the length of Grant's spine. "A third?"

"In an alley behind a club in Piccadilly. Same mark as the others . . ."

"Except there were three lines instead of one or two."

"Exactly, Commander."

"Nice of the bloke to keep track for us," Grant said grimly.

He turned for one last look at Allison's grave, making a silent promise to see her the following Sunday. Then he told Hawley to lead the way. As they walked out of Highgate Cemetery, a thought that had recently become Grant's mantra ran through his head.

I can't wait until New Year's Day, when I can leave Scotland Yard forever.

IV

G rant didn't even know that the Wooten existed. There used to be underground clubs on practically every block in mid-London and Grant hadn't frequented a single one. He'd definitely never heard of Billy Street or his band, the Blasphemers.

The crime team had been working the scene for over an hour by the time Grant arrived with Sergeant Hawley. The club's adjacent alley was so tight between buildings that only a Smart car or the victim's MG could navigate it without scraping paint. It was a space to toss trash, sneak out the back door for a smoke, or send an aging rocker off to meet his Maker. Being Sunday, Street's body wasn't discovered until a neighbor ducked into the alley to let his dog relieve itself. Street had been identified by the driver's license in his pocket, allowing them to run his name through the system, which resulted in the knowledge that his band had played the Wooten the previous evening. As Grant approached the MG, Hawley was already on his mobile, rounding up the club owner and other Blasphemers to put together some semblance of a timeline.

Jeffries, the forensics medical examiner, was taking measurements and notes. Well into his forties but looking two decades older (*Living with the dead will do that to you*, thought Grant), he wore a bulky parka over jeans and a sweatshirt. Clearly his weekend had been interrupted just like Grant's.

"Sorry to drag you out on a Sunday morning, Commander."

"Not as sorry as I am," Grant said. "Seeing how it looks like we have an even larger problem on our hands."

"I'm afraid so," agreed the FME.

Grant peered over Jeffries's shoulder to stare down at the dead rocker. With rigor setting in, Billy Street looked paler than Marley's ghost, but even more anguished. The metal guitar string wrapped around his bulging neck didn't help. But it was the victim's forehead that commanded Grant's attention. Vertical cuts had been sliced directly above the victim's dyed eyebrows.

"Sadly familiar?" asked Grant.

"Without being back at the morgue to compare, I'd say you're looking at the same perpetrator," answered Jeffries. "The marks are identical in width and length; a similar knife was used. The only difference being . . ."

". . . the number of marks," finished Grant. "Bastard must think we can't keep count."

"Any chance this leaked?"

"We've managed to keep it out of the papers and it hasn't been on the telly." The commander indicated the three marks. "We made sure to keep those to ourselves—especially after we got the second one."

"How long do you think you'll be able to keep it that way?"

"I need to figure that out. How soon can I get a full report?"

"End of the day? Good thing about it being Sunday—it's quiet."

"Not for long," Grant said wearily. He wished he wasn't so certain about that—but he could feel the storm rising.

Three murders in a week.

Each more horrific than the last.

V

The first body was discovered on the second of December.

It was an easy enough date for Grant to remember. It had been Allison's birthday. So he was already in a glum mood to begin with.

A visiting Oxford professor of Greek mythology had not returned to the college after lecturing at the British Library the previous evening. When the Yard was alerted, a couple of constables were dispatched to the library, where a search located the dead man stuffed inside a WC off a back stairwell on the third floor.

After the lecture, Professor Lionel Frey had ducked inside the loo but had never exited the stall. His killer had turned out the lights and placed an "Out of Order" placard on the doorknob after carving a vertical line on Frey's forehead to go with the deadly slash across the professor's throat.

The sheer audacity of the murder had drawn Grant into the case.

Grant's brother, Everett, a philosophy don at Oxford, had said someone had done a great service sending Frey to that big university in the sky. The mythology professor was a "pompous arse" who looked down on anyone who wasn't taken with the Greek gods Frey had made his life's work.

None of the other Oxford faculty were as overt as Everett, but Grant could tell that Lionel Frey wasn't going to be missed by his colleagues. But none seemed to have an actual motive or interest in traveling down to London to sit through a two-hour lecture and then kill its orator in a tight-fitting WC stall either.

Grant's thinking went to the obvious—a discarded mistress or some other affronted Londoner, but Frey's schedule, credit cards, and wife's statement showed he hadn't set foot in the city for over six months. Any further theorizing was thrown to the wind when the second murder occurred.

Melanie Keaton.

A sculptor of some renown in the East End, she'd been found in her studio by Thomas Simmons, a prospective buyer, who'd arrived for a scheduled showing that morning. Simmons had sauntered inside the Whitechapel studio five days ago to discover Keaton on the floor with her throat slashed. Surrounding her body were the six figurines she had planned to show him with their wooden heads lopped off.

Grant was summoned to the East End by the constable, who had made a connection between the carefully carved marks (*plural*, yes, because there were now *two*, thank you very much) on Melanie Keaton's forehead and the one found on the Oxford don who'd met his demise on the porcelain at the British Library.

When Grant arrived on the scene, he was immediately drawn to the beheaded figurines with black-feathered wings sprouting from their backs and faces an even darker shade of ebony. One of Keaton's employees told him they were a series of archangels the sculptor had been working on. The studio was filled with a host of carvings in the same vein, causing the commander to wonder if he'd stumbled onto a black magic cult. Grant made a note to check if the murdered Oxford don had similar tastes, then began a round of questioning that proved no more successful than the inquiries days before at the British Library.

No one had seen Melanie Keaton since she'd locked up the previous evening. Grant asked Simmons if he was familiar with the library but it proved to be a tree not worth barking up; the man had just returned from a business trip in Poland where he'd been for the past month, dousing the idea he might have been on the third floor of the British Library on the first night of December.

Grant left the studio with no sort of connection between an Oxford professor of Greek mythology and a Whitechapel sculptor of archangels.

Except for the carvings in their forehead; Melanie Keaton had twice the number of Lionel Frey. Grant felt no better when the FME concluded they'd been administered postmortem. It meant the killer was trying to make a point—as if purposely egging Grant and the Yard on.

Catch me if you can.

VI

The few hours after leaving Piccadilly brought no clarity. Nor did subsequent days.

An Oxford don, an East End artist, and a washed-up rocker—what did they have in common? It was one nasty riddle—and the only person who knew the answer wasn't sharing.

It went further downhill once they rounded up Billy Street's bandmates. They were fairly new additions to the Blasphemers; the original members had fallen to the wayside due to excessive alcohol and lack of gigs. None of the current trio held any enmity toward the lead singer. It was Billy's band—they were just playing in it. With his passing, they were talking of forming a tribute group, but were unsure if it was a good idea because there was just one song to pay homage to.

The next dead end was Lisa Gosden. Jeffries had found trace evidence in the MG that Street had been with a woman the night he was killed and it didn't take long for Grant's team to run down the Gosden girl. She'd attended Billy's swan song and reluctantly admitted to leaving the club with him that night.

Grant found it hard to believe she could have wrapped an E string around the musician's neck as well as dispatched an Oxford don and sculptor all within a week. She fumbled through the details of her rendezvous with Billy—expressing frustration at his lack of prowess as a lover (more information than Grant needed). And she hadn't been aware of being watched by anyone in the MG or during her "walk of shame" out to Charles Street.

By Thursday night, when he headed up to Hampstead for his weekly dinner and chess match with Everett, Grant felt further astray than ever on the case. The Thursday dinners had started, at Everett's insistence, at his brother's house shortly after Allison's passing. Grant appreciated Everett taking it upon himself to look after his older brother.

"I won't have you wasting away," Everett had told him the night of the wake. "I can't tell you how many geezers at the university I've seen go belly up right after their loved ones passed. They just seem to give up on living."

Everett said he would miss Allison as well. He'd actually known her longer than Grant. Everett had introduced them during his last year as a student at Oxford when he'd come home to Liverpool for the holidays. Everett and Allison had briefly gone out but her heart quickly went to Grant. She'd jokingly say she hadn't felt smart enough for Everett, a brilliant budding theologian. This made Grant feel slightly inferior, to which Allison would say "Nonsense." At least the two of them could talk about normal things and affairs of the heart.

The chess game came about gradually. They played a few times those first few months, then it became a challenge that Grant actually looked forward to. During their matches, Grant would often discuss his cases with Everett. His brother was a good listener and usually offered a fresh analytical view. Sometimes, it was just enough for Grant to lay out the entire matter—hearing it leave his lips often helped him locate the missing piece to the puzzle he'd been trying to unravel.

But not this time.

"This 'Counter' . . ." began Everett.

"An awful moniker, you must admit." A colleague of Grant's had come up with the not-so-clever-label and it had unfortunately stuck.

"Well, I'm sure he, or she, though I doubt it's a woman, would probably like the idea they've been given a nickname."

"What makes you say that?" Grant asked.

"Why mark his victims unless he's boasting? I'd wager he's frustrated that you haven't been giving him his fair share of press. If it should leak to the press, I wouldn't be shocked if it was your killer who sprung it."

A frustrated Grant rested his finger atop his black bishop. "Wonderful. If that happened, I'd need to claim the source as 'Anonymous' because the killer isn't going to identify himself—and I'd be back at square one."

"Which would be what?" prodded Everett.

"Damned if I know!" cried Grant. He moved the bishop diagonally three spots and plopped it down on a black square.

His brother gave him a disapproving look and moved a rook sideways. "Afraid that's checkmate, dear Austin."

Grant didn't see it at first. Then he realized his fatal mistake was four moves down the line. He rose to his feet and started pacing in Everett's library, where they had set up the board beside a dwindling fire.

"I can't concentrate on anything."

"So try and narrow it down," suggested Everett. "What does your gut say?"

"My gut says this can't be random."

"And why not?"

Grant stopped midstride. "Because the killer went to the unnecessary trouble of selecting these particular victims."

"You're saying he chose them for a specific reason."

"But why? Why a professor who bores people with tales of mythic beings no one cares about, a sculptor who makes strange idols, or a washed-up musician in a band more interested in taking the Lord's name in vain than making something that passes for music? It's beyond me."

Everett suddenly stood up as well. "Say that again."

"It's all beyond me."

Grant's brother shook his head. "No. No. The Lord's name part."

"Taking it in vain? That part?"

"Yes. Why do you say that?"

"Because Street's band is called the Blasphemers."

Everett made a beeline for his bookshelves.

"What are you doing?" Grant asked, intrigued.

Everett didn't answer. His eyes crisscrossed the various shelves until he spied a black bound book.

"Ah, here we go."

He held up a thick tome. A King James Bible.

Grant's eyes widened. "Isn't that the one that Dad gave each of us?"

"I'm surprised you even recognize it," said Everett with a smile. "I figure yours must be gathering dust somewhere, you good-for-nothing heathen."

"You're going to start quoting scripture? This is what my life has come to?"

Everett was silent while flipping pages. "Ah, here we go. Exodus, chapter twenty, verse one. I quote: *'And God spake all these words, saying, I am the Lord thy God, which have brought thee out of the land of Egypt, out of the house of bondage. Thou shalt have no other gods before me.'*"

Everett looked up. "As opposed to Lionel Frey, who devoted his life to other gods—the Greek variety, not Jehovah or whatever the Good Book says he should be doing . . ."

"Everett . . ."

His brother quieted Grant with a look and continued. "Number two. *'Thou shalt not make unto thee any graven image, or any likeness of any thing that is in heaven above. . . .'* Like your sculptor of archangels."

"You can't be serious."

"Deadly." Everett tapped the Bible passage. "Number three. *'Thou shalt not take the name of the Lord thy God in vain.'* Sound familiar?"

He lowered the book and stared at Grant, whose mouth had dropped open.

"Good God. The Blasphemers?" said the stunned commander.

"I think we might have stumbled onto your connection, dear brother."

Grant shook his head in disbelief. "The Ten Commandments?"

"He's even numbering them for you. Right on their foreheads."

Grant shook his head in disbelief as he uttered the words. "Someone's killing people according to the Ten Commandments."

"Do you have another link in mind?" asked Everett.

Grant wished he did.

The thought running through his head was much, much worse.

Three down. Seven to go.

VII

Grant kicked himself for not putting it together on his own. The killings wrapped up in some sort of misguided religious fervor made perfect sense. Someone was traipsing around London doling out their own form of judgment on people they deemed to have committed punishable sins, even if they were far-fetched and not actual transgressions. Clearly, the killer was bent, so his choices needn't make sense to a normal person, only to the delusional one who had declared himself judge, jury, and executioner.

Leave it to his brother, "the educated one" as their father used to say, to figure it out. If his Ten Commandment theory held, he knew Everett would lord it over him forever, even if Grant caught the killer and put him away.

"Seeing as how I'm not up to speed with the Good Book, remind me what the Fourth Commandment is."

Everett turned back to the King James Bible and found the passage again. " '*Remember the sabbath day, to keep it holy. Six days shalt thou labour, and do all thy work: but the seventh day is the sabbath of the Lord thy God: in it thou shalt not do any work . . .*' " Everett closed the book.

"Splendid. I'm looking to protect a person who works on Sunday."

"Or Saturdays if we're adhering to Judaic law. But seeing as how Jews are outnumbered by Christians at a rate of over one hundred to one in Britain, I think we're safe sticking with the Sabbath being a Sunday."

"You have any idea how many people in Greater London we're looking at?"

"Probably a whole lot more than the men you have at your disposal. What sort of folks are we talking about?" asked Everett.

"Well, there's every bartender, waiter, or kitchen hand in a restaurant, café, or bistro. You have your ticket takers at the cinemas, shop girls up in Notting Hill and Marylebone High Street to name a few hundred. Men working tube stations, black cab and Uber drivers, museum docents—need I go on?"

"No, though I quite enjoy hearing you prattle away. I'd say you have your work cut out for you." Everett laughed. "Any thoughts where you might begin?"

"I don't have a bloody clue!"

A frustrated Grant grabbed the Bible from his brother and flipped through its pages. He slammed it shut just as quickly. "What the hell am I doing? It's not like I'm going to find an answer in here."

"You wouldn't be the first to go looking. Father Talbot up at Oxford chastises us on a weekly basis for not keeping up with our Bible studies."

Grant started to respond, then checked himself. "Of course."

Everett's brow raised. "What are we talking about—of course?"

"A priest," answered Grant. "That has to be it, don't you think?"

Before Everett could reply, Grant was back up and pacing. For the first time since Frey's body had been discovered in the library loo, the commander could feel life pumping back into his veins. He turned to face his brother and pointed at the Bible as if answers had just sprung from it like a fountain of truth.

"Whose work is defined by them working on the Sabbath? Who spends every Sunday morning front and center before Londoners, come rain or shine?"

"Your friendly neighborhood parish priest," Everett responded. "You think he's going after a priest?"

"It's just twisted and specific enough to fit your theory."

"Do you have any idea how many priests, pastors, and reverends there are in Greater London?" asked Everett.

"A lot more than I'd like."

VIII

The number turned out to be way higher than he anticipated. There were thousands of Catholic priests in the UK, with at least a quarter of those practicing in the London environs. Grant realized he couldn't rule out altar boys, assistant clerics, and the like, as they worked the Sabbath as well and could fit the same criteria laid out in the Fourth Commandment.

The good news was that it was only Friday, which gave his team at the Yard a two-day jump. First, Grant went to see Franklin Stebbins, the Yard's deputy commander and head of the Metropolitan Police—the man he answered to. He painstakingly convinced his superior that Everett's Ten Commandments theory was their prime (and only) lead, and they formulated a plan on how best to prevent a fourth murder from occurring right under their collective noses.

Stationing a constable at every church in London was obviously impossible, so they considered how to get the word out without yielding a mass panic. All the Yard needed was screaming headlines in the *Daily Mail* or the *Daily Mirror* informing Britain's citizenry that a knife-wielding lunatic was threatening to disrupt their Sunday sermon or the baptism of their newborn child.

It was decided that Grant's team should reach out one by one to every church with a very specific warning. Rather than tell clergy they were possible prey for a serial killer, the party line would be that the Yard had received a veiled threat of violence against a priest that coming Sunday. Extra patrols would be provided wherever possible and priests would be urged not to venture into solitary places on that particular day and not to hesitate to report anything suspicious. Grant told the clergy he personally contacted to keep this information to themselves as he didn't want to start full-fledged hysteria within their congregations.

Not a single priest or pastor uttered a protest. Grant figured as men of God they had been trained to take on burdens to ensure the common good. Many asked if they should cancel services. Grant said it was their choice, but not a bad idea.

Miraculously, the media didn't catch on until Saturday evening.

That was when Monte Ferguson, a veteran reporter for the *Daily Mail*, appeared outside Grant's office just as he was heading home after calling hundreds of London churches. Bespectacled, wiry, and desperately hanging on to his few remaining wisps of unkempt hair, Ferguson was polite but dogged, a journalist who Grant knew from experience he'd need to tread lightly with. Their history of give-and-take had been rocky; not enough giving on Grant's part for the reporter, with Ferguson taking a bit too much when allowed the opportunity. Most recently, Grant had been criticized by Ferguson in a Sunday editorial after the Fleming mess. It still rankled.

"No better place to hang out on a Saturday night, Monte?" Grant asked, turning the lights off in his office.

"Better than going to church in the morning," said the smiling journalist.

"I'd say that all depends on the sermon."

"Well, in my parish, Father McGuinness has canceled services."

"Consider yourself blessed."

"He's not the only one," Ferguson added. "I've found at least a dozen other churches that will be closed as well."

The reporter checked a pad for notes. Ferguson was a bit of a Luddite, refusing to subscribe to the marvels of iPhones and other devices. Grant could appreciate that, being somewhat of a technophobe himself—but it made him aware that Ferguson had done enough digging to compile a list of his own.

"Must be something in the holy water," chided Grant, taking one last stab at getting Ferguson to look a different way.

"Or receiving the same call from the Yard earlier this morning telling them about a threat against the church."

So much for that.

"I don't suppose you'd care to share who told you this?" asked Grant.

The scribe gave Grant a look that screamed *You can't be serious.*

"What do you want, Monte? You know I'm not going to confirm such a claim."

"How about giving me a reason not to run with it in the *Mail*'s morning edition or popping it online right now?"

"How's not starting a mass panic through London sound?"

Ferguson shrugged. "Just more news for Monday."

Grant had to hand it to Ferguson. The man was most comfortable once he got a bone in his mouth. "What would you need to not print something before tomorrow morning?"

"An exclusive of some sort."

"Some sort being what?"

"A statement by day's end tomorrow from you acknowledging the existence of a threat that didn't come to pass or an exclusive interview with details about a crime should it occur."

"I think I can promise that."

Grant felt Ferguson's eyes focus in on him. "That was easy enough," said the journalist. "Too easy actually. What gives?"

"I've had a long day, Monte. I expect an even longer one tomorrow. So I'd like to get some sleep while I still can."

Grant started to move past but Ferguson shifted enough to cause the commander to stop in his tracks. "What time?"

"What time what?"

"What time do we chat tomorrow?"

"Monday morning."

"I thought we agreed on day's end."

"That would be midnight. A threat on Sunday could be at any time."

"That means I don't get an exclusive in the paper until Tuesday."

"But you'll put it online with your byline within minutes of us talking."

Grant watched Ferguson chew on that. Finally, the reporter nodded.

The commander was satisfied. At least Ferguson was a solid newsman who had enough integrity to stand by the veracity of his findings.

Grant was halfway down the hall when Ferguson called out.

"Would you advise me to skip morning services, Commander?"

"Totally your decision, Monte. Unfortunately, I don't get a choice."

IX

Grant had kept going to church each week after his wife passed. At first, he did it out of respect for his better half who was the church-goer in the family. But as the weeks and months pressed on, he had found deep comfort there. Not wanting to admit that loneliness was settling in, especially with retirement on the horizon, Grant had convinced himself that Sunday mornings at Saint Matthew's were something he could rely on, a constant in a world that had changed more in the past year than the previous half century.

But on this particular Sunday morning, all of Grant's synapses were on full alert. Not that he expected chaos to erupt in his very own church, but he spent the majority of the priest's sermon watching his fellow parishioners' every movement, looking for anything that seemed out of the ordinary. Thankfully, the service concluded without interruption and Father Gill still in one piece.

Afterward, Grant approached the priest, whom he had personally called the previous day to warn him to be extra careful on this Sabbath. Grant had told him that once midnight rolled around, they'd be able to take a communal deep breath.

"If nothing happens, are we supposed to go through the whole thing again next Sunday?" Father Gill had queried.

Grant hadn't even considered that.

"I think we take this one day at a time," Grant had replied.

The priest had thanked Grant for coming, then retreated with the other clergy into the church. Grant couldn't help but admire his calmness, the dedication to his flock and service to God. The commander wished he believed in something so pure—but he'd witnessed too much horror in his three decades of public service.

It was one of the many reasons he was retiring.

He skipped the weekly visit to the cemetery, promising Allison that he would make it up to her. Soon enough, Grant would have plenty of time on his hands. He spent the remainder of the day checking with patrols, churches throughout London, and with any member of clergy he could find.

As each hour passed, Grant could feel his insides churning more, convinced that the killer was torturing him and his brethren, stretching the moment till the last possible second when he would unleash his knife and make his literal mark—throwing Grant and the whole of Scotland Yard into complete chaos.

Eventually, the midnight hour arrived. And nothing came to pass.

"I guess I'm happy to be proved wrong," said Everett when he phoned Grant shortly after twelve and was told all of London's clergy were safe and accounted for.

"I feel the same way," agreed Grant, as he tossed his keys on the hall table of his house in the Maida Vale section of London and locked the front door.

"What happens now? Same thing next Sunday?" asked his brother.

"Right now, I just want to get some sleep," answered Grant.

X

He got about three hours.

When the phone rang, it was 4:15. By the time Grant picked it up, he was wide awake. Nothing good ever happened at 4:15 in the morning.

Especially when one was a commander at Scotland Yard. "Grant here."

The first thing he noticed was the faraway hiss and ever-so-slight delay that signaled the call wasn't local. "Commander Austin Grant?"

The next thing was the voice. Officious—yes. British—no.

"Yes, who is this?"

"My name's Frankel. Detective John Frankel, NYPD. Sorry to wake you; I know it's early there."

"That's all right, Detective. How can I help you?"

The question was easy enough. He had a sinking feeling about the answer.

"I got pointed in your direction by reports that came over the homicide wire about a series of murders you've had there in England. Throats slashed. Marks carved on foreheads."

"Yes," replied Grant. "That would be my investigation."

"Well, I've got a DB here with the same MO."

"DB?"

"Sorry. Dead body. Guess you have different terminology over there. My victim was impaled on a cross above the altar in Saint Patrick's Cathedral."

Grant felt his mouth dry up. "By any chance, is your victim a priest?"

"Father Adam Peters. He's been at Saint Paddy's for over forty years."

"And the marking on the forehead. A capital I and capital V—like a Roman numeral four?"

Grant heard the detective's intake of breath on the other end of the line.

"A number. That answers a few questions. We thought maybe someone was trying to spell out something—like a name." Frankel cleared his throat. "I don't suppose this is a lucky guess on your part?"

"No. Not lucky." Grant sighed. "Not lucky at all."

PART ONE

Little Town Blues

1

G rant hated heights.

He blamed it on the family cat and Everett. His younger brother had let Frisky slip out the door and the pet had promptly chased a bird up a giant elm. The next thing nine-year-old Austin knew, he was climbing after him and up fifty feet in the air. When he reached the top, Frisky was back on terra firma and Austin was holding on to the tree for dear life. Yelling, he lost his grip and dropped twenty feet before grabbing a branch, where he swung until his father rushed out to rescue him. Young Austin ended up blubbering uncontrollably all night. The tears subsided the next morning, but the feeling of nausea and panic he'd suffered when up on high returned again and again.

So Scotland Yard Commander Austin Grant made sure to book an aisle seat on the 777 British Airways jet to JFK out of Heathrow. Intellectually, he knew he was firmly ensconced in the finest machinery that brilliant engineers could devise. He'd read the statistics—the chance of being involved in a fatal auto crash was a thousand times more likely than an air catastrophe. That didn't alter the fact that an airplane window provided a forty-thousand-foot view of the Atlantic Ocean. Grant was totally content limiting his line of sight to the well-worn airline magazines and boring rom-com on the TV monitor on the seat back in front of him.

He resisted the urge to kiss the Jetway upon arrival at JFK and entered the terminal on somewhat wobbly feet. He didn't relish a return across the pond and having to be sky-high soon; he figured his presence wouldn't be required that long by NYPD Detective Frankel.

It was still light out when he reached the cab stand, a benefit of catching the morning flight and getting to turn his Tag back five hours. He was on the Long Island Expressway (which his cabbie called the "world's biggest parking lot") when the sun began its descent behind the massive Manhattan skyline—bathing the city in a pinkish glow that could have come courtesy of Monet's water lily palette.

The gargantuan buildings left him awestruck. He was immediately aware of what was missing: the Twin Towers. It had been nearly two decades since they crashed down with a roar that changed the world, but it was still impossible to imagine the city without them. Thoughts of an early retirement had swirled through his head right around the Millennium, but those disappeared after 9/11. That tragic day on the tip of Manhattan had left him determined to do his part in keeping his countrymen and loved ones safe. He realized if the Towers were still there rising in front of him, he might not be heading into New York City on the trail of a maniac who was well on his way to holding two cities hostage.

A jolt courtesy of a pothole snapped Grant from his remembrance and he discovered that they were suddenly in a Midtown traffic jam. He wondered if rush hour was a 24/7 occurrence that plagued New Yorkers and mentioned as much to his driver, a dark-haired, overweight escapee from the Bronx.

"Who the fuck knows what's going on?" cried the driver. "Probably some Third World cocksucking country having their weekly parade down Fifth Avenue." The cabbie slammed the taxi into park and jumped outside. Grant could hear him screaming at someone. He marveled at the man's ability to string so many invectives into one run-on sentence. Seconds later, the driver had returned.

"Fuckin' garbage truck. Asshole decided to take up half the street to grab a cup of coffee." He glanced in the rearview mirror, meeting Grant's eyes. "Bet you Brits wouldn't stand for this kinda shit."

"Absolutely not," replied Grant, putting on his best faux upper-crust Bond Street accent. "We'd guillotine the tosser in the middle of Trafalgar Square."

"Seriously?"

"We'd sell tickets too. All in the good name of the Queen's Trust."

"You're shitting me now, right?"

Grant smiled. "A smidge."

"You know, if you don't like the way we do things here, you should just go back to where you fucking came from."

Welcome to New York City, thought Grant.

———

When making rushed arrangements that morning, Grant had searched for places to stay near Saint Patrick's Cathedral. It seemed like Divine Providence when a certain hotel popped up, so he chose it as a home away from home.

"Welcome to the London," greeted the doorman as he swung open his charge. Grant was taken aback—not just by the friendly smile (after enduring over an hour of expletives and Brit bashing) but the dark suit the man wore. He had expected to find employees of a hotel with such a moniker wearing something more Anglo-Saxon—if not a Beefeater's uniform, at least a traditional morning suit.

Thus began the Americanization of Austin Grant. The lobby with massive jutting abstract pieces someone called "art" was as far removed from the tea-serving sanctuaries he and Allison had taken Rachel to every Sunday in her youth as Grant's cabbie was from applying for a British passport.

Grant approached the reception desk, where he was handed a registration slip along with a hot towel dipped in a "mixture of regenerative herbs." Grant dabbed a cheek gently, then gave the towel back to the female receptionist who could double for a flawless mannequin in one of Harrods display windows.

"You'll be staying with us for a week?"

"I'm not quite sure," Grant replied. "I might be leaving tomorrow or I might have to extend. Can we leave it open-ended?"

She worked the keyboard with perfectly violet-manicured fingers. "I'm afraid that might be difficult, sir. It's actually our busiest season with Christmas rapidly approaching. And the New Year immediately after."

"So, what happens if I need to stay longer?"

"I'm afraid you'll need to make other arrangements. We can help you find another accommodation, but I wouldn't wait long. The city gets crowded this time of year. Perhaps your business will wrap up before your departure date."

For all Grant knew, the killer was upstairs in his room waiting for him, wrapped up in a pretty bow, ready to confess. Along with Father Christmas. Grant sighed inwardly, signed his name, and took the key.

"We'll have to see. Thank you."

"I'm sure you'll be happy to get back to your family in England." She leaned forward, as if about to impart a secret that would totally enlighten Grant. "You don't want to be here near Christmas. People tend to go a bit nuts."

Grant nodded.

I know one person in particular.

The room was smaller than small, barely enough space for Grant and his carry-on bag. The walls were bright—he was tempted to turn off the lights to see if they actually glowed in the dark. Grant crossed to the window and opened the shade. He had a very nice view of a brick building across a service alley. And this was a deluxe room. He had figured, *Why not splurge while on the public dole?* He couldn't even imagine the view a standard room offered.

Way too wired to consider sleep and realizing he would just stumble over himself in the tight confines of his room, he decided to go for a walk.

Once outside, Grant was fully aware of what the receptionist had been talking about. Even at nine o'clock on a Monday evening, the city was buzzing with yuletide cheer, even if it was more like "Christmas—The Infomercial." Every window celebrated, announced, or pushed the upcoming holiday. From "Xmas Slash Sale" to giant Advent calendars, from plastic blow-up reindeers to Santa-clad mannequins, each storefront vied for the consumer's eye and pocketbook.

It reminded Grant that he wasn't going to have to rack his brain to come up with the perfect Christmas gift for Allison. As much as he hated the pushing and shoving he had to endure each December to get the desired item, it was worth it seeing Allison's face light up each Christmas morning as she unfurled the gift his hands had clumsily wrapped in too much paper. Now, with Allison gone forever, a daughter who wouldn't answer his e-mails, let alone accept a gift, Grant's Christmas list was quite empty. He understood why so many called these weeks the Most Dreadful Time of Year.

Suddenly, Grant was swallowed up by a horde of happy Manhattanites exiting Radio City Music Hall. Many were jolly families, some executing ridiculous leg kicks. The placards in the building's showcases advertised the "Holiday Show Featuring the World-Famous Rockettes." He was swept up by the masses down Fiftieth Street, where the largest Christmas tree he had ever seen was aglow in all its glory with a host of ice skaters swooshing in circles below it.

Grant took it all in and tried to get in the spirit of the season. But this proved difficult, knowing that evil had made its way across the Atlantic to wreak havoc on unsuspecting New Yorkers.

Happy Holidays, everyone, from the worst of Merry England!
Turning away from the holiday lights, he shuffled on.

Saint Patrick's Cathedral.

It encompassed the city block between Fiftieth and Fifty-First Streets on Fifth Avenue. Grant stared up at the humongous structure. There were cathedrals in Britain that rivaled and surpassed Saint Patrick's in ornate design and size, but it was the setting that amazed him. Having read up on the cathedral's history on the plane, he'd learned it was an early nineteenth century Jesuit college that was abandoned to become a cemetery. It had been saved by Reverend Michael Curran, an energetic priest who raised funds to construct the cathedral starting in 1858. Upon completion, it was the seat for the archbishop of the Roman Catholic Archdiocese of New York and had borne witness to celebrations, weddings, and requiem masses for famous New Yorkers like Babe Ruth, Bobby Kennedy, and Ed Sullivan.

And now it was a Manhattan crime scene.

Most remnants of a police presence were gone. There wasn't a squad car in sight, and only one local news van was present, with a roving reporter doing filler follow-up. Clearly the cops had moved on to the next-worst thing—which suited Grant. He had agreed to meet Frankel the following morning. This way he could get a good look at the church beforehand without being there in an official capacity.

Once inside, he was surprised to see a few dozen people moving through the church, even though it was ten o'clock on a Monday evening. A few were sprinkled in pews, others by small side altars lighting candles. Some sightseers strolled in the back, poring through guidebooks detailing the church's history and highlights.

But most had gathered up front, where Grant saw the all-too familiar yellow crime tape spread around the altar steps. A gigantic cross hung above it, wrapped in clear plastic. A uniformed patrolman was stationed there, motioning for the curious to keep their distance.

"I heard he was missing his entire head and you're still looking for it," one female tourist in a camel coat said to the patrolman. "Is that true?"

"I'm not at liberty to say, ma'am," was all the man would offer up.

"They wouldn't have allowed us inside the place if the head was rolling around in here somewhere," muttered her companion, a beefy sort wearing a Syracuse sweatshirt. "Isn't that right?"

Grant was taken aback realizing that the Syracuse man was addressing him. "I've no idea—but I suspect you're correct."

The camel-coated woman's eyes widened. "Are you from England?"

Grant couldn't hide his accent if he tried. "I just arrived this evening. I'm all bollixed by the time change. Thought I'd go for a walk and take in the sights."

"And stumbled right into a murder scene."

"I thought that looked out of place," Grant replied, pointing at the yellow tape. "What happened exactly?"

He knew he could learn a lot by not flashing his credentials until necessary. People usually buttoned up around authorities. The woman was eager to oblige.

"A priest lost his head and was crucified right up on that cross."

"He didn't lose his head, Marla. You watch too many crime shows."

"Charles!"

"They can be quite addicting," Grant acknowledged. "Did they catch the person who did it?"

Charles shook his head. "It would have hit the news by now. The body was taken away a while ago—otherwise they wouldn't have let us in here."

Grant noticed that one of the pew sitters, a man in his midthirties wearing a winter coat, had risen, looking irritated. Grant lowered his voice, worried they were disturbing praying parishioners. "What would possess a person to do such a thing?"

"I have my theories," Marla eagerly offered.

"This ought to be a doozy," murmured Charles.

Marla lowered her voice as well, conspiratorially. "It has to be one of his former altar boys. Getting revenge for some kind of abuse. Some of these priests . . ."

"Marla! You know no such thing!" Charles face reddened. "This gentleman isn't interested in your fanciful theories. Not to mention disrespect for the dead." Charles started to guide her from the altar. "I'm sorry, sir."

"It's quite all right," Grant assured him. "I actually found it quite fascinating."

"See!" protested Marla to no avail as Charles led her away. The Syracuse man nodded an apology to the gentleman in the winter coat as well.

The man nodded and watched the couple walk toward the church exit, then turned back to face Grant. "Interesting theory, though."

Grant started to answer but stopped. Something about the voice.

"But we both know this isn't some killer just targeting men of the cloth. It's a much larger problem. Isn't it, Commander?"

Grant's eyes narrowed. "Detective Frankel."

"I see why you earned that highfalutin title they gave you over there at Scotland Yard." Frankel's smile wasn't exactly welcoming. "You might have given me a call."

"And you could've told me where you'd be tonight, Detective."

"Well, here we both are," Frankel pointed out. "So we might as well start talking."

2

The waitress at the Astro poured half the chocolate milkshake into a tall, narrow glass and placed it directly in front of Frankel. She left the rest in a metal mixing cup with a long spoon sticking out of it.

"Thank you, Phyllis."

"Pleasure, Detective. How goes the bad-guy catching?"

"Still trying to keep up."

Phyllis, who Grant thought must be pushing seventy years and looked like she'd been working at the coffee shop for most of them, nodded. "You'll get there. We're counting on it." She turned to Grant. "More tea?"

"I'm fine, thank you. I'm just pleased you have English breakfast."

She moved to the empty counter and wiped it down with a rag. Frankel took a big sip from the shake, then waited. Grant watched the detective repress a shudder, make a slight choking sound, clear his throat, and bring a finger to his head.

"Brain freeze," explained Frankel. "Gets me every time."

"You come here a lot?"

"Ever since I made the squad. Going on fifteen years now."

Grant indicated the glass. "Been drinking those all the time?"

"Long as I remember."

"And you don't weigh twenty-five stone."

"Is that a lot?" Frankel asked innocently.

"Three hundred forty, say fifty, of your pounds."

"What can I say? I was blessed with a healthy metabolism."

Not to mention a sweet tooth, thought Grant. He studied the New York cop. The man dressed well, not going for the polyester numbers detectives wore on the telly programs that made their way across the pond. Frankel was handsome enough that the ladies wouldn't turn away but the men wouldn't feel threatened. He possessed a frame that stretched just over six feet and had dark hair whose length probably pushed NYPD restrictions. Film-star piercing blue eyes were an added bonus, and Grant was fairly sure the man used them to his advantage.

Frankel put down the glass without taking said eyes off Grant. "You want to tell me why you didn't give me the head's up about your little trip to Saint Pat's?"

"I had some free time on my hands and took a stroll."

"And ended up at the crime scene you traveled across the Atlantic for."

"Like you said—some of us are blessed. Tonight, I just caught a bit of luck."

Frankel laughed. "You don't expect me to believe that."

"As much as I do that you were waiting for midnight mass to start."

"We both know that wasn't the reason," said Frankel.

"What were you expecting to see?" asked Grant. "The killer return to the scene of the crime?"

"No one catches *that* kind of luck," grumbled Frankel. He drained the glass and moved on to the milkshake container. "It's a habit I've developed—soaking it all in after the fact. You get all sorts who come to check it out. Can't keep them away—kinda like rubberneckers on the road after a six-car pileup."

The detective poured the rest of the shake into his glass. "And the theories they come up with? They'll blow your mind. Some guy a half hour before you showed up was sure it was an archangel sent to wreak vengeance on us because we are on the verge of eternal damnation." He licked the spoon clean. "Like we already don't know that."

Grant couldn't help but smile. "You've been down the abuse road, naturally."

"Everyone loved Father Peter and there isn't even a whisper of it being anything but in a platonic, God-blessed way. Plus, it doesn't sound like it's personal, especially if this is really connected to your killings in London."

"I'm completely convinced."

"There are plenty of fruitcakes out there. Could be a copycat."

"We've made sure this hasn't leaked yet."

Frankel shook his head. "There are always leaks."

Grant didn't correct him and took another sip of tea. The cup was full. Phyllis smiled from the counter, having topped it off when he wasn't looking. "I presume the accent gave me away in the church."

"That and the picture on your Wikipedia page," Frankel said. "It's rather old by the way—no offense."

"I didn't put it there. My late wife's doing."

"I read that you lost her recently. My condolences."

An uneasy silence followed. The type where strong-willed men try to figure out what the other is made of.

"So, how are we going to go about this?" Frankel finally asked.

"Work together?"

"That seems to be the issue. You've got three murders on your hands where I've just got the one. But seeing as how you didn't get the job done on your side of the Atlantic, it now falls to my department to pick up the pieces."

"I closed every church in Greater London," Grant said, defensive.

"I'm sure Father Peters would be the first to applaud you." Frankel finished off the rest of the shake.

"I'm sorry the bastard didn't leave a travel itinerary."

"I suppose the killer could have gone anywhere to spread holiday cheer."

"Have you checked out passenger manifests for all the major airlines?"

"Of everyone who left London for New York since the musician's murder?" asked Frankel. "When did he die? Five days ago?"

"Six," corrected Grant.

Frankel waved the spoon for emphasis. "I don't need to tell you how many people flew over that period between Heathrow and JFK. For all you know they could've left from Gatwick or flown into one of the other major airports here. Or they could have taken the Chunnel and hopped a plane from Paris to throw us off track . . ."

"You've made your point."

"I know everyone wants to think we've cracked down on our security since 9/11 but technology has grown by leaps and bounds. It's easier than ever to forge documentation and the TSA can't begin to keep up with it."

"I'd still be looking at those lists."

Frankel offered up a slight smile. "Ever since I hung up the phone with you earlier today."

This produced another go-round of silence. Phyllis came over and asked if anyone wanted a refill. The two cops said they were fine and she scribbled out a check. Grant tried to reach for it.

"Not on my turf."

Frankel dug a twenty out of his wallet and handed it to the waitress. He told her to keep the change and that he'd see her in a day or two. As she walked away, Grant thanked Frankel for the tea.

"If I'm ever over your way, you can return the favor," Frankel told him.

"On my turf," Grant echoed.

"Exactly."

"I understand I'm the guest here, Detective. What do you say we start over bright and early tomorrow at the precinct as previously agreed?"

Frankel gave Grant a nod. "A fresh slate sounds good." The NYPD detective got up and handed Grant his heavy overcoat.

"I even have the perfect place to start," said Frankel.

"The Fifth Commandment?"

Frankel laughed. "Ever been told you're a pain in the ass, Commander?"

"Constantly."

3

Honor thy father and thy mother.

That only narrowed the field to the entire human race. Everyone had one of each. Sure, there were orphans to consider and those who had lost their parents—but even those people dishonored those who brought them into the world. And what exactly constituted a transgression against one's parents? Disobeying their orders? Not heeding sage words of advice? Lashing out at them verbally or even physically in public? Forgetting a birthday? Interpreted differently, it could be putting an elderly mother or father away in an old folks' home.

Or none of the above.

Grant shoved the room service table away with a sigh. His first morning in Manhattan wasn't off to a good start. It had taken three tries to produce English breakfast tea after they brought obscure herb varieties. The kitchen's idea of a scone resembled a rock and the concept of porridge was lost on them altogether.

Getting to the Midtown North precinct proved equally challenging—even though it was only six blocks from the London. The skies had opened up to greet Scotland Yard's Finest and with temperatures hovering in the low thirties, the precipitation was stinging pellets of ice. Finding a cab in these conditions was foolhardy; how hard would it be to navigate six bloody blocks?

Ten minutes later, soaked to the bone (his umbrella flipped inside out when the icy wind gusted at typhoon speed), he had his answer.

Upon pushing through the precinct's heavy double doors and depositing his crumpled brolly in a trash bin, Grant shed his drenched raincoat and shook himself dry like a sodden Lab. Moments later, he was led by a uniformed officer through a bullpen where detectives busily mapped out their days while washing breakfast burritos down with cups of hot coffee. The uniform escorted Grant to an office at the back of the precinct and knocked on the door.

"Detective Grant is here to see you, sir," the cop said.

Grant considered correcting him but figured the title "Commander" or "Chief Inspector" would seem pretentious and curb no favor from either man. He nodded thanks to the uniform and turned his attention toward John Frankel.

The detective had his feet up on the desk, a huge file in his lap, and was sipping from a blue-and-white pinstriped coffee cup with a Yankees insignia. Frankel gave Grant a good once-over and didn't bother to suppress a grin.

"We could've sent you a car, Inspector."

Now he tells me.

"Seemed silly to waste funds and manpower on a six-block jaunt."

"Six blocks in Midtown during the holidays can seem like a suicide run."

"I prefer to consider it a character builder, Detective."

"Let's make it John," suggested Frankel. "And I'll call you Austin?"

"Might as well. Everyone else will come the first of January."

"I heard you were retiring. How many years with the Yard will that be?"

"Thirty-four, Detective." Grant corrected himself. "I mean, John."

"Well, they picked a hell of a case to send you out on." He glanced at the file on his lap. "You've come to the same conclusion about the Fifth Commandment?"

"I've no doubt of it."

Frankel nodded. "Since every single person in the five boroughs is a potential victim, I'm not even sure where to begin."

"There's no guarantee the killer will limit himself to the island of Manhattan. I was certainly wrong about him sticking to Central London."

"Where would you suggest us starting?"

"With what we already know—the latest victim," answered Grant. "What I don't understand is how the killer isolated Father Peters like that. Isn't Saint Patrick's open twenty-four hours a day? Surely there would have been witnesses."

"He pulled the fire alarm. Then he got even more daring." Frankel tapped his keyboard and swiveled the computer screen around.

A surveillance camera tape from Saint Patrick's began to play. The time code read 9:58 P.M. Two dozen people were milling around the sanctuary. Frankel fast-forwarded to fixate on a portion where the visitors suddenly scurried into motion.

"Obviously in response to the alarm sounding." Frankel tapped the left corner of the screen. "I imagine this is the person you and I are looking for."

A hooded, robed figure entered from the wings. The shrouded person waved their arms toward the exit, beckoning for everyone to head for the street.

"I presume you've tried to enhance this?" asked Grant.

"Of course." Frankel punched more buttons until the cloaked figure filled the screen. "He seems to be wearing some kind of full-face covering."

Frankel freeze-framed the image. The hood and robe concealed a lot, but Grant could make out an ebony full-face mask deep within the folds of the cowl.

"Clever. Didn't anyone find that sort of mask strange?"

"Not in the moment. Chalk it up to yelling 'fire' in a crowded building. The alarm sounds, a man of the cloth flies into the sanctuary and orders people to vacate the building—everyone does a 180 and makes for the streets pronto."

Grant watched the visitors flee until the hooded figure was the sanctuary's sole occupant. He closed the main doors, bolted them, and remained inside the church. Then, just as the man crossed the sanctuary, another entered the edge of the frame.

"The unfortunate Father Peters?" asked Grant.

Frankel nodded. "He was in the rectory when the alarm went off. Probably asleep at the time, seeing as how he's wearing a T-shirt and sweatpants—clothes he would have thrown on quickly before checking things out."

They watched Father Peters advance on the robed figure. Grant could tell that the priest was calling out to the other man.

"Have you been able to determine what he's saying?" asked Grant.

"Best we can tell is 'What is happening?' and 'What are you doing?' " Frankel hit the zoom function and focused on Peters's face.

The priest's expression went from curious to frightened.

"That must have been when he noticed the mask," ventured Grant.

Frankel resumed the tape and Grant watched Peters try to run from the hooded man. The latter was inches from catching the priest when they both exited the frame. The tape showed the empty sanctuary—then the screen fritzed and went black.

"What happened there?" asked Grant.

"Our friend obviously found the camera source and cut the power. Probably right after he knocked Father Peters unconscious."

Grant nodded, somewhat shocked by the killer's audacity. "So once the cameras were off and the doors locked, he was able to cut the alarm and go about his nasty business?"

"Exactly. Might have taken him all of ten minutes to cut Peters's throat and mount him on the cross." He closed the web browser and leaned back.

"Have you been able to ascertain anything from the tape about the man?"

"Based on his close proximity to Father Peters—we're looking for an individual about six feet tall." Frankel shrugged. "Of course, since the robe covered his feet, we can't say for sure that he wasn't wearing lifts in his shoes or large heels."

"Which eliminates maybe half the men walking the streets of Manhattan."

"That sounds right," said Frankel. "But shouldn't we be looking for someone from your side of the Atlantic? This started on your island, not mine."

"That's a fair assumption. But I never imagined he would venture out of the UK. Now that he's done that, he could be practically anywhere."

Frankel extended the file toward Grant. "We've already run a cross-check on the London victims with Father Peters. There doesn't seem to be any connection. Peters has never been to Oxford, didn't collect art by this dead woman Keaton, and it's a pretty safe bet you won't find the Blasphemers in his iTunes."

"The killer doesn't appear to be linking the victims personally. He seems intent on carrying out his own interpretation of the Commandments."

"But why leave England?" wondered Frankel. "It wasn't like he was wearing out his welcome there."

"We did tumble to him wanting to go after a man of the cloth. Maybe he figured we might try and stop him back home, so he took his show on the road."

"But why New York?" Frankel asked. "Wouldn't it be easier to gallivant all over Europe without risking air travel or sticking out like an English sore thumb?"

"I suppose he has some sort of logic that works for him. The biggest questions I have are what set him off and why he is doing this now."

"As opposed to him just being fucking insane?"

"I guarantee it makes perfect sense to him." Grant shook his head. "Why did he start with Frey and only two weeks ago? Why not kill a different professor six months ago—or six years ago, for that matter? That's what I keep asking myself—why now?"

"Maybe it's an early retirement present for you," suggested Frankel.

4

Given a tiny office in the back corner of the precinct, Grant continued to follow up on the Saint Patrick's murder. The room had a desk chair, potted plant (green plastic), blank desk blotter, a cup with blue Pilot G2 pens, a framed picture of the precinct's cops circa 1920, and one rather disgruntled Scotland Yard Commander.

Most of the interviews were to the point—the few "witnesses" they'd tracked down relayed the same story. The alarm blared, then a man resembling a hooded monk appeared to shoo them out of the building. One woman, a matronly sort from Ohio on a tour of the Eastern Seaboard's great cathedrals and churches, had seen the cowled figure enter from a side hallway—the same corridor that housed the fire alarm. It was hard to make out his voice, muffled by the face mask. It covered his entire face.

Grant had called Mrs. Thelma King of Cleveland, Ohio, to reinterview her. By this time, she was taking a break from traipsing through Trinity Church in Boston's Back Bay ("... amazing stained glass, but truthfully, Commander, by the fifteenth cathedral it's hard to differentiate"). Thelma had roused Grant's interest because she'd stayed near Saint Patrick's after the fire alarm had gone off. The first fire truck arrived twelve minutes after the alarm first rang, but the firefighters found the doors locked tight. Even though no one spotted smoke, they couldn't get through the massive bronze doors, so they raced to the side of the cathedral and busted in there.

Thelma had been glued to her section of the sidewalk, intently watching as more fire trucks appeared, immediately followed by a half-dozen squad cars.

"When did you find out someone had been murdered?" Grant asked.

"It came out in dribs and drabs. First, I heard someone say there was a body inside. I thought it was the monk who chased us out—that maybe he'd died in the fire. Then I overheard one of the police radios saying it was actually that poor priest."

When he asked if she'd seen the hooded monk again—possibly slipping out a side door—Grant could practically hear Thelma shaking her head.

"Not after we fled the sanctuary. Do you think he killed the priest?"

Grant sidestepped an answer and told Thelma they were still pulling facts together. He thanked her and hoped she enjoyed the rest of the tour.

And so went the morning. By the time they headed to Saint Patrick's to check out the crime scene in the daytime, Grant was only too happy to leave the tiny office.

The rain had stopped and the sun was poking through cotton candy clouds gliding across the Manhattan skyline at a furious pace. Grant was certainly used to the dampness that pervaded his London streets, but the wind tunnel effect between the avenues, caused by being squeezed between skyscrapers and the Hudson and East Rivers, was an altogether new, and unpleasant, experience.

Sadly, the daylight investigation of the cathedral yielded nothing worth noting. The perpetrator either entered the church with the general public or snuck in the back service entrance. As for changing into the monk's robe, that wasn't caught on the surveillance cameras; neither was the alarm being pulled.

Grant didn't think it a coincidence—with each successive murder it became apparent their quarry had carefully planned every step.

Grant and Frankel made their way to the office of Father Timothy Polhemus, the senior priest at Saint Patrick's. With gray hair and rosy cheeks that Grant imagined came from sampling the sacramental wine a tad too often, Polhemus said his colleague Adam Peters was a priest loved by all and a threat to none.

"You don't remember a disagreement with a parishioner?" asked Grant.

"I've met my share of testy and opinionated clergy," answered Polhemus. "But Father Peters had a disposition that never changed. He was even-keeled, always making sure to leave you with a good word and a blessing."

This didn't surprise Grant—the only thing the priest had probably been guilty of was working on the Sabbath. He told that to Frankel as they left the office.

"So you're basically saying this maniac could have killed *any* priest."

"I'm afraid so."

Frankel shook his head. "And he had to pick my precinct to do it in."

"The frightening thing is that next time he might venture somewhere completely different. There's no specific reason for him to stay in Manhattan. Every bloody person has a mother and father—he could choose anyone."

"You really know how to cheer a fella up," chided Frankel as they entered the sanctuary.

Before Grant could respond, Frankel's cell buzzed. The detective glanced at the readout and motioned that he was going to take the call. As Frankel moved off, Grant's eyes were drawn to a side altar where a lean man was lighting a candle.

"Did they finally come to their senses and kick you out of your parish for a multitude of sins?" Grant asked as he approached the man.

Monte Ferguson straightened up and faced Grant.

The *Daily Mail* reporter appeared to be wearing the same ill-fitting suit Grant had seen him wearing over the weekend. He suspected Ferguson was the type of man who bought half a dozen identical off-the-rack suits, ties, and shirts—never wanting to be a distraction when pursuing a story, preferring to blend in unnoticed.

"You didn't call me yesterday," accused Ferguson.

Grant had been in such a rush to get himself across the Atlantic that he had forgotten he owed the journalist a phone call. By the time he remembered midflight, he figured the man was still pursuing connections to the murders back home.

Clearly Grant had been mistaken.

"The circumstances changed," Grant told him. "Obviously, you figured that out—otherwise you wouldn't be standing here. And just how did that happen?"

"Have you ever known me to reveal a source, Commander?"

The Scotland Yard man shook his head. "Though I wouldn't be surprised if Sergeant Hawley were a bit forthcoming when you rang yesterday looking for me."

"I leave that for you to discuss with your subordinate," Ferguson said, obviously not wanting to discuss the subject of his arrival further.

Grant let that pass without comment. "What exactly do you want from me?"

"A reason not to tell the world you're chasing a serial killer across two continents."

"If that's what you think, why haven't you gone and published this already?"

"Corroboration from a credible source adds veracity to any story. And despite our past differences, I've always appreciated the fact that you've never outright lied to me, Commander."

"And why would I corroborate this theory of yours?"

"Because you've been the lead investigator on three murders taking place over a ten-day period and have now flown across the ocean to look into a fourth. Not to mention that this one is a *priest*. I find it hard to believe *that* is a coincidence—given the church closings you orchestrated back in England over the weekend."

"It could just be a nasty stretch we're going through. You know what they say about people this time of the season."

"Perhaps I'll talk to your American colleague over there." Ferguson indicated Frankel, who was still on his call by the entrance. "I could ask about the marks on the priest's forehead and how it matches up with the bodies you found back home."

Grant's eyes narrowed. This was the first thing that Ferguson had uttered that took him by surprise. He thought they had successfully clamped down on the particulars of the crimes. He chose his next words carefully.

"If I asked how you got that information, I suppose you'd fall back on your precious sword of privileged information."

"I'm glad you've been paying attention all these years," replied Ferguson. "Are you going to stand here and deny all four bodies had the same mark?"

He doesn't know that they were numerical in order.

Which meant that Ferguson hadn't tumbled to the Ten Commandments connection.

Grant considered the ramifications of a published story linking the crimes to a serial killer working two sides of the Atlantic. It wouldn't hurt for people to be a touch more careful around strangers in the coming days—at least until he and Frankel figured out who wasn't honoring their mothers and fathers.

"Suppose I was to acknowledge the existence of such a person. Would you be willing to hold back the information concerning the 'markings' as you call them?"

"I think that can be worked out," Ferguson replied.

Grant, his mind already made up, pretended to consider the deal. He went on the record with the journalist about a serial killer being in two nations' midst. He was about to send Monte on his merry way when Frankel joined them.

Grant made introductions. The two men nodded, then Ferguson headed out, clearly wanting to file his story before Grant rescinded their agreement.

As Frankel stared at the departing Ferguson, Grant said the newsman might actually be an asset to their investigation. A dubious Frankel told Grant he might want to explain that on the way to the morgue.

Off Grant's questioning look, Frankel explained. "That was the ME. He's done the autopsy on Father Peters and is ready for us."

In the cab on the way to the coroner's office, Grant was happy to learn Frankel agreed on the deal he'd made with the reporter.

"I think it's time we let this nut know we're not far behind him," Frankel said.

He asked Grant if he wanted to grab a bite before the autopsy. The commander felt his stomach turn and suggested perhaps waiting till afterward.

One look at Father Adam Peters's body on a metal slab and Grant knew he'd made the right decision.

It had been only a day since the priest had been murdered, but he looked like something that had rotted in a closet for weeks. His face was blue tinged and bloated from his eyebrows to his cheeks. His neck bulged from a wire wrapped around it tight enough to not just extinguish his life, but hang him from the cross atop the main altar.

Marcus, the African American coroner, was in his late forties and told Grant he couldn't remember performing an autopsy on a holy man, even though hundreds of unfortunate souls had found their way to his table. The coroner relayed his findings while massaging a thin goatee that was starting to go gray.

"The first blow he received was to the back of the head." The ME indicated a bruised section on the dead priest's skull that had been shaved and cut open.

"Is that what killed him?" Frankel asked.

Marcus shook his head. "I'm getting to that."

Marcus pointed to a tray that held various instruments, bagged fluids, and specimens extracted from the corpse.

"The blow definitely subdued him; probably knocked him unconscious—but it looks like your killer wanted to keep him alive long enough to give him this."

Grant and Frankel stared at the item in question.

It was silver and a perfect circle—much like a coin but a bit larger.

"May I?" asked Grant, holding up a gloved hand. Marcus nodded and Grant held it up so both he and Frankel could study it.

"It's a souvenir coin," remarked Frankel.

Grant gave him a curious look.

"You must have something like them in London. They're all over the city—particularly in Times Square and other tourist traps. You pay a dollar or two and create your own New York City souvenir with the Statue of Liberty, Central Park, or some other landmark on it." Frankel took the coin from Grant and flipped it over. "This one has the Empire State Building. You choose which you want and then engrave a message on the other side."

Grant thought the temperature in the room had just dropped, but then realized it was his body reacting to whatever was coming next.

"And I presume there's one on this particular coin?"

Frankel pointed at it with his forefinger. "9888."

Grant turned to face Marcus. "The killer kept Peters alive long enough to make him swallow this? So that we'd find it?"

"That's what I'm figuring," the ME responded. "But for the life of me, I've no idea what it means."

"It means this asshole is really starting to fuck with us," said Frankel.

Grant would be the first to say there was quite a difference in the way Americans and Brits described things.

But he couldn't have put it better if he tried.

5

Sitting in a cafeteria in the bowels of the building that housed the morgue, Grant found the concept of food nauseating after Marcus's discovery from the dead priest's stomach. It didn't stop Frankel from gobbling down two hot dogs slathered with mustard, sauerkraut, and ketchup. The detective polished off the second with a swig of Coke, then wiped his mouth and noticed Grant staring at him.

"I know. My ex used to say I was raised in a barn."

"I didn't realize you were divorced," Grant observed, his eyes drifting to the detective's left ring finger and the simple, slightly tarnished gold band on it.

"This?" Frankel waved the finger. "Almost two years now. I keep meaning to take it off but then don't know what to do with it. I'm not going to throw it in the trash and it'd just clog up a toilet. I stick it in a drawer, I'll come across it when I least expect and it'll make me feel like shit for not working things out with Julia."

"Does that mean you hope she's coming back?"

"Fat chance of that. She took off with the super in my building. They're running a beach bar on the Big Island in Hawaii." Frankel shook his head. "A shrink told me I keep wearing it so I won't have to explain what happened. If I take it off, it's going to end up being some kind of big thing." He polished off the rest of the Coke. "Maybe I'm just waiting for the right girl to get rid of it for."

Grant, not knowing how to respond, retreated to an old British standby: polite empathy by way of a simple nod. It seemed to do the trick as Frankel switched the conversation to their current conundrum.

"9888," Frankel said. "What do you suppose we're looking at here?"

"First thing that comes to mind is a location or address," suggested Grant.

Frankel already had his iPhone out and started to work Google Maps. "988 Eighth Avenue is an apartment building on the corner of Fifty-Eighth Street and Eighth Avenue—that puts it just south of Columbus Circle."

"How many apartments or tenants are we looking at?"

"I've got no idea till we get there," Frankel replied. "But I imagine a whole bunch of them are occupied by mothers and fathers."

"Or their sons and daughters," said Grant.

As Frankel navigated the unmarked sedan through clogged Midtown Manhattan, Grant suggested making the twenty-block journey on foot.

"Some days you don't move two blocks an hour, others you sail right through," Frankel pointed out. "You used to catch the stagger up and down the avenues but it's gone to hell ever since Uber and Lyft, along with apps like Waze and Tell-Me-the-Fucking-Best-Way-to-Get-There." He finally gave up honking and dug up a portable red light encased in a plastic bubble, tossed it on the dashboard, and clicked a siren switch that let out an annoying *whoop-whoop*.

"That seems to help considerably," Grant commented a minute or two later when they had barely budged an inch.

"If our friend's intent on killing someone in that building, let's pray he's stuck in the same traffic jam."

Grant glanced at a city map to get his bearings. He'd earlier asked Frankel about Eighty-Eighth Street; what if the address were either 98 West or East Eighty-Eighth Street instead? A quick check revealed that those locations would be the actual middle of intersections, as both directions of Eighty-Eighth Street ended with the number 88 before jumping to 100.

At least they were looking at one building instead of three. Still, 988 Eighth Avenue was fifteen stories high.

Frankel used "police privilege" to deposit the sedan in front. He slapped a police banner on the dashboard, then motioned for Grant to get out of the car.

The commander glanced up the gray edifice—it was completely nondescript and probably only got washed by the splatter of wind-based thunderstorms. He started, then quickly stopped, counting windows.

"This is going to take us forever."

"Hopefully this guy will prove useful."

Frankel indicated the doorman stationed outside massive glass doors. He produced his NYPD shield, then proceeded to give the semi-lowdown on the situation they were facing to Jordan Sanchez, a hefty, handsome Latino who commuted from Queens every day except Sunday.

"And why do you think someone here is going to be targeted?" Jordan asked.

"Afraid we're not at liberty to share that information," Frankel responded.

They got Jordan to discuss the recent nonresident visitors to the building. Unfortunately, with over sixty apartments, the figure was in the dozens over just the past couple of days.

Guests were asked to sign and check in, but formal identification wasn't required. Visitors wrote down the apartment they were headed to, then the doorman buzzed the resident to inform them of their arrival. But that wasn't a guarantee the visitor went directly to the apartment in question; it was easily possible to make a stop or two on other floors of the building.

There was also the matter of deliveries. Tenants were accustomed to takeout and online shopping, so things appeared at all hours. Jordan provided the register for the past three days, then took them to meet the super, who could assist further and provide access to the building's security system.

Grant thought George Tompkins must have come with the building, his age anywhere between seventy and the century mark. The super possessed a full head of hair the color of Wite-Out but had enough energy for someone half his age. He was the third generation of Tompkinses to oversee the goings-on at 988 Eighth Avenue, dating back to Grandfather Hal, who took occupancy of the same basement apartment shortly after World War I.

Tompkins led them belowground to the space where he had basically spent his entire life. Crammed with mementos, it was a visual history of Manhattan since WWI, from the glory of V-Day in Times Square to the tragedy at the tip of lower Manhattan that September day early this century.

The security cameras were orderly stacked in a tiny closet and Tompkins showed the two men how to play them back. Frankel lined up entries from Jordan's logbook with the digital time readout to watch guests enter and exit the building.

"The tenants overwhelmingly voted down cameras in the hallways," Tompkins explained when asked about additional coverage. "Felt it was an invasion of privacy. It was a huge expense for management to take on anyway."

Frankel fast-forwarded through the footage. None of this was likely to help, especially since the last dead body found in the building was poor Mrs. Simmons, who had passed away three months before.

"What other ways can a person get into the building?" asked Frankel. "Besides the front door."

Tompkins mentioned the maintenance entrance off Fifty-Eighth Street, but only a select few had keys to it. None of the employees would let someone they didn't recognize slip inside, but he provided the cops with their names.

Then it was on to the painstaking part of the process—interviewing the occupants of the building. Grant and Frankel had discussed this on the way over during their lengthy (one traffic-snarled mile) trip up the West Side.

"We agree that we're looking for a potential victim here, not our killer, right?" Frankel had asked between blasts of the horn.

"Seems far-fetched that, despite his bravado in trying to engage us, he would provide his actual home address. Plus, it would make no sense to start a killing spree across the Atlantic, only to go and bring it back to one's own doorstep."

"And we're definitely pursuing the mother-father angle?"

"Unless you have a better idea?"

Frankel said he didn't.

Grant realized that getting a forthcoming answer from the building's tenants was no sure thing. If one of them had done something horrible to their folks, he couldn't imagine that person owning up to such a transgression.

Frankel set himself up in the game room and Grant sat behind a table in a lounge near the building entrance. They'd decided to conduct the interviews separately to move more quickly through the tenants, then regroup and compare notes.

It was early afternoon when they began, so most of the interviewees were stay-at-home moms, pensioned elders, and those who worked at home. Only a few were worthy of discussion. One had written off her parents because they had refused to pay for her child's schooling. Another had stopped talking to her widowed father, citing him as a hopeless drunk, her mother having passed when she was a teen.

"If anything, I should be killing him," she told Grant. Then she burst into tears realizing what she'd said and he'd spent ten more minutes consoling her.

As evening rolled around, the work force returned to 988 Eighth Avenue, surprised to find policemen from two different countries occupying the public spaces in their building. The majority dutifully submitted to interviews with Grant and Frankel. To a person, they only had glowing things to say about their parents. By the time Frankel and Grant called it a night, they were convinced they'd been run ragged by a killer who must have been laughing himself silly.

Before leaving, they sat again with Tompkins to figure out how many tenants they still needed to reach. They'd made a sizeable dent and were down to fewer than a dozen. The super said he'd check on who was out of town and provide numbers for the rest.

On the way out, Frankel handed Grant a copy of the remaining list, which they divided in half. "Feel free to call them from your hotel or the precinct in the morning. Want to meet around eleven to see where we end up?"

Grant was so tired he could barely manage a nod.

The only place he wanted to end up was back home in Maida Vale with his head buried under a pillow until the new year.

"It isn't necessarily an address," said Everett.

Grant repressed a sigh. It wasn't like that hadn't already occurred to him, but it was painful hearing it spoken aloud. Especially after ten hours at 988 Eighth Avenue.

"At least it's a place to start," Grant told his brother.

Everett had left two messages asking Grant to call him back whenever he returned to the hotel; never mind the time change. He wasn't surprised. His sibling was a self-pronounced insomniac and often worked into the wee hours.

"It could be an invoice number," added Grant. "Coordinates on a map we're not getting?" He threw up his hands, frustrated. "The possibilities are endless."

"Did you consider it being a date?" Everett asked.

It had floated through his mind briefly, but that would translate to September 8, 1988—and three decades seemed like an eternity in these days of instant gratification and social media. He said as much to Everett but made a mental note to look into it later.

"You're probably right," Everett replied. "There are obscure references to try—the numbers for californium and radium on the periodic table of elements, ninety-eight degrees in a normal temperature Fahrenheit, eighty-eight keys on a piano . . ."

"Are you suggesting I should be searching for a radioactive Steinway?"

Everett chuckled. "Who knows how this bugger thinks?"

Grant smiled as well. The next night was supposed to be his weekly rendezvous with his brother. He actually found himself yearning to be seated opposite Everett, getting obliterated by a confounding series of chess moves.

Still, Grant found it edifying to review the case with him, much as they had that night—*Was it only a week ago?*—in Everett's study when his brother had helped discover the crimes were being plucked directly from the Old Testament.

They spent a few more minutes debating various parts of the investigation until Grant remembered the voice messages that Everett had left earlier.

"You said it was important I should call—no matter what time," Grant reminded him. "What did you want to tell me?"

Everett hesitated. Then he cleared his throat and began with, "I need you to listen to me for a minute, Austin."

Uh oh, thought Grant. *This can't be good.* But he listened anyway.

———

At first, Grant tried to go to sleep but he couldn't get the end of the conversation with Everett out of his head.

So he distracted himself by looking up the date: 9/8/88.

On that day, Yellowstone Park was closed for the first time in history due to massive forest fires. Bart Giamatti was unanimously elected the Commissioner of Major League Baseball. Grant couldn't see either event spurring the killer to take out a particular sinner, be it an arson-setting park ranger or irate fan who didn't approve of the baseball vote, let alone relating those things to dishonoring a parent. He searched crime blotters and, like any day in America, it was filled with atrocities. On that September day in the tristate area there had been three armed robberies, a nasty home invasion killing a couple on Long Island, and a rapist caught after an hour-long chase through Central Park. All horrendous occurrences, but trying to connect them to the present just made Grant's head hurt further.

He should have nipped Everett's idea in the bud. But he was often cowed by his younger brother, who was so much smarter that it was difficult for Grant to stand up to him.

So, naturally, he had agreed to do what Everett had asked.

———

The dining room at the Surrey reminded Grant of a London hotel tearoom. The finest china, silverware, and linens were on display, with each table featuring a simple but elegant flower arrangement that wouldn't distract a conversation or the bite of a delectable dish. The walls were adorned with Impressionist-style drawings that could have been masterpieces for all Grant knew.

When asked by the maître d' for a reservation, he gave him the name "Grant" and was told the other person in the party had just arrived.

Grant followed the tuxedoed man through a dining room populated by Upper East Siders and moneyed Manhattanites eating omelets and closing deals. As they neared the table, Grant slowed, filled with sudden trepidation.

Even with her back to him, it was clear the woman seated at the table was attractive, and from the way she carried herself, someone to be reckoned with.

"Enjoy your breakfast, Mr. Grant," said the maître d'.

The woman turned and her exquisite jaw almost hit the floor.

"What the hell . . . ?"

Grant noticed that she'd lost some of her British accent.

"Don't blame me—you can put that all on your uncle," he told her.

"That doesn't mean you had to go along with it, Dad," said his daughter.

6

No matter what Grant or Allison tried, Rachel wouldn't stop screaming.

Barely three days old, but already possessing quite the set of lungs. Grant didn't remember their newborn daughter uttering a peep while cradled in Allison's arms in the hospital room or watching her through the nursey window.

She saved it up for the cab ride home. Grant was afraid the driver would drop them off on Hyde Park Corner because he couldn't stand the racket.

The baby kept it up upon entering the flat. No matter what the new parents did, she proved inconsolable. They tried rocking. Cooing. Singing lullabies. Grant even recited nursery rhymes he remembered from childhood. Nothing worked.

Then Grant turned on the big portable radio in the living room hoping to drown out the screaming child and keep the neighbors from making child abuse claims.

It was tuned to the oldies station Allison found so tiresome.

The Beatles' "She Loves You" began to play.

Rachel not only stopped crying—she began gurgling with pure happiness.

Grant thought, *Oh my, she's a lovely British lass through and through.*

From the moment she entered the world, Rachel and Allison were as close as a mother and child could be. But on that wintry morning when Lennon and McCartney calmed his baby girl, Grant's heart had been stilled when Rachel stared up at him with adoring sky-blue eyes. When recounting the story over the years and asked if that was the moment he fell in love with his daughter, Grant would smile and answer, "*Yeah, yeah, yeah.*"

Nothing was too good for Grant's little girl. He was never happier than when pushing the pram in rain, wind, or shine; he never missed a recital; he dutifully helped Rachel with homework even as the math got more complicated; and he was the first shoulder she'd cry on when an adolescent crush wasn't reciprocated. Grant loved that she shared his passion for sixties rock—countless were the times when Allison walked away shaking her head as her husband and child sang along with Petula Clark and the Turtles.

Grant missed her terribly when she went to the States to study journalism. He knew that Rachel's desire to become an investigative reporter stemmed from a fascination with Grant's own profession and he was forever grateful she hadn't signed up to risk life and limb at the Yard. When Rachel got her first job writing for a small paper in New England, Grant couldn't have been prouder—knowing her determination to get to the bottom of a story came from watching her old man work case after case, year after year.

Her semiannual trips back to England (Christmas always and a holiday during the brutal New York summers) were cause for celebration. Despite her mother's prodding as to when she was going to settle down and give them a grandchild or five, the trio were inseparable on these holidays.

So when things changed drastically two years ago, it had left him stunned.

It was like being thrust into a boxing ring and hit from both sides before he could even bring up his gloves. Allison's cancer diagnosis had been a punch to the gut that doubled him over in blistering pain, and Grant knew he'd never recover. Then came the crushing blow—Rachel shutting him completely out of her life within days of the diagnosis for no apparent reason. Grant was reluctant to bring it up to Allison, who was deteriorating before his very eyes. The few times he'd tried, she didn't want to talk about it.

Soon after, Grant found himself totally alone.

Now, standing in the middle of the Surrey dining room, Grant couldn't believe this was the girl he had sung harmony with to Herman's Hermits, read bedtime stories, then kissed and tucked in good night.

She was practically a stranger.

Rachel reached for the bag that she had strung over the back of her chair. Grant took a gingerly step forward and shook his head. "Please, Rachel. Stay." He somehow managed a smile. "I hear they serve a lovely breakfast here."

He watched as Rachel glanced around the room, noticed patrons looking their way, and finally sat back down. Grant took a silent deep breath of relief that he and Allison had raised a young woman who wasn't one for making a public scene.

Grant eased the chair away from the table and sat across from his daughter. The place settings were perpendicular to each other. The commander casually tried to shift the silverware to his side of the table without making a fuss of it.

"You planning on interrogating me?" she asked.

"That's the furthest thing from my mind."

He motioned to a passing waiter, desperate for a pot of tea to calm him. He would also have taken any advice the server had on how to break the ice with a daughter he hadn't seen since they'd buried her mother the year before.

Rachel certainly didn't seem interested in the melting process.

"So why exactly are we here?" she asked.

"I think Everett was just trying to do something nice."

"By pulling a Brother Grant double switch?"

"I told him it was wrong to lure you here under false pretenses. He said you would never show up if you thought you were meeting me instead of him."

"He wasn't wrong," Rachel responded.

Rachel had remained on speaking terms with Everett since things had taken a bad turn. He wasn't surprised; Everett had always been in her life. But as a confirmed bachelor ("You know Allison was always the one for me," his brother would gleefully rib Grant), Everett lectured all over the world and as a result was gone for months at a time. When he'd return to the UK, Everett would visit Rachel first thing, enthrall her with stories, and bestow gifts upon her from faraway lands, often saying Rachel was "the closest thing to a daughter that I will ever have." Grant never begrudged the relationship—all he cared about was that her uncle made Rachel happy and laugh.

"I apologize for not calling directly," he said. "My coming over here was sudden."

"The priest who was murdered at Saint Pat's."

Grant gave her a solemn nod. "What else did Everett tell you?"

"That's it. Don't worry, Dad. I'm not writing a story about it."

"I thought you covered crime for your paper."

"I've moved on to Sunday feature pieces. I was going to do one but passed my notes on to a colleague when I heard you were involved."

Grant suppressed a wince. "What sort of feature?"

"Murder in the church; tying it into religious fanaticism. But I didn't want to step on your toes or try to curry some familial favor."

He took a chance and leaned forward, desperate to engage with his daughter. "The last thing I would want is to come between you and your work."

"And this way that won't happen," she responded, firmly enough that Grant could feel the door slam between them.

"What do you want from me, Rach?" he asked, using the nickname he always thought of as a term of endearment.

"Just to live our own lives. You'd think that could be done easily enough with an ocean separating our two continents."

This was going worse than he'd even imagined. "Like I mentioned, I had no choice coming here. I'm just going to see this through and then go on my way the first of the year."

This seemed to take Rachel by surprise.

"What? You're actually retiring?"

Grant nodded. "I announced it a couple of months ago. I would have told you if we'd talked but . . ."

"But we don't. I know that."

Their server thankfully picked that moment to return with tea and coffee. The hot liquids slightly thawed their icy standstill, at least long enough to order. Rachel asked for a mushroom and bacon omelet. When told they didn't do porridge or kippers, Grant settled for a couple of eggs over easy and a side of ham.

"Can't change those British spots so easily," Rachel mused.

"I'm not planning on staying over here that long."

"Guess that'd depend on what the person you're looking for decides to do."

Unfortunately, Grant couldn't disagree.

He ended up discussing the case with her over breakfast. Not only was it neutral ground to avoid anything personal, it helped to lay it all out. Rachel offered up an occasional observation and a few questions, a by-product of her chosen profession, falling into the old rhythm from her teenage years when Grant would bring his work home from the Yard and discuss it with both her and Allison.

"And what are you holding out on with Ferguson?"

Rachel had spent enough time around her father to know when he was playing something close to the vest.

Grant considered. Then he made a big decision.

He told Rachel about the Ten Commandments.

He wasn't exactly sure why. Maybe he wanted her to get the story out before that bothersome Ferguson. It was also possible that Grant didn't care about playing by the rules any longer. The killer certainly wasn't. He couldn't imagine the Yard suspending him with just a few weeks left before retirement.

Rachel's startled expression made it clear that Everett hadn't betrayed the Commandment connection. Grant was grateful for that small miracle.

When they got to the Fifth, Rachel shook her head. "He could be going after anyone. Everyone's got a mother and father."

Grant went on to tell her a little about John Frankel. He was surprised to hear himself use a superlative or two. Until he spoke them aloud, he hadn't realized how impressed with the NYPD detective he was.

"I met him a few months back at a crime scene," Rachel said. "Seemed very serious and dedicated to his work." She took a purposeful sip of coffee and gave her father a look that could only be interpreted one way.

"Sounds familiar," Grant admitted.

"Must mean he's good at his job."

Grant, happy to accept any compliment from his daughter, gave her an appreciative nod. And decided to wade gently into the unsteady waters.

"So, are you going to at least tell me how you are?"

Grant could see a wisecracking response form in her eyes but was encouraged when it just as quickly faded away.

"I'm fine. Good, actually. I like my job. I've got nice friends."

"I just want to know that you're happy."

"I'm happy enough, Dad."

Her eyes betrayed that there was more as well, but there was also a plea there that she finally voiced.

"Can we just leave it at that?"

"I'll do whatever you want, Rachel. I'd hope you'd know that by now."

"Thank you," she murmured. As she dabbed her lips with the napkin, it didn't escape his notice that she ran it quickly across her eyes, which he could have sworn had begun to well up.

Grant was certain she was holding back something. Whatever it was, he had no idea. But in that moment, he needed to fill the void of silence that was beginning to engulf them once more.

"As for what I revealed about the case . . ."

"Don't worry. You're off the record, Dad."

"I didn't mean it that way."

"You probably did, but that's okay. I wouldn't put anything in print you didn't want me to."

"I appreciate that. There could come a time where I might want you to."

He purposely trailed off again. Rachel got the gist right away.

"If it'll keep someone safe and help you catch this lunatic—I'm your girl."

You'll always be my girl, Rach.

"Good," he simply said.

Rachel started to gather her things. The breakfast clearly over, Grant got to his feet and pulled Rachel's chair out for her.

"Can I see you again before I leave?" he found himself asking.

"That's up to you. Everett obviously has my number," she said, as if he needed reminding. "Maybe this time you'll call instead of him."

She moved for the door before he could even consider a hug or any sort of embrace. He wasn't sure it would have been accepted.

As he watched her leave the restaurant, he thought at least they'd gotten through a meal together.

Sadly, it had taken a homicidal maniac to finally bring them together.

7

G rant decided to make the remaining calls to the residents of 988 Eighth Avenue from the precinct rather than the London. The office might be cramped and devoid of style but it had access to all the NYPD resources should he need them.

By the time he was finished, Frankel had contacted his half of the list as well. They met up and compared notes in the ubiquitous coffee corner, where Grant was pleased to see the fresh box of Lipton English breakfast tea that Frankel had requisitioned.

But unhappy to learn they were pretty much where they started.

With close to six hundred men and women interviewed, there wasn't a definitive person to single out as the most likely target. Over ninety-five percent of the residents were automatic throw-outs for one reason or many, and the few they gave a second look were long shots at best.

"I wouldn't be upset if you've been holding on to a major lead, Commander."

"I wish I had one." Grant proceeded to share the ideas he'd kicked around with Everett the previous evening. Frankel paid close attention but each seemed to be its own haystack devoid of needles.

Grant was replenishing his tea when someone cleared their throat behind them. Both men turned to see a younger detective holding an iPad.

"What's up, Morton?" asked Frankel.

"Thought you'd want to see this, sir," Morton responded.

Frankel took the tablet and quickly glanced at it.

Grant would need to have been blind to miss the glower. "What is it?"

"The shit hitting the fan," answered Frankel. He handed over the iPad.

Five seconds later, Grant was sharing the same grim expression.

It was the web page for the *Daily Mail*. A headline screamed out that would have been well above the fold in the print edition.

Serial Killer Takes His Act on the Road.

Monte Ferguson's byline wasn't quite the size of the headline, but close.

Here we go, thought Grant.

Moments later, Grant and Frankel were in the Media Relations office, having been called on the carpet by its head, a man named Little, and Frankel's superior, Desmond Harris, a Black lieutenant in his fifties. Harris told Grant his closely shaved, more-salt-than-pepper hair was due to putting out fires that Frankel had started.

"Like the current one," Harris added.

He indicated a flat screen on the wall that was playing back a just-aired noon newscast. Unlike the stick-to-the-point BBC broadcasts, Grant couldn't help but be aghast at the sensationalistic display that was the norm on America's airwaves. Half a dozen field reporters who looked like rejects from a runway model audition had been deployed to every borough. For a station that plastered red chyrons like STORM WATCH or DEADLY WEATHER, the news that an "international serial killer is on the loose" was like reporting on the End of Days.

Monte Ferguson got barely a mention, merely as "first reported by a British journalist." But Ferguson must have loved the coverage, which had the network's "crack news team covering the story from every angle!" They had already acquired photos of Father Peters along with Lionel Frey, Melanie Keaton, and the *Blasphemers'* Billy Street. The dead never looked so good, like they'd been airbrushed by some Hollywood art department. Someone had even dug up Billy's not-so-euphonious hit, "Ain't I Good Enough for You," and played it in the background of the field reports about a "homicidal maniac preying on New York City."

Harris muted the replay with the remote. "The job is hard enough without these wannabe actors spreading panic in the streets."

"That wasn't the intention when we fed the story to the British reporter," said Frankel.

Grant was taken aback to see Frankel share responsibility for the deal with Ferguson. He couldn't let the detective take heat from his superior for something he'd only agreed to but hadn't instigated.

"I was actually the one who gave Ferguson permission," Grant told Harris.

"And why the hell would you do that?"

"He was ready to print the story a few days ago in England, even before the priest was murdered. I was able to hold him off at the time, but he quickly made the connection when Father Peters died, and then there was no stopping him."

Harris shook his head. "If he'd just gone lone wolf with a random story for that rag of his instead of us corroborating it, we could have issued a flat-out denial. Now we have to spend valuable man hours fending off the national media." He swiveled toward Little. "How many calls have you gotten since this broke?"

Little finally spoke up. "Over three dozen since it went online an hour ago."

Grant's eyes drifted back to the muted television. His very own Sergeant Hawley stood on the steps at the Yard holding up a hand to fend off the barrage of questions from the horde of British reporters.

Explains the missed call and voice mail Hawley left me thirty minutes ago.

He'd have to apologize to the sergeant when he called him back. Clearly this was avalanching beyond any control that the men in this room possessed.

"No one talks to this man Ferguson again unless it's cleared by me or this office," said the lieutenant. "Is that clear?"

"Gotcha, Loot," Frankel replied. "In the meantime, should we scrap the 'denial' idea and just go with 'no comment' when asked?"

"Not so funny, Detective," Harris told Frankel.

Grant looked over at the television again to avoid a fuming Harris seeing the smile on his face. The newscast had moved on to the next story. The red-haired talking head had swiveled in her chair to another camera as a new chyron flashed just below her plunging neckline: *Not So Welcome Homecoming.*

Meanwhile, Harris continued. "We're going to work with Little's office here to prepare a blanket statement everyone needs to stand by until further notice."

The newscast was running old file footage of a night crime scene. Two bodies on gurneys were being wheeled out of a big house. Grant started to look away but then noticed something in the upper-left-hand corner of the screen.

Another chyron.

Then it disappeared as the coverage ended and the redhead appeared again, ready to talk weather.

Grant waved frantically at the television set. "Wait, wait . . ."

An annoyed Harris glared at him. "What is it, Commander? You're already on my shit list."

Grant pointed at the remote control. "Wind that back. Please."

"Why? It's not like we're going to see something we don't already know, especially since these fools know nothing themselves."

Grant snatched the remote control and pressed rewind. The images squiggled by until he got to the old crime footage of two bodies being removed from the house. He freeze-framed the image—and felt a familiar chill run up his spine. Grant grabbed Frankel by the shoulder. "Take a look at that."

The detective was confused. "At what?"

"The upper left corner of the screen," said Grant.

The red chyron was a specific date.

September 9, 1988.

"You're shitting me."

Grant was happy to see the detective was quickly catching up.

"What the hell is this?" asked Frankel.

"It's follow-up on a story they've been running since last night," Little told them. "The Timothy Leeds case."

"Timothy Leeds?" Grant asked. "Never heard of him."

"He got released from prison last night after doing thirty years for a double murder," explained Little.

"A double murder?" repeated Grant.

Something started gnawing deep in his brain, trying to come together.

"Out on Long Island somewhere," Little said. He indicated the chyron. "That's the night it happened. September 9th, 1988."

The crime blotter report.

The one he'd looked up late the night before when he couldn't sleep.

It had been right there.

"Oh, shit," said Frankel. He turned his attention fully to Grant. "I heard a story the other day that this guy was getting released. They made a big deal how he was going to be out in the real world for the first time as an adult."

"And that would be because . . . ?"

"He was only seventeen when he was convicted for murdering his parents," explained Frankel.

<hr/>

Timothy Leeds had been the textbook case where everyone who knew the teen said he was a quiet kid who had never done a violent thing in his life.

Until one night in early September 1988, when he blew both of his parents away with his father's shotgun in the Long Island town of Cedarhurst.

It was probably that reputation and no previous record that got him tried as a minor instead of as an adult. Between that classification and the good fortune that the crime had occurred before the State of New York reinstituted the death penalty, Timothy had avoided being given a lethal injection.

Instead, he got a fifty-year sentence but had been granted his release for model behavior following his first parole hearing, having served more than half his term.

When asked why he killed his mother and father by countless physicians, therapists, officers, and magistrates, Timothy Leeds offered up the same answer.

"They wouldn't let me borrow the car."

It wasn't due to a sordid tale of abuse by sadistic parents or unabashed greed like the Menendez brothers. Three decades ago, Timothy Alan Leeds had a very bad day. He had stopped taking the antianxiety medication that his folks had given him since he was an "overactive toddler," and just acted out in the worst way possible when his parents said he couldn't take his father's new car to impress a senior girl.

He had been found weeping over their bodies when the police arrived (a pair of shotgun blasts in the Five Towns will get 911 calls going fast and furious), saying he only wanted to borrow the Ferrari. Timothy never denied his wrongdoing and accepted his sentence like the man he wasn't yet. He didn't miss a dose of medication in the thirty years that followed and emerged from his confinement as a man who just wanted to peacefully reenter society.

Unfortunately for Timothy, the city of Cedarhurst didn't take to this idea.

The upper-crust Long Islanders weren't about to welcome the town's not-so-favorite son back with open arms. An online petition when Timothy's parole hearing was announced became a full-fledged protest the moment he was freed.

So, despite his desire to return to his hometown as a forty-nine-year-old man wanting to resume the life he'd never had, it was arranged for him to be assigned to a halfway house in Far Rockaway, little more than a stone's throw from cushy Cedarhurst, but more than a few rungs down the class ladder.

By the time Grant and Frankel hit the Long Island Expressway in the unmarked car, the commander had absorbed all of this. They also learned that Leeds had entered the halfway house the previous evening and left shortly after breakfast that morning.

And hadn't returned.

The best thing about Timothy's new digs was the unobstructed ocean view, one of many gone-to-seed buildings adjacent to the dilapidated boardwalk that was still in the urban planning stages post–Hurricane Sandy. Directly in the JFK flight path, the sandstone edifice was probably last painted during his presidency.

For more than three decades, it had been taking in released prisoners whose day-to-day movements were pretty much unrestricted. Their recidivism rate was less than five percent, leading Grant to believe someone was doing something right there.

A Long Island sheriff named Barnes met them at the building's entrance. Stylish, with a white beard and mustache fit for a stint that month as Macy's Kris Kringle, Barnes had been the one Frankel had gotten on the phone when he'd contacted the local authorities. The sheriff had been unable to locate Leeds upon arriving at the halfway house. That was why Barnes was now standing beside Bentley Edwards, the man who ran the facility.

Edwards, in his midforties, had enough bulk to stand up to the residents he watched over but enough caring in his soft green eyes to make Grant believe the man would lend a tender ear and shoulder to lean on when necessary. Edwards told them he'd seen Leeds just before the man left that morning. Frankel asked if it were normal for a newly released prisoner to be allowed to roam freely, especially one with Leeds's notoriety.

"There's a curfew he has to adhere to," explained Edwards. "Anyone assigned here has been triple-checked by medical professionals and prison authorities before being deemed fit to handle a day-to-day life."

"No one's questioning you, sir," Frankel said. "We're just trying to get a complete picture here."

Edwards summarized Leeds's arrival at the halfway house. The Sing Sing authorities had made sure the release ran smoothly, arranged a quick opportunity for the gathered press to take pictures when Leeds exited the maximum-security prison, then secured safe passage (i.e., no media allowed) to Far Rockaway. Leeds had done the standard intake review with Edwards and later took dinner in his room.

"He said he wanted KFC. So, we got him a bucket and he seemed content," Edwards said. "Especially at the prospect of sleeping without other people screaming all night as he has for the past thirty years."

"And what about today?"

"He said he wanted to take a stroll on the boardwalk and dip his toes in the ocean. Can't say I blame him—even though I wouldn't go near it with a ten-foot pole. You can't believe the crap that ends up in there."

"So that's where he headed?"

Edwards shook his head. "I don't think so."

"How's that?" wondered Frankel.

"He got a call on the house phone. Must have been right around breakfast. One of the other residents took it and came to get him. Leeds left a few minutes later."

"Did he say who it was?" asked Frankel.

Edwards shook his head. "I didn't even know about the call until you phoned asking about him. But Chet, the resident I just mentioned? He said Leeds told him it was a reporter who wanted an interview and would pay him good money for his time. So off Leeds went."

Frankel and Grant traded wary glances.

"Chet didn't happen to catch the name of this reporter, did he?" asked Grant.

"No," Edwards answered, his eyes fixing on Grant. "Funny you should ask though. Chet said the man on the other end of the phone had an English accent."

8

The fresh air felt good on Timothy Alan Leeds's face.

For the first time in three decades, he was outside the walls of Sing Sing. It didn't matter that the temperature was barely above freezing, the sky filled with ominous thunderclouds, and the walk to the bar three times as long as the little man back at the halfway house had told him.

He was barely out a day and already looking at making a small fortune.

A thousand dollars. That's what the reporter had promised.

Back when he'd been incarcerated, that amount of money would've kept an angst-ridden teen rolling in dough for six months. Now, he knew a grand would probably not get him very far in life. But with nothing on his résumé except successfully killing both his parents with shotgun blasts, he knew it was an opportunity he had to jump at.

Not that he didn't yearn to become a useful member of society who could hold down an everyday job. It was all he'd dreamed about in his ten-by-twenty-foot cell. But he knew he wasn't going to be anyone's number one candidate.

Therefore, he hadn't hesitated in going to meet the man at Connolly's.

The angry gray surf pounded the shore for miles in either direction. For Timothy, the stark power of the Atlantic and deserted white sand was breathtaking, considering the only view he'd experienced for almost three decades was a metal door and grimy stone walls.

By the time he reached the beach access road where the bar was, he worried he had blown everything by walking instead of trying to cop a ride into town. Connolly's was housed on the bottom floor of a pale blue-and-white Cape Cod structure and Timothy could see through the bay window that it was empty.

He let out a regretful sigh. The offer was too good to be true; or the reporter had second thoughts. Perhaps the guy feared Timothy had acquired an AK-47 and was going to pick up where he left off years before.

But violence wasn't on his mind. He barely remembered that night in Cedarhurst or even Marian's last name (the girl he wanted to take to *Die Hard* in his father's Ferrari). It was all lost in a Tangerine Dream–like haze, the band whose album he'd been listening to when the cops found him sitting between his shotgun-blasted folks.

It was probably a good thing that the reporter pulled a no-show. Timothy was pretty certain he didn't have a grand's worth of memories for the man.

A horn tooted behind him.

He turned to find a midnight blue Hyundai Sonata pulling up. The car braked to a halt and the passenger window slid down. "Mr. Leeds?" It was the same English accent he'd heard on the phone. "Sorry, I got stuck getting out of the blasted city."

"I thought I was getting stood up. So, is this happening or not?"

"I'm ready if you are—as you can see."

Timothy approached the passenger side and leaned inside the window. Colorful bills were spread on the console between the two seats.

Timothy's eyes flickered. "What the hell is that? Monopoly money?"

"It's eight hundred and fifty British pounds. You'd do well on the exchange rate—probably make an extra hundred. I'm sure your bank will convert it for you."

"I don't have a bank. I just got out of prison after thirty years." Timothy was getting cold feet and not just because the wind was picking up and the temperature dropping. "Maybe we should just forget the whole thing."

Timothy straightened up and started to turn away from the Sonata.

"Mr. Leeds, wait," came the plea. "I'm sorry. I just got to the States and arrived ill-prepared. My bad, as you would say. Why don't we go to a bank together, get the money exchanged, and then go about the interview as planned?"

Timothy hovered by the window. It wasn't like he had many options. "Okay, let's do it."

He opened the passenger door and climbed inside. As Timothy buckled himself in, the other man pointed to the money on the console.

"If it'll make you feel any better, hang on to that until we get to the bank."

Timothy reached for the money, then shook his head. "Not necessary."

Timothy looked up just in time to see an elbow come flying at his face.

There were very few things Chet Wilson couldn't break in to. Be it a private home, an auto parts store, a bank vault, or a neighborhood bar's till, finding a way to gain entry had rarely posed a problem for the petty thief.

Sticking around afterward was usually Chet's downfall. It had resulted in three prison terms, the last a ten-year stint that ended with his release six months ago and led to him occupying a small room in the Far Rockaway halfway house.

If pressed, he'd say things were easier behind bars. It was pointless trying to break a jail cell lock with cameras watching one's every move. Three square meals a day and no worries where his next dollar came from; prison had its advantages.

Edwards told this to Grant and Frankel as he walked them through the place. They found Chet in the community room watching *The Talk*. "One thing I'll say about Chet—he's quite forthcoming. Not good at keeping things to himself. He would have been a much more successful thief otherwise. I'd go with whatever he tells you."

When looking at Chet Wilson, he reminded Grant of the men in Liverpool who trudged along with his father to the munitions factory. Chet wore an old denim work shirt and khakis; all that was missing was the black lunch pail and dour expression of a man who day-in, day-out, dutifully provided for his lower-middle class family. The former thief was content getting three hot meals every day at the halfway house and watching the roundtable discussions on the all-female talk show. Today's topic was "My Favorite Christmas Party" with their very special guest, Sarah Michelle Gellar. Chet was glued to the set because he'd spent the past five holiday seasons locked up where Christmas was crap eggnog and the men's chorus singing off-key carols.

The two cops apologized for dragging Chet away from his program to question him about Timothy Leeds.

"No problem—I'll catch the rest later." He muted the program and indicated the remote control. "The DVR's an incredible thing."

"Tell us about your discussion with the man on the phone," said Frankel.

"Ain't much to say. He asked if Timothy Leeds was around and I said I'd check. I hadn't met the guy yet, but we all knew who he was because he arrived last night with all that fuss on the news."

Grant stepped forward. "You said the caller had a British accent?"

"He talked like you, if that's what you mean," Chet replied.

"Do you think you'd recognize his voice again?"

"Probably not. Don't take this wrong, but you all sound alike. It could've been you I was talking to."

"Did you happen to overhear Leeds's end of the conversation?" asked Frankel.

"I gave him his privacy. Most of us round here came from some place where we were on top of everyone else."

"Then how'd you find out he was meeting a reporter?" wondered Frankel.

Chet indicated the door leading out to the main hallway. "He ducked his head in here and asked me how far Connolly's was."

"Connolly's?"

"A dive bar down on Ninety-Fifth Street," explained Edwards.

Chet nodded. "I said it was a ten-minute walk. That's when he told me he was going to meet this reporter who wanted to pay him for his story."

"I know Miles, who works the day shift at the bar," Edwards said. "I texted him a photo of Leeds. He said he hasn't been in there today and Miles would know. The place is pretty much dead until happy hour."

"Did Leeds mention the reporter's name?" asked Grant. "Monte Ferguson?"

He had tried Ferguson's cell the second Edwards had mentioned the phone call Leeds had received. It had gone directly to voice mail.

"Nope. I just told him how to get there, then wished him good luck. Figure he had it coming after doing his thirty in Sing Sing."

Frankel's expression tightened. "The man murdered his folks in cold blood."

"And served his time," said Chet. The ex-con's voice had turned serious. "Everyone deserves a second chance," said the thrice-convicted thief. "Hell. I'm working on my fourth."

—————

Timothy opened his eyes, then immediately shut them again.

Sand was pouring inside his eyeballs.

He tried to open his mouth to scream but it was covered in duct tape. Trying to move his arms produced a similar result—they had been pulled behind his back and tied together with a tightly-knotted rope.

He was being dragged across a stretch of white sand. Ironically, it might have been the same piece of shoreline he'd been admiring just a short time before.

"Ah, you're back with us," came the now-familiar British voice that Timothy finally understood he never should have trusted.

The man pulled Timothy to his feet. Totally immobilized and still hurting from the sucker punch to the face, Timothy had no choice but to yield to his captor.

The man was a whole lot stronger than he looked.

Not that Timothy had gotten a good bead on him. His brain was really scrambled.

As the sand blew away and his eyes cleared, Timothy saw the massive building he was being shoved toward. It resembled a beached gray whale crossbred with one of those alien ships in that movie *Independence Day* someone with a warped sense of humor showed every Fourth of July back in the joint.

As if the broken-out widows and dead landscaping surrounding a structure that looked ready to topple any second weren't enough, a sign near the rickety building entrance sealed the deal.

Condemned! Stay Out! This Means You!

It might as well have read "Abandon All Hope Ye Who Enter Here."

Though Timothy's screams were muffled by the duct tape, it didn't stop him from continuing to try and be heard.

Until his captor punched him in the head again.

Miles, the thirtyish bartender at Connolly's, was blond and looked like he belonged permanently atop the surfboard he took out at dawn and dusk. There had only been three customers that morning—a young couple looking to wet their whistles shortly before noon that Miles carded and sent thirstily on their way, and an older woman who had gotten lost looking for Coney Island.

"Definitely not this guy," Miles said, holding the photo that Edwards had sent over. Frankel gave Miles his card and told him to call if he saw any sign of Leeds.

Minutes later, the two cops stood outside the bar, equally frustrated.

"We're getting a line on the calls coming into that phone back at the halfway house to see if one lines up with Ferguson," Frankel told the commander.

It wasn't like Grant had another bright idea. He had tried Ferguson again and once again it had gone directly to voice mail.

They began canvassing the shops and streets near Connolly's to see if anyone had spotted Leeds. Being the peak of winter, this part of Far Rockaway resembled a ghost town. Most shops were shuttered for the season, and the few yearlong denizens they spoke to had been cooped up all morning, not brave enough to confront the close-to-freezing temperatures.

Grant was in a tiny corner grocery ordering hot tea when his cell rang.

Monte Ferguson's name appeared on the mobile screen.

Grant took the call immediately. "Where have you been all morning?"

"Talking to the press. Print. Television. Online bloggers," answered the *Mail* man. "What did you think I'd be doing? Or haven't you seen the news today?"

"Oh, I've seen it."

"Sorry if it's caused you any inconvenience," Ferguson said.

That's one big fat lie.

"Are you on your way to Far Rockaway to talk to Timothy Alan Leeds?"

"Far Rockaway? I don't even know what or where that is," responded Ferguson. "And who the hell is Timothy Alan Leeds?"

This time, it was excruciating pain that woke Timothy.

Worse than any he had experienced in his forty-seven years, emanating from the center of his forehead. Blood dripped into both of his eyes.

He tried to bring his hands up and wipe it away, but they were still tied behind his back. And his mouth continued to be sealed tight with the duct tape.

Timothy violently shook his head, clearing enough blood from his eyes to make out the hideous shape of his captor standing inches away from his face.

The man was wearing plastic gloves and held a knife dripping with blood.

Timothy's blood.

"Figured that might bring you around," the man said. He made a grandiose motion with the knife. "Bring back old memories?"

The first thing Timothy noticed were the stone walls and metal door. He started to shake uncontrollably.

"They don't have actual cells here," explained his captor. "I think they're more like holding rooms for their 'problem children.' Seemed appropriate."

Suddenly, the man spun Timothy around 180 degrees in a swivel chair.

Timothy saw the wall behind him for the first time.

It was covered with old newspapers and photos. All featured either Timothy, his parents, or their dead bodies. The headlines practically screamed at him—*Teen Brutally Murders Parents* and *Leeds Gets Fifty Years—Is It Enough?*

Timothy screamed—in spite of the duct tape.

"Sorry, I didn't catch that," the man said. "But I get the gist."

The man pointed with a bloody glove at the collage.

"I understand. You think you did your time after being tried and convicted in criminal court."

His captor turned back to look directly at Timothy.

"But now you're in *mine*."

The man reached in to his pocket and pulled out a cell phone. Then he punched a couple of buttons with a gloved finger and placed the cell on a table behind him.

He gave a slight nod of satisfaction. Then turned his attention back to Timothy.

"So, do you want to begin praying—or should I?"

9

G rant couldn't get Ferguson off the phone quickly enough.

Unfortunately, the man from the *Mail* wasn't interested in ending the call so fast. A barrage of questions followed, and as much as Grant wanted to hang up, he knew Ferguson could drip enough poison from his pen to worsen the situation.

"You're thinking this bloke Leeds will be victim number five?"

Grant considered his options. Leeds was all over the news and, having already given Monte his name, it wouldn't take long for him to learn everything about the released convict. Grant realized a denial would only come back to haunt him, especially if Leeds ended up with a Roman numeral *V* etched in his forehead.

"It's looking that way," Grant admitted. He begged Ferguson not to go public with the information. By letting the killer know the authorities were casting their net over him, they risked the man fleeing. As for Leeds, if he saw his name listed as an intended victim, there was an equal chance he might head for parts unknown instead of coming directly to the cops for protection.

Monte agreed to keep quiet for the moment but Grant knew the reporter would try to find Leeds himself, so he asked Ferguson to contact him or Frankel if he got a line on the man.

"If Leeds is in the killer's sights, you might be putting yourself at risk, Monte."

"Duly noted, Commander."

The call ended with a click. Grant put the odds at fifty-fifty that Ferguson would honor any of his requests. He turned to find Frankel on his cell as well.

The NYPD detective looked impatient. "On hold," he murmured.

Grant brought Frankel up to speed on his conversation with Ferguson.

Frankel shook his head. "Doesn't matter where they're from. Here, England, wherever. Reporters hide behind that freedom of the press crap and tell you they're only interested in the truth but all they want to do is promote themselves."

Grant didn't disagree.

"So, if Ferguson wasn't the one who contacted Leeds, how likely is it a second British reporter called wanting an interview with the guy?" asked Frankel.

"You know as well as I do who that was on the other end of the phone."

"Shit." Frankel suddenly held up his hand; his call had resumed. "Yes, I'm here. Gimme one second."

Frankel dug into his pocket for a pad and pen. Grant noticed his expression darken the more he scribbled. Frankel finally mumbled thanks, disconnected, and held up the notepad.

"Looks like there were only three calls to the house phone this morning. One was from the cook's mother who had locked herself out and needed a spare key. They tracked another to a resident's girlfriend."

"And the third?"

"Traces to a burner phone. Prepaid for thirty minutes of use; not registered to anyone."

But both Grant and Frankel knew who had bought it.

"The phone's on and working," said Frankel. "They pinged it to an address less than two miles from here."

Within seconds they were back in the sedan. "More than likely another dead end. I bet the asshole just dumped it near this place and took off," Frankel said as he started the engine.

"Why would you say that?"

"The building's been abandoned for thirty years," Frankel replied. "It used to be an mental hospital."

The Neponsit Health Care Center.

That was still the officially designated name, even though it hadn't been operational for a couple decades. Originally, it had been called the Neponsit Beach Hospital for Children, a facility treating youngsters suffering from tuberculosis in the early twentieth century. In its day, it was among the most prominent pediatric hospitals in the country, offering top-notch treatments like Alpine sun lamp usage and supervised bathing in the adjacent Atlantic.

During World War II, it had been taken over by the Department of Public Health to treat merchant marines who had contracted TB. After the war, it had resumed tending children until its doors closed in 1955. It reopened in 1961 as a nursing home renamed the Neponsit Home for the Aged.

For the next few decades, it looked after elderly people and thus took on its current name. Few of its residents appreciated the white sand beaches below and the majestic Atlantic beyond, as many were mentally ill, some in the late stages of Alzheimer's, and may not have noticed the difference from living out their days in a windowless building in Queens.

Then, in September 1998, ten years after Timothy Alan Leeds's life had changed forever, a vicious storm pounded Far Rockaway, forcing everyone in the hospital to be evacuated to the aforementioned Queens property. It happened so fast that two patients died during the transfer and another went missing for weeks.

The hospital survived the brutal assault of the storm but the powers that be didn't let the patients return, citing health hazards. Naysayers believed the late-night emergency evacuation was a ploy to take advantage of the property's beachfront location so the owners could turn it into a luxury resort hotel. But no such renovation ever took place. One reporter unearthed a copy of the original deed to the hospital stating the land could only be used for a medical facility or public park.

As a result, the building had sat neglected for over twenty years. Battered by winter storms and the deadly Hurricane Sandy, the structure continued to sit atop the white sands of Far Rockaway like a monolith on the brink of collapse.

Frankel told Grant that every summer a few drunk teens or vagrants would be pulled from its run-down corridors and gone-to-seed rooms, having ventured inside either on a dare, looking to party in private, or looking for a place to crash. They all agreed it was spooky as hell and most weren't sure if they were hearing the wind blowing through cracks or the haunted screams of former inhabitants.

It wasn't quite the Overlook Hotel, but the redbrick, five-story structure emitted a feeling of impending doom from the long shadow it cast on the lot's white concrete. Weeds poking through the crevices cowered in its presence, having turned brown while trying to shrivel their way back below the surface.

There wasn't a car or person to be seen. Frankel checked out the edge of the parking lot closest to the building and tapped a foot beside some tire skid marks.

"These are recent. Otherwise, the rain the other night would've washed them away. If our guy ditched his phone, it should be somewhere around here."

Frankel moved to a rusted dumpster. Grant walked over to join him. Both men peered inside to see a few broken bottles and crumpled fast-food bags.

A search of the parking lot and nearby sand didn't produce a discarded burner phone either.

Grant studied a fence and the chain-link gate that separated the parking lot from the former hospital's grounds. "Might have been more than just a quick stop."

He pointed to a broken lock lying on the ground by the gate.

Frankel reached inside his coat and pulled out his service revolver. He looked over at Grant.

"Oh, right," Frankel said. "You fellas over there don't carry these."

Grant realized he must have visibly reacted.

"And our murder rate was quite below yours last time I checked."

"Need I remind you this maniac started on your side of the ocean?"

"He hasn't used a gun," Grant added. "At least not yet."

"I've got a spare underneath the front seat if you want it."

Grant shook his head. "I've managed to get this far in life without one."

"Suit yourself."

Grant asked about backup. Frankel indicated the skid marks. "If this was him, he's long gone. It's probably a wild-goose chase and would be a waste of manpower; plus, it'd take them forever to get here."

They moved through the gate and onto the white sand.

A set of footprints led toward the building. The sand's surface had been uniformly scraped directly behind the prints, resembling a narrow path.

"Looks like somebody has been dragging something," Grant observed.

"Something or someone," agreed Frankel.

They followed the tracks until the sand met up with a huge concrete pad.

Suddenly, the two cops were standing in the former courtyard of the old hospital. Two redbrick wings rose on either side of the concrete, half the windows boarded shut. A maroon-colored cylinder resembling a lighthouse rose above the west wing. Its fenced-in circular observation platform reminded Grant of a prison watch tower.

Dead ahead was the entrance to the hospital. It was partially boarded up—one wood panel had been pulled off its hinges and cast aside. It looked like the gaping maw of some behemoth that had risen from the murky depths of the Atlantic waiting to be fed.

"You sure you don't want to go back for that spare?" asked Frankel.

I probably couldn't hit something five feet in front of me, thought Grant. *But I'm not going to tell him that.*

Grant shook his head. "You said wild-goose chase, right?"

Grant was fairly certain the last time a cleanup crew had been inside the hospital had been around the time it shuttered for good. It was a sharp contrast to the building's exterior which had been clear of debris and graffiti. Frankel surmised that the fact it was a "former mental hospital" was bad enough; the Far Rockaway tourism board needed the outside to appear as palatable as possible if it was trying to attract New Yorkers to its white sandy shores.

The main entryway could have passed for the county dump. Papers and old beer cans were strewn everywhere. Sky-blue wallpaper meant to give a feeling of peace and tranquility to the troubled residents had peeled away in mottled patches from cut floor to ceiling. The space was devoid of furniture except for one mattress shoved in a corner that had probably been used by vagrants until they crawled back out into the cruel, hard world.

The two cops moved through massive clutter until they reached a perpendicular corridor running off the back of the entryway. It went both directions with doors upon doors on either side of the hallway. It was nearly impossible to see as the only light came from the room they'd just left and windows at opposite ends of the corridor that seemed to be miles away.

"Where the fuck do we even start?" grumbled Frankel.

Grant started to respond, then noticed something on the wall to his left. He pulled out his cell and used the lit screen to illuminate that section of the wall.

It was a left-pointing arrow—scrawled in fresh blood.

Grant motioned. "I'd say that way."

Frankel raised his gun a bit higher and Grant didn't protest when he took the lead. Frankel dug out his iPhone and punched on the flashlight app to provide light as they slowly moved down the long corridor.

Some doors were cracked open, others closed. All had glass windows halfway up so that back in the day the staff could check on their charges.

The first dozen rooms they checked were either locked or filled with the tattered remnants of drunk-fests and homeless sleepovers.

They were in the darkest part of the hallway when they reached a door with another message in dripping crimson blood.

V.

They exchanged woeful looks, then stood silently on either side of the door. They listened intently, waiting for any sort of sound.

Frankel peeked inside the window.

"Goddamn it." He quickly brought the iPhone up, shined the light inside for a second, then brought it back down again. "Fuck this asshole."

Before Grant could respond, Frankel threw open the door.

A worn chair was in the center of the room; a man was sitting in it.

His head was covered by a bonnet hair dryer attached to the back of the chair. Even in the dim light, Grant could see he was dead, with pools of blood beneath him.

Frankel approached the chair and carefully lifted the hair dryer for a closer look.

The man's head rolled off his neck and plopped onto the floor beside their feet.

Both men jumped backward.

"Jesus," Grant muttered.

Frankel recovered enough to aim the light toward the decapitated head on the floor.

Timothy Alan Leeds stared up at them with blood-filled vacant eyes and a carved *V* in the middle of his forehead.

Grant was still trying to slow his heartbeat when he caught sight of the wall behind Frankel. "John," he whispered to the detective. "Shine your light behind you."

Frankel did just that.

And illuminated a small wooden cross in the middle of the wall.

He widened the flashlight's scope. It revealed numerous photographs and news clippings taped up on either side of the cross.

All were of Leeds or the murders he'd committed thirty years ago just a few miles from where they now stood.

Frankel shook his head. "I guess it's the last thing he wanted Leeds to see before he sent him off to meet his Maker."

"I think it might actually be another message for us."

"What are you talking about?"

"It's arranged in a specific pattern." Grant pointed to the wall again. "Unless I'm totally wrong—that looks like a big Roman numeral seven to me."

Frankel trained the flashlight on the wall one more time.

Sure enough, two sets of photos and clippings were arranged in a *V* and an *I* on one side of the cross.

A second Roman numeral *I* was on the other.

VII

"Seven?" asked Frankel.

He glanced down at Leeds with the freshly carved *V* in the middle of his forehead.

"This is definitely the Roman numeral five," observed Frankel. He looked back up at Grant. "But if he's moved on to seven already, what the hell happened to six?"

10

As dusk fell over Far Rockaway, the Neponsit Health Care Center was teeming with people for the first time since it had closed its doors decades earlier. The crime scene was led by Marcus, the medical examiner Grant had last seen talking about a Manhattan souvenir pulled out of a holy man's stomach.

Marcus was carefully studying Timothy Alan Leeds's mouth when Grant appeared beside him. "Just wondering if he left us another gift like Father Peters."

"I think you were saved the trouble this time, Doctor," Grant said, motioning toward the stone wall. A steady stream of flashbulbs illuminated the morbid photo and clipping gallery, each bright pop shoving the killer's message in Grant's face.

VII.

Grant didn't need a cheat sheet to remember the Seventh Commandment. *Thou shalt not commit adultery.*

The fact that the killer had either skipped the Sixth (*Thou shalt not kill*) or committed another murder they'd yet to come across was simply maddening.

It had been difficult enough hunting a fifth victim with everyone having a set of parents. And though the number was certain to be much less, Grant imagined the number of adulterers in New York City would still be staggering. And none would want to own up to their transgressions—an affair was something both parties did their utmost to keep from being discovered.

The medical examiner took one look at the wall display.

"I wouldn't want to be you guys," Marcus said. This was clearly meant to include Frankel as well, who had taken that moment to join the ME and Grant.

"I'd rather be anyone than me just about now," Frankel conceded.

Grant managed a sad smile.

"What can you tell us so far?" asked Frankel.

"Nothing earth shattering. I see a couple of bruises developing on either side of the head. Administered separately, I'd guess." Marcus pointed out the spots and continued. "Lines up with your theory he was dragged from the parking lot. No way of telling yet which blow was administered first, but playing fast and loose? I'd say he needed to subdue Leeds a couple of times. That would account for the second bruise. Not that either was the killing blow."

"Any idea what was used to decapitate him?" Frankel asked.

Marcus shook his head.

"A preliminary glance at the jagged marks on his severed neck make me think we're looking at an industrial saw. It'll be hard to identify the brand unless I find trace material during the autopsy. I won't know until I get in there—but these tools are practically indestructible, so I wouldn't count on it."

"It's hard to believe he killed Leeds with a saw," Grant said. "Sort of unwieldy, wouldn't you say?"

"Absolutely," Marcus answered. "Look here."

He placed one gloved hand on Leeds's chin and used the other to indicate two gashes directly below the part of the neck that was still attached to his head.

"Two deep slits—thinner and smoother than the jagged ones I mentioned. They're very similar to those I found on the priest at Saint Pat's."

The ME turned to Grant. "I'd wager they resemble the ones on your three bodies back in England."

"I don't share your expertise—but I'm inclined to agree with you."

"These were made with a sharp knife and probably killed him. That left him free to do his dirty work with whatever portable saw he brought along." Marcus gently lowered Leeds's head back down onto a plastic sheet. "I'll compare these marks with those on Father Peters, but I suspect they'll confirm that you're dealing with the same perpetrator."

Grant's eyes took in the clipping collage again. He turned to see Frankel doing likewise. The message might as well have been in flashing neon.

"Yeah," grumbled Frankel. "It's the same fucking guy, all right."

It was after midnight when Frankel and Grant returned to the sedan. They had watched Marcus's crew bag Leeds's body and place it on a gurney, wheel it down the same corridor that only hours before they'd crept through with iPhones in hand, and into the entryway bathed in electric light (courtesy of massive floodlights brought in by Con Ed) for the first time since the hospital's patients had been evacuated decades ago.

Now, as they swung onto the LIE, Frankel told Grant he should take note of the rarest of the rare. Cars were actually moving—some exceeding the speed limit.

Grant remembered his cab ride in from JFK a few days earlier. "Beats being stuck in the world's biggest parking lot."

"Look at you. Stick around long enough, we'll turn you into a real New Yorker."

"I just want to book a return trip for two," replied Grant. "Bring this lunatic back to England and put him in the docket where he can answer for what he did."

"Might have to arm wrestle you for that. Though you are ahead three to two." He ducked over and jumped into the carpool lane. "Of course, it might be all tied up and we don't even know it."

"I just don't see him moving on to the Seventh Commandment unless he's already gone and murdered a sixth person."

"Maybe he's changing things up—keeping us on our toes."

Grant shook his head. "He's been systematically working a very specific pattern. My concern is that the murders are becoming increasingly extravagant—not to mention happening more frequently. If there's a sixth victim out there, he killed them within hours of Leeds."

" *Thou shalt not kill.*' So, what are we looking for? Another killer?" Frankel switched lanes again. "Maybe he's still talking about Leeds. Figures he could knock off two birds with one stone. The guy was a murderer who offed his mom and dad. Violates both the Fifth and Sixth Commandments."

"Wouldn't he have etched a Roman numeral *I* to go with the *V* we found on his forehead?"

"Just wishful thinking on my part," said Frankel. He indicated the police radio below the dashboard. "I've got them running the system for released killers in the Tri-State area. See if any are missing or if one of their bodies showed up."

"It doesn't have to be a convicted-and-released killer. Might be a murderer who has gotten away with their crime so far."

Frankel stared out at the Manhattan skyline rising in front of them.

"Most times I think there can't be a more magnificent place to live. But tonight? All I see is how damn big the city is and wonder how the hell we're going to find a dead murderer's body we're not even sure exists yet, let alone the right cheating spouse. It makes my head hurt."

Grant heard a slight gurgling sound and saw Frankel rubbing his stomach.

"Not to mention my insides grumble. Hungry?"

Grant tried to remember when he last ate. He realized it hadn't been since breakfast with Rachel at the Surrey. He couldn't believe it was the same day.

"It's one in the morning."

"You know how they call New York 'the city that doesn't sleep'?"

"I know the song," Grant said.

"They should've added another verse. Called it 'the city that always eats.' "

⸺

The line was at least thirty deep and curved around the southwest corner at Fifty-Third Street and Sixth Avenue.

The Halal Guys, more commonly known as "Fifty-Third and Sixth," had been serving New Yorkers from their hot food cart since it had first appeared next to the New York Hilton in 1990. It opened every night at seven o'clock and closed at four in the morning. The most popular dish, and what Frankel insisted Grant try, was a simple combination of chicken, rice, and pita bread with their famous "white sauce," whose recipe the Egyptian proprietor would take to his grave.

While waiting a half hour in the slow-moving line, Frankel explained how it had started out as just another Manhattan hot dog stand. The owner, Mohamed Abouelenein, had claimed that a frankfurter wasn't a satisfying meal and switched to a Mediterranean-inspired menu a couple of years later. There had been no advertising; its popularity spread by word of mouth. Its first real appearance in the news had been in 2006 when a fight broke out ending with one man stabbed to death. The reason: cutting in line, naturally.

"I've been coming here since high school," Frankel said as they crossed the street with their stuffed-to-the-brim metal tins.

Grant studied the concoction. "I think I'd be dead by now."

They sat on the edge of a fountain beside two kids wearing Hunter College sweatshirts. Frankel watched Grant dip his fork and told him to make sure he got a lot of sauce.

"So?" the detective asked after Grant had taken a bite. "Pretty great, huh?"

"Better." Grant didn't elaborate; he was too busy loading up the fork again.

"They've franchised all over the country. But nothing beats the original."

"Coming from a people who take great pride in tradition, often to a fault, I would have to concur."

Frankel dug into his own platter. The next few minutes were spent making huge dents in their dishes. Frankel finally paused between bites.

"Speaking of England—have you given much thought to what you're going to do once the new year rolls around?"

"Not really. For years I figured when the time came, Allison and I would get to do all the things we never got around to."

"Of course. I'm sorry," Frankel said apologetically.

"No. It's a fair question." Grant repressed a sigh. "Right now, I'm just praying this is all over by then."

They went back to their meals. Then the NYPD man resumed the conversation. "You've really been at the Yard thirty years?"

"Just finishing thirty-four, actually."

"I haven't been in this job half that time. I can't imagine doing it that long."

"Things are different over there." Grant finished the last bite and indicated his empty plate. "Places like this, for instance. The fact this city never seems to stop—twenty-four-seven as you say. That pace has to take a toll. Things move a bit more leisurely in England."

"I haven't been to London since I went with a few buddies after college. We spent most of it drunk in pubs, but I remember it being a happening place. I hear it's even more so these days."

"It's there if you want it. Just not in your face every single moment." Grant shrugged. "I'm perfectly content curling up with a good book or sitting across from my brother getting my hide fleeced in our weekly chess match."

"I hope you get a chance to return to that." Frankel deposited his plate with Grant's in a nearby trash can. They headed back for the sedan.

A few minutes later, Frankel pulled up in front of the London.

"I talked to Harris right before we left Far Rockaway," Frankel said as he placed the car in park. "He's arranged with Little for a press conference at eleven in the morning. They're insisting the two of us be there."

"Inevitable, I guess."

"It'll be a shit show for sure. Starting with your friend Ferguson, I imagine."

"I haven't heard a peep out of him since we found Leeds."

This time it was Grant who was rubbing his stomach, wondering what had just hit it. He unbuckled the seat belt and thanked Frankel for the ride and late-night meal.

"Hope it doesn't keep you up," Frankel told him.

"I'll be asleep before my head hits the pillow."

Of course, two hours later he was still wide awake.

It hadn't been the chicken and rice roiling around keeping Grant from falling asleep. Whenever they would treat themselves to a five-course meal at a fancy restaurant, Allison used to marvel at how Grant could just roll over and be out before she could even utter "good night."

Grant knew it was the enormity of the case and its rapidly increasing body count that was causing this bout of sleeplessness.

His first mistake had been turning on the television and catching the tail end of a local newscast reporting the discovery of Timothy Alan Leeds's dead body. The anchor informed Grant's fellow insomniacs that NYPD was conducting a press conference later that morning and the station would be there to cover it live with all the other networks.

So much for the idea of sleep coming any time soon.

He spent a half hour scrolling through news blogs and internet sites to see what was being reported. No one had any more information than the newscast. Ferguson, the British tabloid writer, was curiously silent. This worried Grant—he couldn't imagine Monte staying on the sidelines knowing what he already did about Leeds. It was only a matter of time before Ferguson dropped some bomb—the only question was how and where it would detonate.

By three in the morning, he had come to terms with suffering through this night by himself. He suddenly realized it was past eight in the morning in London. He picked up the phone and dialed a particular number. It rang once, and the call was picked up with a distinct click.

"I was wondering when I'd hear from you," said Everett.

"How'd you know it was me?" Grant asked.

"The wonder of caller ID. Who else would call me from America at—what is it over there—half past three in the morning?"

"Don't remind me." He glanced at the digital alarm clock by the bed. It was actually 3:39 A.M. "Why would you expect to hear from me?"

"The morning shows over here have been reporting a fifth murder."

"I'm surprised you didn't call to gloat about your theory being right."

"In the middle of your night? Don't be daft." He could tell Everett was doing his best not to chuckle aloud. "Though I probably would've done so later if you hadn't."

Grant proceeded to bring his brother up-to-date with Leeds's murder and what they had found on the walls of the abandoned hospital in Far Rockaway.

"Perhaps it's time you and your New York policeman stop hanging on to the Commandments and let the public know what they're dealing with."

"All that will do is cause a full-fledged panic."

"Sounds like you've already got one on your hands," Everett said. "It might actually help matters. If you haven't killed someone or committed adultery, it would put you at ease, don't you think?"

"I guess you could look at it that way. But say you had? Killed someone or had an affair. Then what?"

"You'd worry a bit more. At the same time, it would make it a little harder for your fellow to get at these people if they were more aware as to what was going on."

Grant chewed on the thought. He could see pluses and minuses. "I'm not sure, Everett. The carving marks are the one thing that would separate the pretenders from the genuine article when it comes to a confession."

"So, hold back on them. Going public with the Commandments doesn't mean you have to reveal the other."

Grant told his brother he'd given him something to think about.

Everett then asked about his breakfast with Rachel.

"At least she didn't walk out the moment I arrived," Grant told him. "Though I could tell she was considering it."

Everett asked if Rachel had given him an inkling as to what was causing the rift between them. Over the past year, Grant had brought it up to his brother, hoping he could help get to the bottom of it with his niece. But Everett hadn't been able to make any headway and remained as perplexed by it all as Grant.

"I made a point of staying clear of the subject," Grant said.

"Next time perhaps."

"If there is one. She does seem open to it though. Which reminds me—I'm supposed to get her number from you."

Everett was happy to provide it as they continued chatting to well past four. Everett finally told Grant to stay in touch and hoped that he got some sleep.

But he was still wide awake. He crawled into bed anyway and started flipping around various stations, trying to avoid any newscast, knowing it would just aggravate him further.

He finally came across *Notting Hill* playing on a movie channel. It had been one of Allison's favorites—one in a series of movies that she kept on the DVR. She used to say they would lull her to sleep, like comfort food, in the sense that they were "lovely bedtime tales" that didn't require much deep thinking and she would drift off to sleep sooner than later.

Grant had paid little attention to these films.

At least so he thought.

Over the years he'd heard them so often from the other side of the bed that Grant realized he was able to practically recite them word for word himself—and they became a sleeping tonic of sorts for him as well.

So he settled in and began watching it.

He didn't realize he'd fallen asleep until he got to the part of the movie where Julia Roberts tells Hugh Grant that she's "just a girl trying to find a boy who would just *kill* her."

That was when Julia turned around to reveal dozens of Roman numerals carved into her forehead.

Grant bolted up from the nightmare, barely able to catch his breath.

He glanced over at the window. The morning light was trying to slip through the slight separation in the curtains.

Lovely.

11

The room was packed.

Grant couldn't imagine squeezing in another soul. The space was normally used for roll call or an occasional closed-door meeting between detectives and their superiors. The NYPD media liaison Little had dragged in fifty more chairs to accommodate the gathered press. Grant hoped they'd be so crammed in they'd be unable to raise their hands when it came time for questions.

He sat up front with Frankel behind a long rectangular desk. The other two seats there were occupied by Little and Lieutenant Harris. With the local networks broadcasting live, the session started right on time.

"I know it's crowded in here," said Little. "If you want some breathing room, we've got a live feed going in the room next door."

Grant and Frankel exchanged glances. Grant was certain his colleague was thinking the same thing. He'd gladly be in a different room. For that matter, a different building.

Little introduced Harris. The lieutenant's opening remarks didn't offer up anything new. He vowed that the "NYPD's finest men and women" were working day and night to bring the case to a rapid conclusion. "I'm now going to turn things over to our lead investigator, Detective First Grade John Frankel."

More like throw him under the bus, thought Grant. Wasn't that the American expression? Grant figured he'd be joining him under it in a matter of minutes.

Frankel confirmed that it was Leeds's body that had been found in the shut-down Far Rockaway hospital. He acknowledged that they believed Leeds to be the fifth in a series of murders that began in London. Frankel named the other victims, reciting dates and the locations where their bodies had been found.

Grant could hear dozens of styluses tapping iPads and fingers clacking on laptop keyboards.

Frankel urged the public to remain vigilant and calm. It was a standard request that Grant knew Frankel was wasting his breath on. If anything, the Manhattan citizenry would just panic further. Frankel opened the floor to questions.

For the next thirty seconds, everyone called out at once.

Little let loose a shrill whistle, regaining a semblance of peace. Grant wondered if this ability to bring sudden order to chaos was what had landed the man his job. Little started calling on the journalists one by one.

The first question, from a *New York Times* stringer, was not unexpected. The bald reporter, who'd been covering crime in the five boroughs since Ed Koch occupied Gracie Mansion, asked what made them certain the five crimes were connected to one another and committed by the same person.

"There is a similarity in method to all five," Frankel answered. "I'm not going to go into detail. Per usual, we need to keep certain information to ourselves."

It was the answer they had all agreed on giving to the question they knew they'd be getting. This didn't stop the next half-dozen reporters trying variations of the same query. Grant was impressed watching the detective sidestep each volley with a slightly different response that amounted to the same thing—they'd let everyone know more once they caught the person they were looking for.

The questions settled into such a monotonous pattern that Grant was caught unaware when a familiar voice sounded from a few rows back.

"I have a question for Commander Grant?" came a polite British voice. Ferguson.

The *Mail* journalist rose and stared directly at Grant. "Isn't it true that you had reason to believe Mr. Leeds was going to be the next victim?"

The crowd stirred.

"It was one possibility we were considering," Grant replied. He glanced back over at Frankel, who gave him a tacit nod of approval.

"Then why wasn't he afforded police protection?"

Grant started to respond but Frankel beat him to the punch. "Because by the time Leeds was on our radar, he'd already gone missing and we had to locate him."

"Well, you certainly did that," Ferguson pointed out.

This produced enough chortles from the crowd that Little had to issue another reprimand. "You're point being, Mr. Ferguson?" pushed Little.

"That this isn't the first time during this case that Commander Grant has been late on arrival," answered Ferguson. The reporter stared at Grant with a gleam in his eyes.

Here we go.

"Didn't you spend last weekend shutting down churches all over London because you feared for clergy's safety?"

A rumble of reactions circulated through the room. Grant took the microphone and attempted to quell the spreading uneasiness. "It was a supposition we were working on at the time . . ."

"A supposition?" Ferguson mimicked. "It proved to be more than that. Only trouble was you missed it by a whole continent. At least with Leeds you narrowed it down to the proper city."

Grant lifted a hand to quiet the room that was on the verge of exploding. "Besides pointing out what you see as my shortcomings, Mr. Ferguson, what exactly is the question you're asking?"

"I'm wondering if you're ill-equipped to be running this investigation. Your track record is hardly comforting," said Ferguson. "You and Detective Frankel are obviously holding on to information giving you a line on the victims but not following through on time. The public deserves to know what *that* is exactly—as you're not keeping them safe and none have a clue as to what—to use your colleague's own words—they are keeping vigilant about."

Frankel gave Grant a slight shrug. He might as well have been saying, *"Whatever you come up with will be as good as anything I can."*

"It's the Ten Commandments, isn't it?"

Grant was shocked to see Rachel stand up in the next to last row.

"Your killer is murdering people according to the Ten Commandments," she clarified. "Timothy Leeds was number five and the person you're searching for isn't stopping until he reaches ten. Unless someone gets him first."

That was when the room erupted into the shit show Frankel had predicted.

"Your daughter," Frankel simply said.

The implications in the two words were multifold. Not only hadn't Grant mentioned Rachel to Frankel, he'd neglected to say she was a reporter who resided and worked in Manhattan, and with whom he'd discussed the case at length the previous morning at breakfast at the Surrey.

"I thought the two of you knew each other," Grant said to Rachel, trying to calm the situation.

"I said we've crossed paths a couple of times," reiterated Rachel.

"But I didn't realize she was your *daughter*," repeated Frankel.

The three of them were in Grant's cubbyhole of an office after extracting themselves from the near riot that had once been a press conference.

After Rachel dropped her bomb among her fellow Fourth Estaters, Frankel and Grant huddled with Harris in an emergency sidebar. They quickly decided it would be pointless to deny the Commandments connection to the killings.

Grant then walked the press through the victims and parallels that could be drawn between them and the first five of the Lord's laws. By the time he got to Leeds and the theory that the killer had punished him for crimes committed three decades earlier, the press was hanging on his every word.

Grant had purposely withheld how they'd tumbled to Leeds, claiming it was the result of thorough police work. Informing the media that the killer was leaving messages for the cops in the stomach lining of dead priests and all over the walls of abandoned insane asylums would only add to the feeding frenzy.

With everyone checking their smart phones to consult the Old Testament, it was only seconds before Grant and Frankel were assaulted with questions about the Sixth Commandment.

Thou shalt not kill.

"Do you think the killer is targeting another released murderer like Leeds?"

"What if it's someone who's committed a murder you don't know about yet?"

Grant had said these were things they were considering.

He didn't bring up that the sixth victim might already be out there and that they were also now also searching for a cheating spouse.

The questions had moved on to the killer. Did they know for sure it was a man—could it be a woman? Was it some religious fanatic?

Lieutenant Harris, who up until that point had been quietly steaming in his seat watching the presser dissolve into a free-for-all, got to his feet. He said the department was working on a psychological profile for the killer and left it at that. Grant knew a profile was in the works, but highly doubted it would ever be handed over to the media.

At that point, Harris had mercifully brought the press conference to an end, citing the need for the NYPD and other agencies ("of which Scotland Yard is one of many"—a dig that wasn't lost on Grant) to bring the perpetrator to justice.

The second it was over, Grant had moved into the dispersing crowd of journalists to find Rachel. He was relieved to see she hadn't tried to slip out a door in the rear.

She'd started speaking right away. "Dad, I was only . . ."

He'd cut her off with a look. "Right now, I need you to come with me. There will be plenty of time for talking—but not here." Grant couldn't remember having used such a firm tone with his daughter. But he also couldn't recall where he felt it necessary.

That was when Harris had descended on the Scotland Yard commander.

"What the hell is going on here?" Harris had demanded.

"Please give me and Detective Frankel a few moments to get to the bottom of this," Grant had requested.

"See that you do," ordered Harris, already being pulled by Little back into the fracas to rework a new statement on the case.

While escorting Rachel to his cubbyhole, Grant had also been able to commandeer Frankel. Once he locked the office door, Grant had made the proper introductions, which seemed to make Frankel's head spin.

"I thought the only reporter you'd been talking to was Ferguson."

"Rachel and I only had breakfast yesterday."

"And we don't talk that much," Rachel added. "In fact, that was the first time in over a year."

Frankel looked at them in disbelief. "But you managed to lay out your entire case over tea and biscuits—including the connection we've held back from everyone, particularly the media, of which your daughter happens to be a card-carrying member."

"It's something we've always done. I'd share what I was working on and Rachel would listen, then usually offer up fresh insight."

Frankel turned to Rachel. "And what did you conclude? Other than the idea of sharing with the world the one thing we were trying to keep for ourselves?"

"Besides the fact that you and my father have a real mess on your hands?" Rachel gave Frankel a slight shrug. "Not much."

"I thought we'd agreed you weren't going to write this story," Grant said.

"Did you see it in print, Dad? If this was meant to be self-serving, I think an exclusive edition would've hit the streets by now."

"Then why bring it up when you did?"

"Because doing it this way makes your lives easier. And lets the people in the city sleep better at night." She shrugged again. "Well, unless you happen to be a killer or an adulterer. Then you might have to keep an eye open and double-lock the windows and doors."

Grant tightened. "Jesus. You've been talking to Everett, haven't you?"

Rachel didn't exactly nod, but her eyes betrayed the truth.

Meanwhile, Frankel was still trying to keep up. "Wait. Everett? Everett—your brother, who you first figured this all out with? *That* Everett?"

"Yes. *That* Everett," replied Grant.

"He called me this morning—just as I was leaving for work," said Rachel. "He said he was worried about you and repeated the suggestion he gave you and it made a whole bunch of sense."

"Suggestion? What suggestion?" asked Frankel incredulously.

Grant told Frankel how Everett urged them to come clean with the Ten Commandments connection for the precise reasons Rachel had just echoed.

"You could have told me what you were going to do," Grant said to Rachel.

"Frankly, Dad, I didn't know I was going to until it happened. I sat and listened to Ferguson make both of you look like accomplices in these last two crimes by blaming you for not reaching the victims in time. Everett's idea suddenly made more sense than ever."

She turned slightly to address both men. "You have to admit anything that simplifies your job and makes this guy's process a little tougher can't be all bad."

Frankel rubbed eyes that hadn't gotten much sleep since Grant had flown in to town. "Some kind of fucked-up family you've got," the detective told them.

Grant thought about it. By supper time, every media outlet would have broadcast the story and it was certainly all over the internet by now.

"It will make this fellow's ability to move around more difficult," Grant admitted.

"So, what do we tell Harris?" asked Frankel. "Right now, he wants both of our asses in a sling."

"I could say we planned it that way," Rachel suggested. She turned to her father. "You can tell him you took me aside before the press conference and fed me the information about the Commandments for the exact reasons we're talking about. But the story you go public with is that I managed to figure out the connection myself and the two of you just confirmed it."

"And you're not self-serving at all," said Frankel with a slight grin.

"Absolutely not," Rachel told them. "While I'm sitting with you two, I've probably been beaten at my own quote-unquote *scoop* by at least two dozen bloggers and news organizations."

"Point taken," Frankel said.

"So, what do you think?" asked Rachel.

Grant turned to Frankel. "Unless you have a better idea, I say we give it a try."

"If it'll keep Harris off our tails and let us do our job, I'm all for it," said Frankel.

"Does this mean I don't have to get grilled by your lieutenant?" asked Rachel.

"I think we can cover you there," Grant told her. "Provided we meet for dinner later."

Rachel raised an eyebrow. "Two meals in two days, Dad? That's . . ."

". . . twice as many as we've had in a couple of years," Grant said, finishing the thought. "If we're going to continue this charade, it's probably a good idea to make sure our stories line up going forward."

"Strangely enough, that makes sense to me." Rachel looked at Frankel. "Maybe you want to join us, Detective? Bring along a whistle and a striped shirt?"

Frankel let out another laugh.

"Like I said—you're one fucked-up family."

Harris seemed to go for it.

Either the lieutenant thought revealing the Commandments to make the killer's life harder and warn New Yorkers was a good idea or Harris had no one to replace the two top cops in the investigation.

Grant suspected it was a bit of both.

He offered up an apology for keeping Harris in the dark about the "plan" he'd worked out before the news conference with Rachel (whom he'd told to head home). Grant wasn't sure which he felt worse about—apologizing for something he hadn't really done or outright lying to the lieutenant. When Frankel said he was sorry as well, Grant figured they were both on the hook—so that made him feel slightly better.

Harris had just handed them a revised official NYPD statement to the media when someone knocked on the door. "What is it now?" he barked.

Winona Lopez, a female detective in her forties, poked her head inside the office. "Sorry to interrupt sir, but I have a call from a Sheriff Barnes in Far Rockaway. He says it's urgent. Line two."

Frankel got up and started for the phone. "Thanks, Detective."

"Oh, I'm sorry," said Lopez. "He asked specifically for Commander Grant."

Grant's surprise matched the look on the faces of the other two men in the room. He picked up the receiver and punched the appropriate button. "This is Grant."

He heard Barnes's gruff voice on the other end.

"Looks like we located the car your guy used to transport Leeds from Connolly's to the old hospital yesterday."

"Where?" asked Grant.

Barnes told him it was a blue Hyundai Sonata found that morning, dumped in a back alley. "It was stolen from a local woman yesterday."

"What makes you so sure it was used to grab Leeds?"

"There are traces of blood on the passenger's side," said the sheriff. "And it looks like he left a message as well."

Can this possibly get any worse?

"What kind of message?"

"I'm not exactly sure," said Barnes. "But I'm fairly sure it's meant for you, Commander."

12

Barnes was patiently waiting when they pulled up to the mouth of the alley. It had been cordoned off with bright yellow police tape and, being the dead of winter in a beach town, only a few curious locals stood on the sidewalk across the street. Not that there was much to see, just a midnight-blue Hyundai Sonata tucked up against the wall of an ice cream shop that closed down late each autumn.

The sheriff introduced Grant and Frankel to the Sonata's owner, Josephine Tuttle, a woman in her late seventies. Poor Josephine couldn't understand why she couldn't just take her car home—wasn't it bad enough that "some hooligan had swiped it" and left her stranded?

"I told you, Mrs. Tuttle, we will return it once we've concluded our investigation," Barnes assured her. "We'll even give it a wash and fill up the tank."

"That's the least you can do," muttered Josephine.

Barnes said it'd be helpful if she answered Frankel and Grant's questions.

"I don't see what I can tell them that you didn't write down in that little black notebook."

"They might have different questions," pointed out an exasperated Barnes. "Commander Grant has come all the way from England. The least we can do is show him a little bit of American hospitality and help him out."

This opened the floodgates and soon Grant and Frankel knew more than either had bargained for about Josephine Stuart King Tuttle (she'd refused to drop her first husband's name when she'd married Maurice twenty years ago). The names and occupations of her children (they'd all moved away and Grant was starting to see why), her gallbladder operation (Frankel passed on looking at the scar), and Maurice's dying three years earlier ("a summer cold that didn't get better") worked their way into the recital of events that led them to this alley.

As for the theft and return of the Sonata, she didn't have much to say. She'd parked it near the laundromat and had come outside with a full load to find it wasn't there. When she hadn't found her keys, she realized she must have left them in the ignition while struggling with her laundry.

"And how long were you in the laundromat?" asked Grant.

"Three loads, what's that? An hour and a half, maybe?"

"And you didn't see anyone approach the car?"

"Didn't I just tell you I parked it *down* the street? Am I supposed to have X-ray vision and see through buildings like Superman?"

"No, of course not. But wouldn't it be wonderful if you did?" asked Grant.

Josephine frowned. She didn't seem to appreciate his attempt at a joke.

Frankel jumped into the breach. "Did you hear the car start up?"

The NYPD detective received a diatribe all his own—Josephine doing chapter and verse on the faults of industrial washers and dryers. "With that racket? I keep forgetting my earplugs. How am I supposed to hear a car a block away?"

Frankel ended up apologizing as well.

They finally got the whole story. She'd filed a stolen car report with the sheriff's office. One of Barnes's officers had given Josephine and her laundry a ride home. She'd been "stuck" there until she got a call that the car had been located.

"And now I'm going to be stuck again," she practically moaned.

"I told you the department would provide a rental," Barnes said.

"It's not the same. I've got my stations and seat arranged just so . . ."

"I'm afraid it's evidence in a crime, Mrs. Tuttle," explained Frankel. "I'm sure the sheriff will return it good as new. He might even throw in an oil change."

He gave Barnes a pleading look. The sheriff nodded, anxious to move on as well. "I think that can be arranged."

This seemed to appease Josephine. Somewhat.

"I'm telling you right now, I'm not paying for mileage."

"Wouldn't think of it, ma'am." Barnes indicated a uniformed officer standing nearby. "Officer Kelly will take you to the rental agency and get you settled."

Josephine emitted a *harrumph* and crossed the street without saying goodbye.

Frankel and Grant moved with Barnes toward the Hyundai Sonata. "Kelly was the one who found the car. It's not like we get tons of stolen vehicles this time of year. Having just been reported, my guys were keeping their eyes out for it."

Barnes slipped on plastic gloves, then dug out pairs to give Frankel and Grant. The sheriff nodded at the steering column. Josephine's keys dangled from the ignition. "I imagine that's what your fellow hoped to find when searching for a car. Didn't even have to hot-wire it."

He pointed a gloved finger at the beige faux leather directly below the passenger window. Specks of red and a similarly colored small blotch were on it near the door handle. "Here's the blood I mentioned."

Frankel took a closer look. "Hardly anything to write home about."

Barnes nodded. "We're assuming he didn't cut off the man's head here."

Grant took his turn examining the stains. "The ME told us Leeds was hit twice in the head. The first blow probably happened right here." He straightened up. "Delivered from the driver's side; Leeds's head would have hit that spot below the window. It certainly would account for the blood traces."

Barnes walked around to the driver's side. "Fact is, Kelly didn't notice the blood right away. He only started to look around more carefully after seeing this."

The sheriff pointed to a folded newspaper lying on the driver's seat.

The paper's masthead could be easily seen.

The *Daily Mail*.

Barnes let Grant lean in and carefully remove it with his gloved hands.

The now-familiar headline *Serial Killer Takes His Act on the Road* screamed up at him. Monte Ferguson had managed to get his name above the fold.

Grant flipped the paper over to find the story's copy and a few photos. One was from the Saint Patrick's crime scene, another of the dead Father Adam Peters. There were also pictures of the two cops leading the investigation—NYPD Detective First Grade John Frankel and Commander Austin Grant of Scotland Yard.

Grant's picture had been X-ed out repeatedly with a black marker.

Practically obliterated beyond recognition.

Frankel peered over Grant's shoulder. "Looks like someone doesn't like you very much."

Grant was starting to feel like a genuine New York commuter. For the third time in four days, he found himself back on the LIE into the city. With rush hour approaching, it gave him and Frankel plenty of time to discuss the killer's latest parting gift.

"We're getting stuff from this lunatic on a daily basis," said Frankel, inching the sedan along. "I'm starting to think he's confusing the Ten Commandments with the Twelve Days of Christmas. All we're missing is an Advent killing calendar."

Grant looked down at the newspaper residing in a clear Ziploc bag. His own marred image stared up at him behind the black crisscrosses. "I suppose it's pointless to try and trace where this came from."

"You can't get it on every corner like in London. But plenty of newsstands carry international papers. Not to mention subscribers."

Grant surmised fingerprinting wouldn't help. The Sonata had come up empty, everything wiped clean from the door handle to Josephine's set of keys.

They had walked the street near where the car was found, as well as the one by the laundromat where it had been stolen. The citizenry of Far Rockaway had been easier to question than Josephine, but their answers had yielded a similar result. Nobody recalled seeing the Sonata, let alone a just-released convict inside it.

Grant wasn't surprised. Not only did the killer cover his tracks, he had only left behind things he specifically wanted found. And it appeared that Commander Austin Grant was the person he was leaving them for.

"You got an idea who you might have pissed off so much?" asked Frankel.

"Do you know how long I've worked at the Yard?"

"You told me last night," replied Frankel. "Thirty-four years."

"And how many cases have crossed my desk during that time? Thousands." Grant shook his head. "Not that we convicted and put away that many—but more than our fair share. I'm sure a few have gotten out over the years bearing some sort of grudge. But it's not like I kept track of them for any reason."

"Doesn't necessarily have to be someone you tossed in jail. Could be a loved one who thinks you ruined their life by doing so."

After leaving Barnes, Grant had phoned Hawley in London. He had caught the Sergeant just as he was leaving the Yard for the day. The commander had updated him on the newspaper discovery and asked the sergeant to start compiling a list of those that Grant had arrested over the years who were back on the streets of London.

Now, he realized Hawley had to spread a wider net and would need help. Grant had an idea where that might come from. His thoughts were interrupted by Frankel.

"If it's really revenge, he's certainly going to elaborate extremes."

"Especially as I've no connection to any of these victims. At least none that I know of. If, like you say, I've pissed him off so much, why such a roundabout way of going about things? Why not take a shot at me and get it over with?"

Frankel indicated the Ziploc-bagged newspaper in Grant's lap. "Seems to me he wants you suffering through all this."

Back in the city, they returned to the morgue to check in with Marcus. Frankel had worked it out with Barnes to get Leeds's body transferred. The sheriff was happy to turn over the dead parolee; his sleepy department was ill-equipped for a case this size and Frankel had caught the priest murder to begin with.

Marcus had already ID'd the blood samples from the Sonata as type B, the same as Leeds. He wouldn't have a definite match for a while, but that was enough for Frankel and Grant—especially coupled with the newspaper found on the front seat. As suspected, Marcus hadn't found any trace material from the saw used to decapitate Leeds. But the blood on the Sonata's door lined up with the bruise found on one side of Leeds's head.

Frankel and Grant returned to the precinct and ran into Little the moment they arrived. The media man looked ready to tear out the little hair he had left.

He had a stack of different newspapers under his arm and thrust them in their faces. "Just got these."

Each had its own seventy-two-point headline.

THOU SHALT KILL! FIVE AND COUNTING? MURDER, I COMMAND THEE!

"You can only imagine the internet," said Little. "It's completely blowing up. Please tell me you're closing in on this maniac."

Grant didn't think telling the media liaison that the killer was leaving messages all over New York (and specifically for the Scotland Yard Commander) would make him feel any better.

Frankel and Grant watched the harried man move down the hallway. Grant couldn't be sure, but he thought he could hear Little mumbling to himself.

"This is just the tip of the iceberg," Frankel said, watching Little depart. He turned back to face Grant. "That sergeant of yours. . ."

"Hawley."

"We need that list he's been working on pronto," said Frankel.

Grant nodded.

The restaurant Orso was on Forty-Sixth Street just west of Eighth Avenue, situated on the edge of the Theater District. It was always packed prior to Broadway curtains being raised and after they fell. But in between, Rachel told them, you could shoot a cannon through the place and not hit a soul. Plus, the food was good and you could hear what the other person was saying.

When Frankel and Grant stepped inside shortly after eight, Rachel was one of only five diners. She was halfway through a glass of chardonnay and the cops didn't need any convincing to get drinks of their own.

"It's been that kind of day," Frankel said, taking a seat.

That kind of month, thought Grant. He sat down on his daughter's other side, then glanced at his watch and the date in the Tag's little window.

The nineteenth.

Only twelve more days and I'm retired.

By the time their drinks arrived (a Heineken for Frankel and a scotch and soda for Grant), they'd told Rachel about their trip to Far Rockaway. Frankel pulled out his iPhone and showed her a picture of the newspaper he'd snapped.

Rachel stared at Grant's marked-up face. She turned to her father, her eyes filled with clear concern. "Oh, my God. What are you two doing about this?"

"Not letting it hit the papers, that's for sure," replied Frankel.

Grant could see his daughter stiffen. "If either of you think I'd . . ."

Grant held up a hand. "No one's accusing you of anything, Rachel."

"Sorry. That didn't come out right," said Frankel. "I know you put your neck on the line for us today after the press conference. Particularly for your father."

"I keep telling you both that I just want to help."

"Which is one of the reasons we're here," Grant said. "Besides me getting the opportunity to share another meal with my Americanized daughter."

"C'mon, I ain't changed that much," she said with a smile while putting on a Queens accent.

Grant laughed for maybe the first time since arriving in the States. "Why don't you suggest what to order and then we can tell you the rest?"

Rachel insisted they have both the basil and garlic flatbreads and a margherita pizza. She chose a couple of pastas that they could share from the daily printed menu and the waiter left to put in the order.

A second round of drinks arrived right around the time Grant finished telling Rachel about his discussion with Sergeant Hawley at the Yard and how she might be able to help them.

"Your father reminded me that he spent years going over his cases with you," Frankel told her.

"Since I was a child," Rachel said. "I used to find crime scene photos and evidence bags he'd brought home and they fascinated me. I had tons of questions and Dad was more than happy to answer all of them."

"Naturally, it horrified her mother. But I kept telling Allison that curiosity was something that needed to be encouraged, not stomped on, in a child."

"Mom completely gave up on us both after I asked Dad to bring specimens from the lab back home and she found them in the fridge."

"I only did that twice," Grant insisted.

"That's because I made him take me with him to work on the weekends," Rachel explained. "I got to see plenty of good stuff there."

"I see how you ended up becoming a journalist," Frankel observed.

Grant went on to explain how they'd decided it was best to keep a possible connection between the killer and himself out of the papers until they knew more.

"I thought once Hawley had compiled his list, you two could go over it. If someone is really acting out a grudge, it has to be one of those old cases. Between what you remember about them and making a few quiet inquiries saying you're doing a feature piece on your dear old dad, it might help narrow the field."

Rachel nodded. "I'd say anything is worth trying at this point."

"You must promise me that you won't approach any of these people directly," Grant said. "That's to be left to Hawley and the others at the Yard."

"Or if someone happens to be here in New York—me or your father will deal with it," added Frankel.

"Quiet inquiries. Feature piece on my dad," Rachel recited. "Got it."

The waiter chose that time to return with the flatbeds and pizza. He had no sooner left the table when Rachel turned to look back at her father.

"So, when do I start?"

Grant got a text from Hawley shortly before the entrees arrived saying he'd have a preliminary list by the time the sun rose on their side of the Atlantic. Grant was pleased, but not surprised, to see the man working into the wee hours of the London night. He gave Rachel the sergeant's contact info and told her to check with him when she got up in the morning.

Rachel got the two of them to trade war stories—their favorite NYPD and Yard tales—and by the time dessert came, they had gone through enough to fill quite the rogue's gallery.

They departed the restaurant shortly after ten-thirty. Though it was in the low forties, Rachel pointed out the evening was clear enough to walk the ten blocks to Grant's hotel. Once there, she and Frankel could grab a couple of cabs or Ubers and head home themselves.

But as it's wont to do in a city where you look the other way and the weather changes, the skies opened up and the trio got caught in a torrential downpour six blocks from the London.

Grant asked if they wanted to come in and dry off, but both said they would be fine. Rachel insisted that her father go inside before he caught his death of cold. The London doorman offered to find Rachel and Frankel taxis and Grant handed the man ten dollars for his trouble.

Grant decided to risk giving his daughter a goodnight hug and was pleased when she didn't pull away. He knew there was still plenty unresolved between the two of them, but at least it was a start. Grant told Frankel he would see him bright and early in the morning, then sloshed his way into the hotel.

He was halfway to the elevator when the night manager called out.

"Sir?"

Grant caught a glimpse of himself in a nearby mirror—he resembled a drowned rat. He could only imagine what kind of vagrant the man behind the desk thought had wandered into the hotel. Grant pointed to the elevator. "I'm on the fourth floor. Room 412? Grant?"

The night manager nodded. "Of course, Mr. Grant. I know who you are."

Grant nodded and resumed his journey to the elevator. The night manager called out once again.

"I just wanted to remind you that tomorrow's the twentieth."

"Yes."

It usually follows the nineteenth—even where I come from.

Grant turned around. The only thing he wanted to do was soak in a hot tub.

"So, you'll be checking out as planned?"

This stopped Grant in his wet tracks once again. "Checking out?"

"I believe you were informed at check-in that we had no availability starting this weekend due to the Christmas holiday."

"I thought you were going to let me know if something freed up."

"I'm letting you know now that unfortunately nothing has."

Grant couldn't tell if the man was enjoying this or not. He suspected the former.

Half an hour later, Grant finally made it into the tub.

Unfortunately, now he was on the portable phone with the night manager, who said he had checked with every hotel in the area but regretted to inform Grant that they were also fully committed through Christmas Eve.

"But I do wish you the best of luck hunting down this maniac you're looking for, Commander," the night manager said before disconnecting.

Grant stared at the phone for a moment.

How much worse could this day possibly get?

Grant suddenly realized he'd forgotten to bring the soap into the tub. He could see it on the other side of the bathroom lying next to the sink.

13

G rant's stay at the London had been anything but ideal. But as he went to check out, he couldn't help but wonder what sort of refuge he was going to find in the Big Bad City, already fondly recalling the four nights spent in a room where the only perk had been a different chocolate left by the bed each evening.

The same woman who had registered him was behind the desk.

"I hope you enjoyed your stay, Commander." She produced a credit card slip.

"I would've preferred it to be a little longer," he said, scribbling his signature.

She gave him a sympathetic smile that he figured she'd been taught during employee training. "Our busiest time of year, I'm afraid."

He knew it would be pointless to make another inquiry about extending his stay, certain he had other frustrating conversations ahead of him on this day.

Like the one about to occur a dozen steps away—where Monte Ferguson sat in a wingback chair sipping coffee. The reporter had obviously chosen that spot as it was situated between the main entrance and elevators. Unless Grant used the fire escape, Ferguson knew he'd eventually have to pass him.

"Buy you breakfast, Commander?" Ferguson asked.

———

They ended up at the Astro Diner—the coffee shop Grant had gone to with Frankel on his first night in Manhattan. Grant knew he could avoid Ferguson for only so long. Might as well get a meal out of what was sure to be an uncomfortable chat. As they reached the coffee shop, Ferguson indicated Grant's carry-on luggage.

"Giving up the ghost already?"

"No room at the inn, I'm afraid. That time of year," Grant told the journalist, who still had enough good breeding to hold open the door.

"Any idea where you're moving to?"

"Not yet. But I'm sure you'll find me when I do."

They settled into a booth. Ever since the news conference, Grant had expected to be confronted by Ferguson. The man didn't disappoint—they had been seated less than a minute when he asked Grant how long he'd known the killer was selecting victims according to the Book of Exodus. "You certainly did when you closed down all those churches."

"We suspected it then," Grant admitted. "But it wasn't until Father Peters's murder that we knew for sure."

"And you still didn't think it was worth sharing with the public?"

"We were trying to get a handle on what we were dealing with. It didn't make sense to send Londoners into an all-out panic when the killer had come over here. And there's no telling he'll stay put in America."

"So, you're confirming it's a man you're hunting," Ferguson asked, jumping on Grant's pronoun usage.

"I can't confirm that, no. But statistically—"

"I know—men are more likely to go on killing sprees than women."

Phyllis, the waitress who had served him and Frankel, picked that time to take their order. She smiled at Grant. "Nice to see you again."

"Nice to see you as well. I'm surprised you remember me."

"It's the accent. Plus, the detective usually eats here by himself."

"I thought you worked evenings."

"I basically come with the place, darling. What'll you boys have?"

Ferguson ordered scrambled eggs, crisp bacon, rye toast, and coffee. Grant said he would have the exact same except he'd prefer English breakfast tea.

"It'll be up in a jiffy," Phyllis told them and moved back to the kitchen.

"You and Detective Frankel seem to have hit it off," said Ferguson, picking up on Phyllis's mention of the NYPD man. "Two peas in a policeman's pod."

"We have a similar goal in mind."

"And the ability to cover for each other as well."

Grant felt the hair on the back of his neck rise. "Meaning what, precisely?"

"This nonsense with your daughter. You don't really expect me to swallow the notion that she came up with the Commandments angle herself. Why don't you admit that you fed it to her?"

"Rather than you admit she beat you to the punch?"

"Because she's your *daughter* and had inside knowledge," argued Ferguson.

"What can I say? Something rubbed off being raised in a copper's home."

Ferguson muttered to himself. Grant could see his mind switching tracks.

"Let's talk about Leeds. How do you go from interviewing every single resident of an apartment building to suddenly focusing on a parolee just released to a halfway house in Far Rockaway who just happened to murder his parents?"

Grant must have reacted because a smile curled on Ferguson's face.

"You're not going to slip everything by me, Grant. Hard as you might try."

"You know how it works, Monte. One thing leads to another. And I'm under no obligation to detail that process with you."

Phyllis arrived with pots of tea and coffee. Grant thought her timing perfect, giving him a chance to steer the conversation in a direction that would get the *Mail* journalist off his back. By the time Phyllis went to check on their breakfast, an idea formulated in his head that might prove advantageous to both him and Ferguson.

"Shall we talk about a potential victim number six?" asked Grant.

The reporter practically choked on his coffee.

"Am I sitting across from Austin Grant? Commander at Scotland Yard?"

"For twelve more days. But who's counting?"

"What gives?"

"You know as well as I do what comes next. '*Thou shalt not kill.*'" Grant took a sip of tea. "Sort of narrows the field, wouldn't you say?"

"You're looking for a killer. Someone who's out and about—like Leeds was."

Grant nodded. "But he was murdered for a different reason."

"Because he killed his mother and father. That was made quite clear after your daughter dropped her little bomb." Ferguson shook his head. "I'm sure all the agencies working on this are combing databases for killers as we speak."

"No question."

"So why are we even discussing it?"

"Because those lists will only contain murders on the record. They won't account for ones that we haven't heard about."

"And you think someone like me would?" Ferguson wondered. "For once, you're giving me more credit than I'm due."

"You hear things in your line of work, Monte. Rumors, innuendos. You can make the sort of inquiries men like myself and Detective Frankel can't because we are burdened by badges, rules, and such." Grant mustered up his most casual shrug, then finished the train of thought. "At this point it can't hurt working every possible angle."

"Except the one you're not telling me about," countered Ferguson. "What's in it for me?"

"Besides getting a serial killer off the streets of New York?"

"That's your job, Commander. Not mine."

"There might come a day when I will need to remind you that you said that."

Grant was well aware of the high-wire act he was walking. Even though he and Frankel suspected the killer had already dispatched a sixth victim, they still had no idea who it was. If Ferguson figured that out before them, it benefited everyone.

"In the meantime, go do what we can't," continued Grant. "Come back with a name or two. If it leads to something, I'll make sure you get full credit and the exclusive you're looking for. You'll have certainly earned it."

Ferguson leaned back and considered Grant's offer as Phyllis placed their food in front of them. She refilled their cups, told them to let her know if they needed anything else, and moved off.

"You know I'm a man of my word, Monte. I let you run with that story—and believe me I still haven't stopped hearing how I shouldn't have done it."

"I've never accused you of not telling the truth. Bending it, perhaps." Ferguson twisted a fork full of scrambled eggs in the air for emphasis.

Grant just waited. Ferguson finally took a bite, then lowered the fork.

"Okay, let's give your way a try."

"I appreciate it."

And he truly did. He believed he'd gotten the reporter to take a side-step that might actually pay him and Frankel dividends as well.

"I do have one more question, though," Ferguson said.

"Just one?"

"Why is he killing people according to the Ten Commandments?"

Grant had been asking himself the very same question since he had sat in his brother's study a week ago. And for the life of him, Grant had to admit that he didn't have a bloody clue.

Neither did Rachel or Frankel when they sat and talked in the basement of the precinct.

Grant had arrived to find Rachel knee-deep in paperwork in an office Frankel had set up for her. Not only did it afford her a modicum of privacy, it allowed Grant and Frankel the opportunity to drop down and see Rachel at any time while keeping her out of Lieutenant Harris's direct sight. Frankel had informed his superior what they were having her work on and, though Harris wasn't exactly jumping up and down about it, the man was in such desperate straits he seemed willing to grasp at any available straw.

Rachel had gotten in touch with Hawley bright and early and, as promised, his trusty sergeant had sent along his first pass at Grant's old cases. She handed her father and Frankel each a printout that exceeded fifty pages.

"You were right," said Frankel. "There have to be at least a thousand here."

"Try thirteen-hundred and seventy-four." Rachel turned toward Grant. "A lot died while serving their sentences or have since they got out."

"Have you been able to break it down further?" asked Grant.

"We're working on it."

She flipped pages in a notebook where she'd established different categories.

"It looks like half have finished their prison time, so we're talking in the six to seven hundred range that are no longer behind bars."

Frankel was shocked. "That many? High turnover rate you folks have there."

"Different class of criminal," explained Grant. "No guns equals less violent crimes. We don't have as many men and women doing life sentences as a result."

Rachel flipped to another page. "Even with those who have passed away, we still have close to three hundred to check up on."

"Any idea how many still reside in England?" Grant asked.

"Sergeant Hawley and I were just trying to figure that out." She indicated the computer screen and a small window in the bottom right corner. "We've got an open chat going so we can keep updating each other."

Grant nodded, happy to see his daughter throwing herself into the investigation with such vigor. "Please say hello."

Rachel did just that and received a similar typed greeting back from Hawley. Grant then told them about his unexpected breakfast companion and the deal he'd struck with the journalist.

"Smart," said Frankel. "Getting him to look in that direction while we work on this." The detective indicated the computer screen.

"He did happen to bring up one other thing." Grant repeated Ferguson's questioning the killer's motive for using the Ten Commandments.

"I've been racking my brain over that since you told me at breakfast the other morning," said Rachel. "Some fanatic who spent his entire life tethered to the teachings of the church until some crazy switch flipped?"

"Or just some nut job looking for a reason to kill a bunch of people but didn't know where to start," countered Frankel. "Maybe he was watching that Charlton Heston movie one night and thought, hey, now there's *something* I could use!"

"It might be either—but neither sheds any light on why he's reached out to me specifically." Grant glanced at his daughter again. "Your mother was the one who insisted on going to church every Sunday. I basically went in deference to her."

Grant paused a beat. When he resumed, his voice had dipped. "Though the truth is I've been going more often since she passed."

Rachel looked surprised. "I had no idea you did that."

Grant offered up a sad smile. "Perhaps you'll come back and go with me one Sunday."

"You never know," Rachel told him.

Grant managed to pull himself together by looking at Rachel's computer screen and the work at hand. "Whoever is doing this, I think it's clear there isn't anything random about it. There has to be a connection here and this is the probably the best way we've got to go looking for it."

"I don't have a better suggestion at this point," admitted Frankel. Rachel's response was a nod of agreement and a resumption of her computer chat with Sergeant Hawley.

The two cops took their leave and let her get back to work.

The rest of the day was spent doing what all cops spend most of their time doing—good old-fashioned grunt work. Whether one was a commander at Scotland Yard, a first-grade NYPD detective, a sheriff in a Long Island suburb, or even a constable in a Northern Ireland village that Rachel had talked to about a former killer who had moved there, nothing substituted for working a real case.

Back when Grant first started, most investigations had been done on foot or by putting lots of mileage on their personal vehicles. It had taken longer but questions were answered face-to-face. Nowadays, ninety percent of what a detective needed to know could be discovered without leaving his desk, courtesy of the internet, cell phones, and satellite tracking. True, it was accomplished quicker, but Grant still missed talking to people in person. It was the only way to get a true read on someone.

One more reason Grant was convinced he was retiring at the right time.

But he held out hope that before he was done, he'd get to sit across from the person responsible for this chaos. It might be the only way to find out what was motivating the person that he, Frankel, and now his daughter were hunting for.

Frankel and Grant went over a few lists as well—the ones culled from various databases about possible Number Six victims, the men and women currently residing in the Tri-State area that had once taken a life themselves.

"These lists are longer than the ones Rachel and Hawley are looking at," Grant observed, sitting across from Frankel in the detective's office. They had chosen to work here because Frankel's room had a window, even though it looked directly into the rear of another building.

They spent the next few hours contacting names on the lists. Frankel mentioned that one of the good things about the Ten Commandments being out in the open was that they could be upfront with people.

As for the few ex-killers they couldn't reach, uniforms were dispatched to make sure they weren't lying in their apartments, on a street corner, or on a Hudson or East riverbank with a Roman numeral *VI* carved in their foreheads.

Frankel had Philly cheesesteaks brought in from Shorty's around one o'clock, which they devoured, washing them down with cold Coca-Colas.

"I'm going to have to buy a new wardrobe if I keep eating with you," Grant grumbled at Frankel.

After lunch, Frankel and Grant further split up the lists and spent the rest of the day in their offices contacting as many former felons as possible. Meanwhile, Rachel didn't emerge from her cocoon in the basement until seven o'clock, when she appeared in her father's cubbyhole.

"How's it going?" she asked.

"We've gotten in touch with maybe seventy-five, eighty percent," Grant informed her. "No dead bodies yet."

"I guess that's a good thing."

"What's happening with you and the good sergeant?"

"We're working our way through—I think I've narrowed it down to fifty or so. I told him to head home; it's past midnight over there. I think he's put in a long enough day."

"We all have," agreed Grant. "You should be heading home yourself."

Rachel indicated Grant's luggage on the floor behind him. "What about you? Any luck finding a hotel?"

Grant searched his desk and found a piece of paper he'd scribbled on. "A place called the Holland in Jersey City said I could check in tonight and stay indefinitely."

"Oh, I'm sure you can." She reached over and crumpled up the piece of paper and tossed it in the trash can. "You're not staying in Jersey, Dad. You'll never get back into the city this time of year."

She crossed over and picked up his bag. "Come on. Let's go."

"Go? Go where?"

"You'll stay with me. My apartment's not much bigger than this but I've got a fold-out couch. And it sounds better than Detective Frankel's place."

Over lunch, presented with Grant's housing predicament, Frankel had said he wished he could help him out. "But after Julia left, all I could afford was this studio apartment in Murray Hill with a Murphy bed. When you open it, there isn't even room for me to stand up, let alone a houseguest."

Given the state (or nonstate) of their relationship the past couple of years, Grant would never have presumed to ask his daughter to *put him up*—let alone *put up* with him.

But once she made the unexpected offer, he certainly wasn't going to refuse.

Perhaps there was hope for the two of them yet.

If he ever did come face-to-face with the killer, Grant realized, he might very well have something to thank him for.

14

Rachel lived on Ninety-Seventh Street between West End Avenue and Riverside Drive. The neighborhood had undergone a total face-lift and now boasted a condo conversion rate that was off the charts. Many buildings that had once been destined for demolition or considered eyesores now had five-year waiting lists.

But a few, like Rachel's, had refused to succumb to the Manhattan makeover due to residents refusing to give up their rent-stabilized apartments. Their monthly payments were locked in at a rate lower than some paid to secure a spot in a parking garage.

Grant watched as Rachel used her key to let herself into the glassed-in vestibule of her building and check the mail. He pointed at the name tag affixed to the box his daughter had just unlocked. "Who is G. Fletcher?"

"Gretchen—a girl I went to college with," Rachel answered.

She explained how Gretchen had gone to Norway two years earlier on a one-week vacation and had a fling with a then-married local TV newscaster; they were now living together in Oslo and expecting their first child.

"No way she gives up this place—not with what she's paying."

When told the amount, Grant completely understood it was a deal one couldn't pass up, even if you lived in a distant country where half the year you couldn't sleep because the sun never set.

"That's why as far as building management is concerned, there's a tenant—Gretchen-married-name-Fletcher—and I'm her sister back home after attending college at Oxford, where she picked up a bit of an accent."

As they climbed the four flights to the walk-up apartment (Rachel considered it good exercise), she reiterated what she'd told him on the subway ride uptown.

"I absolutely can cancel my dinner plans. They'll totally understand."

"You'll do nothing of the sort. I can use a quiet night to hear myself think."

She used two different keys to undo a pair of locks, then opened the door.

"Make yourself at home."

The entire apartment was maybe a touch bigger than his room at the London. It consisted of a living room with a designated "kitchen area," a barely-able-to-squeeze-into bathroom and an adjacent bedroom the size of a tiny walk-in closet. Grant was happy to see that even though his daughter was living practically on top of herself, it looked quite comfy, and he told her as much.

Rachel took his bag and placed it on a small couch that rested beneath the only window. "It folds out easy enough. I've got a set of sheets and blanket tucked away in the bedroom closet."

"I'm sorry to put you to all this trouble."

"Really, Dad, it's not a big deal." She pointed at the fridge. "Help yourself to anything. There's also a stack of menus in the top drawer—you can get anything delivered here within thirty minutes."

"I'll be fine."

"I'm just going to get the bed stuff. Be right back."

She took two steps and disappeared. The place was *that* small.

Even though the apartment was full of Rachel's things and some that Grant presumed belonged to the Norwegian transplant, it didn't feel cluttered. The bookshelves were lined with paperbacks and an occasional hardcover bestseller. Two tiny plants served as bookends and Rachel had managed to keep an orchid alive by placing it in a corner of the window that got morning light. A few framed art posters hung on the walls—the obligatory one any millennial had from a Met show, but Grant was pleased to see the Tate Modern represented as well.

He peeked into the well-stocked fridge—there was certainly enough on the shelves to fashion a meal (sandwich and salad fixings, Chinese takeout cartons), along with a corked half-filled bottle of chardonnay. He found the menus Rachel mentioned—there must have been thirty different cuisines available within in a ten-block radius—and opened a cupboard to discover a box of English breakfast tea.

He found a kettle under the sink, filled it with water, and set it atop the stove. As it heated up, he continued his unguided tour, moving toward a corner where a small table served as the dining area and Rachel's makeshift office.

Her laptop was open beside a bottle of water and a box of little cookies in the shape of bunny rabbits. Grant couldn't resist trying one. The bunny was actually tasty enough that he feared its mates might join it in his stomach later for a postmidnight snack. The kettle whistled him back to the kitchen and he prepared the tea. A couple of sips later, he crossed to a wooden chest against the wall opposite from the window.

The smallest Christmas tree Grant had ever seen was perched on it. Barely two feet tall, Rachel had decorated it with a few ornaments, blinking colored lights, and a gold star to top it off. Grant reached out to touch it, wondering what kind of synthetic material it was made from. He was surprised to find genuine pine needles.

"It's real, believe it or not," said Rachel behind him.

He turned to see that his daughter had changed into jeans, a T-shirt, and a pullover sweater. She'd taken down her hair from the professional bun she'd worn at the precinct and put on fresh lipstick.

God, she looks like her mother, thought Grant—remembering the girl he had fallen in love with all those years back in London.

"They have some even smaller," she continued. "Space is at a premium in Manhattan—especially at Christmas."

"At least you didn't get one of those pink-colored ones with the fake snow."

His eyes were drawn to a gold ornament. The light above the stove reflected off it, causing it to glitter. He carefully lifted it off the tree. It was a small cameo that had the tiniest picture imaginable inside. It was of a smiling woman who looked like Rachel, holding a baby girl with two ribbons in her hair—one green, the other red for the holiday. There was an etched inscription opposite the photo.

Merry Xmas. ILY. R.

"I remember when you gave her this."

"I think I was nine. Maybe ten." She shook her head, trying to make light of it. "A silly arts and crafts project."

"She loved it so much. I didn't know you had it."

"She gave it to me that Christmas, right after she found out . . ."

Rachel broke off as her voice caught. She gently took the cameo from Grant and rehung it. Grant's eyes strayed to the framed photographs on either side of the tree. A few featured Rachel with secondary school and college friends Grant vaguely remembered dropping by the house. The others were either of Rachel and her mother—or just Allison.

Grant couldn't help but notice that one person was missing. Him.

"Rachel—" he began.

"No, Dad. Don't."

"I just don't understand . . ."

"I'd really rather not talk about it. Please."

But now that Grant had opened the door, he couldn't bring himself to close it. Not yet—not without giving it one more try.

"No one loved your mother more than me, Rachel. You must know that." Grant felt himself start to tremble deep inside. "But if there's one person I've ever loved more than her—that would be you."

Rachel started to turn away. Grant placed a hand on her shoulder.

At least she didn't brush it away.

"I can't imagine what I said or did to drive you away. Whatever it was, I didn't mean it. The only thing I can say is that I'm truly sorry. But I'm completely in the dark here, Rach—and have been ever since I—"

Grant stopped and corrected himself.

"Ever since *we* lost your mother."

"It's really complicated, Dad."

Grant's eyes flickered. "So, I *did* do something . . ."

"No. It's not what you did. It's what . . ."

Rachel threw her hands up in clear frustration and moved away from her father, who couldn't recall a more heart-wrenching moment in his entire life.

"What? What did I do or not do?"

"I can't tell you," Rachel replied. There were tears in her eyes now.

"Why not?"

"Because I promised Mom that I wouldn't!"

Suddenly, he couldn't have felt further away from his daughter if they'd been back on opposite sides of the Atlantic instead of three feet away from each other.

When Rachel finally broke the silence, her voice had softened.

"Please listen to me, Dad. Nothing either of us can say or do will bring her back. We both know that." She wiped a tear from her cheek. "I miss her as much as you do—every single damn day. But we have to get on with our lives."

"I realize that but . . ."

". . . but reopening old wounds won't help us do that." She pointed toward the bedroom. "You might not believe this, but when I woke up this morning, I was the happiest I've been in a long, long time. Probably since Mom passed away."

She turned back to face Grant. "And I'm pretty sure it's because you're here."

Grant stood there speechless.

"I'm actually glad to see you, Dad. I'm happy to help you do something important."

Grant was finally able to find his voice. "It means so much to me too."

"So can't we start with that?" The plea was now in Rachel's eyes and voice. "Can't we just begin there and see what happens next?"

"I'll do whatever you want, Rach. I just want you in my life."

Rachel gave him a grateful nod. It wasn't quite the "I do too" he would have hoped for, but in that moment, he'd gladly take what he could get.

She picked her purse off the chair and moved back over to Grant.

She leaned in and gave him a small peck on the cheek.

"I shouldn't be very late," she told him.

Then she was out the door—leaving a stunned Grant still holding his hand up to the side of his face. As grateful as he was for the ice melting, he couldn't stop thinking about one thing.

What had Allison forbidden Rachel to tell him?

An hour later, it was still the only thing on his mind.

Grant had tried reading a dozen books he'd picked off the shelves and had barely gotten past the title pages or dedications. He'd made up the sofa bed, plopped himself down on it, and tried finding something on television to distract him, but unless there was a reality show called *What Your Daughter is Keeping from You and How to Find Out What It Is*, that wasn't going to work either.

More than once he'd passed the open laptop on the table. He could practically hear it beckoning him.

Austin, come over here and see what I have for you.

He resisted the temptation to pry and gobbled up a handful of bunny rabbit cookies instead.

That's when he knew it was time to go out.

A subway ride and two-block walk later, Grant was back at his now-regular table at the Astro Diner with the ever-present Phyllis there to serve him. He ordered one of the shakes Frankel loved so much. Phyllis tried to tell him that was no dinner for a grown man and she was right. The shake was rich and tasty but, coupled with the bunny cookies, it was too much; he left half the glass. He thanked Phyllis, left her a tip twice the amount of the bill, and then ventured back into the cold December night still in search of some semblance of holiday cheer.

Manhattan was in full Christmas spirit. It was nine-thirty and the streets were packed with people teetering with shopping bags. Others toted Christmas trees and the corner bars had patrons spilling outside singing raucous carols.

All Grant heard in his head were two words—*Bah* and *Humbug*.

Right around ten o'clock, he found himself outside Radio City Music Hall. A man in town from Dubuque, Iowa, was trying to get rid of a spare ticket for the late *Christmas Spectacular* as his teenage daughter had refused to go. Grant bought it, figuring seeing what was so *spectacular* might put him in the holiday mood, or at least take his mind off Rachel and Allison.

There was something impressive about the Rockettes with their precise choreography in a chorus line that stretched the length of the largest stage Grant had ever seen. The crowd was in a jolly mood and sang along with every number.

But a full-frontal assault of that much yuletide joy only made Grant recall Christmases past with his wife and their little girl.

He remembered bringing home a lifelike electronic Saint Nicholas and how when he plugged it in to the wall, the figure had immediately started to whirr and bow—letting out a huge "Ho-ho-ho—Happy Christmas!" with a hearty guffaw. He thought it the most joyous thing he'd ever seen, until a four-year-old Rachel walked in on Boxing Day, took one look at the bearded robot twice her size, and ran upstairs to hide under the bed. Grant spent the rest of the morning coaxing Rachel out from under the mattress with numerous presents. The rest of the holiday found Rachel walking cautiously around the house afraid that "Saint Electronick" (as Grant had dubbed him) was going to pop out of a closet and "Ho-ho-ho" her to death.

The following year Rachel kept asking if Saint Electronick had returned to the North Pole and she giggled when it reappeared by the tree on Christmas Day. By the time she was six, Rachel was bringing friends over to see the bowing Father Christmas and Allison had to sit their daughter down and tell her she couldn't charge admission.

After that, the ritual of "The Plugging In of Saint Electronick" had been the most anticipated moment of the holiday season in the Grant household. The parties had continued way into Rachel's adulthood and only stopped the Christmas when Allison was living out her final days.

Grant wasn't even sure where Saint Electronick resided now—somewhere deep in the cellar, he thought. He was certain that if he went down and saw it, he'd burst into tears.

He got up halfway through the show and left.

Once again, he stood and watched tourists and New Yorkers skate below the gigantic Christmas tree at Rockefeller Center. He knew it was time to move on when he started wondering where he might find the cord that disconnected the speakers blasting the nonstop holiday music.

He ended up on Fifth Avenue walking past department store windows—all brilliantly decorated for Christmas. He stopped in front of Saks Fifth Avenue and took in the Burberry display, staring for a long time at the pink and brown patterned cashmere scarf on a festively dressed mannequin. He thought how lovely it would have looked draped around Allison's neck. It would have gone perfectly with her auburn hair and coloring.

For that matter, Rachel's as well.

Grant let out a heavy sigh. Christmas was never going to be the same.

Especially this one—as a widower searching for a maniac in a foreign land.

<hr>

It was just after midnight when he returned to Rachel's apartment.

She wasn't home yet—the lights were on exactly how Grant had left them a few hours earlier.

He passed the table with the laptop again.

This time, he stared at it a little longer, then went back to the foldout couch. He opened his carry-on bag and dug out his pajamas and toiletries.

He tried unsuccessfully to avoid glancing at the computer on his way to the bathroom.

Finally, giving in to temptation, he sat down at the table. He glanced over at the door—prepared to jump up the moment he heard the knob begin to twist.

Grant tapped the keyboard.

The computer screen lit up and asked for a password. He thought about it. He typed in *Allison*—and got back the message *Access Denied*.

He figured what the hell and tried something else. *Austin*.

And got the same message for his trouble.

Grant shook his head. After the past two years—what did he expect?

What he expected was better of himself. True, he was a policeman and it was second nature to be inquisitive. But not spying on his one and only daughter.

He got up out of the chair, returned to bed, flicked on the television, and started flipping through the channels.

Perhaps they were showing *Notting Hill* again.

"Silver."

Grant's eyes flickered open.

Gray morning light was coming in through the window and Rachel was hovering above him. Disoriented, Grant sat up.

"Silver?"

He looked from Rachel to the table and laptop. The screen was powered back up. He wondered if she had realized he'd tried to access it and was telling him the password.

"Prior Silver. Remember him?" prodded Rachel.

The name rang a bell—but not very loudly.

Grant tried to get his bearings and realized he must have fallen asleep right after he sat on the bed. He noticed that Rachel was in the same outfit she'd been wearing last night.

"What time is it?" he asked.

"Just after seven. I thought I'd just stay with my friend—give you the place to yourself. I tried you around eleven or so to tell you, but you didn't answer. I figured you were already asleep."

"I went for a walk."

"Well, I was worried I'd wake you if I called again. Good thing—you were dead to the world when I came back an hour ago." She pointed to the computer. "I've been online with Sergeant Hawley and I think he came up with something."

Grant suddenly felt pieces falling into place as he fully woke up.

"Prior Silver," he repeated. "A thief, if I remember correctly."

Rachel nodded. "Multiple robberies in the London financial district. He stabbed one customer, who nearly died."

He straightened up; she had his full attention now. "Back about the time you were in upper school."

"I remember it as well. He said all sorts of nasty things about you."

"He wouldn't have been the first."

"Still, it frightened me and Mom."

"So, he's out and about?" asked Grant.

"For over two years. But according to Sergeant Hawley, he 'found the Lord' while serving his time."

"He wouldn't be the first that happened to either."

Rachel was back at the computer screen, scrawling through her text with the sergeant.

"Hawley learned that the man led a Bible group in prison at least three times a week," she continued. "Silver actually wrote a couple of sermons on repentance; one was even published while he was incarcerated."

"Interesting," said Grant as he peered over her shoulder. "And I presume Prior Silver was in London when the first three murders were committed?"

"Certainly looks like it," said Rachel. "He also flew to New York City the day before Father Peters was killed in Saint Patrick's Cathedral."

15

Prior Silver.

Grant had barely remembered the name when Rachel first mentioned it. But halfway through reading the man's file, it came back to him like an avalanche. Strange that he could have forgotten it so easily, but Grant realized he'd put a lot of people in prison over three decades.

Twenty years ago, a spate of bank heists hit London's Financial District—numbering six by the time Grant's team turned their focus on Silver. All the robberies took place during the noon hour, which coincided with the lunch break that Silver took from the garage where he'd been a mechanic for ten years. It had been a colleague of Silver's that had tipped the Yard, having stumbled upon him in the WC picking up bundles of cash that had spilled on the floor in a stall where Prior had been tallying his latest haul.

Grant had set up surveillance on the mechanic and days later watched him leave the garage with a sandwich, only to dump it in a trash bin the minute he rounded the corner. Prior walked two more blocks, dug a kerchief out of his pocket, and donned it as a mask. Then he ducked into a Barclays, where he pulled a knife and demanded the nearest teller empty the till.

When Grant's team descended upon the bank, things took a turn for the worse. Prior grabbed Abby Van Dyke, who'd been waiting to cash her weekly check, and brought the knife to her throat—attempting to use her as a hostage shield.

Abby had started screaming and tried to squiggle free. That was when Silver cut her with the knife. With blood on his hands, Silver had loosened his grip just enough and Abby tumbled to the ground. Silver whirled to make a break for it—only to run directly into then-Sergeant Grant, who threw his arms around the misguided mechanic. Grant was quickly joined by the rest of his team, who leaped onto Prior Silver like he had the ball at the bottom of a rugby scrum.

The crime wave that had brought the Financial District to its knees was over.

Having seen the news on the telly, Allison and a twelve-year-old Rachel had greeted Grant when he returned with hugs and admonishments—his wife taking him to task for putting himself in such danger. He told her it all went with the job, but he was home now, and London was one criminal safer—for at least an evening.

Allison started worrying again when Grant took the stand at Prior Silver's trial. Grant's testimony regarding the knife attack on Abby had been particularly damning. It got Silver a thirty-year prison sentence as opposed to a term half that length if charges of aggravated assault with a deadly weapon hadn't been added to the robbery counts. Silver began screaming during Grant's testimony—shouting he hadn't meant to cut Abby, that the knife had slipped when he was backing out of the bank. Once order was restored, Grant doubled down, claiming Silver's actions had been purposeful and fraught with malice to fend off the police.

When his sentence was delivered, Silver threatened Grant, vowing he "would make him pay for what he'd done"—which kept Allison up for a number of nights. She only relaxed when Grant informed her that Prior's actions had gotten him placed in Wakefield, a prison in West Yorkshire often referred to as the "Monster Mansion" due to the great number of violent inmates incarcerated there.

Grant continued to review the file in the back of a cab, sitting along-side Rachel as they traveled to the precinct. Looking back, Grant didn't regret his testimony. He honestly believed he had kept a violent man off the London streets.

With the steady influx of investigations on his docket, Grant had forgotten about Silver shortly after that. The scarce free time he had was spent with Allison and Rachel, not looking in the rearview mirror at old cases.

So he had been unaware of the turnaround Silver did up at Wakefield, starting with the family Bible his wife had given him on her one and only prison visit. The final straw for her had been having to return the Fiat Silver had given her, the authorities claiming it had been bought through "ill-gotten gains." Prior had told her he'd had a "run of good luck at the races," though she couldn't remember when he'd last backed a winner. She really loved that car, certainly more than she did Prior—and within weeks had divorced him and run off with the owner of the Fiat dealership she had returned the car to.

Meanwhile, Prior Silver got hooked on scripture and spent every possible moment in his cell memorizing passages. He took to spreading the Good Word, enduring more than his fair share of beatings. It didn't prevent him from preaching Gospel, especially Mark 1:15, which preached the kingdom of God was at hand and it was time to repent and believe in the word of Jesus.

The result was Silver becoming a model prisoner, and a few years later he was transferred from the "Monster Mansion" to Hatfield, a more lax facility farther south where he had penned the sermons Rachel mentioned. Grant quickly scanned one published as a pamphlet entitled *Repent + Believe*—where Silver claimed repentance was more than just remorse for one's previous sins; it was also a redirection of the human will.

The sermon was instrumental to his release two years before. Grant wondered if that "will" had been "redirected" to punishing others for their sins—starting with *Thou shalt have no other gods before me* in a loo at the British Library.

"It certainly seems to line up," agreed Frankel.

He had joined the Grants in the basement office. The commander had just condensed the trial and tribulations of Prior Silver for Frankel.

The first thing the detective asked was about Silver's air ticket.

"He arrived early last Saturday, the fourteenth," Rachel told him, providing the specific airline (British Airways) and time (ten in the morning).

Frankel nodded. "Giving him an opportunity to check out Saint Pat's, then come back the following night and kill Peters."

"His return trip is scheduled for this coming Tuesday—the twenty-fourth."

"Wonderful," said Grant. "Back home just in time for Christmas."

"At least New Yorkers and tourists would be safer over the holidays," Frankel pointed out, looking for something to feel good about.

"It's only Friday," countered Grant. "At the rate he's going, Silver could have already dispatched the final five before he takes a plane for Heathrow on Tuesday."

"It could only be four," reminded Rachel. "Remember, he might have already killed number six; we just haven't been able to find that victim yet."

"Aren't you both just rays of fucking sunshine?" grumbled Frankel. He asked Grant if he'd heard from Ferguson since yesterday.

"Not a bloody peep," answered Grant.

Grant hadn't really expected to. The chances of the *Mail* man running down an unknown killer or finding a body first were slim to none with most of the NYPD looking for the same thing. Grant had essentially wanted to put the journalist on a wild-goose chase; if it brought back an unexpected dividend—so be it.

"Unfortunately, the ticket was paid for in cash, so we don't have a credit card yet for Silver," Rachel informed them. "But Hawley and the Yard are working on it."

Ten minutes later, the sergeant had come up with a debit card issued to Silver that had been used three times in New York City over the past week. The first time was at a JFK fast-food restaurant shortly after Silver landed, the second for a cab ride into Midtown minutes later, and the third as a guarantee hold for a room at the Hotel Pennsylvania that same evening.

"A hold means he hasn't checked out yet," Grant surmised.

"There's an easy way to find out," said Frankel.

The Hotel Pennsylvania, commonly referred to as the Penn, had one distinct advantage over every other hotel in Manhattan. It was the closest to Penn Station, situated directly across Seventh Avenue from the massive underground terminal.

"Makes it easy for anyone staying at that dump to get as far away from the place as soon as possible," Frankel told Grant on their way.

Once considered one of Manhattan's Grand Dame hotels, the Penn had fallen on hard times over the years and didn't even qualify as a tourist trap; it was only booked if someone didn't know better or was the first thing one spotted getting off the train from Wichita, Kansas.

Rachel had wanted to come along, but Frankel and her father convinced her this was when reporters did their thing while cops did theirs.

Frankel had tried ringing Silver's room before they'd left the precinct but got no answer. The hotel operator asked if he had a message for the guest. The detective declined, deciding not to leave one saying they were heading over to question him about five, or possibly six, murders he might have committed.

The front desk seemed familiar enough with NYPD, clearly having conferred with Frankel's brethren about the hotel's undesirable guests. After ascertaining that Mr. Silver was still registered, the manager provided the room number and offered to escort the cops upstairs.

"We can find our own way," Frankel told him. "No need to call ahead. We'd rather surprise him, if you get my drift."

The manager looked relieved to not deal with what looked like an unpleasant situation. "By all means," he said and pointed them toward the elevators.

Grant and Frankel exited on the fifth floor. The corridor was dimly lit—it could have been three in the morning. The faded flowered wallpaper was probably put up during the Truman administration, back when the hotel might have had enough stars to warrant a presidential entourage.

They traveled halfway down a corridor that literally stretched a city block and arrived at room 515. A "Do Not Disturb" sign hung from the unpolished knob.

It didn't stop Frankel from knocking on the door. There was no response. The detective leaned his ear against the door panel but neither cop heard footsteps.

Frankel looked down the hallway to see a maid emerge from a room five or six doors away, reuniting with the housekeeping cart she had parked there.

"Excuse me? Ma'am?" Frankel called out.

The maid, a Latina in her fifties who shuffled along, looked up at him. Her eyes flickered with seeming alarm as Frankel pulled out his badge.

He shook his head. "No. Nothing for you to worry about. Really."

"Can I help you?"

Frankel pointed to room 515. "My colleague and I were wondering when was the last time this room was serviced."

"Not since yesterday." She indicated the sign on the door. "That's been there since I started at six this morning."

Grant noticed Frankel give him a look that might have classified as a wink. The detective flipped over the sign so it read "Please Make Up This Room."

"I think it's ready for you now," Frankel told her matter-of-factly.

The maid knocked and announced herself. "Housekeeping."

They waited for an answer the two cops knew wasn't coming.

Frankel nodded to the maid. She used her pass key to unlock the door and Frankel motioned for her to remain outside. The maid was happy to comply.

"Maybe I should go get my cart?" she asked.

"Why don't you finish up what you were doing?" Frankel suggested. "You'll be back here soon enough."

She walked away faster than Grant thought her capable of moving.

Frankel didn't pull his weapon, but he kept his hand close enough to it. "Mr. Silver? NYPD."

Frankel cautiously entered the room. Grant followed close behind.

Unless Silver was hiding in the closet (spoiler alert, he wasn't), it was obvious that the man they were looking for had vacated the room.

The drab decor was a perfect match for the ho-hum hallway they had just left. The furnishings were simple and at best nondescript. A made-up bed, a sofa, and a chair by a wooden desk were basically it.

The detective moved back to the hallway and called again for the housekeeper. "Ma'am? One more moment of your time, please?"

The maid came back into the corridor and headed toward 515 with more than a trace of trepidation in her step. "Yes?"

Frankel waited for her to join them at the threshold. "Not having seen the other rooms in this fine establishment, I was wondering if this was something that came with the other ones?" he asked.

Frankel pointed at the wall directly above the bed.

The maid shook her head. "No, sir. I've never seen that before."

"I didn't think so," said Frankel.

Grant looked from the two of them back at the wall.

And the cross that hung directly above the bed.

—————

A couple of hours later, the cross from the wall of the abandoned insane asylum in Far Rockaway was waiting for them in a plastic evidence bag on Rachel's desk in the basement office.

Grant wasn't surprised to see it could have been the twin of the one found in room 515 of the Hotel Penn.

"Things are looking a little gloomier for your old friend Prior," said Frankel.

"I highly doubt he's going to be waiting for us in the BA lounge on Christmas Eve to have a little chat before he heads back across the pond," agreed Grant.

Rachel was looking at a calendar on her laptop. "He was supposed to stay what—three more nights? I wonder why he left so early." She glanced back up at the two of them. "Do you think he knew you were coming?"

Grant shook his head. "No way of knowing. But it doesn't look like he spent last night there."

"What makes you say that?" Rachel asked.

"The bed was made," explained Frankel. "I don't care if you're a tourist, businessman, or serial killer, no one makes up their rooms when house-keeping will do it for nothing."

"Where do you suppose he went?" she wondered.

"Out disposing of victim number six?" replied Frankel. "Maybe looking for a cheating spouse's forehead he can carve a Roman numeral seven on?"

"That's presuming he's still in the city," Rachel pointed out.

"We're checking flight manifests and waiting for another hit on his debit card," said Frankel. "He hasn't used it since checking in to the Penn."

Grant was only half-listening, continuing to stare at the plastic-covered cross. Something was gnawing at his brain again. He glanced back up at his daughter and Frankel.

"We might be looking at this all wrong," Grant said, tapping the cross.

"How do you figure?" asked Frankel.

Grant shook his head. "I wish I could tell you. I just . . ."

He broke off and simply shrugged.

Rachel looked from her father to the detective. "He gets this way. He used to come home and pace around the living room for hours saying something didn't feel right about the case he was working."

A few minutes later, Detective Morton entered the room holding a piece of paper. The look on his face could hardly be described as happy.

"Bad news, I'm afraid," informed Morton. Frankel took one look at what Morton handed him and cursed out loud.

"Shit." He nodded at Morton. "Thanks, Detective. That'll be all for now."

The second Morton left, Rachel whirled on the NYPD detective. "What is it?"

Frankel extended the piece of paper. "Silver took the red-eye last night. Norwegian Air flight out of JFK into Gatwick. He must have landed a few hours ago."

"Seems our man is on the run," Grant said.

Rachel sighed. "So he's headed back home to spread his brand of repentance and belief."

"With his very special knife and a few crosses," added Frankel.

Grant started to speak, then stopped himself. He turned to Rachel. "Repeat what you just said."

"He's gone back to England to spread his brand of repentance and belief."

"Repent and believe," murmured her father. Grant pointed at the computer. "That sermon you showed me this morning. Can you bring that up?"

It took Rachel less than a minute to find a copy of the pamphlet. Grant was hovering over her shoulder waiting. "There—I knew I'd seen that somewhere. Take a look."

He was pointing at the title of the article.

"Repent and believe," read Rachel.

"Repent *and* believe," Grant said, stressing the middle word. "Look closely enough and you'll notice the 'and' isn't a plus sign."

REPENT + BELIEVE

"It's a *cross*," explained Grant. "A cross that looks just like the one we found in the hotel room and this one from the hospital in Far Rockaway."

He indicated the plastic evidence bag on the desk.

"So Silver sticks with what works for him," said Frankel.

"It's more than that." Grant glanced around the room. "Do we have a picture of the hospital wall down here somewhere?"

"No, but I can get one easily enough." The detective checked himself, remembering something. "Wait. I took a couple of pictures with my phone. Will that do?"

"It should," answered Grant.

Frankel quickly located one and showed it to him. Though the lighting wasn't optimal, Grant could make out the three columns of papers and photos arranged in a Roman numeral *V* and two *I*s with the now-familiar cross situated between them.

Grant's eyes brightened. "That's it."

"What's it?" asked his daughter.

Grant pointed at the picture. "What do you see there?"

"The pictures of Leeds and his parents arranged into a Roman numeral seven," stated Frankel.

"But why is the cross there?" asked Grant.

"Because it's Silver's calling card?" Frankel wondered. "I don't know . . ."

The detective suddenly broke off. His eyes moved from the picture on his iPhone back to the computer screen where Prior Silver's pamphlet was still displayed.

Grant could see Frankel reach the same conclusion that his own brain had been able to unfurl.

"Six *and* seven," Frankel said. "It's not meant as a cross. It's meant to be a plus sign."

Grant nodded.

"It's why we haven't been able to find a sixth body." Rachel had caught on as well. "He hasn't killed them yet."

"Precisely," Grant said.

"So, he's gone back to England to kill numbers six *and* seven at the same time? A murderer and adulterer?" asked Frankel.

Grant started to respond, then stopped. A look of woe appeared in his eyes.

"Damn it to bloody hell."

"What is it, Dad?" asked Rachel.

"That's exactly what he's going to do," said Grant. "And I'm pretty sure I know who he's going after."

16

Stanford Hawley would always remember the first time he'd met Commander Austin Grant of Scotland Yard.

He had been absolutely petrified.

Coming from a working-class family, having spent his youth immersed in P. D. James's Adam Dalgliesh novels and watching *Inspector Morse* on the telly, Hawley had long dreamed of becoming a Scotland Yard man (Morse actually worked at Oxford, but the copper was bloody brilliant). To be assigned to Grant's team as a bright-eyed and bushy-tailed constable was almost more than Hawley could handle—as Grant was well on his way to becoming a legend at the Yard.

When introduced to Grant, he had stammered his name was Hanford Stawley before correcting himself.

"Well, which one is it?" Grant had asked.

Luckily, there had been a trace of a smile on the man's face, otherwise Hawley might have skulked out, never to return. He assured Grant it was the latter, but it didn't stop his new superior from calling him Stawley most of that first year.

This set the stage for Hawley's apprenticeship—where he stuck to his father's advice that he should go about his job with ears and eyes open and mouth closed. Looking back, Hawley recalled that ninety percent of his contributions to conversations with Grant early on were two- or three-word sentences, with plenty of "Yes, sirs" and more than his fair share of "I'm sorry, sirs."

But Grant had stuck with him and soon Hawley was the commander's trusted aide-de-camp. The happiest moment of Hawley's life had been the day he was promoted to sergeant and Grant had tapped him on the shoulder to say, "I'm proud of you, lad." Grant had also been instrumental in helping him through his saddest days—after Hawley's father succumbed to a heart attack a few years back. He had offered sage words of advice and comfort, keeping the sergeant focused on work while allowing him the breadth to grieve at his own pace.

Now Hawley was dreading the arrival of the new year. He already felt rudderless, unsure how things would be without Austin Grant. It would be like losing his father all over again, and he even considered leaving the Yard; it wouldn't be the same without Grant. But Hawley knew he would carry on, if only to avoid disappointing his mentor.

Hawley understood Grant's reasons for calling it quits. Three decades at the same job was plenty long in any vocation; the pressures of police work made it doubly so. When Mrs. Grant had taken ill, Hawley could see the light dim in the man's eyes and a lag appear in his step. Her subsequent passing and Grant's inexplicable estrangement from Rachel had taken their inexorable toll, so Hawley wasn't surprised when he announced his retirement.

And now with this case completely consuming the commander's last days, Hawley wouldn't blame Grant for taking it as a personal affront from on high. How much pain and suffering was one man meant to endure? Especially when he should have been celebrating a career that rivaled that of anyone who had stepped through the doors of Scotland Yard.

At least fate had taken the case to New York City, resulting in a reunion of sorts with Rachel. It had given Hawley solace to know that father and daughter were talking again, and he'd taken great joy working with Rachel the past few days.

But as gratifying as it had been to come up with Prior Silver as the prime suspect, it had been equally frustrating to feel the man slip through their grasp upon his return to England. By the time they'd tumbled to the former mechanic's return flight on Norwegian Air, Silver had been on British soil for hours and was nowhere to be found. There had been no sight of him near his small flat in the East End, and though Hawley had dispatched constables to comb the surrounding area, he had a sinking feeling Silver wasn't returning home any time soon.

If Grant were right, Prior Silver and his trusty knife were on their murderous way to catching up with Jared Fleming and Liz Dozier.

The trouble was that Hawley and his colleagues hadn't been able to get in touch with either of them—and that was of great concern.

The Fleming Mess.

Deep down, both Hawley and Grant had known they weren't done with it; and sure enough, it had raised its ugly head once more. Just in time to put a further damper on the conclusion of Grant's illustrious career.

It seemed appropriate. The Fleming Mess, as Grant referred to it, had probably been what got the commander thinking about retiring in the first place.

Fleming's was a British tobacco company dating back to the eighteenth century, when Joshua Fleming had begun importing crops he owned from the Carolina territories. Now, generations later, Jared Fleming had led the company into the twenty-first century—an industry leader producing cigarettes and a selection of fine cigars. A few years back, Jared had brought Matthew Dozier aboard as a partner with the man's infusion of cash. At first the partnership went swimmingly, but in recent years there had been debate about the future direction of the Fleming's brand.

Recently, Dozier had been a strong supporter of vaping. What had begun with the introduction of e-cigarettes to combat the anti-nicotine campaigns and government restrictions on advertising had blossomed into a craze, with teens and millennials flocking to vape bars springing up all over London, vowing never to buy a pack of cigarettes again.

Jared, ever the traditionalist, had argued with his partner about adding a vaping line to the well-established Fleming products that had kept his family rolling cigarettes and in the money. Jared maintained an impressive estate in Esher, just southwest of London in the county of Surrey, along with a pair of fancy cars and a boat he took out every weekend on the Thames.

The one thing that Jared Fleming desired but *didn't* have was Elizabeth Dozier, his partner's beautiful blond wife.

But if you were to believe Commander Austin Grant (and Sergeant Hawley always did), it had only been a matter of time until that situation was rectified.

Six months ago, Matthew Dozier had accompanied Jared on one of his weekly jaunts on the Thames. Jared had admitted that he and his partner had been in their cups, having polished off two bottles of wine while trying to come to an agreement on which way Fleming's was headed.

The next day, FME Jeffries confirmed that alcohol intake when he found a high level in Dozier's bloodstream after dragging his body from the river.

Jared Fleming had certainly been inebriated the previous evening when he phoned the Yard to tell them his partner had taken a drunken misstep and fallen overboard into the dark waters.

Austin Grant was convinced Jared Fleming had helped Dozier over the side.

The first thing that convinced him was the bruise on the right side of the dead man's head. Jeffries said it could have come from a blow struck by a strong left hook. Even though the FME also pointed out that the bruise could have been Dozier hitting his head on the side of the boat when he stumbled overboard, Grant's mind was made up. Especially since Fleming was left-handed.

Even more damning, as far as Grant was concerned, was the behavior of Liz Dozier—a new widow who didn't seem all that broken up by the sudden demise of her husband. She'd readily accepted Jared's explanation of the accident without bestowing an ounce of blame on him. She didn't find fault with him for liquoring up her husband on their fatal journey or for failing to prevent him going over the railing.

Liz Dozier had told Grant that she was just seeking comfort and friendship from her dead husband's dear business partner.

Grant didn't believe it—and therefore neither did Hawley.

When the good sergeant unearthed evidence of Jared and Liz having spent a weekend at a bed and breakfast under assumed names in the village of Chipping Camden, Grant took it a step further.

He brought a charge of murder against Jared Fleming.

Nothing would have pleased Grant and Hawley more than to slap Liz Dozier with coconspiracy. But try as they might, they couldn't place her in the vicinity of the boat; on that fateful evening Liz had conveniently been enjoying a five-course supper with a friend in Chelsea.

The ensuing trial had been a media circus. Reporters like Monte Ferguson had dined out on the scandalous nature of it all, and despite Grant and Jeffries (along with any other expert witness the prosecution could drum up) doing everything in their power to secure a guilty verdict against Fleming, the tobacco heir was acquitted in less than an hour once the case went to the jury.

Ferguson and his fellow journalists had taken Grant to task in the papers, blaming him for pushing a flimsy case to trial in the first place.

Grant had done his best to appear as though he were taking the defeat in stride, but his loyal sergeant could see the toll it had taken on the man.

When word arose that Jared had put the family estate in Esher up for sale and was moving in with the widow Dozier up on Primrose Hill, Grant had locked himself in his office for an entire day.

And now, if Grant were right, the Fleming Mess was back for one last nasty go-round.

If Prior Silver was going to claim his sixth and seventh victims at the same time, Jared Fleming and Liz Dozier perfectly fit the bill.

Thou shalt not kill. Thou shalt not commit adultery.

One a murderer, the other an adulterer.

I suppose Jared is an adulterer as well, thought Hawley.

He shook his head as he negotiated a roundabout on the southeast outskirts of London. He didn't suppose that Silver cared that Fleming was guilty of both.

Like Grant had said on the phone from New York—it checked all the boxes.

The moment Hawley disconnected from Grant, he had immediately tried to contact Dozier and Fleming at the house on Primrose Hill. No one had answered the phone. Neither picked up their mobiles.

He hoped that the two of them had gone on holiday somewhere far away.

But he had dispatched constables to the north part of London to double-check and see if anyone in the neighborhood knew of their whereabouts.

No one had seen either Jared or Liz for a few days. Hawley told the constables to keep the Primrose Hill house under watch until they returned or responded to the sergeant's messages.

That should have made Hawley feel a touch better. But he hadn't spent all that time with Commander Austin Grant without something rubbing off on him. Hawley wished he could disregard that gnawing feeling at the back of his brain, the one Grant had taught him to never ignore.

One word kept running through it.

Esher.

Despite Jared having listed the family home a few months back, Hawley didn't remember hearing that it had sold yet. It wouldn't surprise him—Esher was a posh village, unaffordable to most, and the notoriety Fleming had undergone in recent months might have made the house hard to sell.

It wasn't like Hawley kept up with real estate sales. He was still living in his father's house in Woking, the middle-class suburb where he had grown up and would most likely never leave. Esher was definitely above Hawley's means.

But it was also on his way home to Woking.

The least he could do was check it out. That way, by the time Grant and the others landed at Heathrow the next morning, Hawley could deliver a complete report when he picked them up.

It was past eight when he hopped on the A3 out of Richmond. About a half hour later, he turned west to cruise through Hinchley Wood. He passed Sandown Park Racecourse, where he'd spent a few lazy afternoons with other punters looking for tips on winners that never materialized, then arrived in Esher proper.

The village, like many of its Surrey ilk, was quaint and quiet. There were a few cars parked outside a pub on the main road. Blinking Christmas lights were strung over a door sporting a golden wreath. Hawley could see a few locals gathered around the tree inside, clinking glasses of eggnog and hurling darts.

Might have to go in and join them after I'm done.

He checked the navigation system and continued down the main road for a spell. When it dinged, he turned onto a side road and headed up a slight hill until it rang again, the computerized voice telling him he'd reached his destination.

The first thing Hawley noticed was the realtor's sign affixed to the iron gate.

Still on the market, he mused. *And still out of my price range.*

Not that Hawley would ever live there. He'd get lost in the place.

The house was gargantuan—New Scotland Yard might have fit inside the classic Tudor. Massive gardens glistened in the wintry full moonlight—leading Hawley to believe Fleming still had a number of people maintaining it to facilitate a sale.

Hawley's attention was quickly diverted from landscaping to the front of the house. A pair of cars were parked in the cobblestone circular driveway. One was a shiny Bentley, the other a dark-colored Audi.

A couple of lights were on in the house as well. One seemed to be just inside the formidable front door, the other somewhere on the second floor.

Hawley parked by the gate and reached out the car window to ring a bell affixed to a wooden post. He waited for some response from the adjacent speaker, but all he got was silence.

He exited the car and tried the bell a second time. He even called out loud in case someone on the other end was listening or the speaker was malfunctioning.

Still nothing.

He was surprised when the gate swung open to his touch.

Hawley hesitated and looked back at his car. He considered calling for backup but realized it would take at least thirty minutes for anyone from the Yard to get out there—if even that soon.

Figuring he was already there, he opened the gate and headed for the house.

He went through the same fruitless ritual at the front door. Ringing and knocking to no avail.

At that point, the feeling Grant had warned him about was resounding through his entire body, even more so when he found the front door unlocked as well.

Hawley swung it open and called out.

"Mr. Fleming? Mrs. Dozier? Scotland Yard here."

The light he had seen from outside came courtesy of a Chihuly chandelier hanging above. It illuminated an entryway that led off to massive rooms still staged with furniture that Fleming had kept to show off the house to potential buyers.

But these rooms held no interest for Hawley. His eyes were on the staircase directly in front of him.

And the bloody footprints on the carpet covering it.

⁂

He found them upstairs in the master bedroom.

That had been the other light he'd seen from the driveway.

At first glance, one would think he had interrupted Liz Dozier and Jared Fleming in bed together. But Hawley quickly realized they'd just been staged that way.

Especially as they were both still clothed—and complete bloody messes.

Hawley moved closer to the bed, carefully trying to avoid anything that might later be classified as evidence.

It wasn't like he wanted to ensure they were dead. No one could have survived the slaughterhouse the bed and two bodies resembled.

Hawley just wanted to double check.

Sure enough, a Roman numeral *VI* had been engraved on Jared Fleming's head. A carved *VII* adorned the brow of the woman he would never get to wed.

Hawley straightened up as he heard a sound.

And realized his big mistake.

There had been *two* cars in the driveway.

He had assumed one belonged to Fleming and the other to Elizabeth Dozier.

As opposed to the blood-soaked killer he turned to find standing directly behind him.

"Ah, Sergeant Hawley," he said. "You and Commander Grant will be happy to know that I got Fleming to confess to killing his partner, the late lamented Mr. Dozier, before we finished our work here."

He waved the dripping bloody knife at his handiwork on the bed.

As the Commandment Killer moved toward him, the sergeant found himself thinking of Austin Grant.

Stanford Hawley truly regretted that he wouldn't get to tell his mentor everything he had just figured out.

PART TWO

London Falling

17

Prior Silver was agitated.

He stood by the newsstand in Stepney, three blocks from his flat. Silver had spotted the two constables watching his street in an instant. The former garage mechanic retreated down the steps into the Underground, mumbling to himself.

Things were rapidly spiraling out of control.

New York had been a total fiasco—he should have stayed home in England.

Silver continued down the escalator into the depths of the Stepney Green station. He searched for and found a phone booth.

Once safely inside, he closed the bright red door and reached into his overcoat. He pulled out a small wooden cross and Bible. He flipped to the Book of Mark, clutching the wooden cross.

"The time is fulfilled, and the kingdom of God is at hand," he read aloud. "Repent ye, and believe the gospel."

He closed the Bible and shut his eyes, grasping the cross even tighter.

"Repent ye," he repeated.

When Silver opened his eyes, they were filled with a renewed determination.

He started pumping shilling after shilling into the coin slot, dialed a number he had committed to memory, and listened as the call went through.

Then Prior Silver waited for the one person in the world who might be able to help him to answer his desperate call.

18

Detective First Grade John Frankel felt completely helpless and disconnected from the world.

That's what happens when you're stuck thirty-five thousand feet in the air on a 777 flying across the Atlantic.

He looked across the aisle. Rachel had fallen asleep on the red-eye, snugly tucked under a courtesy BA-logoed blanket and the eyeshade that came with it. But her father was wide awake beside her, staring straight ahead. As frustrated as Frankel felt, Grant had to feel doubly so as they winged their way back to the UK.

It was becoming abundantly clear that Austin Grant had become the focal point for the killer. From the crossed-out picture in the stolen Far Rockaway car, to the emergence of Prior Silver as the prime suspect, and now the "Fleming Mess" (Grant's words); it couldn't be a coincidence.

Frankel had been fascinated listening to Grant recall his pursuit of Jared Fleming and Elizabeth Dozier. He vaguely remembered seeing it in a tabloid, but burdened with his own caseload, Frankel didn't pay much attention to a trial happening on the other side of the Atlantic. But the pair certainly fit the criteria as Silver's intended victims.

It hadn't taken much convincing to get Lieutenant Harris to authorize Frankel's heading to London alongside Grant. Frankel was sure his superior was breathing a sigh of relief that the killer had taken his serial spree to a distant shore.

There had been much debate about Rachel accompanying them. Grant hadn't thought it a good idea, but his daughter argued that having helped unearth Prior Silver she was now part of this, and that she was concerned for her father's safety and didn't want to be up all night worrying on a separate continent. Plus, she was a grown woman who made her own choices as to where and how she spent her time.

Frankel smiled; the last reason was enough to know this was an argument Grant would never win.

He checked his watch; still three hours till they landed at Heathrow. Frankel tried watching some action movie with Dwayne Johnson but quickly lost interest.

Instead, he replayed where they were in pursuit of Silver. It wasn't great.

The former thief had been in England for nearly a day by the time the three of them boarded the British Airways jet. There hadn't been a sighting of Silver since he'd stepped off the Norwegian Air flight. And Hawley had reported he hadn't been able to locate either Jared Frankel or Elizabeth Dozier.

He glanced over to find Grant watching him.

"We should try and get some sleep," murmured Grant.

"*Try* being the operative word," Frankel corrected.

Grant nodded in agreement, then shut his eyes. Frankel, knowing it was hopeless, leaned back and attempted to do likewise.

He was startled awake by the cabin lights coming on and the steward's announcement that they would be landing in twenty minutes. Frankel noticed that Grant was in his familiar post—staring into space, lost in thought. He wondered if the Scotland Yard man had fallen asleep from pure exhaustion like he had.

Frankel suspected he had not. He noticed Grant was finishing a cup of what he figured must be English breakfast tea.

Rachel stretched and looked at the two of them. "Did either of you sleep?"

"One of us did," Grant said. He motioned at Frankel. "He snores."

Rachel chuckled. Frankel gave an apologetic shrug, then gratefully accepted a cup of coffee from a steward pushing a beverage cart up the aisle. He wanted to be wide awake to hear whatever update Sergeant Hawley had for them.

⸻

But Hawley wasn't there to pick them up.

Grant said it was unlike the sergeant; punctuality could have been Hawley's middle name, especially in all matters commander.

Rachel suggested Hawley had gotten the arrival time or terminal wrong.

"Does that sound like the man you've been chatting with?" Grant asked.

Rachel didn't argue the point.

Frankel watched as Grant tried to reach Hawley on his cell but the call went directly to voice mail. He could feel that concern increase when he contacted the Yard and learned no one had heard from the sergeant since the previous evening.

Frankel looked up at a digital clock on the arrivals/departures board. Eight-fifteen A.M. "Perhaps he's stuck in rush hour traffic?"

"And not picking up his mobile?" Grant hit redial and asked someone on the other end to run a trace on Sergeant Hawley's car and phone.

Less than five minutes later, the Scotland Yard man's phone rang.

"I'll bet that's him circling the terminal," Rachel said hopefully.

Grant looked at the display on the cell. "It's the Yard." The conversation was brief. "Thank you," Grant said. "I'll start heading that way."

He disconnected and turned toward his daughter and Frankel.

"They traced his car to Esher. It's also the last place his cell registered."

"Escher like the artist?" asked Frankel.

"It's a village in Surrey. Not far from here actually," said Rachel. She glanced over at her father. "Did they have an exact location?"

"I don't need one. I know exactly where to go."

Frankel didn't like the way those words came out of Grant's mouth. They had the finality of doom all over them.

———

They caught a taxi and headed south for thirty minutes.

Once on the road, Grant called back the Yard with an address to send reinforcements. He'd just finished telling Rachel and Frankel about Fleming's Surrey estate and how he'd interviewed the tobacco tycoon twice there.

"You might want to tell Jeffries to have a team ready as well," Grant informed his colleague before ending the call.

"Who is Jeffries?" asked Frankel.

"The forensics medical examiner."

Frankel wished he could tell Grant he was overreacting. But Hawley's car parked outside the Esher mansion did nothing to dissuade that feeling of dread that Frankel knew they all shared by now.

They removed their bags from the cab and placed them beside Hawley's car. As the taxi moved off, Frankel glanced through the gates at the mansion. A Bentley was parked in a circular cobblestone driveway. The only sound came from chirping birds brave enough to stay in the barren trees for another dreary winter.

"Do you want to wait for your colleagues?" Frankel asked.

Grant placed a hand on the hood of Hawley's car. "Ice cold," he observed. "It's been here since at least some time last night. I say we head inside."

Rachel visibly reacted. "Dad, maybe you should wait for someone."

"It would be helpful if you'd do that for us," Grant told her.

His gaze returned to the mansion lying behind the massive gates.

The only thing missing is that "Keep Out" sign at the Far Rockway hospital, thought Frankel.

Grant echoed the unspoken sentiment.

"We're too late to stop whatever happened here."

Sergeant Hawley had been unable to prevent anything either, as evidenced by his dead body having been draped over those of Jared Fleming and Elizabeth Dozier atop the bed in the master bedroom. It resembled a twisted version of Michelangelo's *Pietà*, with Fleming added to the tableau as a second parent grieving the loss of their grown child.

Frankel knew the killer had staged the display for Grant. It was as if he were saying, "I hereby offer you your son, the good Sergeant Stanford Hawley."

For the first time since he'd met Grant, the detective saw pure anguish appear on the man's face. Along with a fair share of rage.

"I'm so sorry." They were the only words Frankel could muster up, knowing there were none in the English language that could be strung together to offer Grant any form of solace.

Grant barely nodded.

Frankel knew he would have reacted the same way with the sudden loss of a close colleague in the line of duty. The only choice was to focus on the work at hand and redirect one's grief and fury to try and make things right.

London was on the verge of spontaneously combusting with fear.

Merry Fucking Christmas.

Jeffries showed up with his team shortly after a couple of Scotland Yard detectives had arrived as backup. Grant introduced Frankel to his superior, Deputy Commander Franklin Stebbins, who had made an appearance—having left his family at a holiday brunch at his golf club. The NYPD detective could tell Stebbins wasn't overjoyed to make his acquaintance—probably because his presence meant a homicidal maniac had returned to the British Isles.

A debate ensued on whether to release Silver's name and description to the media. Grant argued for the public to be made aware that a suspected killer was back in their midst to make it harder for Silver to hide. Stebbins urged delaying the pronouncement, not wanting to create chaos just prior to the holiday.

With Stebbins pulling rank, the discussion was tabled. The deputy commander implored them to solve this bloody case once and for all.

"Why do I get the feeling he was blaming me when he said that?" asked Frankel as Stebbins drove off, presumably to return to his holiday festivities. "Like it was my fault for not catching the guy when he went around garroting New Yorkers."

"Probably the same way your Lieutenant Harris felt about me letting Silver cross the pond in the first place."

They moved toward Sergeant Hawley's car, where Rachel was waiting. Neither man had been able to dissuade her when she'd insisted on seeing what they had discovered on the second floor of the house. And though she had tried to keep the proverbial stiff British upper lip, Frankel saw her start to crumble when she encountered the carnage. He had quickly put his arm around Rachel and escorted her down the stairs and out to the car.

"You really should head back to the house," Grant told her.

Once it was decided she'd accompany them to London, Grant had gotten Rachel to agree that she would stay with him in Maida Vale.

"I'm not going back there without you, Dad," she said. "I'm fine."

Frankel could tell she wasn't but had been around her enough to know there was no budge room either.

One of the Scotland Yard men came up and told them Jeffries was ready.

A few minutes later, Frankel and Grant returned to the master bedroom.

A lot had gone on in their absence.

The bodies had been photographed from every possible angle. The bloodstained carpet had been covered in plastic; strings had been pulled and mounted off walls tracing the presumed footpaths of the killer and the victims.

The FME corroborated a number of things both Frankel and Grant suspected. The carvings on Fleming's and Dozier's foreheads corresponded with the ones found on the three bodies Jeffries had examined earlier that month.

"I've already sent pictures to your colleagues in the States," Jeffries told Frankel. "I presume they'll match the priest and the other victim you found."

"I don't have your expertise," Frankel responded. "But they look exactly the same to me."

Jeffries thought the couple had been attacked by the fireplace where they had probably been sitting when the killer arrived. "They were fully clothed and the blood spatters indicate they were moved to the bed after their necks were slashed." The FME brought a finger to his forehead. "Stains on the pillowcases make me suspect the numerals were carved after they'd been, shall we say, laid to rest there."

"And Sergeant Hawley?" asked Grant.

The pain behind the question was written all over his face.

"I suspect the killer caught him by surprise near the door."

"While he was looking at Fleming and Dozier?" suggested Frankel.

"Seems more than likely."

The FME pointed to a puddle of blood on the plastic-covered carpet. "The sergeant would have turned to find the killer right behind him. Once dispatched, his body was placed on top of the others in what seems to be a very precise position."

"Staged," said Frankel.

"Quite," agreed Jeffries. "If he had just been tossed there, his limbs would have been all askew."

Grant delivered the sign of the cross over his fallen comrade. When the commander looked up, Frankel could see the emotion brimming in his eyes.

"I haven't done that since I was in first form," Grant said softly. The Scotland Yard man turned to Jeffries. "Did you find any mark on him?" he asked the FME. The desperation in his voice was audible. "A Roman numeral somewhere?"

"Nothing like that," Jeffries answered. "We'll continue to look but I think it's safe to assume the sergeant was just at the wrong place at the worst possible time."

Grant turned back to look directly at Frankel. When he spoke, his voice was laced with fury.

"This has to stop. Now."

Frankel had barely touched the room service tray. Even the chocolate milkshake he'd found on the all-day menu had no appeal.

He had spent the first hour in the tiny but well-appointed room at the boutique Covent Garden Hotel (suggested by the Grants) pacing. He finally realized he hadn't eaten since whatever had masqueraded as food on the flight and thought it wise to order something.

Once the hamburger, fries, and shake had arrived, it already confirmed what Frankel had suspected.

He'd completely lost his appetite.

Upon exiting the Esher mansion, Frankel and Grant realized they were no further along than when they had left the States.

The crime scene team had found evidence of another car parked outside the mansion but there was no way to tell what the make had been. Seeing as how Prior Silver had never owned a car, and there was no record of him renting one, it seemed likely he had boosted it or found one with a key inside, like Josephine Tuttle's Hyundai Sonata in Far Rockaway.

In a small village like Esher, where everyone was home wrapping holiday gifts or hoisting hot toddies, it came as no surprise that no one had seen anyone in the vicinity of the Fleming house the previous night.

Maybe I should just get soused like last time I was here with my college buds, thought Frankel.

But he knew that wouldn't help him forget the image of Austin Grant standing over his dead sergeant, crossing himself for the first time in over fifty years.

The man was taking it personally now.

A few minutes after placing his room service order, Frankel's cell had rung. He'd taken one look at the number and answered it.

The conversation had been brief.

Once he'd disconnected, Frankel had stared long and hard at his left hand.

A few moments later he had removed the gold ring from his finger and placed it inside his toilet kit.

Frankel was still staring at the shake an hour later, wondering how long it would take the milk to curdle, when the knock came on the door.

He rose and crossed the room to open it.

Rachel stood there.

"You going to just stand there staring or are you going to invite me in?" she asked with a slight smile.

"I can't believe you actually came," Frankel replied, opening the door for her. "What did you tell your father?"

"That I was going to visit a friend."

She stepped inside and Frankel shut the door.

"So, I'm a friend?"

"I'd like to think so," Rachel answered.

She moved a step closer and gave him another smile.

"I did tell my dad not to wait up."

Frankel took her into his arms and kissed her for the first time.

And realized that he was starting to take this whole thing personally as well.

19

I t had started that night in the rain outside the London.

Once the commander had headed inside, Frankel and Rachel tried in vain to find a couple of cabs. Even with the doorman waving frantically and blowing his whistle like calling a foul at the Garden, there wasn't a cab in sight, let alone two.

It was the classic New York City situation. On a bright sunny day on a leisurely stroll, you stop at a corner and a dozen taxis descend on you like a school of sharks. The skies open up, you had a better chance of finding Jimmy Hoffa's body (Frankel subscribed to the under the fifty-yard line at the old Giants Stadium in the swampy Meadowlands theory) than finding an available cab.

Rachel had suggested Uber—but with the theaters having just let out, thousands of soaked patrons were working their apps and when she finally found one, it called for a triple peak surcharge, the same cost as getting to JFK normally. They'd barely had time to debate clicking "accept" when it was gobbled up by some desperate theatergoer and they remained stuck under the London awning.

Frankel grumbled it was enough to drive a man to drink. Rachel thought that sounded like one hell of an idea.

She'd pointed out that Rue 57, a French bistro with a nice bar, was two blocks away and said she was up for braving the storm as they were already soaked to the bone. Frankel agreed, so they splashed their way to the corner of Sixth Avenue and the street that gave the bistro its name.

After they were given bar towels to wipe themselves semidry, they'd been shown to a booth, where they ordered Irish coffees to warm the chill. By the time they'd moved on to hot toddies in honor of the season, Frankel knew he was in big trouble.

Not only was Rachel beautiful, smart, and opinionated, there was something he couldn't put his finger on that differentiated her from any woman he'd ever met. Was it the hint of vulnerability behind her smoky gray-blue eyes that awoke the protective nature in him? The way she laughed with the slightest of rasps that made him want to keep her amused just so he could hear it again? Or that she actually found him interesting to talk to and was still sitting there when their waiter came by three hours later to say it was "last call"?

To say that Frankel had quickly grown infatuated was the understatement of the year, and there were only twelve days left in it.

For the first few minutes, they'd talked about obvious things—the crappy weather and the case. They agreed that sleet and slush sucked, and it should either "warm the fuck up" (Rachel's words, which pleased Frankel immensely) or "Let It Snow" and give us a "White Christmas" (he resisted the urge to offer a rendition of either song). Their discussion of the Commandment Killer had been brief; both happy not to talk shop at eleven in the evening.

More than once Frankel had seen Rachel's eyes stray to his left hand and the slightly tarnished wedding band. He told her the same story he'd shared with her father over lunch a couple of days earlier.

"A beach bar in Hawaii. Sounds lovely," she mused, looking out at raindrops falling in Technicolor, courtesy of reflected holiday lights. "Did you go after her?"

"I learned a long time ago when to stop pursuing a dead end." He had hoped that would finish the topic, but Rachel seemed extremely interested in Julia.

"How did you two meet?" she'd asked.

"Actually, I arrested her," Frankel had replied sheepishly. "You'd think that would have been my first clue."

Rachel started laughing.

"It's not as bad as it sounds," Frankel said.

The Tragic Tale of Julia Molinari and John Frankel followed.

"Italian girl," Rachel observed.

"With all the feistiness and nutso family you'd expect."

Case in point—the evening they met.

Frankel had been working undercover outside the Garden, trying to break a scalping ring that was driving licensed ticket brokers in Jersey City on a road to ruin.

"There was this one girl who kept trying to hawk a couple of nosebleeds for a crappy game. The Grizzlies were in town and no fan wanted to watch the Knicks go against up against some lousy Canadian team they could actually come out of the stands and play for in the fourth quarter."

Rachel laughed again. "Vancouver did suck pretty bad."

Frankel raised an eyebrow.

"My dad's an avid Liverpool booster, just like my granddad—but it never took with me," Rachel explained. "Men running around in circles for a solid hour with nothing to show but a scoreless draw. I started watching the Euros play on the telly and once guys like Dirk headed to the NBA, I was hooked. My folks thought I came to America to get a master's in journalism but it was more about going to the Garden and seeing the Knicks and Celtics battle live.'"

Frankel thought about checking to make sure his jaw wasn't hanging open.

"So, you were saying?" Rachel asked after taking a sip of the hot toddy.

"Huh?"

"Julia? Outside the Garden?" There was a twinkle in her eye.

He checked. Yup. Jaw definitely hanging. He resumed his story.

As tip-off approached, the pesky but striking willowy brunette had already passed by him a number of times. Finally, absolutely desperate, she thrust the tickets in Frankel's face, blatantly asking what he'd give her for the pair.

Frankel pulled out his badge.

The girl didn't miss a beat when she told him she'd take face value.

He'd cracked up. But still ended up cuffing her.

"You can't be serious," she had said.

Looking back, he realized he'd been a bit of a hard ass. But he figured he had been teaching Julia Molinari a life lesson. It was back at the precinct when he'd allowed Julia to make her one call that Frankel had gotten his first taste of his future father-in-law.

"What'd I get for the tickets?" Julia screamed in the phone. "I got fuckin' arrested for the tickets, that's what I got!"

Frankel could hear the dial tone on the phone. She turned and shrugged. "I was gonna say a thousand-dollar fine or six months, but you hadn't told me yet."

And then she'd smiled at him like no other woman Frankel had ever met.

The DA's office took one look at the case and kicked it (hell, Julia wasn't making a profit selling the tickets at face) and Frankel promptly asked her to go with him to a Knicks game the following week.

He'd proposed less than a month later.

It had been impulsive—but at the time he thought Julia was the best thing that had ever happened to a kid who grew up among the factories in Elizabeth, New Jersey. Julia had been runway model gorgeous and the sex had been incredible—not that Frankel had much experience in that department, having had only two semiserious girlfriends, who paled by comparison.

"Sounds like you were really in love with her," Rachel had said after Frankel offered her a more romanticized and less libido-inspired version of the courtship.

"I certainly thought so."

She indicated the ring on his hand again. "And then she broke your heart."

It hadn't happened overnight. Pablo, the building super that Julia had set up bar and house with in Hawaii, had just been the last nail in the marriage coffin.

They had actually lasted close to a decade. Pretty good for starting out by eloping to Atlantic City because Julia's father didn't approve of his only daughter choosing a cop. It might have had something to do with the shady furniture business that Frankel's father-in-law ran on the Lower East Side. Frankel didn't really look the other way when it came to how Leo Molinari made his money—he just made sure to discuss local sports teams when they got together on holidays. They couldn't even agree on Giants versus Jets—with Leo pledging allegiance to the latter because Joe Namath was a great Italian American, even though Frankel had repeatedly told him that the Super Bowl III hero was of Hungarian descent.

In the end, Frankel realized what had brought them together in the first place had been what drove them apart. Julia would always be that girl looking for a quick score while Frankel was making sure everyone played by the rules.

"Now, with Pablo, I think Julia finally found what she was looking for."

"My favorite band," Rachel said with a grin.

"U2? Isn't that a bit sacrilegious? With your family from Liverpool; the Beatles? Aren't they an Irish band?"

"They're everyone's band," countered Rachel.

"I'll drink to that," said Frankel, ordering another round. "Though they'll have to go into the Octagon with Bruce and the E Streeters. I did grow up off Exit 13 on the Jersey Turnpike."

The next round of toddies allowed Rachel to reminisce about all the boys she'd loved before. There had only been two—and both had ended with the realization that Rachel still hadn't found what *she* was looking for.

The first had been a summer crush—the other reason (besides the Knicks) that she'd headed Stateside. When they met, Tom was an American clerking for a British barrister and Rachel had just finished her undergraduate stint at Oxford. They'd tried the long-distance thing and that had gone well enough, so Rachel had applied to the graduate journalism program at Columbia and gotten in. The pressure of Tom's looming boards and landing the proper job with the right firm had not been their undoing—the old adage that absence makes the heart grow fonder was validated when seeing each other every day on the same continent resulted in Rachel realizing that Thomas Nelson, soon-to-be-Esquire, was nothing but an old-fashioned bore.

Charles Kellerman had been a completely different experiment. Rachel should have known the relationship was doomed from the start. Older by a couple of decades, divorced for five years, and with two teens closer to Rachel in age than their father, Charlie was hardly a snooze. A heart surgeon who literally saved the life of every person who ended up on his table, Charlie knew only one route and that was (as Don Henley sings) in the fast lane. It was ski races down the Vermont slopes in the winter and regattas on the Sound when summer came. Charlie had swept Rachel off her feet and she'd had to strap herself in to try and keep up.

It didn't help that her mother was so horrified that Rachel had taken up with a married man ("though I kept telling her he'd been divorced for five years") that Allison wouldn't discuss it. Though initially infatuated by a lifestyle she'd never known, it hadn't taken Rachel very long after she moved in with Charlie (a week) to realize this wasn't for her—he had already lived a full life that she wanted to experience with someone from the beginning.

"Meaning children?" asked Frankel.

"Building something together, at least."

Hearing Rachel's story brought to mind the fact that he and Julia hadn't had kids. He'd often wondered if it were a purposeful or subconscious decision. Whatever the truth, he would never have built something substantial with Julia.

He had ended up telling Rachel as much and she raised her glass.

"Here's to there still being time," she toasted.

When they'd emerged from the restaurant at two in the morning, the rain had stopped and the wintry sky was clear enough to see a few stars and a full moon shining down on the city. As a result, there were plenty of cabs.

"I could walk you home," offered Frankel.

"It's forty blocks from here."

"I'm up for it if you are." He nodded at the holiday light display hanging off the lamps on Fifty-Seventh Street. "It's a special time in the city, particularly when you have it to yourself."

Rachel had said why not. Like Frankel, she hadn't been ready for this evening to end quite yet.

It took just over an hour to walk the forty blocks to Rachel's apartment, and Frankel thought it was the most beautiful stroll he'd ever taken through the city.

It was as if Manhattan was putting on a Christmas display just for them. Whether it was giant glistening snowflakes, trees laden with lights and ornaments in every store window or lobby they passed, or Lincoln Center lit up with enough vibrant colors that Santa Claus could see it from the North Pole, it was their own private winter wonderland.

Along the way, they had reminisced about Christmases past, Frankel talking about the yearly trek into the city with his father to Macy's at Herald Square, where he'd sat on Santa's lap and asked for things he almost never received. Rachel had told him about some contraption her father brought home that they'd christened Saint Electronick—starting a family ritual that continued years into her adulthood.

It was nearly three-thirty when they reached Rachel's walkup.

"Thank you," she'd told him. "That was . . ."

". . . unexpected," Frankel had said, getting to say aloud what he'd been feeling for the past few hours.

They stood there awkwardly for a moment before he took a step forward and gave her a friendly but very quick hug.

"Good night, then." He gave her a genuine smile.

"Good night, John," Rachel said, returning one of her own.

He'd watched her unlock the door to her building. Then he asked her the other question that had been on his mind the entire evening.

"Will we be telling your father about this?"

Rachel thought about it for a few seconds. She scrunched up her nose. "I don't think so."

"Probably a good idea," agreed Frankel.

He'd asked her what she was doing the following night.

After telling her what he had in mind, he was a little surprised when she actually said yes. "Sounds like fun," she told him.

And then Frankel realized something else.

He'd suddenly felt happier than he'd been in the longest time.

Later that day, he had kept expecting her to cancel as they'd worked the case that brought them all together. Rachel never brought it up, so Frankel didn't either. He wondered if she'd forgotten about it or if maybe he'd had one too many and only imagined that he'd asked her out in some kind of drunken stupor.

But shortly before Rachel had left with her father to get him situated at her place, she'd ducked her head into Frankel's office and asked if they were still on.

It had caught Frankel off guard. "Absolutely," he practically sputtered.

"I'll meet you at the corner at eight-thirty like we talked about," Rachel said.

The conspiratorial way she'd uttered it actually caused butterflies to start fluttering in Frankel's stomach.

But when she climbed in the car at the agreed rendezvous, Frankel didn't need his first-grade detective classification to see that her mood had changed.

He immediately asked what was wrong.

"Just some stuff with me and my father." She tried to make light of it by shrugging it off, but Frankel noticed her eyes drift back toward her building.

"Want to talk about it?" he'd asked.

"Not particularly."

Frankel told her if she didn't want to go, he would completely understand. "Maybe you want to go back up and hash it around with the commander."

"That will definitely not be happening." She'd managed a smile and gave him a small nudge. "C'mon, I'm looking forward to this. You can tell me more about this Stone Horse you're taking me to."

"Stone Pony."

"Right. That one."

A few minutes later, they were headed east on the George Washington Bridge into Jersey and Frankel was giving her a brief history of the Stone Pony, the club in Asbury Park that had been his father's musical touchstone back in the '70s.

The emergence of Bruce Springsteen, then other local acts like Bon Jovi and Southside Johnny, had given a voice to men like his dad (who'd spent their entire lives in shipyards and factories) by transforming the Jersey Shore into a force the music scene needed to reckon with. He'd inherited his father's musical taste, and then his record collection after he'd passed away (including a mint pressing of Springsteen's *Greetings from Asbury Park*). The albums were the one thing he wouldn't let Julia near before she fled for sunnier skies with Pablo the super.

On this night, Frankel had been lucky enough to snag a couple of tickets to the Pony's annual Christmas show, with Southside and his Jukes as the headliner. Each year, the club played host to a number of local bands doing their renditions of yuletide classics, raising funds for charity, with gospel singers from neighborhood churches who would do Aretha and Mavis Staples proud.

And there was always the possibility that Springsteen might sneak in during an encore and treat his rabid fan base to a few rockin' carols and some of their favorite hits.

The show had been in full swing when Frankel and Rachel got their hands stamped by the bouncer at the door. They'd ended up in the back of the small club, but it didn't matter as Southside and a six-piece horn section were blowing the lid off the joint with a rendition of "Christmas (Baby Please Come Home)."

By that time, whatever had been troubling Rachel was left back in Manhattan. For the next two hours there was no talk of commandments, serial killers, or suspects—just pure rock and roll, and they liked it.

Yes, as the Stones would tell you. Yes, they did.

Then, around one in the morning, sleigh bells had begun to shake along with the entire building when a gravelly voice called out from the side of the stage. "So, tell me, New Jersey—have you been naughty or have you been nice?"

And suddenly Springsteen, the Boss himself, was up on stage.

The first thing he did was let all the die-hards who were "freezing their asses off outside" waiting for a ticket come into the club and "let the fire marshal be damned!" Then Bruce made good to rock the place "all night long"—or at least for another hour—pounding out hit after hit and a version of "Merry Christmas Baby." A finale of "Santa Claus Is Coming to Town" left every person in the place exhausted but exhilarated.

Rachel had tears of joy in her eyes when she turned and gave Frankel a hug. "Thank you for bringing me here," she whispered in his ear.

"My pleasure," Frankel told her. "It was . . ."

"Unexpected," she'd replied with a smile he knew he would never forget as long as he lived.

About an hour later, Frankel had taken Exit 13 off the New Jersey turnpike in Elizabeth.

There had been a short discussion about heading back to the city but neither wanted the evening to be over. Going back to Rachel's was out of the question with her father sleeping on the foldout couch. And with Frankel's Murphy bed being the only piece of real furniture Julia had left him, he didn't want to force an issue that he wasn't sure either he or Rachel was quite ready for.

They ended up stopping at a White Castle drive-through and picked up burgers dripping with all the fixings, fries, and the obligatory choco-late shakes.

Then he'd headed up a hill not far from the tiny house he'd grown up in.

At a stoplight, Frankel flipped through his music on his iPhone. He punched a few buttons until Springsteen's "Drive All Night" poured softly from the speakers.

"Nice," murmured Rachel.

Frankel had turned the wheel and brought the car to a stop on a small ridge.

"I've been coming here since I could look over the dashboard of a car," Frankel told her. "It might be my favorite place in the entire world."

He pointed out the windshield—a drop-dead view across the Hudson of lower Manhattan was spread out in front of them.

Rachel audibly gasped at the endless brilliant vertical string of lights.

"I see what you mean."

"You should see it first thing in the morning."

"I'm willing to wait if you are."

Frankel pointed out that dawn was still three hours away.

"Well, we haven't had dinner yet," Rachel responded.

The burgers, fries, and shakes were gone in a flash. Frankel had checked his watch. "I think we have two hours and fifty minutes left till the sun comes up."

"I'm just happy to sit here for a while."

So, they'd leaned back and listened to *The River*—his all-time favorite album.

He didn't realize he'd closed his eyes and fallen asleep until he heard Rachel murmur beside him.

"Oh my God."

Frankel glanced over to see her face dappled with the first strains of morning light coming from the east. She was also wiping tears from her eyes.

"It might be the most beautiful thing I've ever seen," she whispered.

It was the sun rising over the East River and illuminating New York City.

And directly below them—a glistening Statue of Liberty.

It looked close enough to touch.

"You should have seen it when the towers were there."

"I really wish I had."

"It's not the same thing but . . ."

He had dug around for his phone and scanned through his photo file.

"I took this back when I was in college." He showed her a picture of the same view—only this one had the Twin Towers rising majestically at the tip of Manhattan.

"Wow. It's breathtaking."

Frankel nodded. "I think about it all the time."

Rachel handed him back the phone. And gave him a mischievous grin.

"What?"

"You took that from a car? Just like this?"

"Pretty much."

"With a girl like me?"

"Definitely not one like you."

Rachel had laughed. "I bet you bring all the girls up here."

"Sheila Rice was the only other one."

"Not Julia?"

Frankel had shaken his head.

"Why not?" Rachel had asked. She inched a teensy bit closer to him.

"She wouldn't have appreciated it."

"Her loss."

"Yeah. Well." Frankel found himself moving closer to her as well.

"So, what did this Sheila Rice think of it all?"

"Not that much. She was sort of interested in other stuff."

Rachel raised her eyebrow. "What kind of stuff?"

She had moved even closer.

"You know," Frankel murmured. "Stuff . . ."

"Mmmm."

Then something in the car had buzzed.

An alert on Rachel's phone from Sergeant Hawley.

It was the information about Prior Silver having taken a flight to New York City the day before Father Adam Peters was murdered in Saint Patrick's Cathedral.

All hell had broken loose after that.

The frantic search for Silver, Hawley dropping off the radar, and the three of them winging across the Atlantic only to discover the massacre waiting for them in the Esher mansion.

During that time, Frankel and Rachel barely had a moment to themselves.

She'd spent the whole trip from New Jersey texting back and forth with the now-dead Sergeant Hawley.

It was only when they had both ended up near the bathroom on the 777 together that they managed to have a regretful quick chat about what might have been.

"I feel awful about the bad timing yesterday morning," Rachel told him.

Frankel let out a sigh. "Duty calls, I guess."

"Duty sort of sucks if you ask me."

"Pretty damn much," agreed Frankel.

So when she had called him at the Covent Garden Hotel that night and asked if he wouldn't mind some company, Frankel hadn't hesitated.

He had told her to head right on over.

And this time, he made damn sure that he kissed her.

20

Rachel woke up to the first rays of light coming through the window. For a moment, she needed to shake the cobwebs out of her brain and get her bearings.

She had slept the last three nights in completely different places—none of them her own. Going from the passenger seat of an unmarked police car to the 777's window seat and now in the comfy queen bed at the Covent Garden Hotel—she was entitled to being a little out of whack. Not that she was complaining.

She turned to see John still asleep beside her.

The sex had been alternately passionate and tender—exactly the way she would have imagined and desired if she'd taken the time to consider what she was getting herself involved in.

The past few days had been such a whirlwind that Rachel hadn't thought about where things were headed; hardly her norm. She usually explored any given situation from every angle, trying to make an informed decision before making any definitive move. She would invariably regret her choice and spend the next few hours, days, sometimes even months thinking about the road not taken.

But this time Rachel had thrown caution to the wind and didn't regret for one second where she now found herself.

Except that it was almost seven in the morning and she was certain her father was wondering where the hell she'd disappeared to.

"Hey."

She glanced from the clock on the nightstand back over at John.

His baby-blue eyes were half-open. She felt a fluttering deep inside.

"Hey," she said back.

John stretched, then gently reached for her. She folded into the crook of his arm and shoulder—where she fit quite nicely, thank you very much.

He smiled. "That was . . ."

This time they said it at the same time.

". . . unexpected." Both laughed.

John looked past her at the clock.

"You've got to go, I bet."

"They taught you well in detective school."

"Graduated top half of my class."

"Higher than that, I bet."

John gave her a tiny shrug. "First, actually."

"False modesty," Rachel said with a smile. "I sort of love that."

"We aim to please."

"You did just fine in that department." She kissed him on the cheek. More than a peck; she let her lips linger, then eased herself out of his arms. "I really have to go."

"I wish you didn't."

"And I'm really glad you said that."

She planted a similar kiss on his other cheek. Then she got out of bed and started putting on the clothes she had left draped over a small sofa. Rachel could feel him watching her but didn't mind. She didn't make a show of it, but didn't rush to cover up either.

When she had finished putting herself together, she turned to see he was sitting up in bed—still watching her. The sheet covered him from the waist down, but his naked sculpted frame was tempting her to think about another go-round.

"That isn't exactly fair," she told him.

"What's that?"

"Me all dressed—and you sitting there like—that."

"I'm not meeting your father until nine-thirty at the Yard."

"Dear old Dad." She rolled her eyes and smiled. "Had to bring that up, huh?"

"This is going to be rather awkward, isn't it?" he asked.

"Oh yeah," Rachel said as she climbed back onto the bed.

As Rachel approached the house in Maida Vale, she considered climbing up the trellis to her second-floor bedroom. More than once in secondary school Rachel had done just that when she had stayed out past curfew—until the time she found her mother waiting by the bed. She moved on to a method suggested by her best friend Matilda (Mattie for short). Rachel would dial home and as soon as one of her parents answered, she'd say "Don't worry, I've got it—you can hang up"— pretending like she was actually in the house on a different extension. It had initially worked with her father, but when she tried it again, her mother had just remained on the line.

"I suppose you find this amusing, Rachel Michele Grant," Allison had said. "Your father and I are here waiting for you."

Mattie's Folly, as Rachel came to think of it, resulted in her being put under Grant House Arrest—no telly or socializing for the better part of a month. Sometimes Rachel thought her father might have only been the second-best detective to reside under the roof of the small Maida Vale house sandwiched among the posher ones on the Grand Union Canal.

Rachel reconsidered the trellis as she walked down the street. Less nimble and daring than in her adolescent years, she abandoned the thought when she saw it. It looked rather rickety, and Rachel suspected dry rot had set in; further proof that her father wasn't the same since her mother had passed away. Allison never would have let it get to that point.

She headed up the stone walk and through a barren garden (another sign of Austin's increasing neglect) and pulled out the key he'd given her the day before.

Before she could place it in the lock, the door was thrown open from inside.

"For a moment, I thought I was going to be denied the pleasure of your company." Everett stood there with a beaming smile.

Rachel grinned and gave her uncle a giant hug.

As they broke apart, Rachel's eyes welled up with all the emotions that had been bubbling under the surface the past few days: sadness, frustration, and a melting heart all rolled into one big mess.

"What's wrong, sweetheart?" Everett asked as Rachel wiped her eyes.

"Everything. Nothing." She hugged him again. "I'm just really happy to see you."

Rachel had always treasured the relationship with her father's brother. She could talk to him about things she had difficulty bringing up to either of her parents. Everett knew about her struggles with hard science and he'd patiently helped her study until she passed with flying colors. She had told him about Teddy Chapman, the first boy who'd ever tried to kiss her, and he had sworn not to tell his brother, knowing her father might court-martial the lad. (She'd lost track of Teddy over the years—the last she heard he'd been living with a lovely chap named Ralph in Bath, much to her amusement and chagrin.)

Even during the estrangement with her father, Rachel had remained in close contact with her uncle. On more than one occasion, Everett had urged her to make peace with his brother—but also knew better than to push the issue.

Now, he ushered Rachel inside the tiny foyer and hung up her coat.

"You and your father have had quite the few days."

"Tell me about it," Rachel said. "I'd no idea you were coming here today."

"Austin called me shortly after you left to go see Mattie last night."

Rachel breathed a sigh of relief, realizing her father had bought the story she'd pulled out of thin air the previous evening.

"He told me the news about Sergeant Hawley," Everett continued. "Such a tragedy. This entire mess seems to be spinning out of control."

"I can't imagine how it could get much worse."

"Well, numbers eight, nine, and ten for starters."

"Heaven forbid."

"Your father wanted me to know about the sergeant before I saw it on the news. I said I'd come right over, but he told me he really wanted to be alone."

"He said the same to me. It's why I ended up going off to see Mattie."

Everett nodded. "So, I insisted on the three of us having breakfast instead."

"I'm so glad you did."

"What else is family for but to be there in times of need?"

It was Rachel's turn to nod. "Hawley was like the son Dad never had. I don't think I've ever seen him like this—even after Mom died. It's different; that was pure grief. But this . . ." She hesitated, fumbling for exactly how to put it. "This is something else entirely," she said, finishing the thought.

Everett was quiet for a moment. "Anger?" he finally suggested.

"Yes. I think that's it exactly," agreed Rachel. "I've just never seen it before."

"Probably a long time coming," said Everett. "At least since your mum died."

Rachel felt the tears coming again. She linked her arm through Everett's and they moved forward. "Did I tell you how happy I am to see you?"

"Yes, but I will never tire of hearing it." He smiled and motioned toward the rear of the house. "Let's see if we can cheer up the old man and keep him from burning down the house."

"Oh God." She managed a laugh. "He's cooking?"

"Attempting."

They took a couple of more steps. Then Everett stopped. "You do know that I'm very friendly with Mattie's family."

"I know you and her father teach together on occasion."

"And that the whole family heads to Saint Moritz to ski each Christmas."

Crap. So much for pulling stories out of thin air.

"You didn't tell Dad, did you?"

Everett gave her a big grin. "Your secret—whatever it might be—is safe with me, darling."

Rachel was glad to see some things hadn't changed.

But as they resumed heading toward the kitchen, she knew she wasn't ready to tell Everett about Detective John Frankel.

Not just yet.

"How is Matilda?" asked Grant as he set a plate down in front of Rachel.

"She sends her love." Rachel glanced out the breakfast nook window at the narrow canal to avoid lying directly to her father or catch the gleam she knew had to be in her uncle's eye. When she turned around, Everett was already digging into the eggs Benedict his brother had prepared and served them.

"Delicious as always," Everett said. "The one good thing you know how to make."

"The only dish I'd dare serve."

"Reminds me of our childhood. Have I mentioned that before?"

"Only every time I make it," Grant responded.

Rachel had often heard the story of her grandfather cooking up eggs Benedict for his wife and two boys every Sunday morning before they headed to church back in Liverpool. He had substituted buttered toast and real bacon for English muffins and ham, claiming that was how retired stockbroker Lemuel Benedict had ordered it in the late nineteenth century when he stumbled into the Waldorf in New York City seeking a hangover cure. Her father had continued the tradition when he'd married Allison. Sunday was the one day he didn't leave for the Yard at the crack of dawn—he was happy to give Rachel's mother a morning off. But Rachel always suspected her father just loved the dish and he knew he'd get it at least once a week this way.

"I fancy it wasn't easy getting a flight this time of year?" Everett asked as he scraped his plate clean.

"It's more common for Brits to flee for warmer climates or the ski lifts instead of staying put when the holidays roll around," observed Grant.

Rachel wondered if her father was calling out her Mattie fib. She looked at her uncle and sure enough, there was that gleam in his eye.

"But we were lucky just the same," her father continued.

Rachel felt her body relax. Safe. At least for now.

"I'm glad you're both home for Christmas, though I'm sure we all wish it were under different circumstances," said Everett.

"Agreed," Grant concurred.

"If you'd care to come to the house for Christmas Eve dinner tomorrow night, it would be my joy to host you both."

Rachel looked directly at her father for the first time. Grant took a final bite, then motioned with his fork. "Whatever Rachel wants."

"That sounds wonderful," she said. "Of course, it totally depends on what's going on with . . . everything."

She wasn't even thinking of John at that moment. Like Everett had said, the case was spinning in so many different directions.

The continued search for Prior Silver. Canvassing the streets of Esher and other nearby villages for possible witnesses. Jeffries performing autopsies on Liz Dozier, Jared Fleming, and the unfortunate Sergeant Stanford Hawley.

Not to mention a potential eighth victim arriving just in time for Christmas.

"Can't imagine him missing an opportunity to make a splash on the holiest day of the year," Grant said, discussing the case.

"Don't forget that the Ten Commandments are from the Old Testament," reminded Everett. "The celebration of Christ's birth stems from the New."

"I'm not sure Prior Silver, if it's indeed him, is playing things that close to the Good Book any longer," Grant countered. "The rules seem to have changed."

"You're talking about Sergeant Hawley, I presume?"

Grant nodded at his brother.

"From what you told me last night, Austin, that sounds more like bad timing."

"I'm just thankful Stan's father is dead and buried all these years. At least that was one call I didn't have to make."

All went quiet in the breakfast nook.

Rachel felt a tug at her heart as she realized how much this was tearing her father apart. She finally broke the silence with a thought she'd had ever since breakfast with him at the Surrey.

"Whoever is doing this—it would've been nice if they'd let you retire in peace."

"But that's exactly the point, isn't it?" wondered Everett. "From what you've said, this whole thing seems directly pointed at you."

"Certainly appears that way," agreed Grant.

"So, what's next?" Everett asked. "Besides the obvious manhunt you've got going for the elusive Mr. Silver?"

"We search for an unlucky thief," answered his brother.

Rachel quoted the Eighth Commandment: "*Thou shalt not steal.*"

"Precisely," said Grant.

"A born-again former thief killing another thief," mused Everett. "There's some sort of intriguing paradox in there somewhere."

"Maybe Silver will just carve a Roman numeral eight on his own head, kill himself, and we can have ourselves a happy Christmas," Rachel said.

Everett looked from his niece to his brother. "I think our Rachel might be spending a little too much time around you, Austin."

⸺⸺

An hour later, Rachel was glad she'd accompanied her father to New Scotland Yard. It was the first time that Grant had been there since Sergeant Hawley's body was discovered. Rachel hoped her presence made it a little easier for him to accept the enormous outpouring of sympathy and condolences foisted upon him.

Rachel hadn't been to the Yard since her mother had taken ill but wasn't surprised to see her father's office looked exactly the same as on her last visit. Upon further examination, however, Rachel noticed the place appeared more lived-in—and not in a good way. The carpet seemed a bit more worn, the books laden with dust, the slipcover on the couch frayed. It felt like a room where someone was biding time—all that was missing was a wall with chalk marks, counting the days until Grant no longer needed to come to the Yard.

There were only eight more until the end of the year.

She remembered how her mother used to stop by at least once a month under the guise of accompanying her husband to a restaurant they favored, but she'd always gotten there an hour early to tidy up the place, usually arriving with a houseplant in hand.

No foliage was in sight and Rachel could guarantee her father would only let the Yard cleaning crew do the absolute minimum—finding it too painful to be reminded of Allison's personal touch.

Walking together in Hawley's smaller adjacent office was no easy task either. Yellow tape stretched across the doorway, ordered by Grant the previous morning after receiving reports of "nothing of interest" from his colleagues conducting a search for anything that might shed light on the sergeant's tragic end in Esher.

Grant told Rachel he thought it a good idea if she sifted through Hawley's computer and scribbles—figuring the two of them had spent the last few days together trying to narrow the suspects that produced Prior Silver.

"As the two of you were compiling lists of my old cases, now with Sergeant Hawley gone . . ."

Her father stopped midsentence. Rachel placed a soothing hand on his shoulder. "I'll give it my best effort, Dad. I can't promise I'll recognize anything if I see it, but it's certainly worth trying."

"Thank you." He reached over and patted her hand still resting there.

She motioned him back toward his office. "Go do whatever you need to do. I'm sure there's plenty for both you and John when he gets here."

Grant nodded and moved off. Rachel winced, realizing she'd just called Frankel by his given name. But her father hadn't reacted and she was appeased by the fact the two cops had been using each other's first names since the day they met.

No harm, no foul, thought Rachel, using one of her favorite NBA expressions.

She lifted the tape and entered Hawley's office.

A little while later, John ducked his head inside the door. Rachel looked at the clock on the desk—it was past ten. "You're just getting here?"

"Your father called and said he was running late. Something about breakfast with you and your uncle?"

Rachel quickly told him what had occurred when she'd returned to Maida Vale. John looked at the wall behind her. They both knew her father was working away on the other side of it.

"So?"

"So?" Rachel asked, genuinely confused. "You mean there at the house 'so' or here at the office 'so'?"

Her eyes strayed to Hawley's computer and paperwork.

"Oh, sorry." John smiled, apologetic. "This really isn't going to be easy, is it?"

"Probably not."

"Oh."

She sensed the sudden disappointment in his voice. "John . . ."

"Huh?"

"I didn't mean it like that. I don't regret anything that happened."

"That's a good thing, right?"

"Yes, John. That's a really good thing."

She could literally see the tension drop out of his ruggedly handsome face. "Yes. Definitely."

Rachel smiled. "At least we got that straight."

John nodded. He started to exit the small office and Rachel turned back to the computer. She punched some buttons on the keyboard.

"So?"

She looked back up. John had reentered the room.

"So?" she wondered.

He pointed at the desk and computer. "Anything?"

"I'm just getting started. I'll let you know when I find something." She motioned behind her. "Now go see my father before he wonders what the hell is going on in here."

This time, John took his leave and Rachel resumed working.

An hour later, she heard a ding and looked around for her phone.

A few minutes later she walked into the office next door.

She found her dad and John hovered over printouts—various lists compiled by the Yard, other agencies, and the ones she'd worked up with Hawley.

John was the first to catch her eye.

"You found something?" he asked.

"Not exactly," replied Rachel.

She placed her iPhone on her father's desk.

"What am I looking at?" asked Grant.

"The text I just got," Rachel responded.

The two men read it together.

How come I haven't heard from you since yesterday?

"It's a continuation of the chat I was having with Sergeant Hawley."

Her father looked up, incredulous. "That's ridiculous."

"One would think," concurred Rachel. "But it was sent to me less than three minutes ago."

21

Frankel took a step forward and picked up Rachel's iPhone off Grant's desk.

"I'm willing to bet this isn't the sergeant's ghost," he said.

"It's *him*," Grant expressed with certainty.

Neither Rachel nor Frankel disagreed.

With Hawley's phone not found on his body or elsewhere in the mansion, they assumed it was in the possession of the person they were hunting.

Frankel scrolled up the phone screen to look at the previous text messages from the sergeant.

Checking something on my end. Will let you know if it amounts to anything.

It had been sent to Rachel the night before last—around seven. Right before Hawley made an unfortunate stop in Esher on his way home.

Rachel took the phone back from Frankel.

"Hawley had just sent a pair of constables to Primrose Hill to check on Dozier's house, but they didn't find anything. I just wish I'd pressed him more on what he was thinking."

"You can't blame yourself," said Frankel. "We were too busy figuring out how to get over here as quickly as possible."

"Not quickly enough," said Grant.

Frankel felt the same regret, and he knew Rachel did as well. She asked the question at the forefront of all their minds.

"So, do we answer him?"

Frankel looked to Grant. Now that they were on the Scotland Yard man's turf, he knew the commander should be leading the show—but Frankel couldn't help his take-charge instinct.

"Anyone around here that can run a trace?" he asked.

Grant pressed the intercom button on his phone. "Get Mr. Morrow, please; come here right away," he said into the speaker.

They had tried running a trace on Hawley's iPhone when they'd realized it was missing at the crime scene, but there had been no signal coming from it—meaning either it had been turned off or the battery had run down.

Less than a minute later, a harried tech in his late twenties with close-cropped hair poked his head into Grant's office. "Sir?"

Grant brought the man up to speed. Now that the iPhone was apparently back on—he asked Morrow what the chances were of being able to run a trace.

"If the Find My iPhone function has been activated, it should be a matter of seconds," answered Morrow. "I can do it from my phone right here if you want."

Grant told the tech to proceed.

As Morrow fished his own cellular out of his pocket, Frankel shook his head. "Our guy is too savvy for that."

Morrow punched a few buttons and confirmed Frankel's guess. "Looks like whoever has the phone has the function button turned off."

"What else can you do?" asked Grant.

"Well, now that it's up and running, we can run a normal trace. Pinging off cellular towers and so forth," the tech responded.

"How long will it take?"

"Depends where the phone is. If it's in London proper, it would be easier to locate; more cell towers. In the suburbs or more rural areas, longer."

"Hop to it then," Grant ordered.

Morrow started to walk out of the office, then turned back. "Sir, I should mention this is providing the phone is kept on. If it's powered down, then all bets are off."

"I understand," Grant told him. "Thank you, Mr. Morrow."

The tech took his leave and they were back to staring at each other—and the iPhone on the desk.

"We could do nothing and hope he keeps it on long enough for the trace to kick in," Frankel said. "But he could get frustrated not hearing back and decide to turn it off—then we'd be screwed."

Grant looked thoughtful, as if considering options.

Finally, he extended his hand to Rachel. "Let me have that blasted thing."

She handed her father the cell phone. Frankel and Rachel watched him open the text icon and type one word into the conversation line.

Prior?

Frankel raised an eyebrow. "That certainly puts the ball in his court."

They stared at the phone like parents waiting for a toddler to utter its first words. Though the wait seemed interminable, a response was almost immediate.

Well, it's definitely not Sergeant Hawley.

"Looks like we're in business," said Frankel. "Now we just need to keep him on the horn."

Grant nodded, then typed some more. *It's been a long time, Prior.*

Grant hit "send," then glanced up at the detective.

"Figure it doesn't hurt to engage him personally," said Grant, explaining his decision to address Silver by his given name. "Plays to his ego a touch and might continue to keep him distracted while Morrow keeps at it."

"Or it might frighten him off," Rachel suggested.

Frankel felt himself holding his breath this time as Grant's message hung at the bottom of the text chat like an aerialist dangling on a tightrope with no net.

Fifteen seconds went by with absolutely nothing.

"Damn it," Frankel muttered, certain Grant had overplayed his hand and that Prior Silver had ditched the chat.

"There." Rachel pointed at the screen. "He's typing something."

An ellipsis had appeared, indicating a return message was in the works.

Ah, is that you Commander?

"Bingo," Frankel exclaimed.

Grant started to type again. *Yes . . .*

Then he seemed to think better of it and deleted his affirmative response.

"Enough with formalities," Grant said. "Time to engage this asshole."

Frankel's eyes widened. It was the first time he'd heard Grant swear since they had met in Saint Patrick's Cathedral a week ago.

"Go for it," encouraged Frankel.

Grant waited a few seconds, then resumed typing his message.

Isn't it time you stopped all this nonsense, Prior?

This time the response was practically immediate.

I would hardly call it nonsense.

Frankel couldn't help smiling. "*That* got his attention."

"So it would seem." Grant's fingers hovered over the phone screen.

"Is that a good or bad thing?" wondered Rachel.

"Whichever one, it's keeping him on the hook," said Frankel.

Grant moved his fingers again.

A poor choice of words.

Another response shot right back.

To say the least.

My apologies, Grant quickly wrote—and sent.

"Good idea," Frankel told him. "Placing him in the superior position."

Haven't you punished enough people for their sins?

This elicited another quick answer.

You don't believe in what I'm doing, Commander.

Frankel and Rachel continued to be spellbound by the chat between the killer and the Scotland Yard Commander, which continued as fast they could both type.

I'm not talking about me, Prior. We're discussing you.

Now you're humoring me.

That doesn't mean you can't stop.

But I'm not finished yet.

Frankel could have sworn a chill had just swept through the room. But he knew it was just an icy threat put before them in the black and white of a text from a dead man's phone.

Grant's response was to hit the intercom button and then redial. "How's that trace coming, Mr. Morrow?"

The tech's voice came back over the phone. "Looks like it's emanating from the East End. We have it triangulated between three towers but it's a lot of ground to cover."

"Keep at it," Grant told him, then returned to his daughter's phone. When he resumed typing, Frankel could feel the fury flying off the man's fingers.

Did you kill Hawley because of me?

The sergeant was a little too smart for his own good.

Meaning?

I didn't anticipate someone getting there that quickly. You taught him well.

Frankel and Rachel watched Grant's fingers hover over the iPhone. But before he could continue typing, another message appeared.

You might like to know I got Fleming to confess to killing his partner on the Thames. I told Hawley that right before I slit his throat.

All three of them visibly reacted. Particularly Grant. He angrily typed a response and sent it.

So this really is all about me.

With no taking it back, they all waited for an answer.

Of course.

Because I put you in prison twenty years ago? You deserved it.

There was a long pause. Frankel wondered if by lashing out Grant had scared the killer away. But then the ellipsis started back up.

I'm not going to debate that. Or stick around long enough for you to trace this further.

"Damn it!" Frankel exclaimed.

You'll hear from me right after the holiday. Happy Xmas!

"What is that supposed to mean?" asked Rachel.

"Nothing good, that's for sure," answered Frankel.

Meanwhile, Grant had continued to type in the message box.

Prior? Still there?

"Bloody hell!" Grant cried out.

Prior!?

He only stopped when the intercom on his phone buzzed.

"We lost him," said Morrow over the speaker. "He's switched off the iPhone."

"How close were you able to get?" asked Grant.

"Maybe a ten-block radius in the East End. But that's thousands of people."

"Put together what you've got and we'll go over it in a few moments."

"I'm sorry, sir," Morrow said.

"You did your best, Mr. Morrow. Thank you." Grant clicked off.

"Isn't the East End where Prior Silver lives?" asked Rachel.

"Yes, but with men all over his flat, I suspect he's not going back there," replied Grant.

"That might not stop him from hiding in his own neighborhood," said Frankel.

"We'll definitely bolster up our surveillance of the area," agreed Grant.

"Would it be helpful for me to continue looking through Sergeant Hawley's computer and notebooks?" asked Rachel.

"It couldn't hurt." Grant turned toward Frankel. "And we should get you situated somewhere to work out of."

"Anywhere with a phone, desk, and computer will do," the detective responded.

"We can manage that. Then we'll have to bring Stebbins up to date and figure out a plan."

Frankel realized Grant might only have a week left in his command, but he was by no means shirking his duty. If anything, a steel-like determination had settled in on the Scotland Yard man since returning to Mother England.

It only took a few minutes for Grant to locate a proper office for Frankel to operate from.

Frankel felt a bit guilty upon entering it. The room was three times the size of the cubby hole they'd given Grant at the precinct. It afforded a view of the Thames below, courtesy of the building being on the Victoria Embankment.

"Hope this will suffice," Grant said.

"It's great. Thank you, Austin."

Frankel motioned back toward the commander's office.

"You did well keeping him going as long as you did."

"I could've handled it better. I sort of lost my temper there."

"It could have gone a whole lot worse."

"I suppose," said Grant, who didn't seem to believe it.

"At least we know who we're dealing with now."

"It appears so." Grant remained in the doorway, glancing around. He seemed to be mulling something over in his head.

"I notice that you're not wearing your wedding ring."

Frankel was so shocked that he went a bit weak in the knees. And quickly tried to fashion some sort of explanation. "I ended up leaving it back home in Manhattan. Figured it was long overdue."

Grant nodded.

Frankel inwardly sighed with relief, thinking that might have been it. Then Grant spoke again.

"Tread carefully, Detective. If she gets hurt, there will be hell to pay."

Before he could respond, Grant turned and left the room.

That was when John Frankel realized Prior Silver wasn't the only person in London whom the Scotland Yard Commander was on to.

22

The phone conversation hadn't gone quite the way Prior Silver had expected.

Somehow, he'd lost control of the situation and had to struggle to get it back on track. He had decided it was best to cut the exchange short and vowed to be better prepared the next time. There was definitely going to be a next time.

Prior kneaded the wooden cross between his hands like rosary beads while stealing an occasional glance at the Bible that was never too far from his heart.

He glanced over the railing at Marble Arch, the white stone monument on the northeast corner of Hyde Park.

"The triumphal arch was designed in 1827 by John Nash to be the state entrance to Buckingham Palace" came a voice through the tiny speaker by Prior's knee. His eyes drifted from Nash's masterpiece to the upper level of the London red bus he was riding on. There were less than a half-dozen passengers up top with him, as most tourists chose to stay below this time of year, watching London's famous sites move past huge windows that also provided protection on such a cold wintry day.

But Prior found the fresh air invigorating, bolstering his spirit and encouraging him to forge ahead with his plans.

He got off in Marylebone, bringing his collar up to obstruct a full view of his face and slinging his cap a little further down over his eyes.

Not that anyone was paying attention to him—they were too busy checking out Madame Tussauds, the famous house of wax, across the street.

Prior ducked inside Saint Cyprian's Church near the southwest corner of Regent Park. Being a Monday morning, it was fairly empty. But the clergy and altar boys were busy preparing the sanctuary for Christmas Eve mass the following night. He walked down the center aisle, glancing up at the white-gold trellis, a crucifixion statue, and the ten magnificent panels of stained glass hanging above the altar. He did the sign of the cross, then moved toward the confessional.

Soon, he was waiting inside, still holding the small wooden cross.

A couple of minutes passed and beads of sweat began to dot his brow. He contemplated taking his leave and was just rising when the panel on the confessional slid open, revealing the shadow of the on-duty priest.

The clergyman began with a prayer. Prior knew it and mumbled along. He thought the priest seemed young but it could've just been the high tone of his voice. The prayer concluded, and the priest continued the ritual.

"Now, let us bring into light anything for which you want to ask God's mercy."

Prior made the sign of the cross again, then recited the string of words he'd uttered more than any in recent years. "Forgive me, Father, for I have sinned."

"How long has it been since your last confession?" asked the priest.

"Just over a week," Prior answered.

It had been back in New York City, on the day that he'd arrived. Prior had meant to return to confession sooner, but so much had happened. As a result, he had a lot to get off his chest with the man from Saint Cyprian's.

When Prior finished, he wondered if the shadowed figure on the other side of the scrim would refuse to absolve him.

But there was only a slight pause before he heard the familiar words.

"You may go in peace, my son—all your sins have been forgiven."

It's nice to know there are some things you can count on never changing.

He had just begun to stand up when the priest cleared his throat. "Forgive me for asking, but have you been to confession before at Saint Cyprian's?"

Prior was taken aback by the question. Maybe he had laid so much on the young priest that he had caused some sort of suspicion.

"No, Father," Prior finally answered. "They're renovating my parish, so I've been going wherever and whenever I can elsewhere."

The truth was that Saint Anne's in Limehouse, only a few blocks from his Stepney flat, was totally open for business. But with constables watching his place and the surrounding neighborhood, Prior thought it best not to take the risk.

"You should know that Saint Cyprian's welcomes one and all."

Prior suppressed a sigh of relief. "Thank you, Father."

"Go in peace, my son."

Double the blessing, thought Prior. *I'll take it.*

Not long after, he ducked into the Marylebone tube station and stopped at a coffee cart for a double espresso. He downed it in a few sips, immediately feeling the caffeine rush that he desperately needed to keep himself going.

The question was where?

He wasn't sure but thought he might start by taking the District Line west. Staying away from the East End seemed like a good idea for now. Somewhere near Wimbledon possibly.

He was just about to head through the turnstile when he caught sight of the television screen above a small newsstand.

Prior's very own face was staring back at him.

It was in the upper right corner of the screen, one of the inmate photos from back at Hatfield.

The blond news anchor sat front and center reading copy behind her desk. The sound was muted but Prior didn't need (or dare) to ask them to turn it up.

He pretty much got the gist from the huge red-and-white chyron on the bottom third of the screen.

SUSPECT IN COMMANDMENT KILLINGS

Prior took a couple steps backward and stood behind a column.

How could this be happening?

He peeked around the column to risk one more look.

This time, his image was filling up the whole screen.

Prior ducked back. Then he lowered his head and pulled his cap down as far as it could go and made for the exit.

He had been right earlier. There was definitely going to be another conversation.

Even sooner than he thought.

23

"I'm afraid he's on to us."

At first, Rachel had no idea what John was talking about.

Wasn't it the other way around? That they were on to Prior Silver?

She said as much to John. That was when he told her about his brief but pointed conversation with her father.

"And you're just telling me this now?"

"Well, this way I figured you couldn't run off somewhere and we'd have to talk about it."

She looked out the glass window and down at nighttime London spread out hundreds of feet below. City lights flickered as they floated up in a glass-enclosed bubble car on the London Eye Ferris wheel.

"Oh, I see. You thought, I'll take her to highest point in London, drop this little bombshell and go—'oh, sorry, hold on to your seat—down we go!' "

"It's a Ferris wheel, not a roller coaster. It doesn't plummet," he informed her. "It just sort of floats down."

"I know what a Ferris wheel does," she said, trying to avoid a smile.

There was something quite charming in the matter-of-fact way he went about things that she couldn't help falling for—even delivering not-so-great news.

"Besides, it's not like we had a lot of time to ourselves today," he added.

She had spent the better part of it going through Sergeant Hawley's computer and desk with the utmost thoroughness but had come up with nothing to help get a further line on Prior Silver.

She did find a small notepad filled with the doodles Hawley must have squiggled during phone interviews. What gave her a moment's pause were the lopsided stars and curlicues he'd scrawled around the word *Esher*, followed by question marks. Rachel imagined the idea fomenting in Hawley's brain that had resulted in his tragic side trip on the way home.

In the meantime, John and her father had brought Commissioner Stebbins up to date. The three of them repeatedly went over the chat transcript between Grant and (presumably) Prior Silver that had alternated between Rachel's cell and the dead Hawley's phone—looking for any clue to Silver's whereabouts.

This yielded the same results as Rachel's search—absolutely nothing.

A lengthy discussion between the three men ensued again as whether or not to release Prior Silver's name to the public. This time Frankel and her father convinced Stebbins it was a good idea, stressing it would make it more difficult for the born-again mechanic to hide. The clincher was getting the deputy commander to imagine what might occur should Silver kill again before such a statement was released. The Yard would be excoriated by reporters like Monte Ferguson and a terrified public for holding on to information that might have prevented it.

As a result, the media outlets were given Silver's name and a photo from his time up at Hatfield prison. Over the next few hours, Rachel watched in amazement as Silver's face and vitals blanketed the UK and beyond.

Almost immediately, the Yard was besieged with calls from people who thought they'd spotted Silver, had a run-in with the man, or barely escaped for their lives when he came after them with a piano wire. One woman claimed to have had a lovely five-course meal with him at Claridge's, then headed upstairs for a matinee.

Naturally, all of these turned out to be blatantly untrue.

"Some people just want their names in the paper," said Grant.

As the sun set over an increasingly fretful London, Grant had urged the two of them to head home.

"We have plenty of people here well-equipped to deal with these calls and even more on the streets looking for Silver."

Rachel had suggested her father call it a day as well, but Grant said he needed time preparing for Hawley's funeral the next day. There were calls to be made, arrangements to finalize—not to mention the eulogy Grant was delivering.

"I've never taken a shine to public speaking," he had told John; something Rachel was well aware of. "But it's the least I can do for poor Stanford."

"Is there anything I can do to help, Dad?"

"I think this is something I have to do myself," he'd replied, waving a pen over a notepad with more crossed-out words than not. "You two enjoy your evening."

Now, looking back, Rachel thought what she'd taken to be a polite good night might have been a not-so-subtle "I-know-what-you-two-are-up-to" shout-out.

If so, she had totally missed it and told John this on the Eye.

"I don't think so," he said. "He was pretty direct with me about it."

The glass enclosed car continued to rise toward the top of the Ferris wheel.

"And he figured that you'd end up telling me."

"I took it as him giving me fair warning. But it did cross my mind that I was glad the cops over here don't carry loaded guns."

John grinned. Rachel couldn't help laughing.

"Lucky for you."

The two of them had left the Yard and discussed getting a bite. Stepping out of the building onto the Victoria Embankment, their eyes took in the London Eye and all its multicolored flickering neon glory across the Thames.

"That wasn't here when I came with my college buddies," John said. "They might have been building it, but we were on an endless pub crawl."

"It went up back when I was in secondary school," Rachel had said.

"Ever been on it?"

Rachel shook her head. "I never could get my father to take me."

"Party pooper."

"He's afraid of heights, actually." Rachel had noticed him raise an eyebrow. "Don't tell him I told you."

"You can totally count on that." He pointed again at the Eye. "You could have gone with someone else."

"I never got around to it. It's one of those things you never end up doing because it's a tourist attraction in the city where you live."

"So, what are we waiting for?"

"Seriously?"

"Well, there was this Jack the Ripper walking tour through White-chapel I read about on the plane—but given how we've been occupying our days, this seems like a much better idea."

Her mind drifted back to the view from his car on the New Jersey ridge.

"I guess you showed me yours the other morning. Since we're here, I might as well show you mine."

"I really like that proposition."

She'd given him a playful shove.

"I was talking about the view, you idiot."

"I knew that."

There was that smile again.

A few minutes later they had walked across the Westminster Bridge and bought tickets. It wasn't very crowded, which Rachel chalked up to the cold evening (it was supposed to snow), last minute Christmas shopping, and the fact that the attraction was shutting down in less than an hour.

Now, having just reached the top of the arc, Rachel shifted around the tight compartment to look him directly in the eye.

"My father isn't an ogre, John."

"You're not the guy taking his daughter away from him."

Her eyes brightened. "Is that what you're doing, Detective?"

"Let's just say I'm on the case."

He gently took her hand and she made sure not to let it go.

As the wheel began to swing them slowly back down, they sat in silence and looked out at the magnificent city. It gave the view from John's ridge a run for its money. With all the London sights lit up and decorated in their holiday finery—Big Ben, Westminster Abbey, the Tower Bridge—it was truly something to behold.

"Wow," John finally uttered.

The first flurries of snow had begun to fall outside the bubble car.

"Ditto," echoed Rachel.

A few moments later, they had reached the bottom. The wheel operator opened the glass door and motioned for them to step out.

"One more go-round?" John asked.

The operator, a roly-poly-jolly sort, who Rachel thought could easily be loading up a sleigh at the North Pole the next night, gave him a polite grin.

"Wish I could, sir, but as you can see, it's closing time."

He pointed at the embarkment area that was completely empty. John reached into his pocket and produced a badge.

"We're not quite done here," he said, giving a little nod toward Rachel, who was trying to keep a conspiratorial grin off her face.

The operator looked up at the cars on the way down behind them. When he turned back, there was a glimmer in his eye. He grinned and shut the door. "You two have a Merry Christmas."

"You too," said Rachel with her warmest smile.

The operator gave the bubble a slap and sent them back on their way.

Rachel looked at John, who was putting the badge back in his pocket.

"It has to be good for something," he said with a slight smirk. "I'll make sure to take care of him when we get back down."

"I thought those payoffs worked the other way with you American cops."

"Ha ha."

The compartment rocked back and forth as it began another climb.

"I bet you did this all the time back in high school, taking that girl of yours—Shirley . . ."

"Sheila."

"Sheila Whatzhername up to the top, hoping to get lucky."

"Sheila Rice," corrected John with another grin. "And that would be no."

"What? No—didn't get lucky?"

"She didn't like amusement parks," he responded.

"Ha ha."

They turned to look out the bubble window as the snow started to fall a little harder, swirling between them and the starting-to-shrink city below.

"Besides, it was to hell and back to get to Coney Island," John said. "And the one that used to be up the turnpike closed a few years before I was born. Palisades Park. Like the song?"

"Song?"

"My dad sang it all the time when I was growing up, telling me he wished he could've taken me there. It was Freddy 'Boom Boom' Cannon's only hit."

He sang a few lines from a fast-paced rock and roll ditty about a guy meeting an awfully cute girl on the Shoot-the-Chute and the romantic evening that ensued in the amusement park.

Rachel thought his voice was pretty good. She gave John a playful shrug—just enough encouragement for him to carry on.

He reached over and took her hand as he slowed the song to a ballad's pace, and she rocked gently in his arms along with the tiny glass cocoon as it made its way to the apex.

John continued to sing of hot dog stands, dancing to a rocking band, and a cruise through the Tunnel of Love. It all culminated with a ride to the top of a Ferris Wheel where there was no better place for a young man to steal a kiss.

And at the precise moment that John leaned in to do just that, Rachel smiled and finished the chorus.

John stopped inches away from her lips. "You *do* know the song."

"My father made me listen to oldies from the day I was born. It made my mom completely crazy. Of course I know that song."

"Then, why did you pretend . . . ?"

She hushed him by bringing a finger to his lips. "Because I liked hearing you sing to me."

She looked up at the clear roof. The snow was starting to blanket the glassed-in car. Rachel pointed down at the city that was beginning to vanish in what was going to be a white Christmas.

"So, here we are at the top," she whispered. "Are you going to kiss me or not?"

Twenty minutes later, when the operator let them out on the bottom of the Eye, Rachel realized she didn't have to go all the way down to Palisades Park to know that she was falling in love.

It was just past one when she got back to the Maida Vale house.

They had gone from the Eye to one of Rachel's favorite places, the Wolseley in Piccadilly Circus. Housed in what was originally a 1921 prestigious car showroom with marble pillars and archways, it had been converted to a new branch of Barclays bank before its current iteration as a splendid café-restaurant.

They sat at the corner end of the bar and ordered up oysters, omelets, and a couple of hot toddies to cozy up in a world all their own.

Shortly before midnight, they'd walked through Mayfair all the way to Maida Vale to find that London had been transformed into a winter wonderland with the snow on the ground glistening in the reflected holiday lights. The only thing missing was a reformed Ebenezer Scrooge racing down the street with a huge turkey earmarked for Bob Cratchit and Tiny Tim.

When Rachel told John she needed to spend at least one night under her father's roof, he hadn't protested—and it made her like him that much more.

"There will be plenty of time after all this madness is over," he'd told her.

In that moment, she'd been brought back to the harsh reality of what had brought them together in the first place. "Do you think it will be soon?"

"It damn well better be."

And Rachel knew he had come crashing back to murderous Earth as well.

This time when she let herself in the house, it wasn't Everett waiting for her.

"It's nice to see he walked you home."

Her father was sitting by the window in the living room. He had the same notepad in his lap that she'd seen on his desk earlier that day.

"Mom used to wait in the exact same place," she said sitting down beside him.

"Except for the times she waited upstairs for you to come up off the trellis."

"She told you about that, huh?"

"There were very few secrets between me and your mother, Rach."

She felt something pull inside of her and turned away slightly.

"I know that."

"Rachel . . ."

She turned back to look at him. "I think he's a good man, Daddy."

"I know he's a good policeman."

"And I probably should have said something to you."

"You're a grown woman—you don't need to explain everything you do."

"Uh-huh."

She watched as her father struggled with what he wanted to say next.

"But you shouldn't feel like you have to hide things from me either."

Rachel closed her eyes briefly. *Oh, if you only knew.*

When she opened them, she realized she had to say something.

"I'm trying, Dad. I really am." She looked around the house she'd grown up in and, though she'd only been gone a few years, those days seemed a lifetime away. "It's just, things are changing so quickly."

"You can say that again."

She indicated the notepad. "Still working on what you're going to say?"

"It's sort of one big mess."

"Can I look?"

Grant hesitated.

"It's a work in progress, I understand," said Rachel. "Maybe I can make a suggestion or two. I didn't know Sergeant Hawley as well as you, but he was in my life for a long time."

Her father reluctantly handed the pad over. Rachel read through it and realized by the end that she was holding her breath.

"I wouldn't change a word."

"Really?"

"Cross my heart." She just hoped he could deliver it. She knew she couldn't.

She leaned over and gave her father a kiss good night.

"Good night, Daddy."

"Sleep tight, Rach."

She started for the door, then turned back. "Dad?"

"Hmmm . . . ?"

"I totally understand if you think John and I should be slowing things down."

"Not so much slow down, Rachel. It's more like I just want you to be careful." He turned and stared out the window. "I think we all need to be extra so right now."

She knew in that moment he was no longer talking about John Frankel.

And it scared the hell out of her.

24

During his tenure with the New York Police Department, Frankel had attended the funeral of a fallen comrade on more occasions than he cared to recall. When a cop died in the line of duty in one of the five boroughs, all of his colleagues showed up to pay their last respects.

The send-off for Sergeant Stanford Hawley of Scotland Yard was sadly no different. The turnout was simply staggering.

The snow had stopped falling, but the temperatures refused to climb above freezing on a cloudy Christmas Eve. The flakes had stuck to the ground and with a touch of morning glare poking through gray skies, the streets of London glistened just enough to leave the impression someone was watching from above.

In a procession that began at the Palace of Westminster and traveled over two miles until it reached Southwark Cathedral, the streets were lined with mourners, well-wishers, and curiosity seekers.

Frankel had no idea how many women and men composed the Metropolitan Police service (the territorial force that patrolled Greater London), but imagined it must be at least ten thousand and all seemed to be present. Many were in uniform—some accompanying the carriage carrying the sergeant's casket, others marching in orderly fashion, and the rest standing in formation on every corner the procession passed—not to keep peace in the streets but to say goodbye to one of their own.

Rachel, walking beside Frankel, basically read his mind. "We Brits actually take it as a personal affront. These sorts of tragedies are not commonplace here."

Frankel knew the statistics supported her claim. England's abolishment of handguns since the mid-1990s had resulted in fewer officers meeting violent ends.

But those numbers had failed to help Sergeant Hawley.

He had been cut down by going the extra yard when he was actually off duty. Stanford Hawley's biggest fault had been that he was just too damn good a detective.

Something Grant spoke directly to as he delivered the man's eulogy to those fortunate to gain admittance into the Southwark sanctuary.

"I actually realized this the first day I met him," said the commander from the podium on the church's altar. "Not that I let him know this. The last thing I needed was a wet-behind-the-ears constable with a swelled head. For starters, I would have had to send him back to fetch a different-sized hat."

There were lots of chuckles, especially from the first dozen rows where Hawley's everyday colleagues sat, the denizens of the Yard building itself. Frankel realized that with neither of Hawley's parents alive, and no sibling or wife to call his own, on this somber morning these people *were* the sergeant's family.

"We'd just gone over the morning report and I was having a devil of a time seeing it because I'd misplaced my favorite pair of reading glasses. I had searched my office, looked in every nook and cranny. When then-Constable Hawley had inquired as to what I was looking for and I told him, he stared for what probably seemed an eternity to him before asking in a voice barely above a whisper if the spectacles in question were the ones resting on my very own forehead."

Laughter circulated through the church.

"From that moment on, I knew I could always count on Stanford Hawley to get me whatever I needed, whenever I wanted, and—more often than not—before I even realized I didn't have or even desired it."

Grant took a deep breath.

"Until right now."

It got quiet once again in the sanctuary.

"Now, when I need something more than ever—he isn't there to help me."

Frankel glanced at Rachel sitting beside him. Her eyes, brimming with tears, were locked on her father as he continued to speak.

"What I *need* is Sergeant Stanford Hawley and the only thing that I can *find* at this point is that I'm at a complete loss without him."

The tears flowed down Rachel's cheeks; Frankel took her hand and she gave him a grateful nod. He noticed her glance across the aisle to offer a sad smile to a handsome man in his fifties who bore a distinct resemblance to Grant. Frankel realized this must be Everett, the uncle Rachel was so fond of. The two men exchanged warm nods, then turned their attention back to the grieving Grant.

The commander took everyone through the "cut too short" life of Stanford Hawley. He recalled his being raised in the southwest London suburb of Woking, the town where his father had worked as a shoemaker in the same shop as Hawley's grandfather. Grant spoke of young Stanford doing his working-class father (who had raised Hawley as a single dad) proud when he joined the Yard. He talked about taking the constable under his wing and watching Hawley transform into a responsible, upstanding keeper of the law.

"The thing I'm most grateful for is when Stanford was promoted to sergeant a few years ago, his father was there that day. He couldn't have been prouder of the young man Stanford had become—and neither could I."

Grant took the time to clear his throat. Frankel could clearly see the man was doing everything in his power to hold it together.

"Even if Stanford had been my own son."

Which in many ways he became, as Frankel and the other mourners learned when Grant spoke of the death of Hawley's father and the subsequent closeness that had developed between the commander and his trusted sergeant.

"Today we have gathered to honor one of our fallen brethren. Stanford Hawley will surely be missed and remembered. And by no one more so than me as I feel like I have lost one of my very own."

The crowd responded "Amen" in unison. Frankel was surprised when Grant remained behind the podium and turned to the casket beside him.

"One last thing, Sergeant. The man who did this *will* be punished. I promise you this—even if takes me till my dying day. On that you have my word, Stanford."

Grant turned around to face the gathered mourners.

"And so do all of you."

"You didn't mention he was going to end with that," Frankel said as he left the church with Rachel.

"I had no idea," she responded as she threw on her coat to ward off the cold. "It wasn't in the draft he showed me last night."

"Maybe he decided to call an audible," suggested Frankel.

"An audible? Like a Peyton Manning, 'Omaha, Omaha' audible?

Frankel raised an eyebrow.

"I'm the girl who went to New York City to hang at the Garden, remember?"

"You certainly are." He gave her a sheepish grin.

"You've spent enough time with my father to know the man doesn't do anything without thinking it through."

"So, why did he do it?"

"I guess we'll have to ask him," replied Rachel.

Easier said than done. It had gotten very crowded outside the church and they had temporarily lost sight of Grant among all the uniforms, exiting guests, and lookie-loo Londoners who were milling around despite the cold.

"There the two of you are."

Frankel and Rachel turned to see that a Grant had found them—though it was Rachel's uncle Everett. He indicated the crowd with a nod, his hands staying in the pockets of his heavy wool overcoat to try and keep warm.

"I had no idea this was going to turn into such a circus."

"None of us did," Rachel said.

Everett extended a hand toward Frankel.

"I'm sorry to meet you under such terrible circumstances, Detective. I've heard nothing but wonderful things about you from both my niece and my brother."

Frankel's eyes widened. "You're sure we're talking about the commander?"

"He checked in with me on more than one occasion while you two were raising such a ruckus across the pond. Austin told me you were—how did he put it? I think the exact words were 'that more than competent detective fellow.' "

Rachel grinned. "Those *are* high words of praise coming from my father."

Frankel glanced back at the cathedral. "If someone said half the things he had about Sergeant Hawley at my funeral, I might think it was all worth it."

Everett nodded while giving his niece a warm hug. "That *was* quite the eulogy your old dad just delivered."

"It was," she agreed. "But I'm worried about the toll this is taking on him."

"We'll have to gang up on him later at Christmas Eve dinner. That is, presuming you and Austin are still coming?"

"As far as I know," answered Rachel.

"Because I would totally understand if you and Detective Frankel had made other plans."

A flustered Frankel looked from Everett to Rachel, who was starting to blush.

"Plans?" stammered Frankel.

"Uncle Everett—"

The younger Grant brother stopped them with a grin. "I admit my eyesight isn't what it once was, but it's still good enough to peer across a church aisle. I also might not be the brilliant copper my brother or the detective here is—but it was easy enough to connect what I saw to my niece's flimsy Matilda alibi yesterday."

Frankel tried to come up with a response and barely managed a word. "Oh."

Rachel ended up doing him one better. "Dad already figured it out."

Everett looked like a child who just had their balloon burst by the neighborhood bully. "Well, like I said, the man's a brilliant copper."

"Sorry if I ruined your fun," Rachel said.

"It was nice thinking I was ahead of the great Scotland Yard commander for a moment."

"Sounds to me like you're selling yourself a bit short," observed Frankel. "I was told you were the first one to come up with the Commandments angle."

"Let's just say I helped get Austin started. So much has happened since, it's been practically impossible to keep up."

Rachel linked her arm in Everett's and they moved away from the church.

"If it's any consolation, I'm planning on being at your house tonight and I will make sure to get Dad there as well."

"Wonderful!" exclaimed Everett. "But given everything we've just been discussing, I think it only appropriate that Detective Frankel joins us as well."

Frankel shook his head. "I wouldn't want to impose."

"Nonsense," said Rachel. "That's a splendid suggestion. This way I won't have to split Christmas between the three of you."

Everett gave a vigorous nod. "Consider it done."

"What's done?"

The three of them turned to find Rachel's father falling into step beside them. He looked even more harried than moments ago at the podium.

"Everett has invited John to join us for dinner tonight," said Rachel.

"Whatever he wants to do," murmured Grant.

Frankel noticed Grant's eyes moving past them all.

"If you really want to be alone with your daughter and brother, Austin, I totally get it. I wouldn't . . ."

Grant held up a hand in abeyance.

"No, sorry. I didn't mean it to sound like that." He turned back to face Frankel. "I'd be happy for you to join us, John."

Rachel continued to stare at her father. "What's bothering you, Dad?"

Grant motioned toward the church. "The constant thorn in my side."

They followed his gaze to see the crowd thinning to expose Monte Ferguson at the bottom of the cathedral steps, his ever-present notepad in hand.

"Son of a bitch," exclaimed Frankel.

"The second I got to the door, he confronted me about his exclusive."

"Exclusive?" asked Rachel.

"It goes back to a deal we made before the Saint Patrick's murder. I thought I had honored it when we let him run the story that the same person committed the murders here in Britain and the States."

"Exactly," said Frankel.

"Apparently, it's not good enough. He thinks it entitled him to getting Prior Silver's name before anyone else, so he's not happy we released it simultaneously to all the media outlets."

"He's a vulture like all of those tabloid twits." Everett shook his head. "They won't stop until they've finished picking at your grave."

"What he should print is your eulogy for Sergeant Hawley," said Rachel. "Word for word."

"I totally agree," added Frankel. "You did the sergeant proud."

"Especially that last part," added Everett. "That packed quite the punch."

"That was the general idea," said Grant.

"When did you decide to add that?" asked Rachel. "It wasn't there when I read it last . . ."

She broke off at the sound of a shrill bird chirp.

"Rachel? Is something wrong?" asked Everett. "You look like you've just seen a ghost."

"Kind of." She dug into her purse and pulled out her cell phone.

"It's a ringtone on my cell. I assigned it to Sergeant Hawley's number—in case he—whoever—texted me again."

Rachel glanced at the phone screen and literally dropped it into her father's outstretched palm like the hottest of potatoes.

Grant and Frankel stared at the latest message together.

You shouldn't make promises you can't keep, Commander.

"What's going on here?" asked a confused Everett.

Grant quickly filled his brother in on the mysterious cell chats. As he did, the gravity of the situation grew on Frankel.

"He's referencing the end of your eulogy, Austin."

"I'm still at a loss here," said Everett.

Rachel nodded. "I am as well, I'm afraid."

Grant motioned back toward the church. "My eulogy was only heard by the five hundred or so people who just left that building twenty minutes ago. It was meant only for Hawley's close friends and colleagues at the Yard—we didn't allow it to be broadcast anywhere."

Frankel indicated the cathedral. "Which means that either Prior Silver was actually in the church at the time . . ."

Grant finished the thought.

"Or someone he's been talking to was."

25

Rachel watched with fascination as the two cops sprang into action. Their first inclination was to cordon off the area and sequester the attendees, but Grant and John realized it was much too late. The service had concluded a half hour ago and many guests had already left to start celebrating Christmas Eve.

They had a list to work from; there had been a checkpoint set up at the cathedral entrance where names were crossed off as they entered the church. But they rapidly abandoned the idea of interviewing everyone as a potential co-conspirator with Prior Silver.

"If, after the funeral, one did get in touch directly with Silver, they're not going to admit having contacted a mass murderer," Grant pointed out.

Rachel thought her father seemed calmer than just moments before, having even caught a bemused smile. "You don't seem troubled by this turn of events."

"I'm actually encouraged," said Grant.

"How so?" asked Everett.

"The last thing Silver texted was that we'd be hearing from him after the holiday," Grant explained. "And here it's not even Christmas Eve and the man has already broken that promise with a threat."

John nodded. "You've rattled him."

"Exactly," said Grant. "And that is when someone who prides themselves on laying out a precise and orderly plan is liable to make a mistake."

Everett smiled and looked at Rachel. "The Yard is going to miss your father."

"You better believe it." She turned toward Grant. "Does that mean you're just going to chuck the list?"

"Absolutely not. We'll begin to cull our way through it. But the first thing we need to do is check and see if our friend Mr. Silver tried to crash the funeral."

—※—

A couple of hours later, they were fairly sure Silver had been a no-show.

Everett had taken his leave before Rachel and the two cops headed back inside the church. Her uncle said he still hoped to see them around eight but would understand if they needed to cancel dinner due to this latest wrinkle.

Once Everett departed, they'd turned their attention to Southwark's security cameras, of which there were plenty. The thousand-year-old edifice had been well-stocked with surveillance equipment post 9/11 and the rash of bombings in the UK.

They were soon joined by Morrow and his tech team in the church basement where the security system was housed. There were over a dozen cameras situated in the cathedral and close to twice as many outside, so they had their hands full.

They scrolled through the extensive coverage to see if the former mechanic had dropped in on the funeral. Paying special attention to men the same size and shape as Silver (he might have been disguised), they eventually eliminated each angle. John fixated on a mannish-looking matronly-type as a sneaky possibility; but using the close-up camera functions, Rachel said it was just a woman possessing an unfortunate set of genes.

The three of them had returned to the Yard, where they ended up in Grant's office deciding what their next course of action should be.

Going over the funeral guest list was an arduous task that could take days and likely end up a fruitless endeavor. That didn't stop Grant from dividing it between them to see what they could come up with.

"Almost all these people are MPS," Grant pointed out, flipping pages.

"It wouldn't be the first time a cop strayed," said John.

But both men admitted it was hard to imagine a policeman working hand in hand with someone like Prior Silver.

"What about the thief angle?" wondered Rachel.

"Pardon?" asked Grant.

"A possible eighth victim? *Thou shalt not steal*? Any luck with that?"

Grant shook his head. "That list would be ten times as long with countless men and women we have no record of having had committed such a crime."

"And given the loosey-goosey way Silver's been interpreting the Commandments—his definition of 'thief' could be anything," John added. "It could be a teenager swiping a scooter or stealing an answer off a math test."

"I was thinking of the personal angle," Rachel countered.

"How so?" asked her father.

"The last two victims, Dozier and Fleming, were known to you. Maybe Silver's targeting someone you've arrested or gone after before," she suggested.

"It's certainly worth considering."

"Sergeant Hawley and I made a lot of progress going over your old cases. Maybe we should be cross-checking them for thieves."

Both men thought that an excellent idea, as they had none of their own.

By the time Christmas Eve fell a few hours later, the Yard detectives had narrowed that list down to six men and a woman Grant had put in prison for some form of theft; they'd served time and since been released. A different constable was dispatched to contact and maintain surveillance on each until further notice.

Keeping with the personal angle, they went through Prior Silver's files to see if they could find a collaborator in his robbery spree that could be a possible target, but there had been none. They even interviewed a few of Silver's former cell-block mates up at Wakefield and Hatfield, the prisons where he had served time. The interviews yielded nothing useful. None of the inmates recalled Silver having any sort of altercation with an imprisoned thief that he might now have his sights set on. Silver had kept to himself, his nose buried in his little black Bible, steeping himself in an ideology that he apparently twisted to fuel his murderous rampage.

As London shut down in preparation for the holiest of nights, Deputy Commander Stebbins suggested everyone go home for the evening. It was a time to be with loved ones; by replenishing themselves they might return from the holiday with a fresh perspective and pick up something they had missed.

Rachel called Everett and told him to expect all three of them for dinner. When she asked what they could bring, all she heard was gratefulness in her uncle's voice. "Just the three of you. It's the best Christmas present I could ask for."

Rachel said they would see him shortly and hung up. She looked across the desk at her father and John. Their expressions remained glum; if Marley's ghost had stumbled in right then, he would have felt right at home.

Rachel and her father arrived at Everett's and saw that the Oxford don had pulled out all the holiday stops. The house just off the Hamstead High Street was all a-twinkle with elegant strands of blinking white lights and had a hearty ivy and berry wreath affixed to the door.

Everett greeted them with warm hugs, took their coats, and ushered them into the library where John was already ensconced, two sips into an Old Fashioned. Her uncle provided them with companion cocktails after displaying the bottle of eighteen-year-old Macallan John had brought. Her father's nod of approval indicated to Rachel that the detective had gone up in his estimation, and it sweetened the pot when he presented Grant a bottle of his very own.

"It's too damned cold for a chocolate shake," John said.

As they worked their drinks, John indicated the chess board and asked if that's where Grant and Everett had first put together the Commandment connection.

Rachel's uncle nodded. "The one and the same."

"I can't imagine where we'd be right now if you hadn't gone and dusted that Bible off the shelf," said Grant.

"I'd think by the time this maniac Silver had crossed the Atlantic and risen the count to four or five, you would have deduced the pattern," Everett told them.

"I'm not so sure about that," John replied. "I played hooky a lot back in Jersey when I was supposed to be in Sunday school catechism."

"Lucky bastard." Everett grinned and knowingly clinked glasses with Grant.

"What my brother's referring to is that our father used to sit in the car outside the church for the first half hour making sure we didn't slip out a window."

The conversation turned to the case as her father and John filled Everett in on the afternoon's futility once they had all departed Southwark. Sensing their frustration and dark mood returning, Rachel jumped in.

"Enough."

She said it with a smile but enough forcefulness to grab all their attention.

"It's Christmas Eve and we're done with shoptalk. I'm going to enjoy my drink and embrace the holiday spirit with three of my favorite men in the world."

This was met with "hear, hear"s and glass clinks by the aforementioned trio, giving Rachel hope there was still time to salvage a bit of Christmas.

Everett had worked his holiday magic with dinner.

A splendid Christmas goose was the meal's centerpiece, replete with homemade stuffing, cranberry sauce, vegetables, and hefty servings of

Yorkshire pudding. Grant and John finished every bite, as did Rachel, who went back for seconds before the men. They toasted Everett for the perfect feast. He claimed no credit save for choosing the menu from a gourmet shop and sending his housekeeper to pick it up. Mrs. Bishop (a blue-gray-haired septuagenarian, who had been coming twice a week to Everett for years) served it on his best china, but politely declined joining them as she was dining with her own family later on.

Upon hearing this, Everett told Mrs. Bishop that he could handle dessert, coffee, and digestifs, and insisted that the "good woman" depart immediately, but not without a sizeable Christmas bonus and leftovers in hand.

Once the woman had gone home, Everett brought a browned-exactly-right pie in from the kitchen. Rachel was the first to notice the twinkle in her uncle's eye.

"You didn't . . ."

"I just might have," admitted Everett.

He sliced the pie open and a rich black-and-red filling seeped out—along with a delicious, mouth-watering aroma.

"Razzleberry pie!" exclaimed Rachel.

"Excuse me?" asked John.

Grant offered up a bittersweet smile. "It was Allison's specialty, made with blackberries and raspberries. She trotted one out every Christmas."

"It's from this cartoon I watched when I was a little girl," explained Rachel. "*Mr. Magoo's Christmas Carol.* It's what Tiny Tim wanted more than anything—'a jar of razzleberry dressing.' I kept begging Mom for one each year and she'd say I'd get sick eating a whole jar of something so sweet, so she went and made a pie."

Everett doled out pieces for each of them. John took one bite and his face practically erupted into rhapsodic ecstasy. "I can see why," he said.

Grant savored each and every bite. "I haven't had this in, what . . . ?"

"It was two . . . no, three Christmases ago," answered Rachel.

Suddenly, the room went quiet.

It had been the last time her mother had Christmas Eve dinner with them.

Two Christmases before, Allison Grant had just been diagnosed with lung cancer and no one had been in the mood to celebrate. She was gone early the next summer, so when December rolled around, the Grant family was still in serious mourning mode without their matriarch.

Rachel raised a glass. "A toast to Mom. We miss you each and every day."

"Especially this time of year," said Everett.

Grant clinked glasses with his daughter. "Your mother *loved* Christmas."

"I think it was because that was when the two of you met," said Rachel. "Christmas Eve dinner at Grandpa's house in Liverpool."

"Is that so?" asked John.

"Well, there's a little more to the story than that," said Everett. He tossed an impish look at his older brother who practically choked on his razzleberry pie.

"Do we really have to discuss this?" her father asked.

"Oh, I think we most definitely should," Everett said with a hearty chuckle.

"What am I missing here?" wondered John.

Rachel leaned over and lowered her voice in a mock conspiratorial whisper. "My mother came to dinner as Everett's date."

"Really?" John looked across the table from Everett to Grant. "And left with you?"

"No, it wasn't like that." Grant shook his head. "Exactly . . ."

Everett, who clearly was enjoying watching his sibling squirm, laughed.

"We hardly knew each other," Everett explained. "I was halfway through my last year at Oxford where Allison had finished her studies the previous term. She worked in the library; we struck up a conversation and ended up going for tea. A few dinners followed where I'm sure I bored her to tears with my highbrow book quotes, but she agreed to accompany me home to Liverpool for the holidays."

John gave Grant a mischievous grin. "Where she took to you instead."

"Not in the slightest. We hardly spoke at all that night," said Rachel's father. "I was headed back to London to join the Yard and she mentioned during dinner that she had secured employment in a Chelsea bookshop."

"And you told her to give you a call?" suggested John.

"My brother ask out a girl he'd just met?" Everett laughed again. "It was actually our mother who suggested to Allison that she should ring up Austin if she found herself with nothing to do," said Everett.

"You could've knocked me off a chair when she phoned out of the blue a month later and asked if I wanted to meet for a drink after work," recalled Grant.

John nodded. "And the rest as they say was—"

"—my brother's gain, but not quite such a loss for me," Everett finished. "I ended up with the most wonderful sister-in-law imaginable."

Everett took a sip of wine, then continued.

"She never would have lasted a year with the likes of me and then none of us would have had her in our lives all those years." He turned to look at Rachel. "Or the blessing she gave us a shortly after they were married, who I think we'd all agree is the reason we're all gathered together tonight."

Grant and John said they would drink to that. Rachel turned toward her father and felt her eyes begin to brim.

"You're going to make me cry," she told them.

The words were barely out of her mouth when she realized it was too late. The tears were streaming down her face, but she was smiling as well, realizing it was the happiest she'd been in—well, at least three Christmases.

―――

There was a whirring noise coming from down the hall as Everett ushered his three guests out of the dining room. Her uncle motioned for Rachel to enter the library first and she opened the door to find a sight for sore eyes awaiting her.

"Saint Electronick!" she cried out.

The automaton looked shiny and bright, his red suit glistening with newly affixed sparkles and a fluffier white beard; it bowed back and forth in front of Everett's Christmas tree and wood-burning fireplace.

Grant stared in disbelief at the mechanical four-foot gyrating Father Christmas. "I was wondering where he had gotten to."

"I removed it from your basement a few months back and thought the old guy could use a going over. I asked Mrs. Bishop to plug it in before she left. I must say it gave her quite the fright when we did a test run earlier."

"I didn't sleep for a week the first time I saw it," recalled Rachel.

Everett moved over and gently patted it on the head.

Saint Electronick blinked and uttered a boisterous "Bah Humbug!"

Grant stared at it. "He never did that before."

"I made a few modifications."

"Isn't that your voice?" asked John.

Everett bowed in unison with the holiday robot. "Guilty as charged." He patted it on the head again and it let loose a holiday epithet not fit for children.

"Everett . . ." Grant began to scold.

"Hold on to your reindeer, brother," Everett said. "We still have Saint Electronick Classico. You just flip a switch here."

Everett indicated a toggle on the back of the automaton's neck and flipped it. Soon their old friend was back to his familiar "Happy Christmas" and "Ho-ho-ho"s. They soon put him on pause and dug in to the Macallan that John had brought.

Even Rachel, who rarely drank a scotch, had to admit the eighteen-year-old digestif was one of the smoothest things she had ever tasted. She could tell that John was particularly pleased that she enjoyed it.

After that, it was time for the exchange of presents. Though Everett had not mentioned gifts, no one had shown up on Christmas Eve empty-handed.

Rachel had swung by Harrods and braved the holiday rush to get colorful socks and ties for both her father and uncle, something she told John was an old tradition when she was young and insisted on giving them presents. They were just what they had wanted and told her so. Then she handed a small package to John.

"No ties or socks for the detective?" mused Everett.

"I haven't known him long enough to get a fashion sense," said Rachel.

"Not much fashion here, and some might say not that much sense," John responded as he opened the gift.

It was a 45 record single.

"*Palisades Park*?" asked Grant, reading the title over John's shoulder.

"Private joke," Rachel said softly.

The look in John's eyes made her heart swell. "I love it." He gave Rachel a warm peck on the cheek, then produced a tiny package of his own for her.

She opened it and emitted a tiny gasp.

Inside the box were two pearl-white earrings with a beautiful impression of the London Eye Ferris wheel etched in black on them.

"They're simply beautiful."

"Great minds think alike."

Rachel returned John's gentle kiss and was grateful that both her father and uncle had the good sense not to interrupt "The Gift of the Magi" moment.

Grant, who always told Rachel and her mother that he was the "world's worst gift giver," didn't disappoint when he handed Amazon gift certificates to both John and his brother. "I had no idea what to get either of you, so I figured you'd manage to find something you want yourselves."

But he subsequently damaged that self-anointed reputation when he surprised Rachel with a gorgeous pink-and-brown cashmere Burberry scarf.

"It's absolutely lovely, Daddy," she said. Genuinely touched that her father had actually taken the time to step into a store and pick something out specifically for her, Rachel give him a big hug.

"My turn now," said her uncle. Everett crossed over to pick up three presents lying beneath the tree. He handed the first to John. "Detective . . ."

John began to protest. "After dinner and such a wonderful evening . . ."

"Indulge me," encouraged Everett. He nodded at his niece and brother. "They have had to for years."

John opened the gift to reveal a DVD and hardcover book. Both were the same title—*Gone with the Wind.*

"The quintessential American book and film for the quintessential American detective," Everett explained.

"Wow. I don't think I've seen this since I was a kid," said John.

"It's definitely worth watching again. And reading, if you never have."

"I haven't," the detective admitted.

"Something for the plane ride home."

"I will take you up on that," John told him. "It'll mean we'll have run down Prior Silver and I can finally relax."

Everett handed identical wrapped gifts to his niece and brother.

Grant motioned for Rachel to go first.

It was a beautiful silver-leaf picture frame holding a black-and-white photograph—taken on a beach featuring a much younger Everett, Allison, and an infant Rachel. They were burying a sleeping Grant up to his neck in the sand. Whatever he was dreaming about, there was a smile on his face.

"I've never seen this," said Rachel. "I certainly don't remember it."

Her father laughed. "I do. You were maybe three or four years old. We'd all gone down to Brighton for the day and I woke up from a lovely nap to find myself sputtering sand." He tapped Rachel's giggling face staring up from beneath the glass. "You thought it was the funniest thing you'd ever seen."

"It's the only picture I can find of the four of us," explained Everett. "Usually you, me, or Allison were taking a picture of the others with the baby."

Rachel ran her fingers lovingly over the picture frame. "It's totally perfect—especially since everyone looks so happy."

"We were," recalled Grant.

"Then hopefully you'll like yours," said Everett, indicating his unopened gift.

The commander tore off bright Christmas wrapping to reveal a similar frame.

This black-and-white picture was of two young boys—clearly her father and uncle. They were maybe five and seven years old. Both were bundled up in ski clothes and old-style parkas; sheaths of ice glistened behind them.

"Top of the world," muttered Grant.

"You remember," said Everett.

"I'm surprised you do."

"It's one of my earliest memories."

John looked at the decades-old photograph. "Explanations, please?"

"Top of the world. It's what we called the peak of the Matterhorn," Grant told him.

"Our first Christmas away from England," added Everett.

"Dad hauled us up as far as you could go in those days and had us pose in front of the glacier," remembered Grant.

"You can go a whole lot higher now. They've got a cable car track that heads up into the mountain; there's an incredible ice palace carved inside the glacier up there."

Grant nodded at the picture. "I think our folks sent this out as a New Year's card right after it was taken."

"Dad loved it so much that when he finally came into a little money, he bought a small cottage in Zermatt down below," Everett further explained. "He ended up leaving it to the two of us, but I can never get Austin to go there."

"I have this thing about heights," Grant told John.

"Yet I keep telling him the cottage is firmly entrenched on terra firma."

"You still have to get up there," Grant lamented.

Rachel couldn't be certain, but she thought his eyes were misting over.

"But this means a lot; thank you very much," Grant said softly. "And who knows, maybe I'll get over there sooner than later."

"I'm headed there next week. Now that Rachel's back for a bit, it would be lovely to see in the new year together and celebrate your newfound freedom."

"Maybe it's something we can talk about," said Rachel. She turned to her father, who seemed to be lost in thought.

He paused before answering. "I think we'll have to wait and see."

The night went eerily silent.

And Rachel realized that all of them were wondering the same thing.

Was there an eighth victim already out there waiting for them in London somewhere? And for that matter—might there soon be a ninth or tenth?

26

I t was Christmas morning.

If someone had told John Frankel a week ago that he would be spending the holiday in a posh London hotel tracking down a serial killer while falling head over heels in love, he would have arrested that person for public intoxication.

But as he wiped the sleep from his eyes and saw Rachel sitting on a plush sofa gazing out the window, he realized it was a cursed but blessed truth.

He thought about the previous night.

Dinner at Everett's had been joyous and festive, but the evening had taken a somber turn when talk turned to Grant's upcoming retirement. Suddenly the pall of the investigation hung over them and Frankel could feel it when he accompanied the Grants to midnight mass at Saint John-at-Hampstead, Everett's local parish.

Frankel spent more time casting sidelong glances at Rachel than listening to the sermon given by an elderly pastor who looked like he had been interred in the nave decades ago. Frankel could see Rachel was having a difficult time.

He knew this homecoming had been bittersweet for Rachel and her father, and that their relationship had been practically nonexistent since the death of her mother. Sitting in Saint John's on this holy night without Allison must have been so painful, and all Frankel could to do was occasionally take her hand. The tightening of her grip each time pulled at his heartstrings.

That night, upon returning to Covent Garden, the sex had been passionate but also filled with a desperation on Rachel's part that made Frankel only want to protect her even further from the harsh reality they were in.

Now, Frankel quietly climbed out of bed and threw on a robe. He crossed to the window and Rachel shifted slightly, clearly aware of his presence.

"Merry Christmas," he said softly.

Rachel turned. "Merry Christmas," she replied in an even softer voice. He could tell that she had been crying. "Hey. You all right?"

Frankel wanted to kick himself. *Of course she isn't all right.* Some detective.

"It's—you know—the holidays," she answered.

He sat beside her and saw she was holding the silver picture frame Everett had given her with the picture of the once happy family at Brighton ages ago.

It confirmed his suspicions; this trip back to London must have been tiptoeing through an emotional minefield for Rachel.

"Maybe coming back home wasn't such a great idea," he suggested.

She shook her head but managed a smile. "It's actually been so much better than I thought. Dinner last night, the Ferris wheel, being here with you . . ."

She motioned out the window. "We even got ourselves a white Christmas."

Frankel followed her gaze. The streets of Covent Garden were blanketed in white, courtesy of a heavy snowfall in the middle of the night. The city looked dazzling, but in his eyes it didn't hold a candle to Rachel.

"Still, I know it must be hard being here this time of year—any time of year for that matter—without . . ." He broke off and nodded toward the photograph.

"That's for sure."

He reached over and took her hand. "Maybe you'll just tell me it's none of my business, but I know there's this thing between you and your father that's gone on since your mom died. But I also see the way that he looks at you, the way he talks about you, and I know whatever it is, it's tearing him to pieces. And with him retiring, something I'm damn sure he's not ready for, I think he'd be lost without you in his life."

"I think those are the most words I've ever heard anyone say without taking a breath."

"Rachel . . ."

"I'm not avoiding the subject, John. I want him in my life more than anything." She shook her head. "And I don't want you minding your business. I've barely known you a week but for some reason I want you to know everything. Warts and all."

"But . . ."

"But I'm afraid if I tell you everything, you might end up running for the hills and never look back."

"First of all, London is pretty flat and I'd collapse before I even got to a hill. And secondly, I can't imagine anything you might have done that would make me even consider it."

"It's not something I did." She shook her head again. "It's something I *should have* done."

"Just tell me, Rachel."

"John . . ."

"You said it yourself. You want me to know everything, right?"

She gently nodded. "I do—but . . ."

"Just like I want you to know everything about me." He held up her hand and clutched it with his other one. "For this to succeed, it needs to work both ways. And I want this to work—more than anything in my entire life."

The tears fell again down her cheek. Frankel gently wiped them away.

"Me too," she whispered.

"Then get that burden off your chest and load it on me. Whatever it is—please just tell me."

He watched Rachel take the deepest of breaths.

And then listened as she told him.

—

Rachel had been reeling for the entire flight across the Atlantic.

She was still trying to come to grips with the phone call she'd had with her parents the night before.

Cancer.

The six-letter word worse than any expletive known to man.

Her mother had always been the picture of health, so the thought of her incurring that dreaded disease was unthinkable to Rachel. And made it so much worse when she was informed that it was a particularly aggressive form of lung cancer.

Rachel had insisted on coming straight home from New York and naturally her mother had tried to talk her out of it. "It's not necessary for you turn your life upside down, darling. You have work to do and you'll come over for the holidays in a few weeks."

Rachel reminded her mother that she was a freelance journalist, emphasis on the word *free*, and there was no place that she would rather be right now. Especially with her father having run up to Scotland on a case he could have let Sergeant Hawley handle, but her mother had refused to allow any upheaval in their lives.

"I will certainly still be alive and kicking when you get back on the weekend," her mother had told her father while they were all on the phone.

After thirty years of marriage, Grant knew better than to start an argument he could never win. It also helped that Rachel said she would be there by the time he'd returned from Glasgow. She had caught the first flight out of JFK the next morning and landed shortly after dusk.

The moment she arrived at the Maida Vale house, Rachel knew something was distinctly wrong.

The front door was unlatched. If there was one rule her father insisted upon, having seen more atrocities than he cared to recall over the years due to people's carelessness, it was that both doors of the house, front and back, were to remain locked at all times.

The next thing she noticed was the living room in total disarray—a small end table by the couch was leaning awkwardly against the sofa, and there were shards of broken glass on the fireplace hearth. Rachel soon found the culprit—the remnants of a shattered unicorn (she had made it in fifth form) tossed in a nearby small trash bin.

"Mom?" she called out. There was no answer.

Then she heard raking sobs coming from further down the hall.

Rachel moved down the corridor, calling out again. There was no direct response, but she heard a quick intake of breath come from her father's study. She moved through the door to find her mother rising from the desk where she'd been sitting behind a laptop. Allison was wearing a robe and looked completely disheveled, her normally finely coiffed hair all astray, and she was using the robe's sleeve to dry her eyes.

Given the recent news courtesy of her doctors, Rachel wasn't surprised. Even someone as stoic as her mother would have to be inhuman not to be shaken.

"Oh darling—I d-didn't realize you were coming tonight . . ."

"I texted you the flight information before I left," Rachel said as she crossed over and wrapped her arms around her mother.

"I-I never looked. It's been a crazy d-day as you can only imagine," Allison said, looking unsteady on her feet.

Rachel hugged her mother tight. And felt her actually shuddering in her arms. "Oh Mom—I'm so sorry . . ."

She kissed Allison and took her hand.

"Shhh, shhh," hushed her mother. "We'll all get through this."

Leave it to her mother. She's the one who just got diagnosed with stage three lung cancer and I'm letting her comfort me.

Rachel started to respond, then noticed blood on her hand—and that it wasn't her own. "Mom! You're bleeding!"

It was oozing through a bandage on her mother's arm that wasn't sturdy enough to staunch whatever had happened.

Allison shook her head. "It was a silly accident. I broke that unicorn you made in the living room . . ."

"I saw it—by the fireplace." Fraught with concern, Rachel took a closer look at the wound. "We should take you to the emergency room."

"Nonsense—it's just a bad cut."

"It's a huge gash and should be looked at!"

A debate ensued, the sort Rachel never got an upper hand in. It ended with Allison agreeing to let Rachel remove the bandage, clean, and redress the wound.

She helped her mother straighten the living room and then, despite insisting she wasn't hungry, Rachel allowed her mother to heat up some leftovers.

They sat in the kitchen for an hour. Every time Rachel tried to broach the reason she'd raced across the ocean, Allison would steer the subject in a different direction—wanting to know about Rachel's job, if there was anyone new in her life, what they should do for the upcoming holidays now that she was home.

The closest thing to an acknowledgment of the elephant that had taken over every room in the Maida Vale house had been when her mother uttered the same sentiment she'd spoken on the phone. "There will be time to discuss all that later."

Finally, Rachel just tried to convince herself to be content keeping the woman she loved unconditionally company.

But a few hours later, after she'd finally gotten her mother to bed, Rachel was still sitting wide awake in the same kitchen chair. Whether it was the time change, the jet lag, or overriding concern for a rotten diagnosis dumped on her mother by some Harley Street practitioner, Rachel was keyed up beyond belief.

And totally positive her mother hadn't told her the complete truth about what had transpired in the living room earlier that day. She couldn't stop thinking about the unlocked door, the half-cleaned mess in the fireplace hearth, and the startled look on her mother's face when Rachel stepped into her father's study.

A few minutes later, she was clicking keys on the laptop. She looked at the search history and the last few entries almost made her keel over. *Sexual Assault Evidence Kit. Rape Kit. Sexual Assault Examination. Sexual Assault Definition.*

Rachel heard someone start to whimper and realized that it was her. She sobbed and sat in her father's chair completely paralyzed.

Her first instinct was to call and wake her father in Glasgow, but there was no way she could do that without talking to her mother first. The next thought was to barge into the bedroom and confront her, but the woman was exhausted and on the verge of who knows what kind of breakdown because she'd kept everything buried for so long.

So she did nothing. Except wait for the sun to come up.

An hour or so after dawn, her mother walked into the study to find Rachel still sitting behind the desk. Allison glanced at the grandfather clock and then out the window, where a wintry gray light had begun to seep through.

"You're up early," she said to Rachel.

"I actually never went to bed."

Allison shook her head. "I hate those transatlantic flights."

"Did someone attack you, Mom?"

Rachel watched her mother stiffen—and felt her own heart break into a million pieces.

"Attack? What?"

"Did someone break into this house and sexually assault you last night?"

Before she'd let her mother try and utter another denial, Rachel opened the laptop. "I read through the search history."

"I really should learn how to work that thing properly," her mother said, indicating the computer. "I thought we raised you better than to go snooping into others' private affairs."

"It's what I do for a living for Christ's sakes!" Rachel shook her head and rose to her feet. "Jesus—why am I even explaining this to you? Mom—please! Were you raped?"

Her mother moved over to the sofa. Rachel could see her hand trembling slightly as she gripped the arm for support and lowered herself onto the cushion.

"It never got that far," Allison murmured.

"Didn't get that far?" Rachel did everything possible not to scream at the top of her lungs. "What the hell are we talking about here?!"

"What happened—and it's not what you're imagining I assure you—was as much my fault . . ."

"Your fault? What the fuck . . . !"

"Rachel—"

"Okay, okay, okay!" Rachel, who had never sworn in front of her mother, tried to stomp down all the bewildering emotions encircling her. "Explain to me how I shouldn't be *concerned* to come home and find you bleeding all over the place, lying to me when I ask about it, and then find you've been combing the net about sexual assault!"

"Because it has nothing to do with you," her mother quietly responded.

Rachel pointed to the hallway outside the door. "What about the person who did whatever they did to you in there?"

"What about him?"

"How about who the hell is he?" Rachel felt her fury rising again. "Is it someone you know? Someone that I know?"

"I'm not going to tell you anything more, Rachel. It's over and done with. And that's all you need to know."

"But you were bleeding . . ."

"Like I told you, things got a little out of hand. That's all."

"Then why were you looking up all that stuff on the computer?"

"Consider my situation, Rachel. I've just been diagnosed with cancer. I'm going to get poked and prodded by more doctors than I've seen in my entire life. I simply want to know if they'd find any sort of bruising I'd need to explain away . . ."

"Bruising? I thought you said you weren't raped!"

"I told you I wasn't, didn't I? Do I need to spell it out more than that for you?"

Rachel started to respond, then stopped. Between the total embarrassment and shame her mother was feeling, and the imploring look on her face, Rachel started to piece the rest together.

"He tried—but then stopped," Rachel realized.

Her mother nodded slightly, then glanced at her bandaged arm. "That's when I stumbled backwards into the table and cut myself on your figurine," Allison said. "He realized things had gotten out of hand and was gone moments later."

Rachel sat there in stunned silence and stared at her mother.

How much is this poor woman supposed to endure? First, she's given a practical death sentence and now this?"

"What are you going to tell Daddy?"

Rachel watched her mother go totally pale. "Absolutely nothing."

Allison sat a bit straighter, reached out, and took her daughter's hand. "And you can't say a thing either."

"Mom . . ."

Allison stopped her with a plea in her eyes that Rachel knew right then would haunt her long after her mother was gone—probably the rest of her life.

"You have to promise me that, Rachel. You can never breathe a word of this to your father. It would absolutely kill him."

⸻

"So, I've kept that promise ever since," said Rachel as she concluded her story. "And while it didn't kill my father, I'm convinced that by my not telling him, it ended up killing her instead."

Frankel had held on to Rachel's hand for the entire gut-wrenching tale.

He didn't know which of the Grants he felt sorriest for—the woman who had taken her secret to her grave, her husband who still grieved every single day, or the girl he had hopelessly fallen in love with.

Frankel realized that the answer was all three of them.

"Your mother had already been given a terminal cancer diagnosis. She was going to pass away one way or another."

"I understand that." Rachel nodded. "But it happened so much sooner than necessary."

"How do you figure that?"

"She started withering away immediately. The doctors wanted to enroll her in all these trials and test studies, but my mom refused treatment, despite how much me or my father would plead with her. She'd just say she was in too much pain and wanted to be left in peace."

Rachel let go of Frankel's hand and pointed to her chest.

"But I'm certain that she willed herself to die quicker for fear my father would somehow find out about what happened that day."

"You can't know that."

"But I do," Rachel said. "She said as much the one time I dared to bring it up. I was alone with her in an examining room and I said not telling my father the truth was literally letting the cancer eat away that much quicker."

She glanced out the window where it had begun to snow again. From her tortured look, Frankel imagined Rachel was reliving that moment.

"She made me promise again to not breathe a word to my father. I reluctantly agreed but said that shouldn't stop her from telling my dad the truth."

Rachel turned back toward him.

"She gave me the saddest smile I'd ever seen and said it was a choice she had to live with."

She shook her head.

"She was gone only a few days later."

"No wonder there's been all this tension between you and your father."

"When she was still alive, I could barely bring myself to be in the same room with him. I was so worried I'd say or do something that would break my promise. And as it got worse, I found myself spending more time back in New York and at the end I was forbidden to come back and even see her—which I now feel completely shitty about."

"She didn't leave you much choice." Frankel took a beat. "And you have no idea who the man was who did this to her?"

"Not in the slightest," said Rachel. "And now all I do is beat myself up because I feel like if I'd gone ahead and told my father, maybe he could've said something to make her try and fight back."

"Sounds to me like you mother's mind was pretty made up."

"That was Allison Grant in a nutshell. She didn't often take a stand, but when she did, she was an immovable object."

Frankel nodded. "And look what it's done to you and your dad."

"At least we're speaking to each other." She offered up a slight smile. "I probably have you to thank for that."

"So maybe it's time to tell him the truth," suggested Frankel.

"And break the last promise I ever made her? Not to mention run the risk of him hating me forever because I didn't tell him the truth before this?" She vehemently shook her head. "I don't think so."

"Your father could never hate you, Rachel. In fact, I'm pretty sure you're the only thing he still really cares about in this world."

"Even more reason I'm not willing to take that chance—especially now with things so much better between us."

Frankel chewed on this a moment, then uttered one word. "Stubborn."

"Like mother, like daughter."

He shook his head. "I hate you carrying this burden."

"Imagine what it feels like in my shoes."

Frankel finally offered up a smile. "Might be a little tight."

She returned a similar grin. "Might be interesting to give it a try."

He took her in his arms and hugged her. Then whispered in her ear. "Just tell me what I can do for you, Rachel."

She stayed in his arms for a moment before she finally whispered back.

"Just hold me tight and keep wishing me Merry Christmas."

So that's exactly what he did.

They ended up taking a walk in Hyde Park.

Even though the snow continued to fall, it felt warmer, certainly more than the sleet-ridden streets that dominated Manhattan at this time of year. Despite it being Christmas morning, they found a vendor selling hot chocolate—a no-brainer for Frankel, the self-confessed chocoholic.

They sipped them side-by-side in a white-covered grove and even took time to build a small snowman. But when the snow began to fall a bit harder, they decided to head back to the hotel.

As they exited the park, they spotted a crowd of Londoners huddled on a street corner around a newsstand. The proprietor had a stack of newspapers beside him that was dwindling rapidly.

Even before he saw the headline, Frankel got a sickening feeling in the pit of his stomach, convinced that while he had been on a literal walk in the park, a thief somewhere in London had become the Commandment Killer's eighth victim.

So both he and Rachel were shocked when they finally had a copy of the *Mail* in hand.

I'M ON A MISSION FROM GOD screamed the headline.

"It's a one-on-one interview with Prior Silver," realized Frankel. "Given directly to Monte Ferguson."

27

I'M ON A MISSION FROM GOD

As told to Monte Ferguson

When one sits across from Prior Silver, one swears they are talking to your average garage mechanic, the forty-five-year-old's former profession, not the man responsible for a string of robberies two decades ago in London's Financial District, or one of the most notorious serial killers to ever prowl across two continents.

Having contacted this reporter directly, Silver expressed a desire to discuss the multiple murders—but only with an assurance that no one else be present, in a place of his choosing, undisclosed to Scotland Yard or any other law enforcement agency.

Mild-mannered, polite, and soft-spoken, Silver could just have been delivering a treatise on the workings of the Alfa Romeos he used to service instead of discussing the murder spree that has recently terrorized London and Manhattan.

Ferguson: Let's start with why you wanted to conduct this interview.
Silver: I thought it was time to set the record straight.
Ferguson: Why? Were there false accusations being made against you?
Silver: Not so much false as misleading.

Ferguson: You don't deny that you brutally murdered eight people, two in New York and six here in Greater London?

Silver: I've been doing the Lord's work.

Ferguson: How so?

(At this point, Prior Silver pulled out a Bible and read from a marked passage).

Silver: Ezekiel chapter 18, verses 21 and 22. "If the wicked will turn from all his sins that he hath committed, and keep all my statutes, and do that which is lawful and right, he shall surely live, he shall not die. All his transgressions that he hath committed, they shall not be mentioned unto him: in his righteousness that he hath done he shall live."

Ferguson: It sounds like you felt driven to commit these crimes out of some desire for repentance.

Silver: Yes. For crimes in my past.

Ferguson: The bank robberies in the Financial District twenty years ago.

Silver: Exactly.

Ferguson: But isn't that what prison was for? That you would repent while you served your time and might possibly find salvation?

Silver: That was only the first step. I vowed that upon my release I would continue my commitment to the Lord's statutes and seek to punish those who did not.

Ferguson: And by statutes, I take it you mean the Ten Commandments?

Silver: That is correct.

Ferguson: And thus anointed yourself judge, jury, and executioner.

Silver: I was only doing the Lord's bidding.

Ferguson: By slaughtering them in cold blood.

Silver: By sending them to eternity marked for their transgressions.

Ferguson: Marked? Marked how?

Silver: With a Roman numeral on their brow to wear until the End of Days.

"So much for holding that piece of information for ourselves," said Frankel.

"It's hard to believe we kept it quiet this long," remarked Grant.

Silver's confession laid out in black-and-white newsprint was the last thing Grant would have expected to find at the bottom of his Christmas stocking.

By the time Rachel and Frankel had arrived at the Maida Vale house to show him the story, Grant was already combing through it online for the umpteenth time.

His mobile and email had blown up with its release. Deputy Commander Stebbins had been among the first to contact him and wasn't pleased to say the least.

"That couldn't have been a very pleasant conversation," said Rachel.

Not only did the story make the Yard look like "complete fools" (Stebbins's words), beaten to the punch by "that thorn Ferguson" (Grant's words), the fact that Silver was still running amok in London was way beyond the pale.

"At least this takes a lot of guesswork out of things," Frankel said, holding up the paper. "Silver walked Ferguson step-by-step through each murder and it lines up with everything we know."

Indeed, the story was a grisly recital of the killings—from lying in wait for Lionel Frey in the British Library's third-floor WC to ending the lives of Elizabeth Dozier and Jared Fleming in the master bedroom of the mansion in Esher.

At least Ferguson had the good graces to call out Silver on what Grant considered the man's greatest sin, the one that would haunt the commander for the rest of his days.

Ferguson: But Sergeant Stanford Hawley wasn't a "transgressor."
Silver: Not as far as I know.
Ferguson: Yet you showed no compunction taking his life as well.
Silver: If you're asking me if I regret the act, I can honestly say no.
Ferguson: But you just admitted the man wasn't guilty of any wrongdoing.

Silver: I have reconciled his death as an unfortunate byproduct . . .
Ferguson: A "byproduct"?
Silver: Of continuing the Lord's work. I couldn't allow someone like the sergeant to stand in the way of my mission from God.

Grant felt his blood pressure rise each time he got to that part of the story.

"What's abundantly clear is that Silver is committing these murders with an interpretation of the Old Testament that suits his particular needs," said Grant.

"In other words, the man is completely off his rocker," suggested Frankel.

"Depends on how you look at it," countered Grant. "Reread the part where Ferguson asks him about the Sixth Commandment."

Ferguson: But each time you took a life, you were violating one of the Commandments, the sixth. "Thou shalt not kill." How do you explain that?
Silver: As I quoted from Ezekiel, all previous transgressions will be forgiven because of the righteousness a man has done once he has turned from a life of sin.
Ferguson: One sin pardons the other?
Silver: According to the word of the Lord? Most definitely.

"That is total and utter bullshit. He's just twisting words to justify his insane actions," grumbled Frankel. "And this man is *definitely* nuts."

"I think I have to agree with my father on this one," said Rachel. "What might seem crazy to us has allowed Silver to stay true to his so-called mission."

"And it's pretty clear he isn't finished yet." Grant scrolled down his computer screen toward the end of the interview.

Ferguson: You say you still have a mission to complete. Does that mean you have set your sights on three more victims?
Silver: You'll understand if I don't answer that question.

Ferguson: I thought you wanted to, using your words, "set the record straight."

Silver: And I have to this point. Austin Grant will know when I'm done.

It wasn't the only time that Silver had mentioned Grant by name. Earlier in the story, while recounting the bank robberies, Silver had confirmed it had been Grant who put him behind bars. His subsequent statement might have been the most chilling of all, at least for those huddled in Grant's study on Christmas day.

Silver: I hope the commander sees how his actions led me to seek salvation, allowing the Lord to send me down the path where I can now set things right.

"He's essentially blaming you for all this," Frankel pointed out.

"The notion wasn't lost on me."

But it wasn't the only thing troubling Grant. He couldn't imagine why Prior Silver had granted the interview in the first place or run the risk of being captured by the Yard when there were no assurances that Ferguson wouldn't renege on the deal to keep the authorities away.

"Something about this doesn't feel right," Grant murmured.

"Why do you say that?" asked Frankel.

"Every move Silver has made to this point has been calculated—from his choice of victims to the clues he's been taunting us with." He glanced at Rachel. "Even the texts from Sergeant Hawley's phone seem to be specifically timed."

"Except for that one outside the church," Rachel reminded. "After your eulogy apparently got under his skin."

"Even so, one could argue that was still on point. That Silver was just marking territory to let us know he was still in control." Grant tapped the computer screen. "I guarantee you he has a very specific reason for doing this right now. Remember, he told us we'd hear from him directly after Christmas."

"But today *is* Christmas," Frankel said.

"One could argue *after* Christmas starts when the clock hits 12:01 on December twenty-fifth," Grant posed. "Silver probably planned on releasing this tomorrow on Boxing Day, fulfilling his promise. Ferguson and Michaels jumped the gun."

"Michaels?" asked Rachel.

"Monte Ferguson's editor at the *Mail*. He should be along any minute."

The only reason Grant didn't throttle Randolph Michaels when he stepped through the door was that the newspaper editor had been one of the first calls the Scotland Yard man had fielded after the story broke.

The key word being *after*. The editor wanted to explain the reasons he had waited until then to tell the commander his side of the explosive Ferguson story.

Michaels was maybe the same age as Grant, his hair gone completely gray—probably from too many years spent trying to find news to print that bloggers and internet trolls hadn't already beaten him to.

"It was one of the caveats Ferguson insisted on when he sent over the interview," explained Michaels. "He demanded that the story be published in a special edition of the paper before it was put online."

"Why do you think?" asked Grant.

"You know the man, Commander. Despite claims the news always comes first, I think we both know Monte Ferguson wants people to see his name right there beneath the headline."

"I presume another requirement was to not contact me or anyone else at the Yard beforehand?"

"Not until the story was published," replied Michaels.

"You could have pulled rank and refused," said Frankel.

"I suppose," agreed Michaels. "But in the end, I'm first and foremost a newspaperman. A dying breed, but I'm still around, and I'm not going to sit on a powder keg like this. Besides, if I hadn't gone and run it, there was no guarantee Silver wouldn't sell it to the *Mirror* or someone else."

"Or that Monte Ferguson wouldn't have leaked it to the internet himself," Rachel added.

"I wouldn't put anything past him at this point," said the editor. "Hell, the man met with a serial killer without telling anyone. Clearly Monte wasn't coming away from this empty-handed."

"The bloody idiot is lucky he came away with his life." Grant shook his head. "What else did Ferguson say when he called you?"

"To be honest, not very much," replied Michaels. "He sounded frightened. Can't say that I blame him. For all I know, Silver was sitting in the same room at the time."

Michaels paused to wipe a dabble of sweat from his head. "It was a very quick call," he continued. "He told me what he had, what he wanted, then emailed the story to me while I was on the phone to make sure I got it. Then he was gone."

"You sure it was Ferguson on the other end of the phone?" asked Grant.

"I think I'd recognize the voice of a man I've talked to almost every day for the past decade, Commander. Who the hell else would it be?"

"Prior Silver, possibly?"

"Wouldn't be the first time a killer tried to hijack the headlines or redirect the news cycle," added Frankel.

Michaels vehemently shook his head and turned to Grant. "You've talked enough to Monte Ferguson to know how distinctive his voice is."

"If by that you mean annoying, yes, I most certainly do. Where is he now?"

"I haven't a clue," said the editor. "I've tried his mobile at least a dozen times, dropped by his flat, even the Chelsea pub where he drinks himself into a stupor most nights, thinking he'd gone there to celebrate. But he's nowhere to be found."

"He's probably hiding out knowing the commander will haul him into jail for interfering with a police investigation," surmised Frankel.

"He'll be lucky if that's all I do to him," said Grant.

Grant asked Michaels a few more questions but there wasn't more to tell. He insisted the editor get in touch immediately once he heard from Monte Ferguson. Michaels promised to do so. The editor wouldn't make the same mistake twice and apologized for any damage that he might have done.

The editor left, and Grant considered the apology. The truth be told, any fallout from the interview had probably been minimal. Except for letting the public know the killer was leaving his calling card on the foreheads of his victims, the story was just a madman boasting with pride about his horrendous accomplishments.

This led to Grant wondering once again why Silver had gone to such lengths to set up the interview with Ferguson. It was hard to believe it was just so Prior Silver could share his twisted journey to salvation with the world.

Grant firmly believed that once he caught up with Silver or, for that matter, Monte Ferguson, he could finally get the answer to that question and others that were nagging him.

Of course, that meant finding them first.

⁂

It certainly wasn't how Grant had planned to spend the rest of the holiday.

Back at the Yard, Grant knew he hadn't done anything to ingratiate himself among his colleagues. He had pulled constables and detectives away from their families, unwrapped boxes filled with cuddly sweaters and scarves, gathered carolers, and anything else that went with the spirit of Christmas.

It also wasn't quite what he'd envisioned for the end of a three-plus decade tenure at the Yard. He'd imagined the time would come when he'd just clean out his desk and quietly move on to the next stage of his life.

Instead, there was now a chance his legacy would be letting a serial killer run rampant all over London (and don't forget, New York City), thus doomed to live out his life with a reputation as a colossal failure.

At least he could be thankful that Allison wasn't around to see it.

He realized he hadn't been to the cemetery since the day Hawley had found him there to say that a Blasphemer named Street had been sent to meet his maker in a Piccadilly back alley. Grant promised to head up there on Sunday and visit Allison one last time before finishing up his time at the Yard. Maybe talking through the case by her grave might give him some perspective he hadn't yet considered.

Grant had plenty to tell her since he'd last sat on that stone bench.

Perhaps he could even convince Rachel to go with him.

By the end of Christmas evening, Grant was wondering if he could even accomplish that.

Because when midnight rolled around and Grant sent everyone home (after apologizing for ruining their Christmas), he felt more useless than at any time since the whole mess started. There still wasn't a trace of Prior Silver to be found.

And now Monte Ferguson had vanished off the face of the earth as well.

———

When the knock came on the front door, Grant turned to squint at his alarm clock and saw it was almost nine o'clock in the morning.

He figured that Rachel would answer it, but then remembered she had spent the night with Frankel at the hotel in Covent Garden.

As he hauled himself out of bed, he thought while he never would have imagined Rachel falling for a member of his profession, he had to admit that John Frankel was living up to being the "good man" his daughter claimed him to be.

At least so far. He had seen way too many relationships go awry in his years at the Yard, so he still thought it best for her to be cautious. Cautious, but hopeful.

The second knock at the door was more pronounced.

"Coming," Grant called out as he came down the corridor.

He opened it to find a delivery man for an overnight package service standing with a clipboard in hand, shivering in the morning cold.

"Sorry," Grant told him. "Overslept."

"Have a pretty good Christmas, did you?" asked the delivery man with a knowing twinkle in his eye.

"Not particularly," answered Grant.

The delivery man frowned, obviously not expecting such a forthcoming response. The man nodded over his shoulder at the delivery van.

"It's a rather large package. Anywhere specific you want me to put it?"

Grant saw a medium sized crate on a dolly beside the van.

"I guess the living room, if you don't mind," Grant directed.

A few moments later, the man had deposited the crate and departed with a few pound notes that Grant dug out of his wallet.

It was only when he took a better look at the shipping label that the sleepy-eyed Grant snapped fully awake. It wasn't his printed name and address that caught his eye. It was the return label in the upper left corner of the crate.

M. Ferguson/The Daily Mail/39092930

Grant presumed the numbers were some sort of account the newspaper had with the delivery service.

Of more interest, and a trifle bit more concern, was what Monte Ferguson had sent him via overnight delivery.

Grant thought about calling Frankel and Rachel but knew he couldn't sit and just stare at the crate until they got themselves together and came over.

So Grant went down to the basement.

He found a crowbar he hadn't used in ages and climbed back up the stairs to the living room. He wedged the tool under a couple of the crate's corners and lifted the lid.

Prior Silver had made good on his word that Grant would be hearing from him directly after Christmas.

The man that Grant, Frankel, Scotland Yard, and the NYPD had been searching for in two major cities was curled up in a heap at the bottom of the crate.

Prior Silver was dead to the world.

With a Roman numeral *VIII* carved into the center of his forehead.

28

S uicide.

Frankel stood beside Rachel and her father in the Grant living room as Jeffries, the FME he'd first met in Esher, shared his preliminary findings.

"We'll run a battery of tests back at the morgue, but everything we're looking at so far seems to be consistent with Silver taking his own life."

"Any idea how long he's been dead?"

"It's only a guess at this point," said Jeffries. "But with rigor mortis still in effect, I'd have to say some time in the past twenty-four hours."

Frankel looked around the room that was wall-to-wall cops and techs. Grant stood beside the open crate, staring deep inside it. He'd been in pretty much the same position since Frankel arrived with Rachel a few hours earlier.

He looks like he's in shock. Can't say I blame him—starting Boxing Day with a dead body dumped beneath his nicely trimmed Christmas tree.

Rachel had been in the shower when Frankel answered Grant's phone call. When she emerged wrapped in an oversized bath towel while drying her hair with another, Frankel had hung up in the same stupor that Grant was now exhibiting.

"Who was that?" Rachel had asked.

"Prior Silver is dead," he had simply answered.

Hearing himself speak the words aloud hadn't made it easier to believe. And now standing over the dead man himself, Frankel felt it was completely surreal.

He suddenly realized what he was feeling was disappointment.

For a search that had consumed them for the better part of a month to end this way, without being able to ask Silver a single question, was beyond frustrating.

It actually seemed unfair.

Even in death, Prior Silver held the same upper hand he had since beginning his killing spree not-so-very-far-away at the British Library in Saint Pancras. With each elaborately staged murder, he had doled out only the precise information he wanted authorities to have.

Even his own death.

"We're still looking at poison?" asked Grant.

"Everything points that way," said Jeffries. "I don't see any of the slashes or knife wounds like the others. Except for the mark on the forehead, naturally."

"And that was self-administered as well?"

"Appears so." The FME indicated the dead man's forehead. "You can spot the hesitation marks. By the *V* in particular—where he must have started. There's also a lopsidedness here compared to the other victims, which indicates he did it in a backwards fashion without being able to see what he was doing. Like so . . ."

He raised a curled fist to his forehead and made a carving motion.

"Do you think he did that before or after he took the poison?" asked Frankel.

"If it were in liquid form, it was likely before getting in the crate because we haven't located a receptacle on or near his body. If it were a pill or tablet, then he could have taken it at any time." He glanced at the crate, then continued. "But given the knife we found inside the crate and the blood splatter patterns, I'd say Silver carved himself shortly after stepping inside it."

Jeffries elaborated on his theory. The bloodstains on the inside wall of the box were consistent with Silver holding on to the crate's edge with one hand while cutting himself with the other. Subsequently, some blood dried on the inner wall, with the rest pooling on the crate's floor once Silver collapsed and eventually died.

"But he managed to lock himself inside beforehand," pointed out Frankel.

"I think he could have secured the box before losing consciousness. Simple enough—given the nature of the crate."

Jeffries had already identified the container as the sort that could be locked from both inside and out. That meant Silver had opted to literally stay buried inside and have himself delivered to Grant's doorstep.

Frankel watched Rachel shudder. "Such a brutal way to die," she said.

She had not strayed far from Frankel's side since they'd arrived and was clearly shaken. Frankel had suggested she needn't be there, but Rachel had steadfastly insisted on staying put. He desperately wanted to reach out and comfort her but knew this was hardly the time or place.

"I guess in the end he decided to save the worst punishment for himself."

"How do you figure that?" she asked.

"The Eighth Commandment. '*Thou shalt not steal,*' " quoted Frankel. "Once a thief, always a thief."

The room went silent as Frankel wondered if Grant and Rachel were thinking along the same lines. They had spent all that time combing lists for a thief to be the next possible victim and the answer had been under their noses all along.

Grant finally spoke up. "I never imagined he would stop at eight."

"Maybe he thought we were closing in before he could finish," said Frankel.

"Or planned it that way all along," countered Rachel.

"I suppose either is possible," Grant conceded.

"Silver certainly made good on what he told Monte Ferguson," said Frankel.

"Which would be what?" asked the commander.

"Silver specifically said that you'd know when he was done." Frankel eyed the crate one last time. "I'd say the man stuck to his word."

You shouldn't make promises you can't keep, Commander.

It practically leaped off the cell phone Frankel was staring at.

They were back in Grant's office and Frankel was scrolling through texts on the cell found in one of Silver's pockets. It had already been dusted and fingerprinted. Two sets of prints were found; both belonged to dead men.

Stanford Hawley and Prior Silver.

Traces of the sergeant's blood had been found on the casing as well and Frankel couldn't avoid flashing on how it had gotten there in the first place. He willed away the disturbing images and concentrated on the text chains on the phone that Silver had purloined from his unintended victim.

Not only did he find the chats the killer had with Rachel, there were subsequent texts to a different number.

The one belonging to Monte Ferguson's cell.

Frankel realized Silver had used Hawley's phone to contact Ferguson and make an offer the *Mail* journalist could clearly not refuse.

I want to tell my story. Interested?

The text chat had started shortly after Hawley's funeral. By scrolling through it, they quickly pieced together how the interview published in the *Daily Mail* came about.

It explicitly outlined Silver's demands, those mentioned in Ferguson's exclusive. The journalist was to show up alone and forbidden to contact the Yard; otherwise the interview was a no-go. The end of the chat shed light on why Ferguson would even consider meeting one-on-one with a serial killer.

Ferguson: How do I know I'll be safe? Why won't you kill me when I step through the door?

Silver: Because you haven't violated one of the Lord's statutes yet.

Ferguson: You mean the Ten Commandments?

Silver: Yes. Have you broken one of them?
Ferguson: No.
Silver: Then you have nothing to fear from me.

That had been enough for Ferguson to take Silver up on his one-time offer.

The chat concluded with a meeting time—six o'clock the following morning, Christmas Day. And Silver had provided Ferguson an address that turned out to be an abandoned warehouse in the East End that the MIS had just checked out.

Not only was it the perfect place for a clandestine meeting (in an industrial section of London that was a graveyard on Christmas morning), it happened to be the same address the crate had been picked up from on Boxing Day to be delivered to the Scotland Yard commander.

The coup de grâce had been the final usage of Sergeant Hawley's cell phone. The search history brought up the package service's website, accessed around seven o'clock on Christmas night.

When Grant followed up with the delivery service, they confirmed the online order for a package pickup the following morning. The information had been entered digitally using Monte Ferguson's *Daily Mail* account. They presumed that Silver had gotten the journalist to give him the name of the package service and account number. There would have been no reason for Ferguson to suspect or even care what the killer was going to do with it. The reporter just wanted to get the hell out of the warehouse and file the story that would change his career.

"Unless Ferguson actually ordered the pickup himself," suggested Grant.

"Why would he possibly do that?" wondered Rachel.

"We'd have to ask him," said Frankel. "But we'd need to find him to do that."

Nearly an entire day had passed since Ferguson's story had stunned London and the world, yet there hadn't been a single peep from the journalist.

Frankel wondered if the newspaperman was waiting for the news conference Stebbins had scheduled in an hour to show his face. He could easily imagine a smug Ferguson basking in the glory of having landed the only interview with Prior Silver and also being the last person to see him alive.

Just one more ignominy to throw into his and Grant's faces.

As Frankel considered this and the upcoming presser, he began to share Grant's feelings about his impending retirement only a few short days away.

Frankel couldn't wait for all this to be over.

But Monte Ferguson was a no-show.

It was the first thing Frankel noticed entering the packed conference room. Michaels, the *Daily Mail* editor, told him and Grant that he still hadn't heard from Ferguson since their phone call the previous day.

Stebbins started out confirming the death of Prior Silver and the surrounding circumstances. There were audible gasps at the revelation that the body had been delivered to Grant's house. Frankel looked over at the commander, sandwiched between himself and Stebbins on the podium; he could feel a wave of embarrassment coming off him.

Stebbins gave way to Jeffries, who played it close to the vest, saying it was suicide by poison, but refused to elaborate without more tests—even though he'd informed Frankel and Grant he'd found traces of strychnine in Silver's system.

When asked by an overanxious journalist if there had been a tell-tale mark on Silver, like the ones reported by Monte Ferguson in the already-famous interview, the FME looked over at Stebbins, who gave him a go-ahead nod.

"We found the Roman numeral eight carved into his forehead," said Jeffries.

The room buzzed again. Stebbins stepped forward and thanked the FME, then proceeded to read aloud the "official" findings.

"This is being deemed a suicide by Scotland Yard. Prior Silver had been the primary suspect in these murders. The forehead markings are consistent with similar ones found on seven previous victims. We also have confirmed that Silver was in New York City when the fourth and fifth murders were committed."

Frankel couldn't help but marvel how smoothly Grant's superior had taken the reporter's question and segued it into the definitive statement by the Yard stating Prior Silver's guilt. It also reaffirmed Frankel's self-knowledge that he didn't have the patience or desire to walk such a political tightrope.

Then Stebbins opened up the floor for questions. For the next half hour, Frankel and Grant found themselves under siege as they had to face reprimands for Silver having outsmarted them right up till the moment he died. More than a few journalists wanted to know what their colleague Monte Ferguson had told them about his conversation with Prior Silver.

"We'll let you know after we've talked to him," answered Frankel, the first time it was asked.

The next time it came up, Grant took the microphone. "If any of you hear from him, you must contact us immediately or risk having charges brought against you for impeding an ongoing investigation."

Frankel could tell Grant was doing the utmost to control his temper.

A journalist popped up in the back. "Are you saying the case isn't closed?"

Stebbins stepped back in and repeated his claim they were no longer searching for a suspect; they were tying up loose ends.

"Detective Frankel?"

The NYPD detective was once again lost in his admiration of Stebbins's tap dancing skills when he realized he was being called on specifically. "Yes?"

"Where does the New York Police Department stand on all this?"

Frankel hesitated. The day had been so crazy he hadn't had time to check in with Lieutenant Harris back in Manhattan. But he knew NYPD would be thrilled at the thought of the Commandment Killer not darkening the five boroughs again.

"We stand by the conclusions reached by Scotland Yard," Frankel said.

"Does that mean you'll now be heading back to the States?"

"Not right away. I'm planning on staying to see some things through."

Frankel couldn't resist glancing over at Rachel, who offered up an appreciative smile. It wasn't the first time Frankel had been reminded of the one very good thing that had come into his life since finding a dead priest impaled on a cross in Saint Patrick's Cathedral.

Soon after that, Stebbins ended the press conference.

Not a moment too soon as far as Frankel was concerned.

And from the look on Austin Grant's face, he knew the feeling went double for the Scotland Yard commander.

"Not even one drink to celebrate?" asked Everett.

"Do I look like I want a drink?" responded Grant.

"You look like you could use a few actually," said his brother.

Grant looked gloomier than when he'd exited the press conference. His expression matched the weather outside, where it was raining in sheets.

They had ended back up at the Wolseley for a late supper—but instead of it just being Frankel and Rachel, they had been joined by the Grant brothers.

It hadn't been planned.

When the trio had returned to Grant's office after the media bloodletting, Everett was there waiting. Being a Thursday, it was the night the brothers had their weekly chess match, but Frankel had heard Grant beg off before the presser when the Oxford professor had called to remind him.

Having followed the proceedings on television, Everett said there was no way he was going to let the three of them sit around and mope when they should be out—if not celebrating, then at least breathing a collective sigh of relief that it was over.

"Let me guess. You're not leaving my office till we agree?" Grant asked.

"You know what happens when I don't get my way," Everett said.

Frankel didn't get a chance to find out what that might be because Grant threw his hands up in dismay and told his brother to "just pick a bloody place."

At the restaurant, neither Frankel nor Rachel followed Grant's tee-totaling lead. They both ordered Old Fashioneds and agreed they were subpar to the ones Everett had made on Christmas Eve.

By the time the appetizers had arrived, Everett had extracted everything about the demise of Prior Silver from Frankel and Rachel, while Grant remained mum the entire time.

"Strychnine poisoning?" Everett exclaimed. "How Agatha Christie of him."

"It supports Jeffries's timeline," said Frankel. "Slow enough to ingest, then carve an eight into his forehead and have his body shipped to Austin the next day."

"Using Monte Ferguson's delivery account. There's an inspired touch for you," observed Everett.

The discussion naturally moved on to the missing Ferguson.

"Where do you think the man could have got off to?" Everett asked.

Grant spoke for the first time since ordering a salad when they sat down. "That's what I want to know. When I find out, I have a whole bunch of questions."

"Such as?" wondered his sibling.

"What was he thinking pulling a foolhardy stunt like meeting a serial killer by himself?"

"Sounds like he was willing to do anything to get a story," said Rachel.

"And what was the deal with him and that package?" asked Grant. "I find it hard to believe Ferguson would just hand over his account number to Silver and toddle on his merry way."

"What other possibility is there?" asked Everett. "Ferguson ordered the crate himself, stuffed the dead man inside, and sent it to you as a belated holiday gift?"

"I'm not sure what I'm thinking." Grant shook his head. "I just know I'm not going to rest easy until I get some of these answers."

Everett gave his brother a pat on the shoulder. "I think you'll be resting plenty starting next week, old chap—what with retirement around the corner."

"Couldn't come a moment too soon."

"Does that mean you'll reconsider my invitation to Zermatt for New Year's?"

"All I'm considering is going to bed and hoping I'll wake up to realize this has all been some horrible nightmare," replied Grant.

"Well, aren't we the life of the party?" Everett quipped. He turned to Rachel and Frankel. "You think you two can work on him to see if he'll change his mind?"

Frankel raised an eyebrow. "I didn't realize I was invited."

"Of course you are," chortled Everett. "What young man doesn't want to ring in the new year with his best girl at his side?"

Frankel glanced at Rachel and could see her starting to blush. Truth be known, Frankel thought he might be getting a little red behind the ears as well.

"It does sound rather fun," said Rachel. "Don't you think so, Dad?"

The only response she got was a subdued *hmmmm*.

"We'll get back to you on that one," Rachel told her uncle.

An hour later, when they were leaving the restaurant, Frankel noticed that Grant's mood had only dampened with the weather outside where, impossibly, it seemed to be raining even harder. As the Grant brothers exited to hunt down cabs, Frankel hung back beside Rachel near the coat check.

"Maybe you should head home with your father tonight," Frankel suggested.

"You trying to get rid of me already, Detective?"

"Furthest thing from my mind actually." Frankel motioned outside. "I think the commander has a lot on his mind right now and you're the only person in the world who can try and help him go a little easier on himself."

"You don't know my father as well as you think. This sort of thing can go on for days," Rachel said. "But I think it's a lovely notion and even lovelier that you suggested it." She leaned in and gave him a healthy kiss.

Frankel immediately began to regret his selfless offer but stayed the course and told her he'd see her first thing in the morning.

Rachel smiled. "So, I'm really one of those 'things you want to see through'?"

"Absolutely."

That earned him another kiss and yet another pang of regret.

After putting father and daughter in the first cab that the doorman had been able to flag down, Everett suggested they share a second—should the drenched Wolseley employee be able to repeat the trick.

"Covent Garden is right on the way up to Hampstead," Everett pointed out.

Moments later they stepped into a second taxi that the doorman had practically done a swan dive in the water rising off the curb to secure.

As they settled for the short ride through the storm to Frankel's hotel, Everett stared out the side window.

Finally he spoke. "I'm concerned about Austin."

"I thought it was usually the other way around—with the older sibling doing all the worrying about the younger one."

"It's a lot for a man to lose in a year. First, the love of his life. Now, the only career he's ever known."

"The second was his choice."

"Yes, but I don't think he's ready for having all that idle time on his hands."

Everett turned back around and shook his head.

"Especially now—what with you taking Rachel away to the States so soon after Austin finally got her back."

Frankel didn't know exactly how to respond, so he just let Everett go on.

"I'm sure she's told you a little about how things have been with them the past couple of years," Everett said.

Frankel thought about how Rachel had opened her heart to tell him the truth about what happened to her mother. He felt that same hollow pit in his stomach.

"Some of it, yes."

"Then you understand what I'm talking about," said Everett.

"I understand we both live in New York," replied Frankel. "But I have no intention of 'taking her away from her father,' if that's what you're trying to say."

"It might help if you told Austin that at some point," suggested Everett.

Frankel had never seen the man so solemn. Clearly, Everett Grant held the notion of family near and dear.

"I'll certainly try," Frankel replied softly.

Everett gave him a grateful smile. "Rachel is indeed lucky to have you."

For the rest of the short journey, Frankel watched the pouring rain, deep in thought himself.

When Everett and the cab dropped Frankel at the entrance to the hotel, he had reached a conclusion.

If there were a way he could offer some sort of salvation to both Rachel and her father, John Frankel was determined to find it.

29

"How many times are you going to read that thing?"

Grant looked up from his desk chair to see that Rachel had quietly entered the study. She was wearing an Oxford sweatshirt and royal-blue leggings, holding the door open with one hand and a cup of hot tea in the other.

"Until I figure what keeps bothering me about it," answered Grant.

He lowered the well-worn copy of Ferguson's interview with Prior Silver. He had been through it at least a dozen times just that morning.

"Maybe the fact that he went off and did it without telling you?" Rachel asked.

"That goes without saying."

She placed the teacup on a coaster with a Degas racing print on it. The Impressionists had been Allison's favorites and she collected coasters with replicas of their works—"the closest we'll ever get to owning one," she used to joke.

"It's just all so perfectly pat. Religious mania begets a killing spree we haven't seen since the Ripper prowled Whitechapel and then ends in the blink of an eye with a confession and dose of strychnine? Doesn't it seem a bit schizophrenic?"

"Sounds more manic depressive to me. Have you spoken with the medical personnel at the prisons? Might be interesting to get their read on the man."

"We did when you and Hawley unearthed him. His psych profile was nil—nothing indicated a criminal mastermind who could pull this off."

"Holed up for twenty years with just a Bible, his thoughts, and a taste for revenge? The man had nothing but time to cook it up."

"I suppose," said Grant.

"And I suppose you have time for breakfast?"

Grant dredged up a smile. "Eggs Benedict à la Grant?"

"I wouldn't dare compete with the master. But in case you've forgotten, I do make a mean stack of hotcakes."

"Lead the way," Grant said and got up from the desk.

A half hour later, the commander shoved himself away from the table with a contented sigh and a scraped-clean plate. "I had no idea I was that hungry."

"You barely touched your dinner last night."

Her Mother Bear concern caused Grant to crack a half-smile. "Have I reached that time of life where the children and parents flip roles?"

"Hardly. But I still worry about you every now and then."

Granted reached across the table for Ferguson's article again. He could see Rachel rolling her eyes. "Maybe I'll have a clearer perspective on a full stomach."

"I know better than to try and stop you from torturing yourself."

"And believe me when I say I appreciate that."

But in that moment, his obsession with the newspaper took a back seat as he watched Rachel move about the kitchen with the same ease that Allison had their entire marriage. The thawing over the past week of their chilly relationship had left Grant willing to let whatever promise Rachel was holding on to for her mother keep until she was ready to tell him.

"What are you smiling about?" Rachel suddenly asked.

"I was just thinking how nice it is to have you back home."

"It feels good to be here."

"Any idea how long you'll be staying?" he asked, trying to keep out of his voice the desperation that went with the idea of her leaving.

"I'm not sure. With the investigation over, I figure John will need to head back to New York soon—probably right after New Year's." She sat down across from him. "Speaking of which—have you thought more about Everett's offer?"

"Five thousand feet above sea level isn't exactly how I'd choose to start my retirement."

"But it would be nice for us all to be together, wouldn't it?"

Grant couldn't deny the warmth of that notion. "This thing between you and Detective Frankel is getting serious, isn't it?"

"I really like him, Daddy."

"I do too."

He saw her eyes drift toward the folded newspaper. "I know things didn't turn out the way you expected. But something good came out of all this, right?"

She reached and took his hand. Grant felt his heart warm as it began to rise in his throat. "Most definitely," he replied.

"Then you'll think about us all going to Switzerland together?"

"Of course I will."

But that didn't mean he was going to stop thinking about what the hell had happened to Monte Ferguson.

———

"I wish I had more news, but I really don't," said Randolph Michaels from behind his desk at the *Daily Mail*. "Not the ideal way for a newsman to begin a conversation, but there you have it."

"Don't you find it odd not hearing a word from the man since he filed the biggest story of his career?"

"I'd expect him to be crowing about it, that's for sure. Most definitely odd."

"So how do you explain it?"

Michaels shrugged. "Fear of having charges leveled against him, impeding a police investigation? It's the only thing that comes to mind."

Grant was considering another line of thought but wasn't ready to share it with Michaels lest he think he'd become a conspiracy theorist. But it was the main reason he headed to the newspaper instead of starting his final Friday of work at the Yard.

"I'd like to get to the bottom of this myself," continued Michaels. "I've got management wondering what happened to their star reporter and if they're going to be held accountable by Scotland Yard for anything."

"You've been completely forthcoming. You're safe in telling them they've nothing to worry about on that count."

"Is there anything I can do to help?"

"Perhaps I could look through Ferguson's desk? See if there's a clue where he's gotten himself off to? Of course, I could always obtain a warrant . . ."

Michaels waved away the notion. "The sooner we put a lid on this mess, the better for everyone concerned."

Moments later, Grant was seated in Ferguson's small cubicle.

To describe Ferguson's desk as resembling the aftermath of a small tornado would be an understatement. He'd obviously never heard of a filing system. Clippings, photos, and paper were strewn everywhere—atop the desk, stuffed in drawers, and crammed into cubbyholes that served as shelves.

Every single item had to do with the Commandment killings.

Grant found himself looking at a vivid record of his investigation spread out in the most haphazard of fashions; Old Testament excerpts with verses highlighted using a fluorescent marker, photos of the crime scenes, mostly featuring Austin Grant, and rival tabloids' stories on the murders.

Of particular interest was the single item on a corkboard that separated Ferguson's space from a sports journalist on the other side of the wall.

A printed out list of the Ten Commandments, with a red checkmark by the first seven. Only the last three remain unmarked—*Thou shalt not steal; Thou shalt not bear false witness; Thou shalt not covet any thing that is thy neighbor's.*

This made total sense to Grant as Prior Silver had still been alive when Ferguson had gone to meet him at the East End warehouse and the reporter had been missing ever since.

Grant took his time sorting through the mess, but in the end, it was literally *old news*—there wasn't anything that the Scotland Yard man didn't already know.

It just fed that gnawing sensation in Grant's brain, something that Michaels inadvertently added to when his head appeared over the partition seconds later.

"Rather obsessed, wouldn't you say?"

"To say the least," replied Grant. He pointed at the Ten Commandment list on the corkboard. "Do you recall when he put that up there?"

Michaels shook his head. "It's not like I make a habit of checking on the idiosyncrasies of my reporters. But I don't recall seeing it before he headed off to New York and that was the weekend before last, right?"

"The priest was murdered on a Sunday night," said Grant. "Ferguson would have gotten to New York after that."

"No, he was actually there that same morning. A total coincidence as it turned out. I'm surprised Monte didn't tell you about it."

Grant suddenly remembered the reporter being evasive when he ran into him in Saint Patrick's and asked how Ferguson had gotten there so fast. The gnawing sensation intensified.

"No, he actually neglected to mention that," said Grant.

———

The first time he had encountered Ferguson on the case was when Grant left the Yard on the Saturday night prior to the Great London Church Clearout. That was when Ferguson had confronted him about the killings and Grant had promised to call him after the weekend. But Grant had neglected to do so when all hell broke loose in Manhattan and he had to hop a transatlantic flight on Monday morning.

The next time he'd seen Ferguson was in Saint Patrick's on that Tuesday morning.

It was certainly worth having Morrow run a quick search of the airlines and Ferguson. By the time he got to the Yard, the tech had done just that.

Monte Ferguson had taken a plane out of Heathrow first thing on Sunday morning December 15th—arriving before noon in the States, at least eight hours before Father Adam Peters met his fate.

According to Michaels, Ferguson had gone to Manhattan because he'd gotten an emergency text; a relative had been in an accident and was on death's door in an upstate New York hospital, and he'd taken the first plane out to the States. He had told the editor someone got their signals crossed because when he arrived Ferguson learned no accident of any sort had occurred—but Divine Providence had put him in the proper spot and time to pursue the developing story.

"He actually said 'Divine Providence'?"

"Something to that effect," Michaels had responded.

Interesting choice of words, thought Grant as he sat behind his desk staring at the airline data. He leaned back and let what had been gnawing at his brain unfold.

Was Ferguson's explanation for his sudden trip plausible? Perhaps. But it also could have been a complete fabrication.

Ferguson had been the only person outside the Yard to connect the first three crimes. He had been on the verge of tumbling to the truth each time he'd crossed paths with Grant. Was it possible his obsession in besting the Scotland Yard man could have led Ferguson to unearthing Prior Silver and setting him up as a suspect in the string of murders? One thing for sure—wherever Monte Ferguson was right now, he'd just scored the story of his life and left Grant's reputation in ruins.

Grant finally let the gnawing question festering in his mind ever since the crate had arrived on his doorstep take full bloom.

Was Monte Ferguson crazy enough to kill eight total strangers and Stanford Hawley, then pin it on Prior Silver in a made-to-look-like-suicide if the reward was worldwide fame?

―――

"That's preposterous," said Deputy Commander Franklin Stebbins.

Grant had considered running all this by Frankel first, but knew he'd be going out on a limb in presenting it to his superior. Grant's career was basically over—no reason to let Frankel crash as well when Stebbins jettisoned his theory.

Like he was in the process of doing this very minute.

"It's a working supposition," Grant said.

"And what about the interview? Prior Silver confessed."

"Ferguson could have made the whole thing up. He poisons Silver, makes it looks like a suicide, and then files the story."

"And the text conversations between the two men?" asked Stebbins, who was becoming increasingly exasperated.

"Ferguson could have manufactured those as well. If he killed Stanford Hawley, he would have had both phones and just texted back and forth with them."

"Are you listening to yourself?" Stebbins shook his head in disbelief. "I know the man is a muckraker you've butted heads with, but he has no record of having ever run afoul of the law. On the other hand, you have Prior Silver, a man who got twenty years for vicious bank robberies, then in prison became a religious maniac and actually *confessed* to all the murders and subsequently *killed* himself!"

"I understand . . ."

"No, you need to understand *me*," insisted Stebbins. "The investigation is officially closed. We have our killer and a confession. I know that neither you or Detective Frankel are pleased it was literally gift wrapped and dropped on your doorstep, but I speak for the Yard, and millions of Londoners and New Yorkers, when I say we are happy to put this to bed and enjoy a *happy* and *safe* new year."

The deputy commander rose and his anger seemed to dissipate, as a look of genuine concern and compassion appeared on his face.

"I know this isn't the end you had in mind, Austin. But it doesn't diminish all the incredible work and dedication you've shown the past three decades."

Stebbins placed a hand on Grant's shoulder.

"It's time, as the poet doesn't say, for you to go 'gently into the night.' I'm sorry if it's with a few lumps you hadn't planned on. But you need to know there are a lot of people here who look up to you and want to wish you well."

Grant began to feel embarrassed. "It's not necessary for you to say that."

"But it's the truth. You'll know that once you arrive on the fourth floor in a few moments . . ."

"Excuse me, sir?"

Now, it was Stebbins who appeared flush. "A going-away party, Austin, which I'm supposed to hand deliver you to in about twenty minutes. So, make sure you act surprised—and let's keep this other nonsense to yourself, huh?"

Grant wasn't sure if he pulled off looking surprised or not. Hardly in the party mood and not one for spontaneous outbursts of joy, looking dumbfounded would certainly not be listed among his top ten talents.

But it didn't seem to matter.

With Prior Silver dead and the case behind them, the staff at the Yard was ready for any sort of celebration, especially with a new year about to arrive.

There were balloons and champagne, trays of appetizers prepared by the lunchroom staff that Grant dare not risk eating lest it begin a new death-by-poison investigation, and a large yellow cake with thirty-four candles (one for each year he'd toiled at the Yard) with a chocolate icing inscription: *Good Luck Commander!*

He had to endure close to a hundred people singing "For He's a Jolly Good Fellow" in four different keys at the same time and then attempt to blow out trick candles—which most found hilarious but just added to Grant's frustrating day.

After accepting well-wishes from more colleagues than he knew he had, Grant sat a corner table with Rachel, Everett, and Frankel, who had all shown up for the occasion.

"You could've said something at breakfast," Grant told his daughter.

"I was sworn to secrecy," she told him.

Everett and Frankel pleaded guilty by association and it was only then that Grant took a sip of bubbly and acknowledged a toast from the three of them—the people in the room who mattered to him most.

After much urging, Grant stumbled his way through a "thank you" speech, specifically expressing gratitude to Stebbins and those gathered at his table, only wishing that Allison and his trusted Sergeant Hawley could share the moment.

When he sat back down, Rachel gave him a nudge. "It's a party, Dad—you really should try and enjoy yourself."

Grant took that opportunity to recount his day and relay how Stebbins handed him his hat and pretty much a dismissal slip on the way to the party.

"I wonder if I'll still get my pension," Grant mused.

"Don't be silly, Austin. Look at this turnout," said Everett.

"Amazing what people will show up for if there's free food and booze."

Everett indicated a barely touched plate of appetizers. "Have you had the misfortune to sample these delicacies?"

Frankel nodded. "I think you guys here share a kitchen with the one in my precinct; Chef N. Edible?"

That brought the first hint of a smile to Grant's face.

"They're all here for you, Dad—like it or not," Rachel pointed out.

"But your Monte Ferguson theory deserves a toast," said Everett, raising a glass. "For originality if nothing else."

"I guess it does sound a bit ridiculous when you hear it said out loud."

Rachel finished off her champagne, then held a hand to her head.

"You okay?" asked Frankel.

"That'll teach me to drink on an empty stomach," she answered a little woozily. She looked around the room. "Anyone else up for a cup of coffee?"

"Why don't we go find some?" asked Everett. He helped Rachel out of the chair. "Hold down the fort lads, and discuss anything except the case."

"I wish you'd called and said something before you took that Ferguson stuff to Stebbins," said Frankel the moment Rachel and Everett were out of earshot.

"I guess I had to get it out of my head and have someone tell me I was crazy."

"I would've been happy to do that for you."

"I'm sure I would've run it by him anyway."

Frankel laughed, then noticed Grant watching his brother escort Rachel across the room. "That's a pretty special relationship they have."

"Rachel and Everett have always been close. Even these past few years."

Frankel nodded. There was a moment of silence between them while music more suitable for a descending elevator poured from the speakers.

"I know it's been difficult since her mother died," Frankel finally said. "For both of you."

"She's told you about that I expect."

Frankel nodded. "We've gotten pretty close in a short period of time."

"So I've noticed."

There was another beat of silence and more bad music.

Frankel smiled. "Is this the part where I'm supposed to tell you my intentions?"

"I don't know, Detective. Do you have intentions?"

"I'm hoping to spend a lot more time together. But the last thing I want you thinking is that I'm trying to take her away from you."

"Why would I ever think that?" asked Grant.

"Well, we both live in New York . . ."

"And with a lot of time on my hands, I can now come for a visit or two."

"I'm sure Rachel would love that."

"If that's really true, I think I have you to thank."

"I'm not sure I understand."

"Wasn't too long ago I thought she couldn't stand the thought or sight of me."

"I think that might be overstating things," said Frankel.

"You weren't in her life these past couple of years. Things have been rather strained—to say the least. I'm sure she's told you as much."

Frankel nodded. "A bit, yes."

A pang went through Grant. He realized that though Rachel had known Frankel a short time, he already knew things about his daughter he didn't.

"And what she promised her mother not to tell me?"

Frankel raised an eyebrow. "You know about that day, then?"

Day?

Grant took a somber moment to compose himself. And then gave Frankel the most honest response he could think of.

"I know enough to wish that I'd been there."

"You were in Scotland. It's not like you could be in two places at once."

Scotland.

Grant shook his head, dozens of thoughts colliding. "Still . . ."

Frankel was looking increasingly uncomfortable.

"This is between the two of you. But I know Rachel really wants things to be the way they were before all that happened."

Grant noticed Frankel glancing past him. The commander turned to see his brother and Rachel on their way back with an entire cistern of coffee and pieces of cake.

"So, what have you two been discussing?" asked Rachel as she placed dessert in front of Frankel and her father.

"Cop talk, what else?" replied Frankel, mustering up a smile.

"The two of us were talking about Switzerland," said Everett as he retook his seat. "We were considering heading over Monday—give ourselves a day to get settled before the New Year festivities. What do you think?"

At that point, Grant wasn't thinking about Switzerland.

For the first time in days, he actually wasn't even wondering where Monte Ferguson had disappeared to.

Grant was trying to remember when he'd last been in Scotland when Allison was still alive.

And what he could have possibly missed on that day.

30

Saturday.

Rachel crumpled up another piece of paper and tossed it across the room at the trash can behind the desk. Swish.

She was sitting in the armchair by the window in Frankel's hotel room, trying to get started on her feature piece. The only thing she'd succeeded in doing was making about fifty percent of two dozen crumpled jumpers—not a bad percentage, even for LeBron James, but an exercise in pure futility for her.

Having fulfilled a promise to her father not to write a story unless the case was over, she had spent a couple of hours trying to find an entry point or angle on the Commandment Killings. But nothing felt right. Either she glorified Prior Silver's grisly accomplishments, or cast her father and Frankel in an unflattering light because Silver had run them ragged on two continents and then further shamed them by killing himself before they could bring him in.

A distinct pall had hung over both her and John since leaving her father's farewell party. Whether it was watching Grant put on a false front for a hundred well-wishers or the toll from being a slave to the stress of Silver's sickening spree (should she use that alliteration somehow?), the last thing either felt like doing was celebrating. They'd just ordered room service and gone to bed early, so down in the dumps that all they could do was cling to each other until they restlessly fell asleep.

She glanced at John sitting atop the bed working his iPad, catching up on the case's endless paperwork. Even with light streaming in from an unseasonably sunny (but cold) wintry day, Rachel could tell John was still troubled, especially when he looked up and gave her a slight smile that disappeared as soon as it formed.

Suddenly, the room was feeling incredibly cramped.

"You getting as much done as me?" she asked, nodding at the crumpled papers surrounding the trash can.

"If that means typing the same statement four times, it's a resounding yes."

"What do you say to getting out of here for a while?"

"Another resounding yes?"

"Good answer."

Since John hadn't been in London since his holiday of debauchery with his college buddies two decades ago, Rachel suggested they do whatever he wanted to do but hadn't gotten around to back in the drunken day.

They did a mini-Beatles self-tour with the obligatory stop at the Abbey Road crosswalk where some teens took their picture. John convinced a couple of them to help form a quartet with Rachel taking the Lennon lead and Frankel bringing up the Harrison rear. After that, it was off to Savile Row, the London street famous for selling posh men's suits, specifically building No. 3, the former home of Apple Records where the Fab Four recorded the second half of *Let It Be* in the basement, then performed a forty-five-minute concert on the roof. John couldn't get over the fact that that had been their last live performance and it had been broken up by local constables for causing too much noise.

"If I'd been on duty that day, I'd have let them play till the sun went down."

Later, Rachel accompanied him to Baker Street where he was disappointed to discover there was no actual 221B, the address that reputedly belonged to Sherlock Holmes. There was a hotel and museum at a different address (with the 221B shingle on the door) that was set up to recreate Holmes's flat where he'd lived and conducted his consulting detective business with Dr. John Watson. Rachel was amused to see John soak in each artifact like the Holy Grail.

"I read all his cases when I was a kid," he told her. "It's the main reason I wanted to become a cop."

"You do know that Sherlock Holmes was a fictitious character and those were stories, not cases."

He bent and nuzzled her ear.

"Indulge an eight-year-old boy's fantasy."

She gave him a mock sexy look. "Right here?"

"That's the thirteen-year-old boy's fantasy," he said, nuzzling her other ear. "Maybe we can investigate that later."

"Whatever you say, Detective."

It was a welcome moment of lightness on a day when their moods were anything but.

By the time they returned to the hotel, after eating fish and chips in a pub that John swore he'd been drunk in before and a West End play through which they took turns snoozing, Rachel was increasingly convinced something was wrong.

It wasn't that she could fault the sex; John had lived up to his Baker Street promise and had delved into, investigated, and brought *The Case of the Passionate Lovers* to more than a satisfactory conclusion, exactly what one would have expected from a Master Consulting Detective.

But something had changed.

She was looking forward to heading to Switzerland more than ever.

Sunday.

Rachel had been sitting on the cast-iron bench her father had donated to Highgate Cemetery for thirty minutes by the time he arrived. She hadn't minded the time alone; it had allowed her to carry on an unspoken conversation with her mother, as this was the first time she'd been here since they had laid her to rest the previous year. Rachel shared the abundance of feelings racing through her brain and heart; the tortuous time apart from her father, their unexpected reunion, the whirlwind courtship with John (she actually said out loud, "I think you'd really like him, Mum"), and, of course, how much she missed her every single day.

"Sorry, time slipped away," said Grant as he sat down on the bench beside her with a bouquet of blush-pink roses tucked under his arm.

"Still looking for Monte Ferguson?"

"That—and a few other dangling threads."

"You're supposed to be retiring, Dad. Remember?"

"Old dog, no new tricks."

Grant nodded at the two flower bouquets lying atop the gravesite—one was another fresh bouquet of blush-pink roses wrapped in cellophane and a pink ribbon, the other just stems, thorns, and some withered brownish petals.

"Nice of you to remember," he told her.

"How couldn't I? They were her favorite. I presume the others were yours?"

"I bring them every Sunday." He bent down to gather up the dead roses and replace them with the new arrangement. "I missed last week. As you probably remember, we were all a little preoccupied."

Rachel thought back to seven days ago. So much had happened, it was almost impossible to keep her head from spinning. That had been the morning they'd arrived back in London to discover Sergeant Hawley's body. She started to shiver—and not from sitting in a graveyard or the dreary weather.

"I most certainly do," she murmured.

She drew the heavy coat she had been smart enough to pack more tightly around her. Her father placed a tender arm around her shoulders.

"Maybe this wasn't such a good idea."

"No, I'm glad we came. Really."

She smiled and he let her go. They sat in silence for a few moments.

"It's really gorgeous here," Rachel finally said.

"It's where she wanted to be." Grant looked down the hill toward a building in the distance. "She insisted I come here and make the arrangements. I kept telling her it wasn't time, but she wouldn't have it any other way."

When he turned back, she could see the mist in his eyes.

"That was so like your mother—taking care of everyone else but herself." Grant brought up a hand and squeezed the tears from his eyes. "I will never forget coming here to do what she asked. It suddenly all became so real. I think that was the saddest day of my life."

Rachel couldn't remember her father speaking so openly from his heart. He'd always been the solid rock, keeping everything bottled up. She felt herself choking up inside as well and took his hand. He clasped it gratefully.

"I'm really glad you came home, Rach."

"Me too, Dad."

"Maybe when the holidays arrive next year, we can celebrate them properly."

"You can come to New York. It's not like you'll have the Yard to deal with."

"I'd really like that."

He gently let go of her hand and shuffled around in his overcoat.

"But more than anything, I'd love to put all this stuff behind us."

He pulled the coat tight to ward off the sudden chill they both felt. But Rachel realized it wasn't the breeze picking up, it was the shift in the conversation.

"Dad, we've been through this . . ."

"Hear me out, Rachel."

His somber tone left her no choice. After all, he was her father.

"I know whatever you promised your mother to not tell me happened when I was up in Scotland."

Scotland? Her mind started racing. *How does he know? Was it something she had said?*

"It was that thing with the broken unicorn and the cut on her arm, wasn't it?" Grant shook his head. "I knew she wasn't telling me the whole story about it just being an accident, but there was so much going on with her sudden diagnosis and everything, that I just let it go. But there was something more, wasn't there?"

And suddenly she knew.

John.

Rachel felt tears of anger and sorrow filling her eyes.

"He shouldn't have told you anything!"

"I don't think he meant to. If anything, all John was doing was trying to help you," Grant implored. "Help the two of us."

"That still didn't give him the right to tell you . . ."

"That doesn't matter right now!" Grant exclaimed vehemently.

His words echoed through the empty graveyard. Rachel, bewildered and upset, openly sobbed. When her father resumed speaking, there was a quiet but desperate plea in his voice.

"Just tell me the rest, Rachel," he begged. "You know me—I won't stop until I find out."

"Dad . . ."

"You're the only thing left in the world that I care about. The Yard's done and I don't know what I'm going to do with myself after this. But if there's one thing the past two weeks have taught me, it's that my life means absolutely nothing without you in it. Whatever you promised your mother can't be worse than that."

"You don't know that's true."

He pointed at Allison's grave. "What I *know* is if your mother was here with us right now, seeing the wedge this has put between us—she'd want you to tell me."

Rachel wiped her eyes dry, then looked from her mother's final resting place back up at her father.

"You know that I'm right," he softly said.

Rachel closed her eyes, took a deep breath, and finally nodded.

"How could you go and do that?!"

"I didn't mean to!" John shook his head in frustration. "I didn't even tell him anything!"

"You told him enough!"

It was early evening and they were standing on opposite sides of the bed in the Covent Garden hotel room. Rachel had spent the grayest afternoon she could recall, traipsing through London, wondering what she would say to John.

She had even ducked into a pub for some liquid courage; but all that had done was feed her anger and sadness. A couple of men had offered to buy her a drink, which she had declined—in a not-very-nice-way.

By the time she returned to the hotel room, she knew John was in a state himself. He had texted her more than a few times and she hadn't responded, saving it all up for the moment she came through the door.

And boy, had she let him have it.

"Your father's actually the one who brought the whole thing up," he said. "He asked me if you'd mentioned the promise you'd made to your mother and I figured he knew more than he was letting on."

"So, you just betrayed what I told you in confidence?!"

"All I said was it happened the day he was in Scotland. He acted like he knew that much!"

"The man's a cop, John! And a bloody good one! All he needs is one bone and he'll dig to the center of the earth to find where the rest have been buried."

John stepped around the bed and Rachel instinctively backed up toward the window.

"But I didn't say anything else. I told him he should talk to you about it."

"Well, he certainly did that!"

Frankel made the mistake of stepping closer toward her. "I'm so sorry, Rachel . . ."

"Don't!"

She pushed him away. Not violently—but enough for him to stand in the middle of the room looking totally helpless.

"What do you want me to do, Rachel?"

"I don't know!" She shook her head. "What I didn't want was you taking something I told *you* in total confidence, the *only* person I ever told, and spilling it to the *one person* I promised my mother I'd *never* tell it to."

She took a deep breath and tried to calm herself.

"How did your father take it?"

"How do you think he took it? He was devastated." She lowered her eyes. "You should have seen the look on his face when I was telling him. It was like he was Old Yeller and I was the boy with the gun standing over him. Only I didn't put him out of his misery; I just caused it."

"That's not fair to you, and you know it."

"Well, that's how I feel," she murmured. She turned her back on him and walked to the window. "I knew something was wrong ever since we left my dad's party at the Yard. You should have told me you'd said something. At least I might have been prepared . . ."

"I guess I didn't know how to tell you."

"Obviously." She stared out into the blackest of winter nights.

"Did he have any idea who the man was who did that to your mother?"

"He doesn't have a clue. But now that he's got nothing to do, I'm sure he'll obsess over that!"

"If there's anything I can do to fix it . . ."

Rachel turned back around and gave John a look that stopped him in his tracks. He immediately corrected himself.

"I guess that's how we got to this spot in the first place," John mumbled. "I have no idea what to do here."

"Neither do I," Rachel told him. "But I have to be able to trust the person I'm involved in a relationship with."

Suddenly she found it impossible to look at him and lowered her gaze.

"Rachel, wait. Are you taking about . . . ?"

When she looked back up, there was a plea in her eyes.

"I need some time, John."

"But I thought we had something special here."

"I thought so too," Rachel said. "Or I think we do. I just don't know! Everything has happened so fast!"

"Rachel, please don't do this . . ."

"Think about it, John. Two weeks ago, we didn't even know each other! And now we're what? Living together? A couple trotting all over the globe?"

"It's been extraordinary circumstances, I'll give you that," said John. "But it's also *been* extraordinary! Unlike anything I've ever experienced in my life."

"The same's true for me," echoed Rachel. "But if it's really meant to be, time will tell. We'll both be back in New York soon enough."

He stared at her, as if not totally comprehending. "So, you're saying I should go back home?"

"Maybe . . . ?"

She barely said it aloud. But the look on his face caused a deep pang in her gut. Somehow in the past two hours, she'd managed to stab the two men she cared about most directly in the heart and only needed a few words to do it.

Rachel started to gather up her things and place them in her duffle.

"If that's what you want," Frankel finally replied.

She turned around. "Don't you get it, John? I don't know what I want."

"So, where are you going?"

"I really don't know." She finished packing. "If I tell you I'm going one place right now, in an hour I'd probably be somewhere else." She threw the duffle over her shoulder. "The one place I can't be right now is *here*."

She gave him a small but sad kiss on his cheek, then made sure she got out the hotel door before she broke down sobbing.

As she stood by the door, Rachel wondered if she'd made a mistake coming there. She knocked anyway.

"Your father thought you might end up on my doorstep."

Everett's warm and sympathetic smile eased at least one burden for Rachel as she let herself fold into his arms.

"He called you?"

"On his way home from the cemetery. He was worried about the way you went running out of there."

"Me? What about him? Did he tell you what happened?"

"Every word," Everett replied, ushering her inside. "You know your old man can't keep anything from me."

"How did he sound?"

"Let's just say he's had better months. First, let's get something in your stomach." He led her toward the kitchen. "Forgive me if I sound indelicate, but you do smell a bit like you've been hanging with a bunch of drunken sailors."

"Only a couple," she said, forcing a grin.

"Thank goodness for small favors."

"Maybe I can take a shower first?"

Everett said his casa was her casa, and that it was an excellent idea. A half hour later, he sat and watched Rachel finish her cereal along with a buttered scone and jam, the only things she could even think of stomaching on a day she thought would never end.

When discussing Allison's secret and her father's reaction, Rachel was happy Everett didn't linger on either for long. But he'd been stunned by the revelation.

"I couldn't believe what I was hearing," he told her. "Your father actually had to repeat himself a couple of times before I could wrap my head around it."

"Mom never hinted to you about something happening back then?"

"Heavens no, child. If she wasn't going to tell your father, I can assure you she wasn't going to tell me."

"I just can't imagine who could have done such a thing."

"If anyone is going to figure it out, it'll be your father."

"I'm pretty sure that's what my mother was afraid of."

Everett showed an exhausted Rachel to a guest room where she'd spent more than a few nights as a teen when she'd decided not to climb the Maida Vale trellis. "Try and get some sleep if you can. Things always look better in the light of day."

But it was still the end of a pretty crummy one for Rachel, and she ended up crying herself to sleep for the first time since the night her mother told her what had happened in the living room while her father was up in Scotland.

Monday.

The morning hadn't brought the clarity her uncle had hoped for.

It had started with a couple of calls from John that she didn't answer. She finally picked up the third to hear him sounding lonely and forlorn. He told her that he wasn't flying back until the next day in case she changed her mind about ringing in the New Year together. She softly reiterated her need for a break but promised him they would talk more when she returned to New York.

She called the Maida Vale house to check on her father, but ended up finding him at the Yard. He told her he was still trying to get a line on Ferguson and tying up those "dangling threads." But Rachel wouldn't have been shocked if he were combing the system (while he still had access) for lists of sexual assault offenders and victims around the time her mother had fended off her attacker.

Everett agreed with her suspicion when she told him. "I wouldn't expect anything less. Did he mention joining us tomorrow?"

"He said it was up to me," answered Rachel. "Whatever I wanted."

"I'm sure the two of you will figure it out."

Rachel looked out the window of the Swiss Air Flight bound for Geneva. She could just make out the top of the Alps a few hundred miles away.

He pushed a button and leaned back for a cat nap in his aisle seat.

She'd decided that morning with Everett to stick with the Zermatt New Year's Eve plan. The idea of staying in London seemed like a recipe for disaster.

As for figuring out what she wanted—she didn't have a clue.

31

Tuesday.

New Year's Eve. His final day at Scotland Yard.

Not only was it the end of a thirty-four-year career, but the last day of as tumultuous a year as he could recall. Grant wasn't even thinking about what the New Year might bring; he couldn't rid himself of the current one fast enough.

Stebbins had told him after his farewell gathering there was no reason for Grant to work the last few days. The Commandment Killings were over, and it wasn't like anyone at the Yard would object to him getting a jump on his new life.

"What are they going to do if you don't show up?" Stebbins had asked with a grin. "Suspend you?"

At first, Grant was going to take him up on the offer, but there was still the unfinished Ferguson business. It had almost been a week since he'd seen the reporter at Hawley's funeral, so Grant had dutifully trudged into the Yard the day before and kept making inquiries into the *Daily Mail* man's disappearance.

He had all but discarded the theory that Ferguson was the actual Commandment Killer and had framed Prior Silver. But not completely. There was something about it that seemed so right, yet simultaneously so wrong.

Wherever the truth lay, Monte Ferguson had dropped off the face of the earth. Grant began to wonder if something had actually happened to the man.

Maybe he was lying dead in a ditch on some British backroad, having swerved off the road from too much drink celebrating his coup. If that was the case, Grant thought, good riddance; the bugger deserved it.

But now Grant was suddenly preoccupied with something else.

Rachel's revelation of the secret she had promised Allison to keep from him had sent Grant into a total tailspin.

Sexual assault. For God's sake. What kind of world were they living in? Why couldn't Allison just have told him?

That should never have been a burden for her and Rachel to carry alone.

If Grant had only known—he could have done something about it. He would have utilized every resource the Yard had to find the monster. He would have hunted the man down and made him pay for attacking a helpless, dying woman.

Austin Grant was certain he would have strangled the culprit on sight.

It was what Allison wanted to desperately avoid—Grant taking the matter into his own hands in a way that would ruin her family's lives long after she was dead and gone.

And that was why Grant had returned to the Yard for his last couple of days—to try and find Allison's attacker while he still had access to the massive database it had compiled over the years.

Massive might have been an understatement—*overwhelming* was more like it.

With no information except the date two years ago, the task was virtually impossible—especially with the little time he had left. He wasn't going to ask Stebbins for more—not when he couldn't give him the real reason. Grant knew it was pointless to lie and say he needed to keep working the Ferguson angles; that case was dead as far as Stebbins and the Yard were concerned.

When Rachel had called the day before, Grant had told her he was still hunting the missing reporter—though he suspected she knew that her father couldn't resist looking into what happened in the Maida Vale living room that day.

Rachel made no mention of it. Neither did Grant.

More bloody secrets.

More than anything, Grant wished he was spending New Year's Eve with her in Zermatt, even if the place was a mile up in the sky.

He would absolutely meet Rachel there—but only if she asked him.

The last thing she had said on the phone was that she just wanted to go to Switzerland with Everett and clear her messed-up head. Grant knew it was best to give her some space. But he was determined not to let them grow apart again.

So, for the moment, Grant went back to the Herculean task of searching through the Yard databases while he still could.

Once Frankel finished packing, he stopped and took in his room at the Covent Garden Hotel.

He couldn't help but dwell on the happy time he'd spent there with Rachel. Despite the way their last evening had ended, Frankel would look back on the week as one he would never forget. He longed to rekindle that perfection once they were both back in Manhattan.

When he'd been married to Julia, he's been wed to the NYPD as well, often to the exclusion of their relationship, and wasn't surprised when Julia found solace in the arms of another man. Rachel was the first woman he had been serious about since the dissolution of his marriage. He had made a concerted effort to be totally present with her, but the last thing he wanted was to be suffocating.

He didn't think twice about giving Rachel the time she needed. But he hoped when she returned to the States, she'd come to the same conclusion as he had.

That he wanted them to spend the rest of their lives together.

It was true that they had been a couple less than two weeks—but standing in the hotel room without her, Frankel felt more lost and alone than he could ever remember. Realizing all he could do was return home and hope for the best, Frankel started for the door.

He was almost in the hall when he realized he'd forgotten the most important thing. He lunged for the door (having left the key on the dresser for housekeeping) and grabbed it just before it clicked shut.

He crossed to the desk and took the framed 45 single of *Palisades Park* off the wall where he had hung it on Christmas Eve. It reminded him of the hour they had spent rising above the twinkling city on the Eye and then heading back down in Rachel's arms beneath the gentle falling snow.

He tucked the record inside his bag and checked his watch. His flight didn't leave for a few hours. He had time for one stop before heading to Heathrow.

Rachel put on one of the London Eye earrings that John had given her, then stopped to regard herself in the small mirror atop the vanity.

She saw a woman who hadn't slept much and wasn't very happy.

She hadn't had a restful night since her father's somber farewell party. She was starting to think she might have made a mistake rushing off to Zermatt.

She loved spending time with her uncle, no question. Ever since she could remember, he'd been the one who made her laugh, the one she would confide in. But in her eagerness to get away, she'd also left two very good men in her wake who, when pressed, would tell you they were waiting for Rachel to come to her senses.

Which she felt was starting to happen on this day.

The last day of a horrible year. The day that one tended to make resolutions for the year going forward. The day that Rachel found herself making a couple of her own—not to let these two very good men disappear from her life.

She just hoped it wasn't too late.

There was a knock at the door. "Come in," she called out.

Everett's reflection appeared in the mirror as he entered the well-appointed guest room carrying a steaming cup of coffee. "Thought you might need this."

Rachel turned and accepted the dose of caffeine. "You're a godsend."

"Did you sleep well?"

"Not really—a lot of tossing and turning."

"The elevation takes some getting used to."

"Maybe. But I don't think that's it." She told her uncle what had been on her mind just before he knocked.

"That would definitely keep me up at night," agreed Everett.

She sipped the coffee. "Exactly what I needed."

"There's breakfast to go with that if you're interested."

"Very interested, surprisingly."

"Meet me in the kitchen when you're ready."

She nodded, then turned to the mirror and put on the second earring.

"Detective Frankel has good taste," said Everett.

"They're exquisite, don't you think?"

"I wasn't just talking about the earrings," he said with a wink.

Rachel waved him off with a laugh and said she'd be right there.

Minutes later, she entered the kitchen to find Everett placing two full plates on a perfectly set table. Each had an omelet bursting with veggies and oozing with cheese, crisp strips of bacon, and sliced potatoes.

"Wow," said Rachel.

Everett pulled out a chair for her to sit down. "I was just thinking about what you said. Maybe we should catch a plane back to London today."

Rachel shook her head. "Don't be silly. I'm sure John's already headed back to New York and Dad's probably chained himself to his desk at the Yard on his last day. I'm really looking forward to getting the grand tour of Zermatt."

"It's not so grand, but it'd be my pleasure. I just hate seeing you like this."

"I'll be all right," Rachel assured him. "I'm just a little sad, that's all."

"Well, let's see if we can remedy that." He indicated her breakfast plate. She picked up the fork and dug in to the omelet.

She gave Everett a genuine smile. "This is a very good start."

The list seemed to go on forever.

Grant leaned back in his chair and rubbed his eyes.

He had the same reaction over the years each time he had to go through the Yard's data on known sex offenders and predators—he was totally gobsmacked. The numbers were staggering and those were just the reported cases. He knew the actual count was at least double, maybe triple, seeing as how domestic violence and sexual assault were the type of incidents many refused to come forward about.

It was one part of the job he wasn't going to miss about the Yard.

Needless to say, he hadn't made an ounce of headway trying to find out who might have attacked Allison.

He was saved having to dive back into the breach by a tap on his door.

Grant looked up to see Frankel stepping into his office.

"John," Grant said with genuine surprise. "I thought you would've been en route to New York by now."

"I'm on my way to the airport. I just wanted to stop by and wish you a Happy New Year before I left."

Grant got up from his chair and came around the desk to shake the NYPD detective's hand. "I really appreciate it. The same to you, John."

"I also wanted to say it was a sincere pleasure and honor getting to work with you these past few weeks."

"Likewise," Grant said. "I wish it had ended differently, but at least it's over."

"So you've given up the Monte Ferguson crusade."

"Stebbins made a pretty persuasive argument against it. And . . ." Grant glanced at the wall clock—it was just past 8:30 in the morning.

". . . in less than sixteen hours, I will no longer work here, and the Ferguson search falls on someone else's watch. If anyone is still even looking."

"If I were in your shoes, I'd feel the exact same way."

They exchanged a few pleasantries, then Frankel said he should go. That was when Grant brought up what had been hovering over both since Frankel stepped into the office.

"You haven't mentioned Rachel."

Grant thought Frankel might have actually gone a little pale.

"I didn't think you'd want me to."

"There's no one I'd rather talk about than my daughter."

"I haven't known her long, but I feel the same way."

Grant nodded. He knew more than ever that Rachel's assessment of John Frankel had been spot on. This was a good man.

"I feel like I might have gotten in between the two of you," Grant finally said. "I just want you to know that was never my intention."

"I never thought it was," answered Frankel. "In fact, I feel like I'd done that to the two of you."

"I know you were just trying to help."

"And look how that turned out." Frankel offered up a slightly sad smile.

The soon-to-be-former Scotland Yard commander nodded again.

"Rachel's a smart girl, John. She'll figure it all out. It just might take a bit."

"I'm willing to wait," said Frankel.

It was Grant's turn to smile.

"Remember the other day, at that bloody party I had to suffer through, when I asked you what your intentions were?"

"I do."

"Well, what you just said is what a father longs to hear."

"I just hope it isn't too late."

"I'll tell you this, John. I've watched the two of you together over these past few days."

"I'm sure you have."

"And I've never seen Rachel look at anyone the way she looks at you."

"Thank you for that," said Frankel. "Whatever ends up happening, Austin, I hope you'll get in touch when you come to New York to see her."

"Without question." They shook hands again. "Fly safely, John. I'm sure I'll see you soon."

He could tell that promise filled Frankel with more than a modicum of hope as he left the office and headed for Heathrow. Grant found himself buoyed by the notion as well.

He returned to his bloody lists.

It was an hour later when his cell phone rang and he was pleased to see that it was Everett.

"How's it going over there?" Grant asked.

"Just giving Rachel the ten-schilling tour of Zermatt," answered his brother.

"Lucky girl."

"The city's grown since you were last here—how old were you—seven?"

"Whatever age I was in that picture you just gave me for Christmas," said Grant. "How is she doing?"

"That's why I phoned."

Grant felt that immediate punch one gets in the gut when they get a call about their child—no matter the age—but then realized his brother had just said they were touring the Swiss city.

But he was still unable to keep the alarm out of his voice. "Everything okay?"

"Yes, yes, of course—sorry," said Everett, obviously sensing Grant's concern. "I didn't mean it like that."

"Thank god."

"She's just down in the dumps."

Grant couldn't tell if he felt good or bad about hearing that.

"What can I do?"

"I was thinking you should hop over here and join us like we planned."

"Seriously?"

"I think she'd be pleasantly surprised," suggested Everett.

"I got the distinct impression Rachel needed some time alone."

"She's with me, Austin—how alone is that?"

"You make a good point there."

"And she told me at breakfast that she really regretted running off the way she did, leaving you and Frankel behind."

"He just left my office an hour ago for the airport. He probably isn't on his plane yet. Maybe we can catch him and see if he can change his plans as well."

"I'm not sure we want to overwhelm the poor girl," said Everett. "Besides, wouldn't it be wonderful for the three of us to be together? Just the family seeing in the New Year?"

"It's a nice thought but—"

"What's stopping you, Austin? Your daughter needs you. Come over and be here for her. Set things right between the two of you. Then maybe we can work on Rachel about seeing the light with the good detective."

Grant looked at the clock. "It's already ten. I'm not sure I can get there."

"There's a three o'clock nonstop to Geneva leaving out of Heathrow. You get in at five-thirty and can be at the house around eight. Plenty of time to have a few drinks, eat a nice dinner, and still sing 'Auld Lang Syne.' "

"You've got it all figured out."

"No one's going to care if you play hooky your last day at the Yard. Just run home, pack what you need—and off you go."

"You really think this is a good idea?"

"It's our Rachel, Austin. Do you need another reason?"

Grant was tempted to mention Everett's house being five thousand feet above sea level but wasn't in the mood for his brother's taunts. Besides, how many times had Everett told him his house was on the ground?

The next thing Grant knew, he told his brother he would come.

"Fantastic! Rachel will be ecstatic," said Everett.

"I certainly hope so."

32

Heathrow was a complete mess.

Frankel exited the cab at the British Airways terminal to find extremely long lines and impatient passengers. He figured that people were flying all over the world trying to get to some party before the clock struck midnight.

But he was in no rush to get back to New York. It wasn't like he was going to stand in Times Square with two million revelers to watch the ball drop and then spend hours trying to get out of the world's largest human sardine can.

He didn't care where he was when the next year started. If it weren't in a Swiss town at the base of the Matterhorn, where the object of his desire was staying, he might as well spend it cramped up in a coach seat above the Atlantic.

And that was the fate he seemed headed for. Once he got through the interminable security line and arrived at his gate, he discovered his flight had been delayed four hours because of equipment trouble back in Chicago.

He plopped down on a chair next to eight-year-old twins, a cute-as-a-button tow-haired British boy and girl totally immersed in a video game and puzzle book respectively while their parents kept looking alternately at their watches, then at the arrival and departure board.

Frankel took a swig from the Fiji water he'd bought at a kiosk and took out his laptop. His first inclination was to log on to the airport wireless and catch up on the slew of emails he'd ignored since being in the UK, figuring it would eat up time.

Suddenly he had a different thought. He reached into his carry-on for the *Gone with the Wind* DVD Everett had given him. Frankel flipped it over to check out the running time—three hours and forty-one minutes. Or, three hours and fifty-four minutes allowing for the overture, intermission, entr'acte (whatever the hell that was), and exit music.

It certainly beat responding to people he was in no hurry to get back to. He placed the DVD in the disc drive, plugged in earbuds, and hit play. Frankel settled in to see what the big deal was with Scarlett O'Hara and Rhett Butler. He'd been maybe eight when his father dragged him to a Jersey retro house to see it. The only thing he remembered was it being super long and Clark Gable saying he didn't give a damn to someone.

It took Grant five minutes to pack a bag once he returned to the Maida Vale house. Given his dislike of higher elevations, he wasn't a winter sports enthusiast, so he didn't need to cram a parka or ski clothes in his luggage. He settled for a sweater Allison had given him five Christmases ago and the overcoat he had on.

He spent more time looking for Everett's blasted house key.

Right before they'd hung up, his brother had asked if Grant could stop by the Hampstead house. Everett and Rachel had been in such a hurry to catch their flight the previous day, his brother had forgotten to take his ski boots. "They're custom made and it's not like I can head down the slope in my tennies," Everett had said.

Why anyone would want to hurl themselves down the side of a mountain was lost on Grant, but he wasn't going to argue with Everett. It was easier to just get the house key, pop up to Hampstead, grab the damn shoes, and head to Heathrow.

His brother told him where to find them in the basement and said while Grant was there, he should pull the bottle of '96 Dom Perignon out of the fridge down there, as he'd been saving it for a special occasion.

"Seriously?" Grant had asked.

"It has a ninety-seven-point rating, worth a small fortune. If I'm not going to pop it open to ring in the New Year and celebrate your retirement, when else?"

Another battle not worth fighting.

He spent ten minutes turning his kitchen upside down looking for the key Everett had given him way back when, only to remember it was in the top drawer of the desk. Grant sighed, went in and found it, then grabbed his bag and coat.

The things we do for family.

He locked up the Maida Vale house, found a cab, and headed up the hill to his brother's house in Hampstead.

Frankel put the movie on pause and rubbed his eyes.

The film certainly took its time to get going. He was already an hour in and nothing had happened. Wasn't it supposed to be about the Civil War? Where were all the battle scenes? What about all those bodies laid out for as far as the eye could see in the picture on the back of the DVD?

Instead, there were all these scenes with Scarlett pining after Ashley Wilkes, the man her cousin Melanie was going to marry. Some epic alright. It was giving him an epic headache. He dug into his bag for some Tylenol and washed them down with the water, then looked over to see the twin girl staring at him.

"Are you sick?" she asked.

"Nah. Just have a bit of a headache."

"If you were, my mummy would make me wear a mask—and I hate wearing masks."

"You're good." He nodded at the book in her lap. "What've you got there?"

"My puzzles."

He saw she was using a red pen to draw lines between a series of dots that turned into various animals. "Connect the Dots. I used to do those when I was your age. Is that your favorite?"

"I like the hidden ones better," she told him.

"Hidden ones?"

She found a black and white drawing of an English country garden. At the top of the page were the words *Hidden Figures and Numbers*.

"See how it looks like a garden? It's really filled with letters and numbers." Her eyes suddenly widened. "See, here's a K!"

Sure enough, embedded in the whorls of the tree bark was the letter *K*. The girl circled it in red with glee.

"And I think that's an upside down seven right beside it," Frankel pointed out.

"It is!" She circled that one as well. "You're pretty good at this."

"Beginner's luck."

The two of them hunted for digits and the twenty-six letters of the alphabet. Most were easy to find, especially the numbers, but Frankel held back and let the little girl (whose name was Claire and her brother, whose eyes never left his video game, was Jack) locate the majority, giving her a hint every now and then.

A few of the letters—the T and X in particular—proved more difficult.

"That's because it's easy for them to look like something else," said Claire.

Both letters turned out to be hidden in the lawn, looking more like scribbles than members of the alphabet.

Eventually, Claire's folks said they should go eat. They managed to tear Jack away from his video game and Claire thanked Frankel for the puzzle help.

"My pleasure," he said and watched them toddle off through the terminal.

It was a nice distraction but the longer they had played, the more Frankel felt he'd missed something. But for the life of him, he couldn't remember what it was. The more he taxed his mind, the further it slipped away. It'd probably hit him thirty-five thousand feet in the air where he couldn't do anything about it.

He picked up the laptop again and let out a sigh. He hoped the battle would start soon and Scarlett would stop whining. But he highly doubted it.

Grant let himself into Everett's house and headed directly into the kitchen. Opening the door next to the pantry, he flipped on the adjacent light switch.

It illuminated a set of wooden stairs that led down to a rather large basement that ran half the length of the Hampstead house.

The room wasn't quite a candidate for that *Hoarders* show Grant caught a few times on the telly, but there was plenty packed inside. There were stacks of books and an equal number of documents and papers that Everett had stored for years.

Grant located the ski boots easily enough in a corner. Everett had been very specific about where to find them. He then moved across the room to the large refrigerator sitting flush against the wall.

Grant knew his brother used it to keep chilled Chardonnays and spar-kling wines, to go with the racks of reds above it that composed Everett's version of a wine cellar.

Grant threw open the refrigerator door to grab the bottle of Dom.

The minute Grant was back in the kitchen and had reception, he began dialing. Everett picked up after barely one ring.

"Don't you have a three o'clock plane to catch?"

"Where's Rachel?" Grant demanded.

"In the other room. We just got back from our tour," his brother responded calmly. "I take it you couldn't find the Dom."

"You know bloody damn well I didn't."

"But you found Monte Ferguson," said Everett.

Staring at him from inside the cleaned-out fridge, his throat slashed and a Roman numeral IX carved into his forehead.

Just when he thought this horrendous year couldn't get any worse, Grant was trying to come to grips with the ghastliest fact of all.

My brother is the Commandment Killer.

Everett had been leading him around by the nose from the very beginning.

Starting in the library down the hall over a game of chess where Everett connected the first three murders *he* had committed, all the way to stuffing the reporter from the *Daily Mail* into the fridge in his basement below.

"Why Ferguson?" asked Grant.

With countless questions racing through his brain, it was the first Grant thought to utter.

"*Thou shalt not bear false witness,*" responded Everett, quoting the Ninth Commandment. "One shouldn't make up stories about other people."

"The interview with Prior Silver?" realized Grant. "But he didn't even write it. You did!"

"About time you finally caught on," Everett taunted. "He might not have written it, but he certainly told that editor of his to go and publish it."

Grant remembered Michaels telling him how frightened Ferguson had sounded on the phone. "Because you must have forced him to do it."

"I might have been holding a knife to his throat at the time, but he didn't say no," Everett said. "I must admit you were getting close when you thought it was Ferguson who made it all up and faked Silver's suicide."

"Right idea, wrong lunatic."

Everett chuckled. The fact that his brother didn't deny it was chilling.

"You have a twisted sense of logic," Grant told Everett. "Washed up rock and rollers, priests just doing their job . . ."

"Means to an end."

"Victim number ten?" asked Grant.

"X marks the spot, as they say."

"Care to tell me who?"

Everett just laughed again. "You're going to miss your plane if we keep this up," he said. "And if you're thinking of calling the Swiss police on your way over here, I would seriously reconsider. Especially if you want to see Rachel. It would be a damn shame if you didn't—considering how happy she would be to see you."

Grant felt his entire body go cold. "You wouldn't dare, Everett."

"I've been known to improvise when the need arises. Just ask Sergeant Hawley."

"Lay one hand on her and I'll slit your throat myself."

"Like I told you before—don't make promises you can't keep, Commander."

There was a click, and Everett was gone.

Grant screamed in anguish at the top of his lungs.

———

Rachel had found the cold crisp walk through the quaint streets of Zermatt invigorating. She'd returned to her uncle's feeling refreshed—her resolutions to keep Frankel and her father in her life gave hope to the new year on the horizon.

After hanging up her parka in the guest room closet and changing into sweats, she walked into the living room just as her uncle put down his cell phone.

"Who was that?" she asked.

"Your father, actually."

"Is he okay?"

"Absolutely."

But Rachel could see the mischievous look in her uncle's eye. "What is it?"

"What's what?"

"What aren't you telling me?" asked Rachel.

"It was supposed to be a surprise, but you'll find out soon enough." Everett made a grandiose gesture. "Your father is on his way here for New Year's Eve."

"Really?"

"I called and invited him. I wasn't wrong to do that, was I?"

Rachel threw her arms around Everett and gave him a big hug.

"You're the best uncle ever!"

"I wouldn't go that far," he said. "But we should get the garret ready."

"The garret?"

Her uncle pointed toward the ceiling. "The apartment in the attic. It's where the two of us stayed when we were boys. I thought it might make him feel at home."

"Sounds like a splendid idea," said Rachel. "How can I help?"

Frankel had paused the movie again at the intermission and was getting another bottle of Fiji water at a nearby kiosk when his cell rang.

He quickly pulled it from his pocket—hoping it might be Rachel.

One look at the caller ID told him it wasn't—but he answered right away. "Austin?"

"I took the chance I'd catch you before your plane left," said Grant.

"It got delayed a few hours," Frankel told him. "What's going on?"

He took a seat halfway through Grant's dumbfounding download because he wasn't sure his legs could support him under the weight of what the commander was telling him.

Everett Grant was who they'd been looking for all along.

As insane as that sounded, there were certain things Frankel realized he couldn't deny and was already kicking himself about. Starting with the fact that Everett put his brother onto the Old Testament tie-in to the murders.

"You'll come to Zermatt with me?" Grant asked.

"Do you even have to ask?"

They were going after Rachel.

He could hear Grant telling the cab driver the quickest way to Heathrow. "I should be there in forty minutes," Grant said after giving him the Swiss Air info.

"I'll have my ticket and meet you at the gate."

"Thank you, John."

"Don't be ridiculous," responded Frankel. "Did Everett give you a clue as to who he's going after?"

"Nothing specific," said Grant. "All he said was 'X marks the spot.'"

X marks the spot, thought Frankel.

Something about that.

X marks the spot.

"John? Are you still there?"

But Frankel was barely hearing him. He was flashing on the puzzle he had been helping Claire with an hour ago and the thing that had been bothering him.

Hidden Figures and Numbers.

"John . . . ?"

And suddenly he had it. *Oh shit.*

"I'll call you right back, Austin. Five minutes."

Before Grant could protest, Frankel hung up and went back to his laptop.

—⁓—

Rachel went up the steps to the attic, her arms laden with a fresh set of sheets, blankets, and pillows.

She reached out with one hand, turned the doorknob, and stepped into the room that had been refurbished many years before—back when her father and uncle were just little boys.

It was fairly dark, as the window shades were down.

She flicked on the light switch. The room was illuminated in a moody glow.

Rachel gasped and dropped the bedding on the floor.

And began to sob.

A distressed Austin Grant was in the back of the taxi thinking of calling the detective back when he received a text from him.

Grant clicked it open and found Frankel had sent him a picture he hadn't looked at in least a week. Not since they'd found it in a stolen car in Far Rockaway.

It was the newspaper photo of Grant that had been crossed out over and over with a black marker.

Grant was still staring at it when his cell phone rang again.

"You got what I sent?" asked Frankel the moment that Grant answered.

"I did. But I'm not exactly sure what you wanted me to see."

"It's the markings, Austin. When you first look at the photo, it seems like a crazy person just went nuts and scribbled all over it in anger."

"I hate to say it, but I think you just described my brother."

"But these aren't just scribbles. They're *X*s."

*X*s.

Like the Roman numeral for ten, Grant suddenly realized.

"And if you take the time to count them," continued Frankel. "You'll see there are *ten* of them. The big one on top—and nine more underneath."

Grant took a closer look and quickly counted. Frankel was absolutely right.

"*You're* his next victim, Austin. It's been about you all along."

Grant thought of the Tenth Commandment and said it out loud.

" '*Thou shalt not covet any thing that is thy neighbor's.*' How am I guilty of that?" asked Grant.

"I guess we'll have to ask him when we get there," said Frankel.

The attic was filled with pictures of her mother.

Dozens of them. At every age from the time Allison was a teenager until the year that she passed away.

The garret could have been a shrine.

Rachel walked further into the room, unable to speak, wiping her eyes.

She noticed something glistening on the night table beside the bed.

It was a piece of glass that looked achingly familiar.

Rachel crossed over and picked it up. It felt like she would pass out right then and there.

It was the head to a glass unicorn. The one she'd made for her mother when she was in the fifth form.

The same unicorn that had been smashed in the Maida Vale living room a couple of years ago.

"She was supposed to be mine."

Rachel whirled around to find Everett standing in the doorway. He carried a wooden box in his hands and a dead-eyed expression on his face.

"It was you?"

She barely got the words out before she started to sob again.

"She was supposed to be mine and your father took her away from me."

Then the monster, whom she'd known her entire life as her loving uncle, closed the door and began to move toward her.

DECALOGUE

Top of the World

I

Everett Grant hung up the phone; he couldn't believe what his brother had just told him. How could that even be possible?

Cancer?

Allison had lung cancer and, according to her doctors, it was inoperable.

Austin had delivered the news matter-of-factly, as if reciting crime statistics. Everett presumed that was his way of dealing with shock; stick to the cold, hard truth and don't let others see how much it affects you.

Didn't matter. Everett was devastated enough for both of them.

He had been in love with Allison for over thirty years—ever since he'd met her at an Oxford library, brought her home to meet his folks, and his brother had stolen her away from right under his nose.

That hadn't been how Austin portrayed it. For years, he'd dined out on the story that Everett and Allison hadn't been serious, just friends. And that shortly after she'd called Austin in London to go for drinks, they couldn't deny their magnetic attraction.

An outright lie on his older sibling's part.

While Everett had been getting the teaching degree that would guarantee him a yearly salary, Austin had gotten Allison caught up in a whirlwind romance. By the time he went down to London with a university job and good intentions, Austin and Allison were engaged to be wed, before Everett had gotten the chance to get down on bended knee and propose.

He was convinced that Austin had been aware of his desires and purposefully preyed on Allison, knowing he had a small window to dash Everett's dreams. He was certain that Austin had meticulously plotted a course that would win her heart—getting back at Everett for besting him at countless endeavors throughout their childhood and adolescence.

Everett had hated his brother ever since.

But he had still been in love with Allison and realized it was better to have her in his life than not at all. He knew if he ever voiced his beliefs about Austin's courtship and motives, Allison would have stuck by her husband. She was a loyal and loving woman—one of the many reasons Everett continued to adore her.

So he'd remained a dutiful brother-in-law and favorite uncle once Rachel was born, hoping Allison would eventually realize Everett was the better man, that she'd fall out of love with Austin and he would be there to pick up the pieces.

Over the years, he'd even entertained some sort of tragedy befalling his brother, imagining scenarios where he helped it along. But Everett couldn't see any of those vicious endings through because he couldn't stand the thought of Allison suffering. He loved her that much.

As a result, he just waited, figuring Austin would pass first, either from the hazards of his profession or the stress of being an overworked male. Even if it had happened late in life, Everett would have taken her for however much time was left.

Now, with this devastating diagnosis, he was going to be denied that as well.

After delivering the news, Austin said he needed to go to Scotland on an investigation—and Everett knew he must go and see Allison.

Looking back, he hadn't shown up at the Maida Vale house with the intention of pouring out his heart. But he must have known it on some level, as he hadn't told his brother he was going there in his absence.

They sat on the living room couch where Allison served tea and scones. He commiserated on the horrid turn of events, saying what one does in such situations—how unfair life could be and there must be a way to get through this. Allison took his hand and said there was no hope for her. But she was certain they'd all be fine afterward and that caused Everett to fall apart.

Suddenly, the woman he'd cherished with all his broken heart was comforting *him*—and three decades of holding everything back poured out of him.

Everett told her he'd always loved her, how he'd do anything for Allison, how she should have been with him all these years, and that there was still time.

Allison let go of his hand. "You don't know what you're saying, Everett."

"But I do." He put his arms around her and started to plead with all of his misguided soul. "Let me take care of you—let me see you through this."

Tears formed in her eyes. "That's impossible, Everett . . ."

But he continued to pull her toward him. "Please, Allison . . ."

He moved to kiss her, but she turned her head away. "Everett, no. Don't . . ."

She began to struggle in his arms, but Everett wouldn't let go. He couldn't. Not when, after all this time, he held her this close. "I love you so much, Allison."

He kissed her neck. Her cheek. Started pulling at her clothes—unable to stop himself.

"No!" she cried out. And pushed him off her.

Everett reached out to grab her again.

But Allison backed away and smashed into the end table beside the sofa. She tumbled off it and there was a crash.

A stunned Everett looked down to see Allison curled into a ball on the floor.

And there was blood. It came from a nasty gash in her arm—caused by falling onto a glass unicorn figurine that had smashed into dozens of pieces.

Snapping back to brutal reality, Everett bent down to check on her. "Allison, I'm so sorry . . ."

She waved him away, her blood tricking on the floor. "I'll be okay."

He offered a hand. "Let me help you up. Please."

She shook her head. "I can do this myself."

Not knowing what to do, Everett began to pick up broken pieces of glass.

"Just leave them be, Everett. Please."

He looked down at her. "What can I do? Please, just tell me."

She sat up and used napkins to stanch the blood. "You need to go. Rachel is flying in and should be here any minute. I don't want her to see me like this."

"Allison, I don't know what to say . . ."

"You must leave. Please."

The desperate look in her eyes left him no choice.

Everett knew he would always do whatever she asked. He left.

It wasn't until he got home that he discovered the unicorn head in one of his pockets. He realized he must have put it there while cleaning up.

He sat down and stared at the remnant of the figurine in his hand.

And understood things would never be the same with him and Allison.

He could feel what was left of his heart breaking.

In the days that followed, Everett kept waiting for his brother or Rachel to confront him with what he'd done. But neither ever said a word.

He gradually came to the realization that Allison had never told them.

She confirmed it a few months later at a small birthday gathering she'd thrown for Austin. Everett had begged off more invitations than he'd accepted, but knew he had to show up on this particular occasion.

He'd ended up alone in the kitchen with Allison for a few minutes while she was preparing the cake. She looked much frailer but maintained an upbeat mood as always, although Everett knew the dreaded disease was ravaging inside her.

"I never said anything," she told him.

"I figured as much," Everett said. "I'm not sure I understand why."

"You and Austin are brothers," Allison explained. "You need to take care of each other afterwards."

She asked him to help her with the cake and that was the last time they ever talked about it.

She was gone a month later.

II

Everett stood in the garret of the Zermatt cottage, studying the broken glass unicorn in his hand.

You and Austin are brothers. You need to take care of each other.

His brother had been the luckiest man on Earth. All because he had taken from Everett what was once his.

Thou shalt not covet any thing that is thy neighbor's.

He looked around the room at the pictures of his beloved.

Thou shalt not covet thy neighbor's wife.

He was definitely going to take care of his brother. Just like he'd taken care of nine others who had violated the Lord's statutes.

His eyes drifted to the floor where Rachel lay motionless.

Everett opened the wooden box he had placed on the bed. He reached inside and chose one of his blessed knives. He lifted it up and stared at it for a long time; thinking how he would be using it again very soon.

Just not quite yet.

He returned it to the box and removed what had lain beside it.

There was work to be done before Austin Grant's commandment ended.

III

"Everett got to JFK on Saturday the fourteenth and headed back to Heathrow the following Friday, the twentieth," Grant said, reading the text sent by the Yard.

"How did you explain asking for your brother's flight itinerary?"

Frankel had just swung the car onto the Swiss A1 Autobahn and started heading east, shortly after the sun set behind the mountains in the west.

"I told Morrow it had something to do with year-end taxes," replied Grant.

The tech guru hadn't seemed very interested. Like everyone else at the Yard, Morrow probably had some place to go on New Year's Eve. Grant couldn't blame him. Anything beat tearing across Switzerland to keep a date with a lunatic serial killer, who just happened to be one's younger brother.

The bored woman behind the Hertz desk said it would take around three hours to get to Zermatt. Frankel had hopped behind the wheel, saying he was a New York driver and would get them there faster.

"He arrived in time to kill the priest," said Frankel, happy for a clear road so he could punch the accelerator. "And then he spends the week getting a line on Timothy Leeds, posing as a British reporter . . ."

". . . who we were supposed to think was Monte Ferguson," added Grant.

". . . steals a car, lures Leeds to Far Rockaway, kills him in the old hospital, and leaves you that love note in the Sonata."

"And we fell for all of it," grumbled Grant.

"What about those phone calls you were getting from him in New York?"

"He obviously placed them from somewhere in Manhattan. When I called his London number, it just forwarded to his cell. For all I know, he might have been staying in the same bloody hotel as me." Grant shook his head in disbelief. "How could I have been so blind?"

"Why would you even suspect him? He's your brother."

"Not the brother I've known all my life."

"How many psychopaths have you encountered where those closest to them didn't have a clue as to what they were really like? It goes with the territory."

"He must have been laughing behind our backs all this time," rued Grant. "Especially with me updating him all the time on the murders *he* was committing."

Frankel flip-flopped between lanes while keeping a steady speed around 125 kilometers an hour. "How about that nifty trick he pulled texting Rachel while he was standing right beside us?"

Grant thought back and recalled the text, the same threat Everett had repeated on the phone a few hours before.

Don't make promises you can't keep, Commander.

Suddenly, Grant remembered his brother keeping his hands buried in his coat, ostensibly trying to ward off the winter chill.

The cocky bastard.

Grant and Frankel had spent most of the flight discussing whether to bring in the Yard or Swiss police—despite Everett's demands to the contrary.

For all the pros and cons, they kept coming back to the same conclusion. Grant would do exactly as his brother had asked because he had Rachel with him.

Besides, Monte Ferguson was already gone in Hampstead. Waiting an extra twenty-four hours for his body to be discovered by the Yard wasn't going to hurt anyone—especially the *Mail*'s former star reporter.

One thing neither of the two cops hurtling toward Zermatt could answer was what Grant could have done to make himself the ultimate target in Everett's Commandment spree. Grant couldn't think of anything belonging to Everett that he possibly wanted, let alone coveted.

But Everett had obviously been working himself up to this point for some time—a murderous rampage that so far numbered ten (nine marked victims and Sergeant Hawley).

As they circled the north shore of Lake Geneva and got on the A9 directly to Zermatt, Grant realized the answer must lie in the cottage he had never been to. Otherwise, why would Everett drag them there?

He shared this with Frankel, who didn't disagree. He asked the detective if they could push the speed limit further.

"Don't see why not," responded Frankel as he tested the limits of the speedometer. "Let's see them try to pull over a couple of cops."

IV

They covered the two-hundred-and-thirty-eight kilometers in just over two hours without being stopped, Frankel making good on his word by besting the Hertz's woman's estimate by almost an hour.

He parked a couple of blocks from the address in Zermatt, made sure that his NYPD firearm was properly holstered, and exited the car. Grant had gotten out and moved to the driver's side of the rental to confer one last time.

Even though they'd heeded Everett's demand that Grant keep the Swiss authorities in the dark, Frankel's presence ran the risk of setting the killer off and endangering Rachel before either could get in the door. They figured Grant should park in front of the cottage and approach on his own.

Meanwhile, Frankel would situate himself somewhere with a direct line of sight to the cottage and wait till Grant went inside. If Everett gave Frankel an opportunity to get off a clean shot without jeopardizing Rachel—Grant agreed that the detective should shoot to maim and ask questions later.

They told each other to be careful and went their separate ways.

A few minutes later, Frankel had traipsed through the quiet Zermatt neighborhood whose denizens were huddled inside working their way through long-saved bottles of bubbly or celebrating elsewhere. He found a black BMW SUV hybrid parked across from the Grant cottage that provided the cover he needed.

Frankel watched Grant pull around the corner in the rental and get out the driver's side. He could tell the Scotland Yard man had just sighed deeply as his breath manifested in the near freezing temperatures.

As Grant walked up the path, Frankel pulled out his gun and perched himself against the SUV, set to fire.

He watched Grant knock on the door and waited for what seemed like forever. Nothing happened. Grant knocked again and got the same result. Twenty seconds later, Frankel watched Grant try the handle and ease open the door.

He felt helpless watching the commander enter his brother's cottage.

This time the wait was an excruciating ten minutes.

Suddenly, the lights on the first floor began to flicker on and off—three successive times. There was a pause and then the pattern repeated. It was the signal they'd agreed on if Grant ended up inside and Everett was nowhere to be found.

Frankel raced across the street, gun raised, and went inside the front door.

He lowered the gun when he saw Grant sitting on the stairs. Frankel might have been mistaken but it looked like Austin Grant had aged a couple of decades in the ten minutes they had been separated.

"Everett?"

"Not here," Grant confirmed in something that resembled a whisper.

The man looks like he's going to have a heart attack.

Frankel imagined the worst. He was barely able to ask the question.

"Is it Rachel?"

Grant shook his head and pointed up the stairs behind him.

Frankel took the steps two at a time. He could hear Grant right behind him.

At the top of the steps was an open door from which an eerie glow emanated.

Frankel stepped through it and found himself inside an attic that had been converted to a quaint apartment. It was lit by at least two dozen candles.

And filled with dozens of pictures of Allison Grant from photos he'd seen on the commander's desk at the Yard and the Maida Vale house.

"Me and Allison," Grant said, appearing behind him. "That's what this whole thing's been about."

In a number of photos—the ones featuring Allison and Grant specifically—the commander's face had been crossed out with a familiar black marker.

"You are in exactly ten of them," counted Frankel. "And each time, he's blotted your face out with a giant X."

At that point, the detective noticed what was above the macabre photo gallery.

He had been so caught up in the candle-lit shrine to Grant's late wife that he hadn't noticed the message on the wall above it.

"What the hell does that mean?" asked Frankel.

"It's where he's taken Rachel," said Grant.

The four words were scrawled in the same black ink.

TOP OF THE WORLD

"That's where he wants me to go now."

V

C old as ice.

It was the first thought that went through her muddled brain when she woke.

Rachel felt like she was in the middle of a kaleidoscope, surrounded by swirling soft magentas, satin reds, dusky blues, and candy apple greens.

Once her eyes began to clear, she realized the multicolored hues were coming from a translucent dollhouse completely made of ice. It jutted out from a snowy glacier wall that was part of a seemingly endless ice cavern.

All that was missing was the Snow Queen.

She still felt pretty loopy, sitting on a blue-lit narrow path between the frozen walls while thoughts of fairy tale princesses and majestic ice halls danced through her head. And suddenly she realized where she was.

The ice palace on top of the Matterhorn.

The one Everett mentioned at dinner on Christmas Eve.

Everett.

Rachel shuddered as those moments in the garret rushed back to her.

Everett was the Commandment Killer.

She remembered standing in the converted attic, surrounded by all those pictures of her mother. And then her uncle had appeared.

She had started to back away and stumbled onto the bed. As she tried to get up, Everett had told her to stay where she was.

"You need to listen to me, Rachel. You need to understand."

Frozen in fear, Rachel had stayed on the edge of the bed. Trying to comprehend what Everett told her, all of which sounded like utter madness.

How he had always loved her mother, how Allison was supposed to marry him, not Austin. How her father had ruined his life by stealing Allison away and now needed to be punished for violating the most sacred of the Commandments.

"Thou shalt not covet thy neighbor's wife."

Her uncle, overwhelmed with jealousy and hatred that had rendered him insane, repeated the Tenth Commandment over and over.

When he'd told her the truth about what happened in the Maida Vale living room, Rachel had wanted to die right there.

It had been Everett whom her mother had refused to name, the man that Allison made Rachel swear she would never tell her father about.

No wonder. He would have strangled Everett.

Rachel had started wailing out loud and that was when Everett pulled the hypodermic out of his wooden box and used it on her.

She remembered nothing else after that.

She had woken up the first time in the passenger seat of the car beside her uncle to see him holding the knife inches away.

"If you ever want to see your father again, you're going to do exactly as I say," Everett told her.

He'd mentioned "a party" and to smile at "the nice man by the cable cars." It hadn't made much sense as she was still shaking off the effect of whatever drug he'd given her. Most importantly, she was told the pointed knife he'd used more than a few times that month would never be far from her throat.

Soon after that, Everett had led her up to an embarking station where a sign read *Glacier Paradise*. Rachel remembered a kind older man waiting for them beside some cable cars, engaging Everett in a muted conversation.

Minutes later, she and Everett were inside one of the cars and heading up the side of the majestic Matterhorn. The twinkling lights of Zermatt were just starting to move away when Everett produced the hypodermic again.

Next thing she knew, she came to on the floor of the glacier ice palace.

"Awake, I see."

She turned her head to see Everett approaching through the cavern of ice. Rachel tried to crawl away but was blocked by the crystal-clear dollhouse.

"If I was going to hurt you, Rachel, don't you think I'd have done that by now?"

Rachel could barely find her voice.

"Is that what you told all those people you killed?"

He shook his head. "There wasn't much chat time with them."

Rachel realized that was probably true. And that the best thing was to keep her uncle talking. "What about Prior Silver? You were certainly speaking to him."

"Prior Silver? Prior Silver was a fool."

Everett chuckled. It wasn't a pleasant sound.

"A fool, but a necessary one."

VI

It had taken Everett a long time to find the perfect person. But when the painstaking search finally unearthed Prior Silver, the man was a literal godsend.

Someone to take the fall for the acts of vengeance Everett had meticulously planned against those who'd violated the Lord's Commandments.

Beginning on what would have been Allison's birthday with Lionel Frey ("Your father even missed that," he'd told Rachel), a heathen colleague who'd dared to bow to other gods, and ending with Austin being punished at the Top of the World on the last day of his command for committing the worst transgression of all.

Silver had met every piece of criteria that Everett demanded.

A man filled with religious mania. Someone who had committed crimes in the past. A man desperately seeking repentance on the road to salvation. And most importantly, a person who had a bone to pick with Commander Austin Grant.

In actuality, Everett hadn't required much from his choice.

He just needed Prior Silver to be in the right places at what would be the exact wrong times. That meant London for the first three murders, New York for the next two, and then back to the UK until Everett decided it was time to dispatch Prior for good as a martyr who confessed to crimes he didn't commit.

Next, Everett worked out a scenario to get the man back and forth from America. There had been a few hiccups along the way but Everett had gotten good at coming up with alternate solutions when needed.

Just ask Sergeant Stanford Hawley.

Everett slowly reached out to Prior through a series of seemingly random emails—posing as Deacon Jeremiah, founder of the Church of the Repentant Soul, an organization made up by Everett. He'd designed an appropriate website and gone online with it just before he first contacted Prior Silver.

Within a few days, Deacon Jeremiah had reeled in the Church of the Repentant Soul's newest (and, unbeknownst to Prior, *only*) congregant. It was really quite simple; all Everett did was feed into the religious mania of the born-again soul who was desperately craving salvation.

Then, in one-on-one text chats (with burner phones for Everett), he filled his mark with the proper mix of scripture and sermons of repentance until Prior was primed to do anything Deacon Jeremiah asked.

So when Jeremiah told Silver he'd been handpicked to speak at the Church of the Repentant Soul's first annual conference in New York City during the third week of December (with round-trip airfare and hotel accommodations included), Prior didn't need to be asked twice.

Everett kept his website-built-for-one current with a fictitious calendar of events, arranged for Prior's ticket to be ready when the man got to Heathrow, and made sure Silver arrived in New York on that Saturday, the day before Father Adam Peters would meet his maker in Saint Patrick's Cathedral.

That part had gone off without a single hitch.

Things had gotten a touch trickier on Monday morning when Deacon Jeremiah received a frantic text from Prior Silver about the conference having been canceled. Of course, Everett had been prepared, having himself sent an alert to Prior's phone about the cancellation and it being rescheduled for May.

That was when Everett had gone to the Hotel Penn and met his disciple Prior Silver for the first time under the guise of Deacon Jeremiah.

The confused and distraught Prior was grateful to be with his mentor, who spent an hour convincing him to take advantage of being in New York at this most blessed time of year.

Everett informed Prior there was enough in the Church's coffers to pay for his time. Prior took the thousand dollars out of Everett's hands in a flash. Everett found that amusing and telling—repentance only seemed to go so far.

Once a thief, always a thief.

Prior Silver would eventually pay the price for violating the Lord's Eighth Statute. Just not yet.

Everett still needed him to stay in the city until the end of the week when he would dispatch Timothy Alan Leeds. After that, Prior could return to the British Isles.

With cash in hand, Prior Silver eagerly agreed to stay.

Prior held up the stack of pamphlets and small wooden crosses he'd taken to carrying since his prison release and told Jeremiah he was happy to continue his work in the Lord's good name.

Everett had asked if Prior would give him a few pamphlets and crosses to hand out on his own. Everett had tossed the pamphlets in a trash can shortly after leaving the Hotel Penn. But he had held on to the crosses.

One eventually made its way to the wall of a room in a condemned hospital in Far Rockaway. The other ended up above the bed in the Hotel Penn after Everett convinced a housekeeper he'd forgotten something in his room when he had checked out a little earlier.

Everett had been concerned when Rachel and Sergeant Hawley stumbled onto Prior Silver's connection to Austin quicker than he'd anticipated. But back in London, Everett had gotten lucky when Prior spotted constables surrounding his East London flat and gotten in touch with Jeremiah, the only man he trusted.

Deacon Jeremiah had assuaged Silver's fears—whatever the Yard was accusing him of was a mistake. He even arranged for Prior to stay under an assumed name in an out-of-the-way hotel near Wimbledon, advising him to lie low until the situation could be rectified.

When Prior Silver's name had finally been released to the media, Everett realized the end of the road had come for Deacon Jeremiah's one and only disciple.

Silver had called in a panic, realizing he'd been set up for a murder spree he didn't commit. He even accused Jeremiah of being behind it.

Everett convinced Prior to let him explain and the man agreed to meet him at the warehouse in East London. It was there that Everett had revealed his true colors. He told Prior what a fool he'd been and that it was finally time for him to be punished for repeatedly violating the Lord's Eighth Commandment years earlier.

By that time, he'd laced Prior's coffee with a healthy dose of strychnine.

He packed the dead man in a crate, got in touch with Monte Ferguson and used him to get an "interview" published in the *Daily Mail*. All that remained after that was delivering a package to his brother on Boxing Day and putting the reporter on ice.

Scotland Yard and the world had gotten the Commandment Killer with a confession wrapped up in a giant bow as a belated Christmas gift.

And the only person who knew the real truth?

The man Everett had vowed vengeance against from the very start.

VII

G rant wasn't sure how long he would be able to keep his eyes shut.
"Just don't look down," Frankel urged.

Easier said than done.

Grant felt sick enough with the discoveries made inside the garret at the Zermatt cottage. As they ascended the Matterhorn in a cable car all their own, Grant could feel his fear of heights kick in—even though they'd just begun to climb.

"I'm trying not to."

He finally managed to open his eyes and concentrate on Frankel.

"Not quite the party I expected when he invited us to Switzerland."

"But I'm sure it's the one he'd always planned on having," countered Grant.

Party.

That's what the older man who operated the cable cars at the foot of the Matterhorn had called it when they had arrived twenty minutes earlier. "But he only left the name of one guest," said the man, whose own name was McCreery, checking his list. "Would one of you be Austin Grant?"

Grant had identified himself with his Scotland Yard credentials that were still legitimate for a few more hours. Then he had introduced NYPD Detective First Grade John Frankel.

"What do you exactly mean by 'guest'?" Grant asked.

A suddenly extremely nervous McCreery had explained. A man had paid a significant amount of money (twenty thousand euros to be precise) to rent out the Glacier Palace atop the Matterhorn for a private New Year's Eve party. It wasn't a normal request but the corporation that operated various attractions on the Swiss Alps' most famous mountain was not immune to sudden windfalls while not asking many questions.

McCreery had thought it odd that the guest list totaled three. But with the unspoken Swiss credo being "money is money," McCreery said he didn't make the rules and just minded his own business.

After ascertaining that the gentleman in question had also been named Grant, they'd asked if he'd been with a younger woman. McCreery nodded but said she hadn't seemed well. The man had told McCreery she was just suffering from altitude sickness and then gave him the commander's name.

At least Rachel's still alive, Grant thought.

Grant told McCreery to call the Swiss authorities and have them waiting for him and Frankel when they came back down the mountain.

"Have I done something wrong?" asked the worried McCreery.

"Not you." Frankel had shaken his head. "Can't say the same for the man up top, though."

Then they had climbed into the car and begun the forty-five-minute ascent to the Glacier Palace.

"Why here of all places?" asked Frankel now, regaining Grant's attention.

"I've been thinking about that," Grant answered.

His stomach lurched again—so he tried to distract himself by remembering the one and only time he'd been up this mountain. The trip mentioned at Christmas Eve dinner—their first journey abroad from Liverpool when he and Everett were young boys.

Austin couldn't remember ever having felt colder and it had seemed like a year to reach the top. The boys had run amok in the glacier caves, then stopped to take a family picture. They convinced their folks to let them head outside the cavern where they found a snow-covered plateau with a view that stretched forever.

"It's the top of the world!" Austin had cried out.

"Top of the world!" echoed Everett, who loved to mimic everything his big brother would say and do.

Then the two brothers had gone and built the snowman.

They rolled the snow into two big balls and placed them atop each other, forming "Mr. Frosty." Austin had found a few twigs sticking out of the snow and some stones he could use for a pair of eyes, nose, and a mouth. He'd just finished filling in Mr. Frosty's face when he felt a tug at his parka sleeve.

Everett was standing there with a woolen cap in his hand.

"Mr. Frosty needs a hat," his baby brother said.

"Where did you find that?"

"On the ground," Everett had told him.

No sooner had Austin placed it on Mr. Frosty's head, when a little girl came running up behind them with her mother.

"There's my hat!" the little girl had screamed, pointing. "They stole my hat!"

"No, we didn't!" cried Everett. "I found it!"

What followed was the sort of screeching argument only two children can have, the girl repeatedly accusing him, while Everett denied having taken it on purpose. Finally, Austin and Everett's father appeared. When the girl's mother explained the situation, their father turned to his youngest son and asked if he had stolen the girl's hat.

Everett had denied it once again.

Their father had turned to Austin.

"Did your brother take this little girl's hat on purpose?"

Austin had looked from his father to Everett. His younger brother was staring up at him with a mix of sibling hero worship and a plea in his eyes.

"Maybe," Austin answered. "I don't know. I was fixing Mr. Frosty's face."

His father had nodded, then removed the hat from the snowman and returned it to the little girl and her mother.

The moment the three Grants were alone, their father had slapped Everett across the face and admonished him in the harshest tone Austin had ever heard.

"It's a sin to steal, Everett! Don't you know that the Lord punishes sinners?"

Over five decades later, sitting in the cable car heading back up the Matterhorn, Grant recalled that previous trip down the other way.

Everett had whimpered the entire time. And never said a single word to his older brother until right before they reached the bottom.

"You always get what you want. I never do."

"I didn't want the hat," Austin had told him.

Everett had shaken his head with tears in his eyes. "I meant you want everyone to like you more."

Everett hadn't spoken to him for almost a week after that.

"That's pretty much how I remember it," said Grant, having finished the story. "You asked me why we're here? That's all I can think of."

Frankel glanced up at the Matterhorn's peak towering above. "Sounds like that day made quite the impression on your brother."

Grant hadn't realized how much until he'd just remembered the story and told it to Frankel.

"Your father sounds like he was quite the religious man."

"He would occasionally get into these fire and brimstone moods but none of it ever really rubbed off on me," said Grant.

"That doesn't seem to have been the case when it came to Everett," observed Frankel.

"Apparently."

They rode the rest of the way up in silence with Grant having a clearer and more painful understanding of what was waiting for them up top.

VIII

The glow reminded Frankel of the snow cone machines he used to see every summer with his father when they would take a trip to the Atlantic City Boardwalk.

Every color of the rainbow seemed to be swirling up ahead like those shaved bundles of flavored ice, as he and Grant made their way on the narrow blue-painted path deep inside the glacier, just below the peak of the Matterhorn.

Once they turned the corner, despite the dire circumstances that had brought them there, Frankel and Grant stared in wonderment at the Glacier Palace.

Exquisite ice sculptures in vibrant assorted colors filled the cavern. Houses, animals, cars, and flowers looked like they had been carved from precious crystal instead of ice from the massive glacier. It was a genuine winter wonderland.

"Was this here when you were here before?" asked Frankel.

Grant shook his head. "Believe me, I would have remembered it."

They resumed walking until Grant stopped in front of a wall of ice with a distinctive jagged pattern. "I remember this though," Grant said.

"I think I've seen it too, but I know I've never been here."

"Because it was in the photograph Everett gave me on Christmas Eve. We took it right here."

"Of course," remarked Frankel. Suddenly, he realized something else. "Oh shit."

"What?"

"Those gifts he gave us," said Frankel.

"What about them?"

"He was telling us what he was up to—flaunting it again in our faces." Frankel pointed at the wall. "Like the story you just told me how it all started with this place. Everett was telling us it was going to end up back here."

He turned back toward Grant. "That DVD and book he gave me?"

"*Gone with the Wind*," said Grant.

"The main plotline has Scarlett O'Hara pining away for the man that her cousin ended up marrying."

Grant's jaw dropped. "Bloody hell."

"I'm sure that picture he gave Rachel meant something too," Frankel added. "But for the life of me, I can't tell you what."

Frankel could see Grant thinking of the snapshot taken long ago at the Brighton seashore. The commander's eyes suddenly widened.

"The family he wanted but could not have," Grant said. "Me dead and buried in the dirt—leaving Rachel, Allison, and him as one happy family."

"Very good, detectives!"

Grant whirled at the sound of Everett's voice behind them.

Frankel reached in his coat for his gun but two sounds beat him to the punch.

The first was Rachel screaming at the top of her lungs.

"John!"

And the second was the blast of a rifle shot.

Frankel was knocked to the ground and his pistol scattered along the icy floor before he even realized what had happened.

He had taken a bullet between his shoulder and chest.

Grant turned to help him but Everett's voice echoed through the glacier.

"Stay right where you are, Austin."

Lying on the ground, Frankel could barely turn his head, the pain was so excruciating. He saw Everett standing in middle of the path with a rifle aimed directly at his brother's chest.

Rachel suddenly appeared. She rushed over and dropped to her knees beside him. "John . . . !"

She tried to cover the bleeding wound with her hand but he writhed away in agony.

"I tried to warn you," she told him.

"It's okay," Frankel grumbled. "*You're* okay . . ."

Rachel nodded, tears falling down her face. "I am," she whispered.

Frankel watched as she turned to look up at her uncle.

"You have to help him," she pleaded. "You have to do something!"

But Everett's eyes and the hunting rifle were trained on Grant.

"I told you to come alone."

"You, of all people, shouldn't be telling anyone what to do," said Grant.

Rachel turned back toward Frankel, her eyes filling with concern.

It must really look bad, thought Frankel. *It certainly feels really bad.*

"Enough of that!" roared Everett above him.

He waved the rifle at his brother. "Get her away from him!" he ordered.

Rachel moved down closer to the fallen detective.

Frankel nodded at her. "Do what he says, Rachel."

She shook her head, refusing to stand up.

"You have to, sweetheart," Frankel begged her. "Please."

Suddenly, Grant was behind her. Frankel could see the Scotland Yard man had no choice but to help his daughter to her feet because Everett had the rifle trained on both of them.

With pain coursing through him, Frankel felt more helpless than ever as Everett grabbed hold of Rachel with one hand while poking Grant in the back with the rifle.

"Let's go." Everett motioned behind him. "You know where."

As he backed them away, Frankel felt his chest seize up.

And then he saw Rachel's lips part.

"I love you," she silently mouthed.

Frankel did everything in his power to not wince as he softly answered her.

"I love you too."

The next thing Frankel knew, they had disappeared around a corner. Seconds later, everything went completely black.

IX

The snow was an endless field of white, untouched by a human soul. If there had been a crater in sight, or if the full moon itself hadn't been shining down from a star-filled sky, one might think they were on the lunar surface.

All of this was lost on Rachel as she was dragged out of the ice cavern by the lunatic she'd until recently thought of as her uncle—because all she could hear was herself screaming.

Her raking sobs and string of scathing epithets ranging from *murderer* to *madman* were the only sounds within hundreds of miles.

Until Everett threw her down in the snow and yelled. "Stop! Enough!"

Her uncle pointed the hunting rifle directly at her and slid his finger onto the trigger guard. Rachel felt herself beginning to tremble. And saw that Everett's finger was doing so as well.

"Everett—no! You don't want to do this!"

Everett swiveled to see that her father had emerged from the cavern. The rifle didn't budge an inch.

"Give me one reason I shouldn't."

"Because you don't want her." Her father raised his hands in the air. "It's me."

He took one step closer and immediately stopped when Everett turned the gun in his direction.

"I've always been the one you wanted."

"It took you long enough to figure that out," scoffed Everett. "The great Scotland Yard detective—outwitted at every turn."

"You can do what you want to me. But this has nothing to do with her."

"You still don't get it, do you, Austin? Aren't you wondering why I went to New York in the first place?"

"I don't really care," her father answered.

"I went to bring Rachel back home."

What? Rachel stared at her uncle incredulously.

"I needed someone left behind who would feel the pain of what it's like to lose everything in an instant." Everett leaned closer to her. "And that person is you, Rachel."

He waved the rifle at Grant.

"Your father's career is in ruins. And now, tonight, he is going to die. Just like your precious Detective Frankel did back there."

Rachel screamed and leapt to her feet.

"Noooooo!"

Everett swung the hunting rifle into her stomach. Rachel doubled over in agony. Everett hurled the rifle away and it vanished deep in the snow.

Grant started to move for his brother.

And stopped when Everett pulled out a knife and grabbed Rachel by the throat.

"Don't even try it," growled Everett. He pulled Rachel closer and waved the knife in front of her face. "Now do you see why I need her, Austin?"

Grant raised his hands up.

"You don't need her. You need me." He pounded his chest. "Take me."

"Someone needs to suffer the rest of their life. Like I have all these years." Everett shook his head wildly. "Someone has to suffer because of what you did to me!"

"You mean Allison?" asked Grant.

"Of course I mean Allison!" yelled Everett. "She was supposed to be mine."

"You've had it backwards all these years, Everett. Allison never loved you."

"Liar!"

"I didn't take her from you. No matter what that twisted brain of yours is telling you."

"Liar!"

Her father inched closer to Everett.

"If anyone is guilty of the last commandment, it's you, *brother*. You're the one who coveted his neighbor's wife. Not me."

"That's not true!" screamed Everett.

Rachel suddenly understood what her father was doing. He was baiting Everett—trying to unnerve him. Just like his speech at Hawley's funeral.

And maybe she could help him.

"Then why did you attack her, Everett?" she asked.

Anger and complete betrayal rose up in her father's eyes like she had never seen.

"You?" her father cried out. "You're the one who did that to her?"

Everett pulled the knife away from Rachel's throat and started waving it at his older brother.

"No! I told Rachel that wasn't what happened—"

Her father leaped on top of him.

Rachel got knocked aside and fell to the ground. She suddenly found herself far away from the two brothers who were rolling in the snow, locked in a mighty struggle.

Everett let out a roar and came up with the knife. He didn't hesitate and lunged at his brother with the razor-sharp blade.

Rachel screamed. "Nooooooo!"

A gunshot split the cold night air and echoed through the towering Alps like a booming cannon.

Everett looked down to see a hole had suddenly appeared in his chest.

He dropped the knife and clutched the gaping wound. A gush of blood sprouted forth.

Everett's lips quivered for a moment, then the life drained out of his eyes and he died right there.

Her stunned father slowly lowered Everett's dead body into the snow and then called out for his daughter.

"Rachel, are you all right?"

"Yes," she answered. "You?"

Her father nodded.

Suddenly, they heard a noise behind them and both whirled around.

Just in time to see John sprawl into the white snow, blood still dripping from his open wound.

He let out an enormous sigh, then dropped the just-fired service revolver from his open palm and passed out.

X

They were halfway back down the southern face of the Matterhorn when Grant closed his cell phone. He looked across the cable car's small aisle at his daughter and the still unconscious Frankel leaning against her. His wound was no longer bleeding; Grant and Rachel had wrapped it tightly in every piece of clothing they could spare without freezing to death themselves.

"The medics down below said we've done all the right things for him."

"It's a miracle," she said.

"The real miracle was that when John passed out in the cavern, he rolled up against that jagged piece of the glacier."

"The one from the picture, right? That Everett gave you?"

Grant nodded. Like he'd told Frankel on the way up the mountain, his father's religious fervor hadn't done much for him. But there were times in life when Grant couldn't deny someone, somewhere, was looking out for certain people.

Case in point: the glacier's ice had stanched the blood long enough to keep Frankel alive, and then the freezing cold had woken him back up. It kept him conscious just long enough to stumble out of the cavern and fire one shot into Everett's chest—saving the woman he loved and her father from getting a Roman numeral ten carved in his forehead.

"I have to say I hadn't planned spending New Year's Eve dressing gunshot wounds," Rachel said.

The rifle had been another oddity.

Rachel said she'd been surprised to see Everett bring it up the mountain with them. Her uncle had told Rachel that if she or Grant had ever bothered to come visit him in Zermatt, they would have known there was a hunting as well as a ski season. "It's good to be overprepared," Everett had said.

"A lot of things happened tonight I never could have imagined," agreed Grant.

Rachel managed a smile. "Some retirement party, huh?"

"Believe it or not, I actually preferred that one at the Yard."

Rachel told her father she was just glad it was finally over.

"For me, maybe," said Grant. "But you still have your article to write."

"Oh. That."

"You'll get to it eventually."

"I guess," she said. "I think I came up with a title for it, though."

"You did?"

"Well, actually *you* did."

"Really now."

"It was something you said up there. *The Last Commandment*. How's that sound?"

Grant thought about it.

And that final moment up there on top of the world.

Rachel had rushed to tend to Frankel, leaving Grant alone with his fallen brother.

Grant had stared down at his younger sibling. It would be hard to remember Everett as anything but like this.

It was then that he had noticed his hand was covered with his sibling's blood.

Grant took a deep breath.

And then traced an *X* on his brother's forehead with Everett's own blood.

Grant knew the next snowfall would wash it away—long before the Swiss police got themselves up there and took his body off the mountain.

But Grant would always remember it there. It seemed appropriate.

Now, he turned to look across the cable car at his daughter.

"I think that sounds perfect."

Before she could respond, Frankel groaned and his eyes fluttered open.

"Hey," said Rachel.

"Hey," murmured Frankel.

"Welcome back," said Grant.

Frankel shifted around and groaned again.

"Easy there," urged Rachel.

But Frankel continued to stare at Grant. "Everett?"

Grant shook his head.

"Good," said Frankel.

Then the detective's eyes cleared with the realization of what had transpired thousands of feet above. "And, I'm really sorry," he told Grant.

"Thank you, John," replied Grant. "And I mean that."

Frankel leaned back against Rachel and started to close his eyes. But then he spotted something out the window.

"Look at that . . ."

Rachel and Grant followed his gaze. Fireworks were arcing and bursting over the twinkling lights of Zermatt down below.

"Happy New Year," said Rachel. She gave the wounded detective a soft kiss on the cheek.

"Happy New Year," murmured Frankel and managed to gently kiss her back.

Then Rachel leaned across the aisle.

She gave her father a kiss and followed it up with a hug where neither one wanted to let go.

"Happy New Year, Daddy," she whispered in his ear.

"Happy New Year to you, Rach," he whispered back.

A moment later, she settled back next to Frankel and they all watched the fireworks for a bit.

Then a smile crossed his daughter's face and she turned back toward him.

"What?" asked Grant.

"You know what that means, don't you?" she asked.

Grant nodded.

I'm retired.

And he had no idea what the hell he was going to do.

But in that moment, he realized it didn't matter. He had everything he could ever want right there.

Acknowledgements

I must begin with Otto Penzler, whose passion and incredible guidance has brought this book to life, like everything else he does at Mysterious Press. Many moons ago, I used to frequent the Mysterious Bookshop on Fifty-Sixth Street, where I would climb the spiral staircase to the second floor and find Otto hard at work on his latest omnibus. Always busy, he still took the time to discuss the latest mystery fiction, and I would happily leave the shop with more than a few soon-to-be-cherished nuggets that filled many page-turning hours. We subsequently lost touch for decades, so it is wonderful to be reunited in such a gratifying way. As Otto recently said, "Here's to the (re)beginning of a beautiful friendship."

Many thanks go to my team out here in California—Robb Rothman, Vanessa Livingston, and Amy Schiffman. Friends first, reps second—your support through this has been greatly appreciated.

To Benee Knauer—your help with this novel is beyond measure. You never lost faith from the time we first discussed it, and I know seeing the book come to fruition this way gives you much the same sense of pride and satisfaction as it does me.

A specific acknowledgement is long overdue to my close friend, Dan Pyne. You've made me a better writer from the day we first met and continue to inspire me all these years later.

I can't thank Cindy McCreery enough for being there every step of the way through this process. Whether it's coteaching or continuing to try and conquer Hollywood together, it means everything to have someone who has your back and you can always count on.

I am grateful to my early readers—Sibyl Jackson, Rodney Perlman, David Reinfeld, Connie Tavel, and Tom Werner—for their thoughts and encouragement. Richard Michaelis—your help with Britishisms proved invaluable. And Bruce Blakely—thanks for some pointers on using refrigerators instead of freezers.

And most of all, my everlasting love to Holly. Everything starts and ends with you. Your absolute belief in me is what keeps me going.